CHESHIRE CROSSING

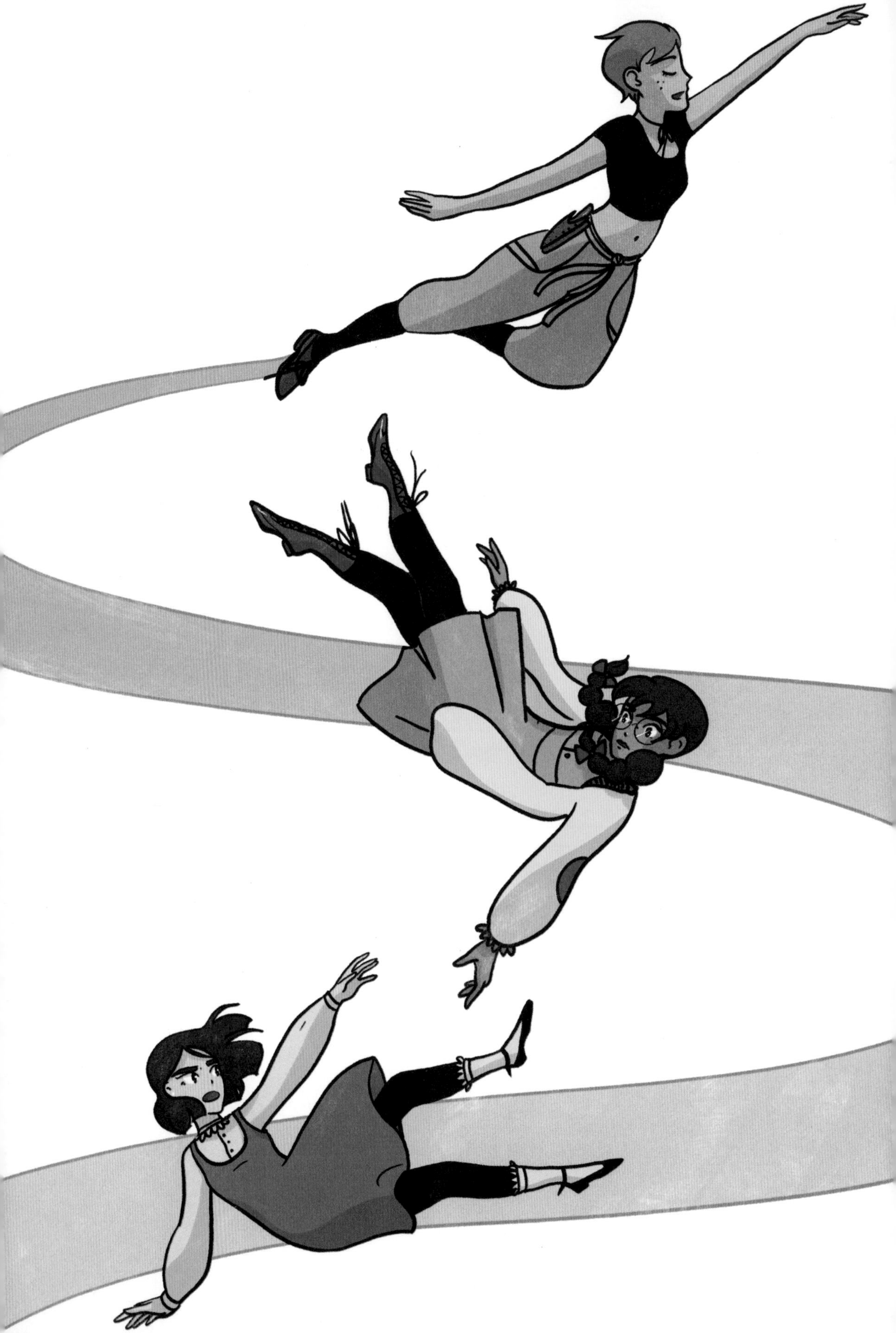

CHESHIRE CROSSING

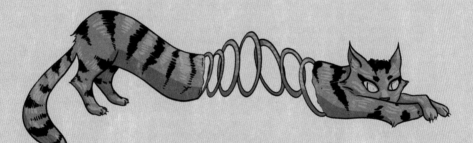

ANDY WEIR

ILLUSTRATED BY
SARAH ANDERSEN

TEN SPEED PRESS
California | New York

FOR DEMI AND JOJO

-ANDY

TO BANI AND PATRICK
FOR THEIR PATIENCE, LOVE, SUPPORT, AND ROOF.

-SARAH

CONTENTS

PREFACE

I know what you're thinking: Andy Weir isn't known for graphic novels, or for fantasy writing. Also he's extremely handsome. Well, you're right. But before I broke into writing and found a niche in hard sci-fi, I wrote a lot of fanfiction, and a few webcomics, and tossed them all up on my crappy website. Hell, I still write fanfiction. It's fun! (Not so much on the comics, though—more on that later.)

Plus, I've always loved crossovers. Give me some *Star Trek* vs. Daleks and I'll devour it. One day back when I was still writing webcomics, I started wondering about how the events of *Alice in Wonderland* would affect Alice later in life. Wouldn't she be a little messed up? She was a little girl who was put in mortal danger repeatedly and saw people die left and right. Then I thought, hey, Dorothy from *The Wizard of Oz* had kind of the same experience. Would she be messed up, too? Oh, and Wendy Darling from *Peter Pan* also had a bunch of horrifying adventures.

I guess that's when the kernel of the idea took root. What if these girls all met? Basically, they're mutants—they have the ability to go to other dimensions. That's kind of cool.

At first, I planned to make them all about 10 years old—the ages they were during their adventures. But I changed my mind on that pretty quickly. First off, I wanted some time to have passed since their previous adventures. Also, I wanted them to be clever. While little kids can certainly be intelligent and wary, after a while, it would start to seem really unlikely that such young kids would be so level-headed in life-or-death situations.

Once I'd decided to make them teenagers, the answer to how to put them together seemed obvious. What else do you do with teenage mutants but send them to boarding school, hopefully with a teacher who understands (or maybe even shares) their abilities?

And then there's the villains. An adventure story is only as good as its villain. *Alice in Wonderland* is sort of a stream-of-consciousness kind of story with no real enemy. Yeah, the Queen of Hearts is insane and generally seen as the Big Bad, but if you go back and read the original book you'll see she's just one of a menagerie of lunatics Alice runs into. So in effect, "Wonderland" is the antagonist of her story.

Luckily for the other two, you couldn't ask for better enemies. Captain Hook and the Wicked Witch of the West? We grew up hearing about those baddies all our lives. Having them team up is, frankly, even more awesome than the protagonists teaming up. And hey—evil love story!

I'm a terrible artist. Always have been. That didn't stop me from making the comic, though. I wanted to tell the story so I gutted it out. During that process I discovered three things:

1. Art is hard work.
2. I don't like doing it.
3. I'm not going to get any better at it.

So I never continued the story beyond the first adventure. In fact, the grueling artwork on *Cheshire Crossing* convinced me to return to narrative fiction. That's when I wrote *The Martian*.

Fast-forward a bit. *The Martian* came out and was successful beyond my wildest dreams, and all of a sudden people started reading that stuff I'd posted on my ugly old website. And interestingly enough, someone got interested in publishing *Cheshire Crossing*.

I reminded them my art was utter crap and they agreed. They said they'd get an artist to redraw everything.

And then came the best news of all! Sarah Andersen would be doing the art.

I've been a fan of *Sarah's Scribbles* for years. So many of her comics speak to me at a deep level. The joys of chronic anxiety, insecurity, and a general inability to get your life together. I think we all feel that way sometimes, and Sarah is excellent at turning it into humor. Her comics aren't just funny, they're therapeutic. And with her illustrations here, we're getting to see a whole new side of her artistic abilities. The only downside is, with the comic already written, we only get to tap into her artistic talents and not her writing talents. But who knows? If this takes off, maybe we can collaborate on future issues.

Anyway, it's fitting that this crossover of classic stories ends up coming to you via a crossover of creative authors.

Enjoy!

–ANDY WEIR

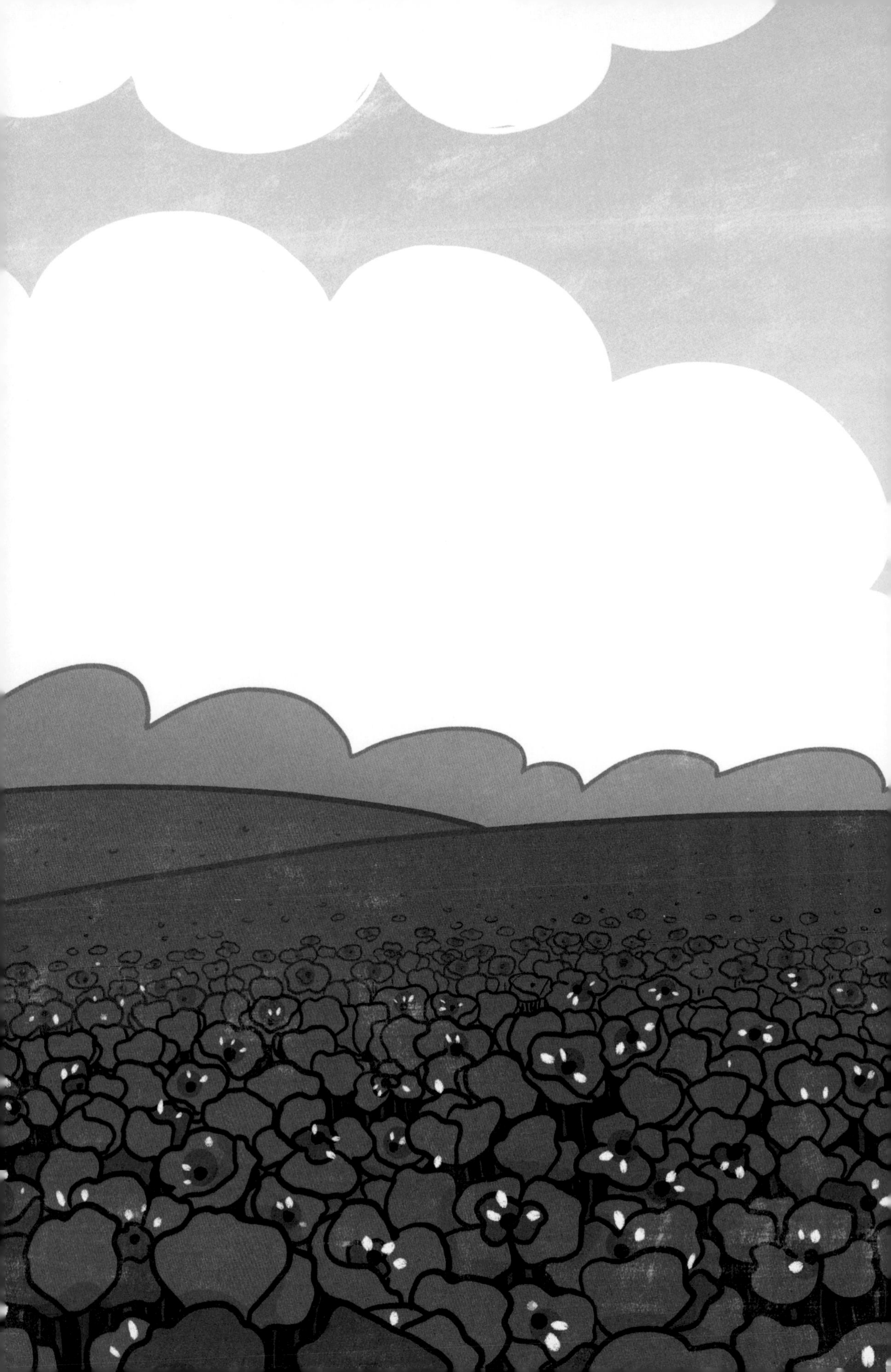

SCHOOLGIRLS

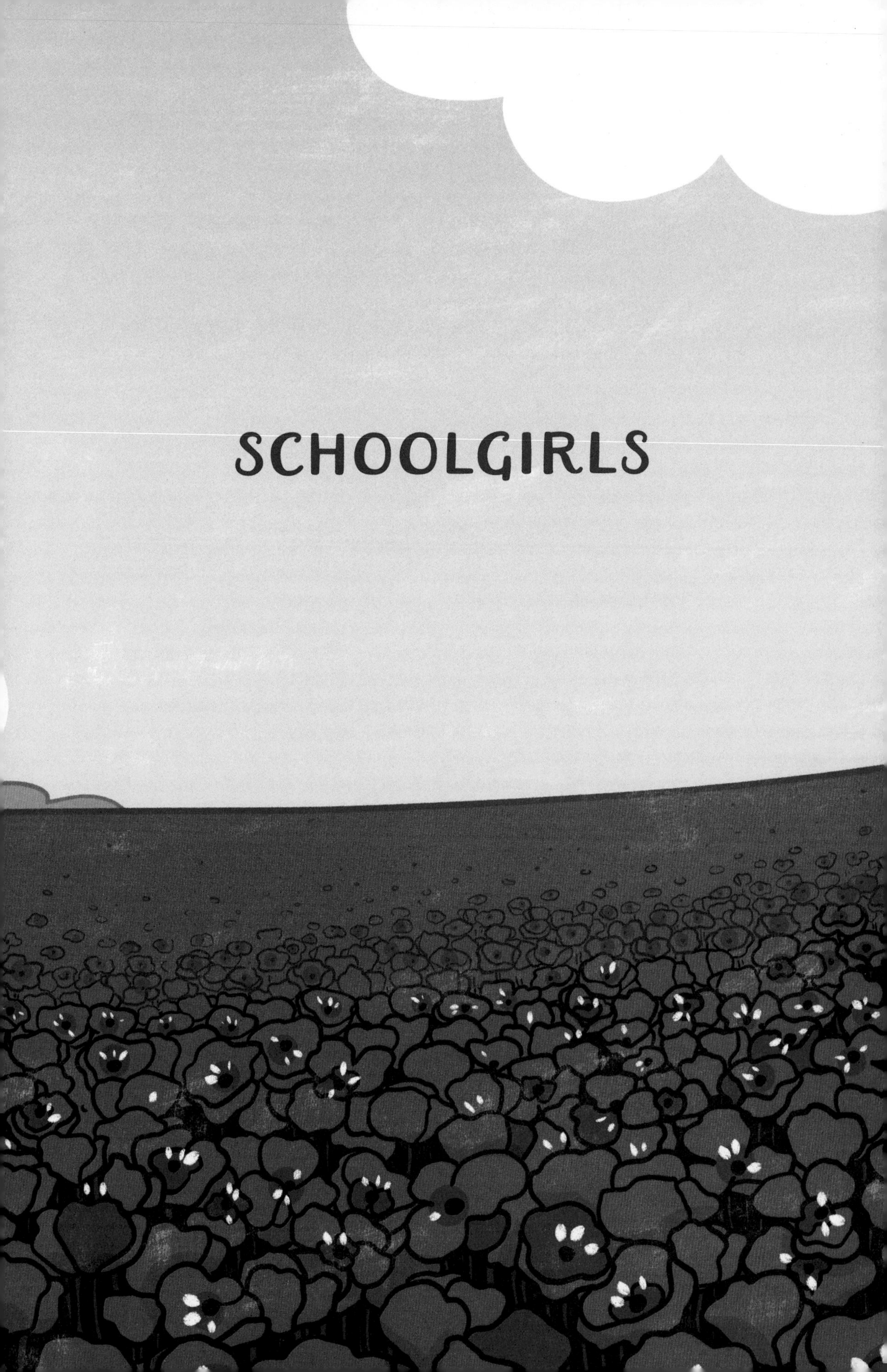

1904

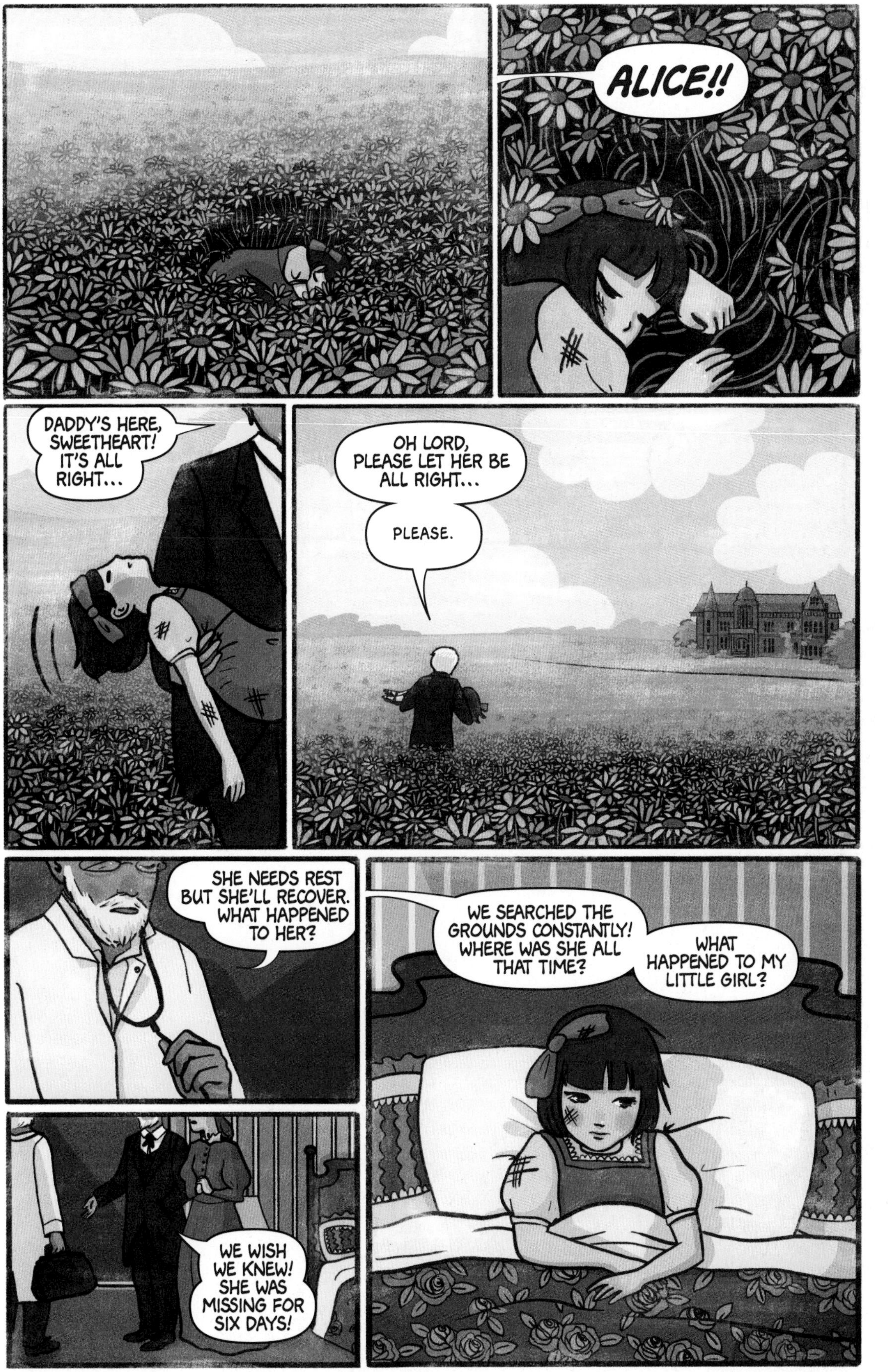
ALICE!!
DADDY'S HERE, SWEETHEART! IT'S ALL RIGHT...
OH LORD, PLEASE LET HER BE ALL RIGHT...
PLEASE.
SHE NEEDS REST BUT SHE'LL RECOVER. WHAT HAPPENED TO HER?
WE WISH WE KNEW! SHE WAS MISSING FOR SIX DAYS!
WE SEARCHED THE GROUNDS CONSTANTLY! WHERE WAS SHE ALL THAT TIME?
WHAT HAPPENED TO MY LITTLE GIRL?

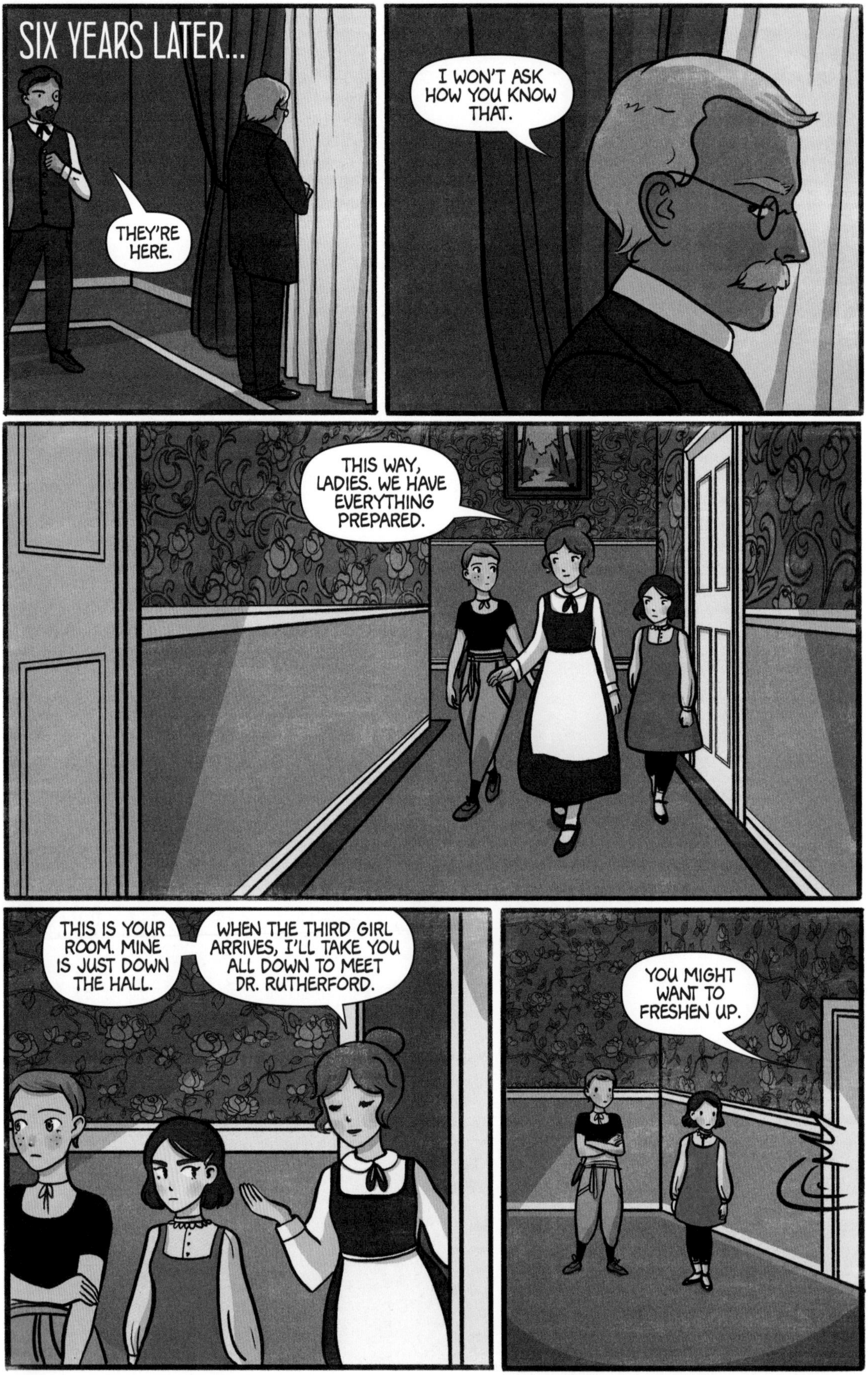
SIX YEARS LATER...
THEY'RE HERE.
I WON'T ASK HOW YOU KNOW THAT.
THIS WAY, LADIES. WE HAVE EVERYTHING PREPARED.
THIS IS YOUR ROOM. MINE IS JUST DOWN THE HALL.
WHEN THE THIRD GIRL ARRIVES, I'LL TAKE YOU ALL DOWN TO MEET DR. RUTHERFORD.
YOU MIGHT WANT TO FRESHEN UP.

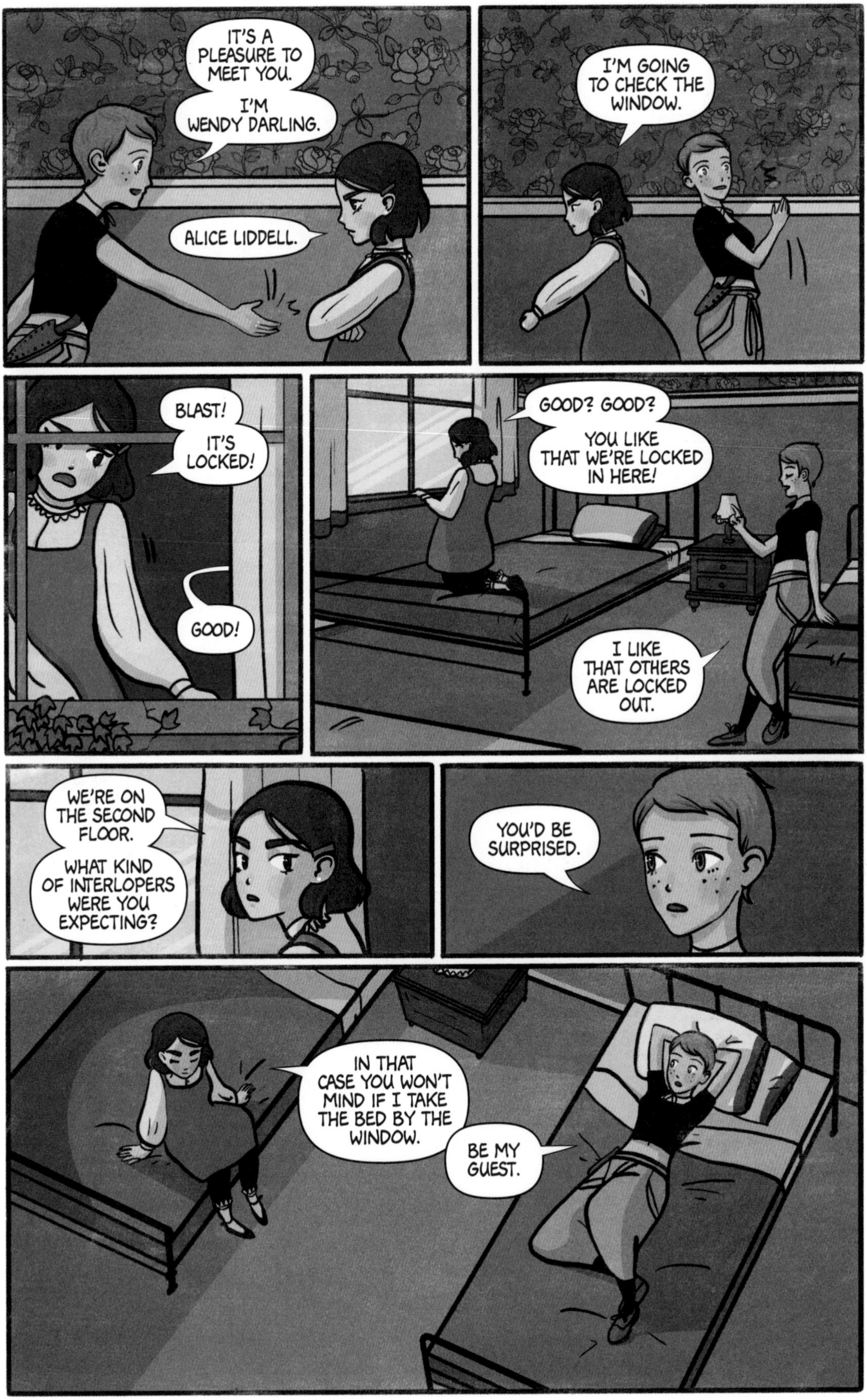
IT'S A PLEASURE TO MEET YOU.
I'M WENDY DARLING.
ALICE LIDDELL.
I'M GOING TO CHECK THE WINDOW.
BLAST!
IT'S LOCKED!
GOOD!
GOOD? GOOD?
YOU LIKE THAT WE'RE LOCKED IN HERE!
I LIKE THAT OTHERS ARE LOCKED OUT.
WE'RE ON THE SECOND FLOOR.
WHAT KIND OF INTERLOPERS WERE YOU EXPECTING?
YOU'D BE SURPRISED.
IN THAT CASE YOU WON'T MIND IF I TAKE THE BED BY THE WINDOW.
BE MY GUEST.

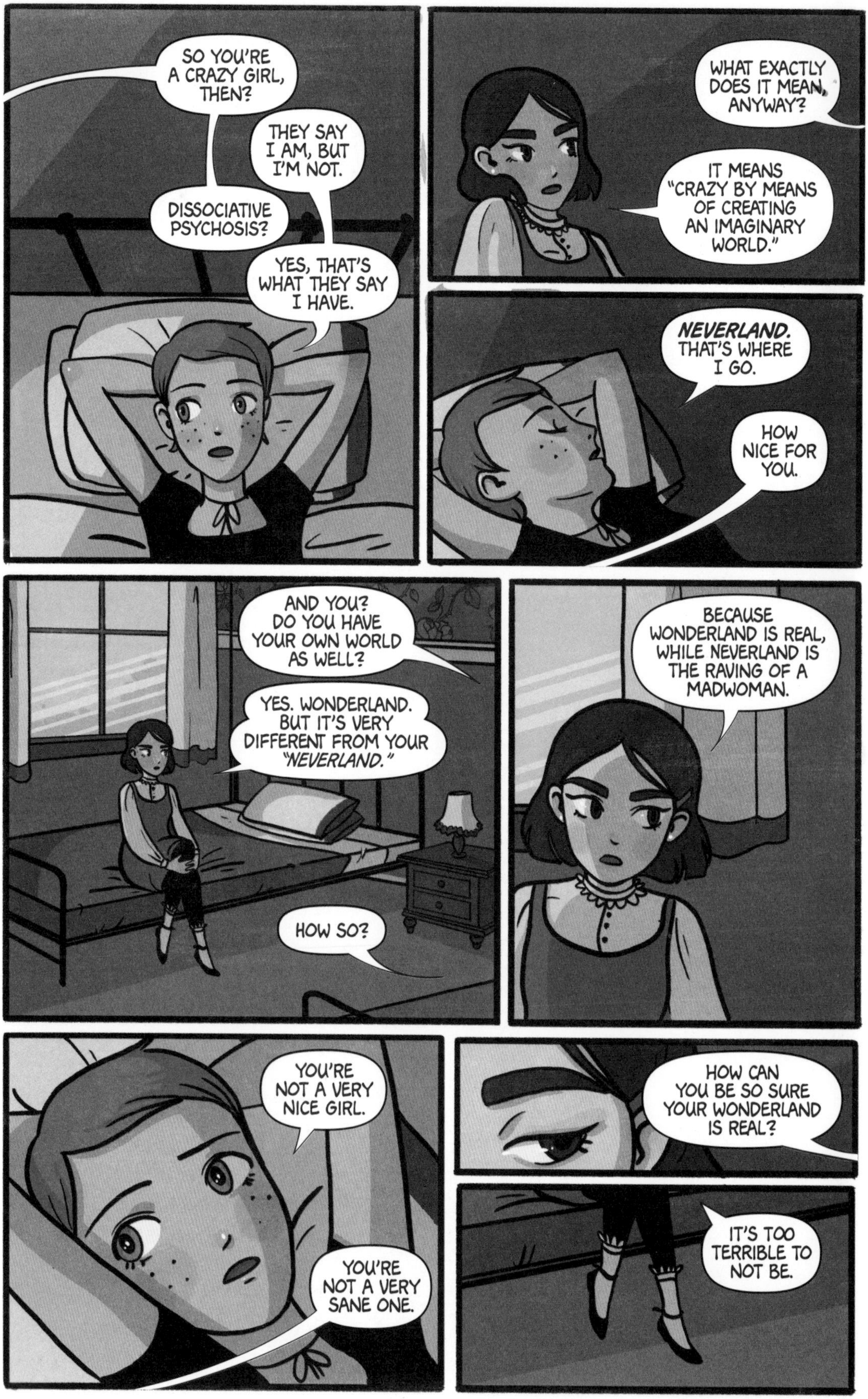
SO YOU'RE A CRAZY GIRL, THEN?
DISSOCIATIVE PSYCHOSIS?
THEY SAY I AM, BUT I'M NOT.
YES, THAT'S WHAT THEY SAY I HAVE.
WHAT EXACTLY DOES IT MEAN, ANYWAY?
IT MEANS "CRAZY BY MEANS OF CREATING AN IMAGINARY WORLD."
NEVERLAND. THAT'S WHERE I GO.
HOW NICE FOR YOU.
AND YOU? DO YOU HAVE YOUR OWN WORLD AS WELL?
YES. WONDERLAND. BUT IT'S VERY DIFFERENT FROM YOUR "NEVERLAND."
HOW SO?
BECAUSE WONDERLAND IS REAL, WHILE NEVERLAND IS THE RAVING OF A MADWOMAN.
YOU'RE NOT A VERY NICE GIRL.
YOU'RE NOT A VERY SANE ONE.
HOW CAN YOU BE SO SURE YOUR WONDERLAND IS REAL?
IT'S TOO TERRIBLE TO NOT BE.

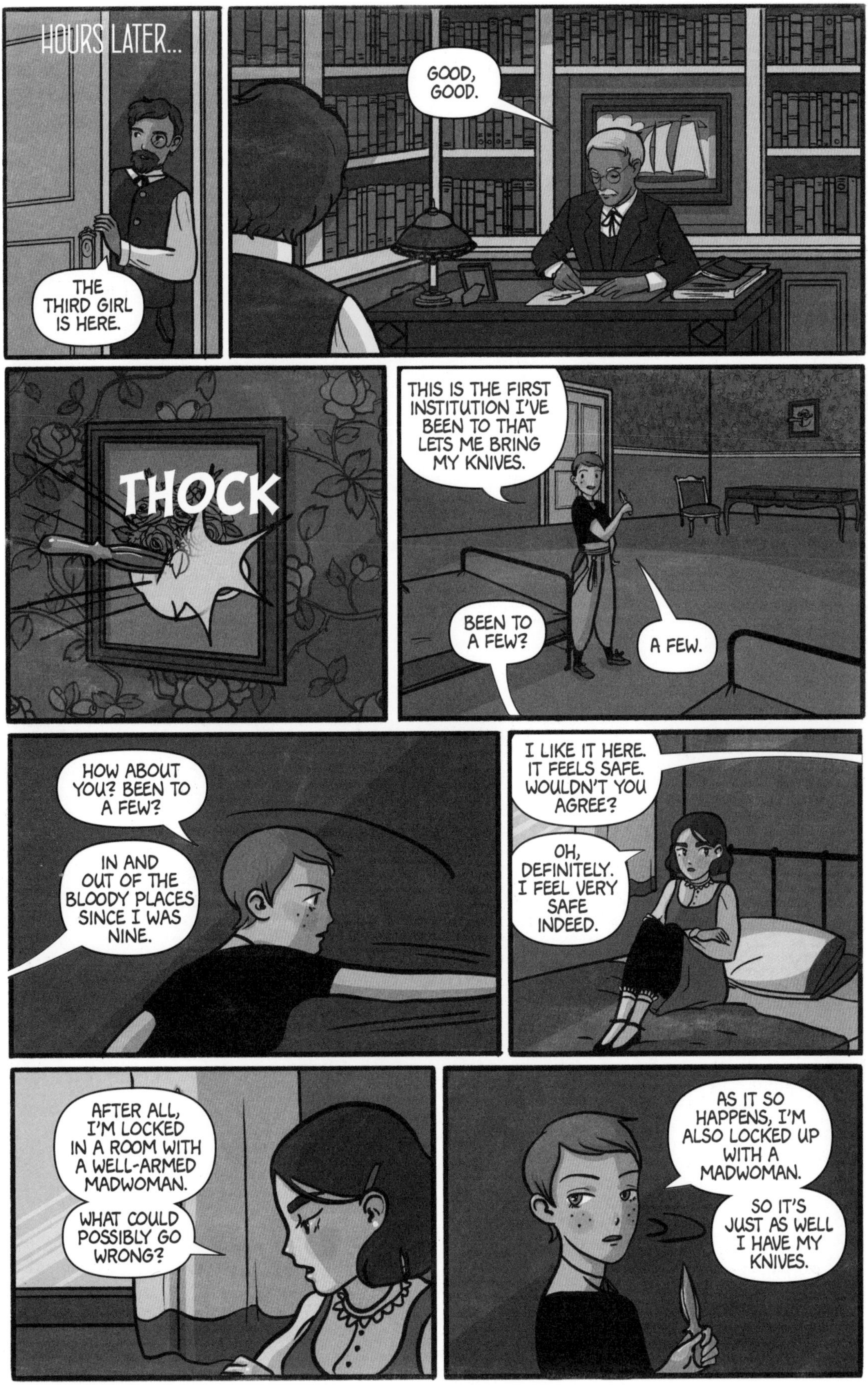
HOURS LATER...
THE THIRD GIRL IS HERE.
GOOD, GOOD.
THOCK
THIS IS THE FIRST INSTITUTION I'VE BEEN TO THAT LETS ME BRING MY KNIVES.
BEEN TO A FEW?
A FEW.
HOW ABOUT YOU? BEEN TO A FEW?
IN AND OUT OF THE BLOODY PLACES SINCE I WAS NINE.
I LIKE IT HERE. IT FEELS SAFE. WOULDN'T YOU AGREE?
OH, DEFINITELY. I FEEL VERY SAFE INDEED.
AFTER ALL, I'M LOCKED IN A ROOM WITH A WELL-ARMED MADWOMAN.
WHAT COULD POSSIBLY GO WRONG?
AS IT SO HAPPENS, I'M ALSO LOCKED UP WITH A MADWOMAN.
SO IT'S JUST AS WELL I HAVE MY KNIVES.

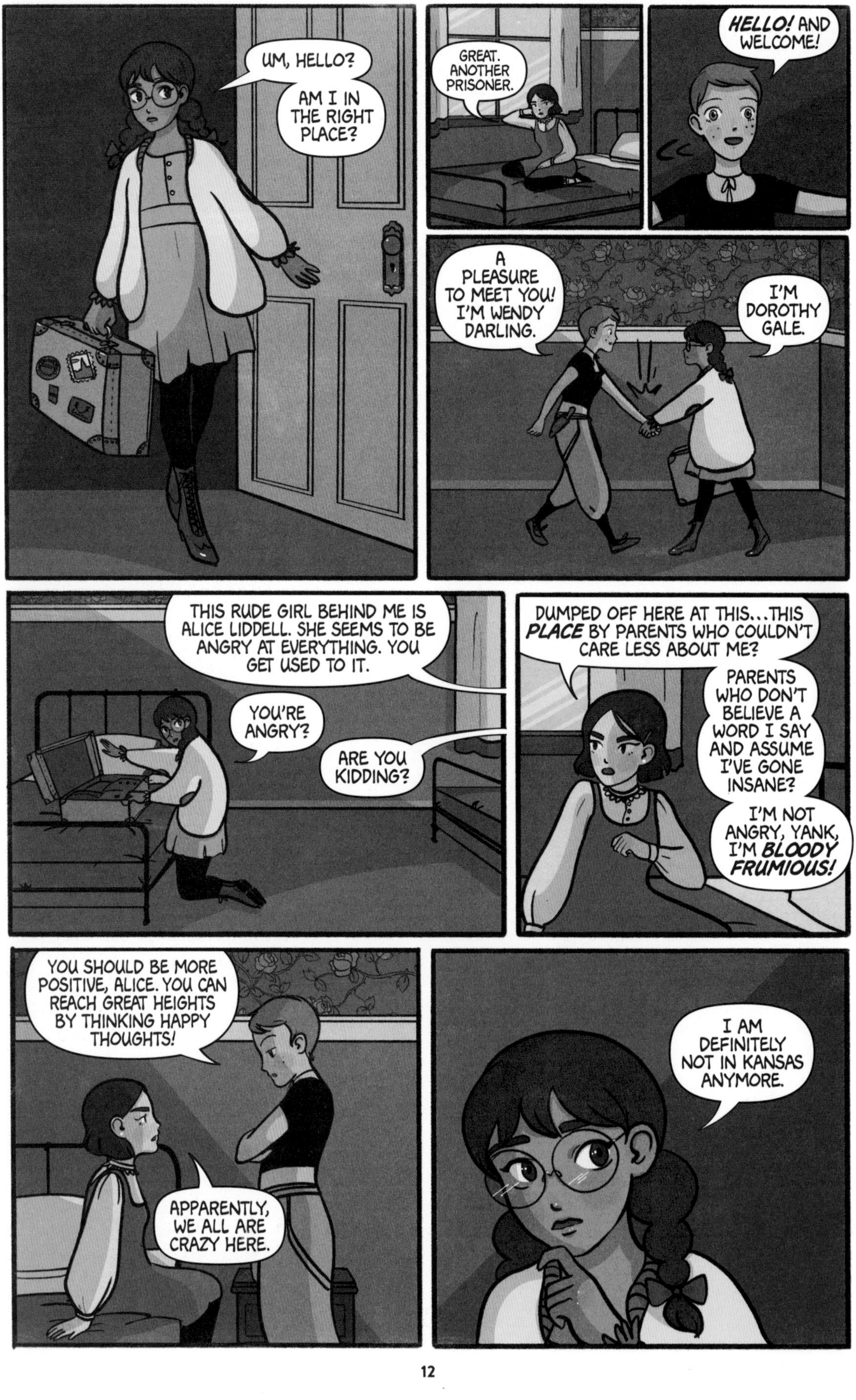
UM, HELLO?
AM I IN THE RIGHT PLACE?
GREAT. ANOTHER PRISONER.
HELLO! AND WELCOME!
A PLEASURE TO MEET YOU! I'M WENDY DARLING.
I'M DOROTHY GALE.
THIS RUDE GIRL BEHIND ME IS ALICE LIDDELL. SHE SEEMS TO BE ANGRY AT EVERYTHING. YOU GET USED TO IT.
YOU'RE ANGRY?
ARE YOU KIDDING?
DUMPED OFF HERE AT THIS...THIS *PLACE* BY PARENTS WHO COULDN'T CARE LESS ABOUT ME?
PARENTS WHO DON'T BELIEVE A WORD I SAY AND ASSUME I'VE GONE INSANE?
I'M NOT ANGRY, YANK, I'M *BLOODY FRUMIOUS!*
YOU SHOULD BE MORE POSITIVE, ALICE. YOU CAN REACH GREAT HEIGHTS BY THINKING HAPPY THOUGHTS!
APPARENTLY, WE ALL ARE CRAZY HERE.
I AM DEFINITELY NOT IN KANSAS ANYMORE.

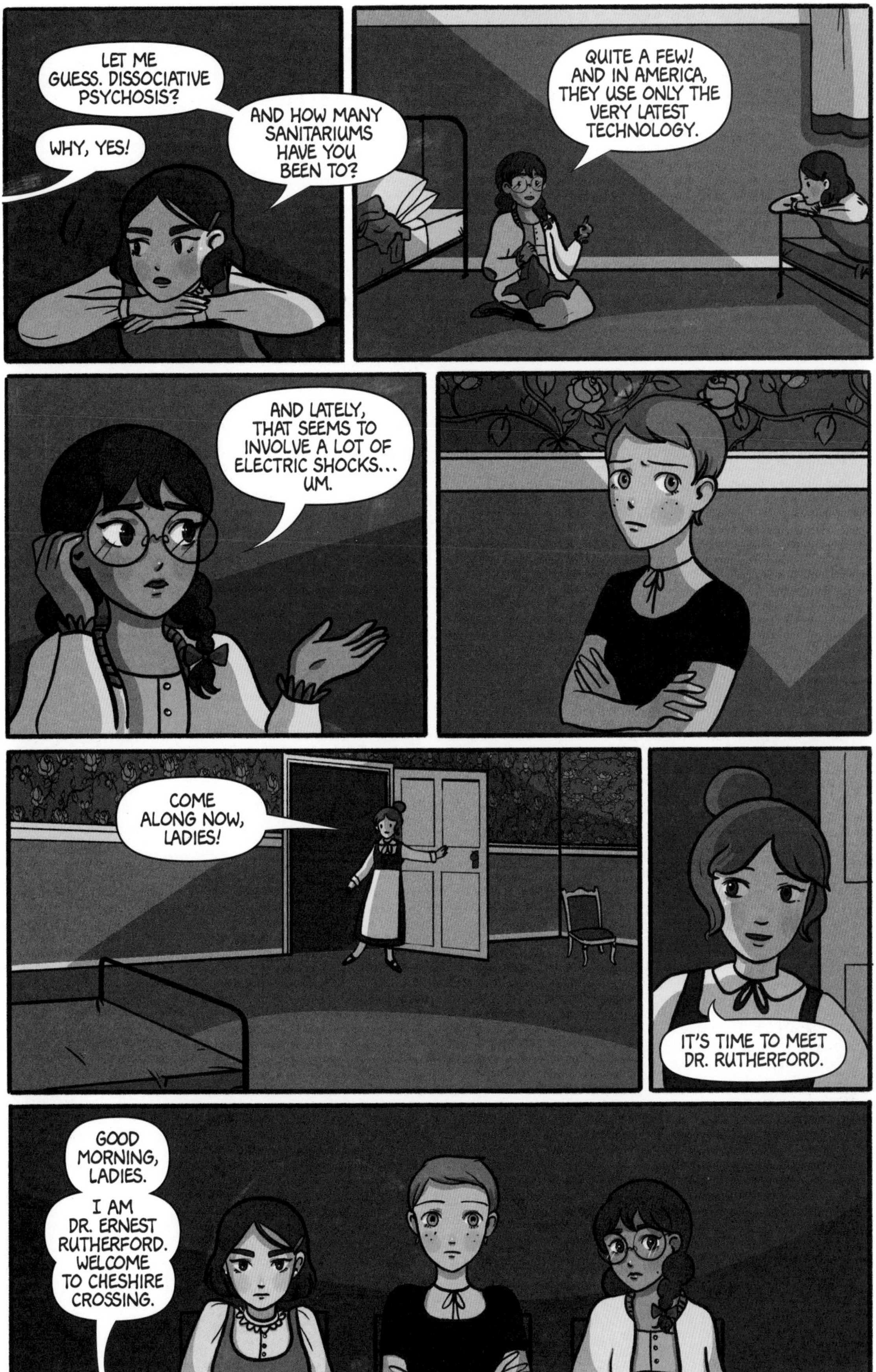
LET ME GUESS. DISSOCIATIVE PSYCHOSIS?
WHY, YES!
AND HOW MANY SANITARIUMS HAVE YOU BEEN TO?
QUITE A FEW! AND IN AMERICA, THEY USE ONLY THE VERY LATEST TECHNOLOGY.
AND LATELY, THAT SEEMS TO INVOLVE A LOT OF ELECTRIC SHOCKS... UM.
COME ALONG NOW, LADIES!
IT'S TIME TO MEET DR. RUTHERFORD.
GOOD MORNING, LADIES.
I AM DR. ERNEST RUTHERFORD. WELCOME TO CHESHIRE CROSSING.

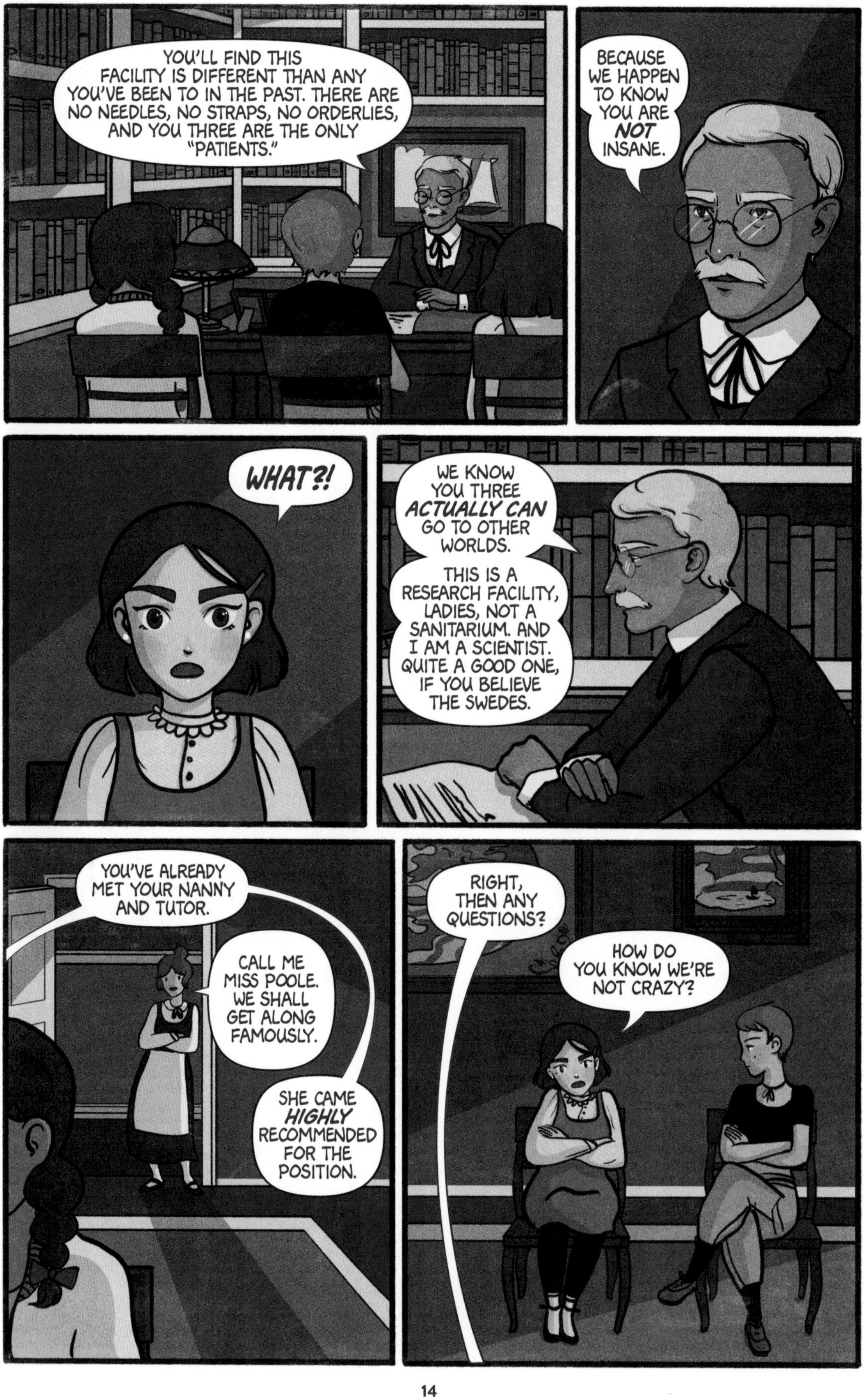
YOU'LL FIND THIS FACILITY IS DIFFERENT THAN ANY YOU'VE BEEN TO IN THE PAST. THERE ARE NO NEEDLES, NO STRAPS, NO ORDERLIES, AND YOU THREE ARE THE ONLY "PATIENTS."
BECAUSE WE HAPPEN TO KNOW YOU ARE ***NOT*** INSANE.
WHAT?!
WE KNOW YOU THREE ***ACTUALLY CAN*** GO TO OTHER WORLDS.
THIS IS A RESEARCH FACILITY, LADIES, NOT A SANITARIUM. AND I AM A SCIENTIST. QUITE A GOOD ONE, IF YOU BELIEVE THE SWEDES.
YOU'VE ALREADY MET YOUR NANNY AND TUTOR.
CALL ME MISS POOLE. WE SHALL GET ALONG FAMOUSLY.
SHE CAME ***HIGHLY*** RECOMMENDED FOR THE POSITION.
RIGHT, THEN ANY QUESTIONS?
HOW DO YOU KNOW WE'RE NOT CRAZY?

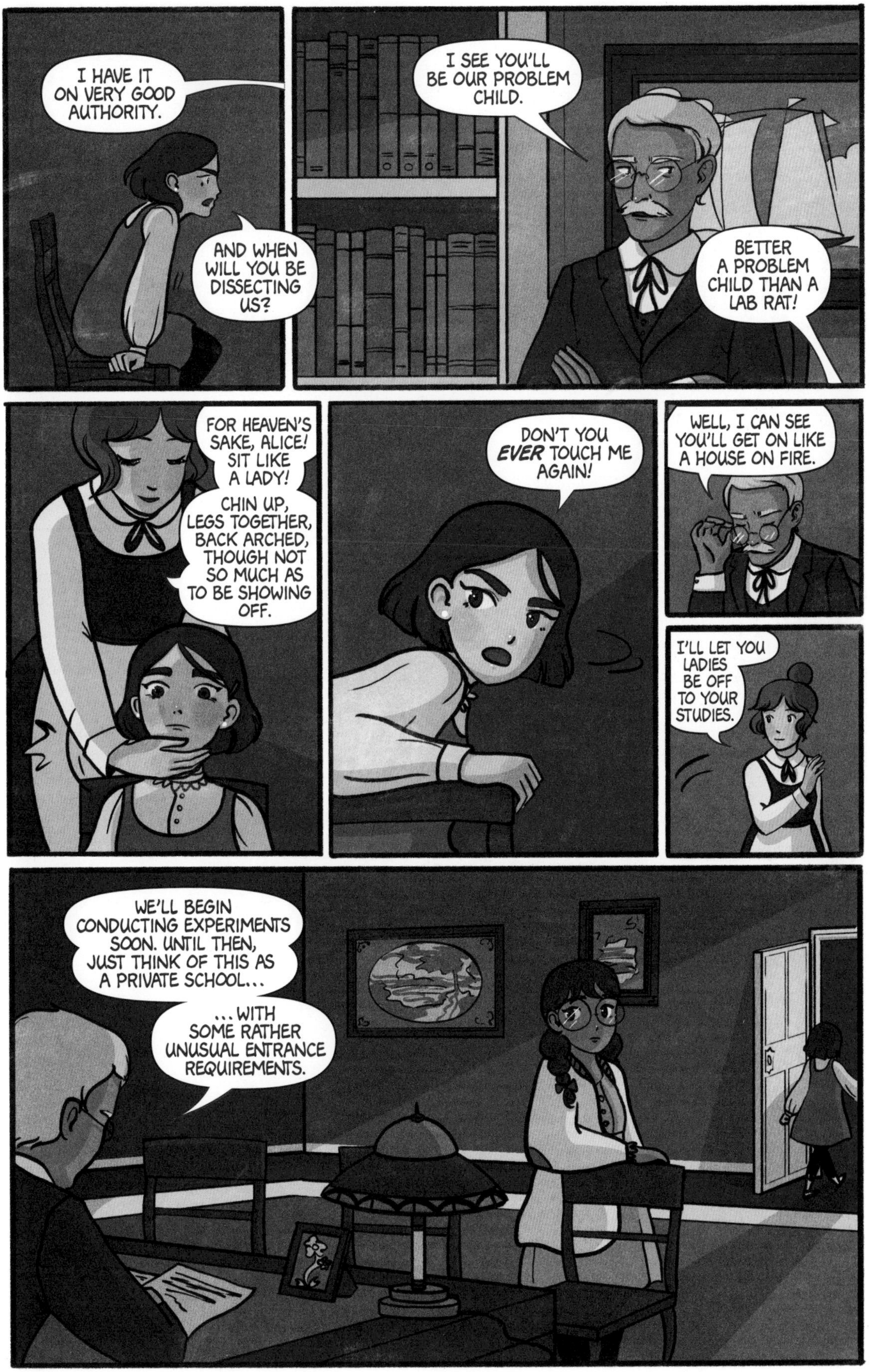
I HAVE IT ON VERY GOOD AUTHORITY.
AND WHEN WILL YOU BE DISSECTING US?
I SEE YOU'LL BE OUR PROBLEM CHILD.
BETTER A PROBLEM CHILD THAN A LAB RAT!
FOR HEAVEN'S SAKE, ALICE! SIT LIKE A LADY!
CHIN UP, LEGS TOGETHER, BACK ARCHED, THOUGH NOT SO MUCH AS TO BE SHOWING OFF.
DON'T YOU *EVER* TOUCH ME AGAIN!
WELL, I CAN SEE YOU'LL GET ON LIKE A HOUSE ON FIRE.
I'LL LET YOU LADIES BE OFF TO YOUR STUDIES.
WE'LL BEGIN CONDUCTING EXPERIMENTS SOON. UNTIL THEN, JUST THINK OF THIS AS A PRIVATE SCHOOL...
...WITH SOME RATHER UNUSUAL ENTRANCE REQUIREMENTS.

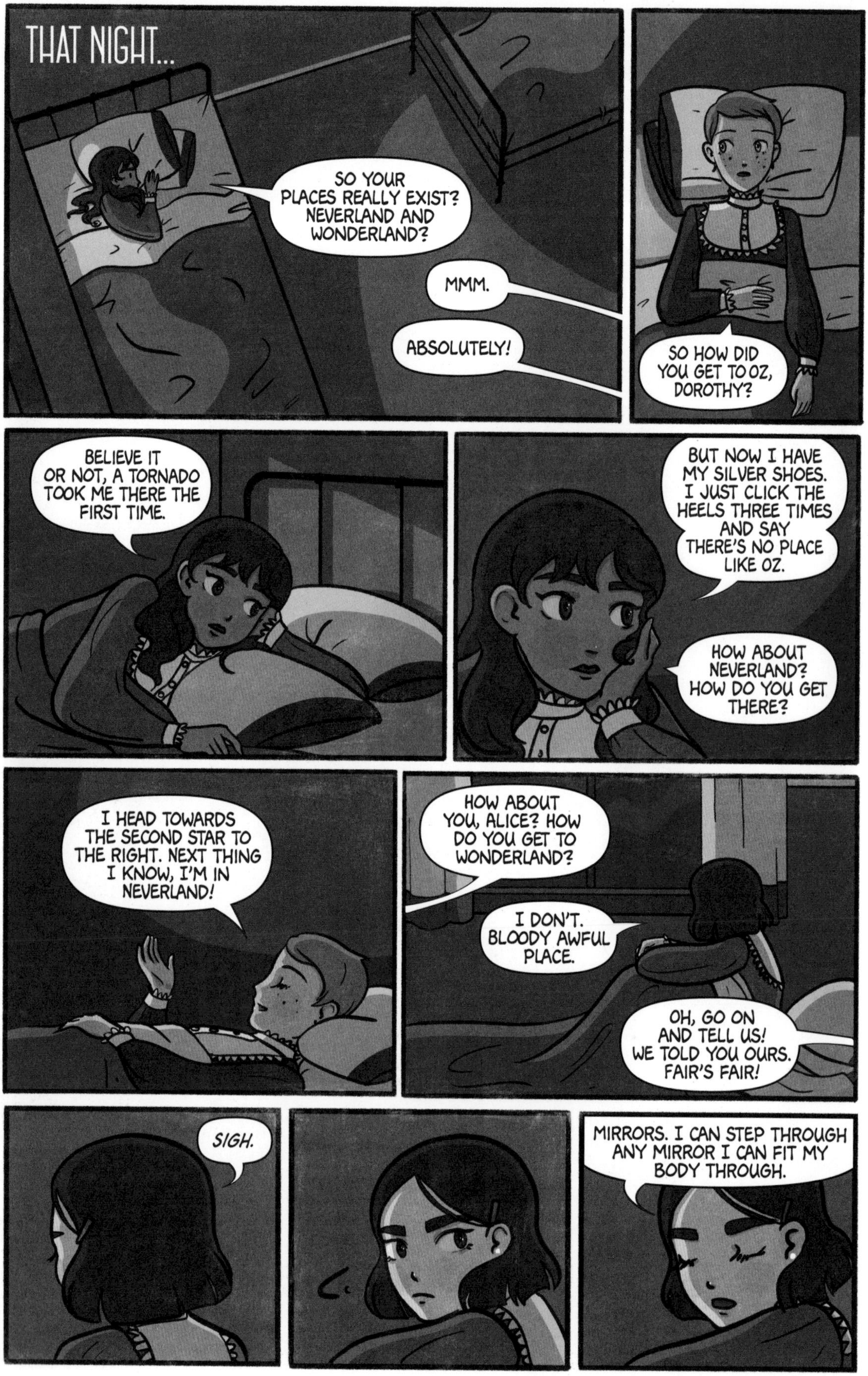
THAT NIGHT...
SO YOUR PLACES REALLY EXIST? NEVERLAND AND WONDERLAND?
MMM.
ABSOLUTELY!
SO HOW DID YOU GET TO OZ, DOROTHY?
BELIEVE IT OR NOT, A TORNADO TOOK ME THERE THE FIRST TIME.
BUT NOW I HAVE MY SILVER SHOES. I JUST CLICK THE HEELS THREE TIMES AND SAY THERE'S NO PLACE LIKE OZ.
HOW ABOUT NEVERLAND? HOW DO YOU GET THERE?
I HEAD TOWARDS THE SECOND STAR TO THE RIGHT. NEXT THING I KNOW, I'M IN NEVERLAND!
HOW ABOUT YOU, ALICE? HOW DO YOU GET TO WONDERLAND?
I DON'T. BLOODY AWFUL PLACE.
OH, GO ON AND TELL US! WE TOLD YOU OURS. FAIR'S FAIR!
SIGH.
MIRRORS. I CAN STEP THROUGH ANY MIRROR I CAN FIT MY BODY THROUGH.

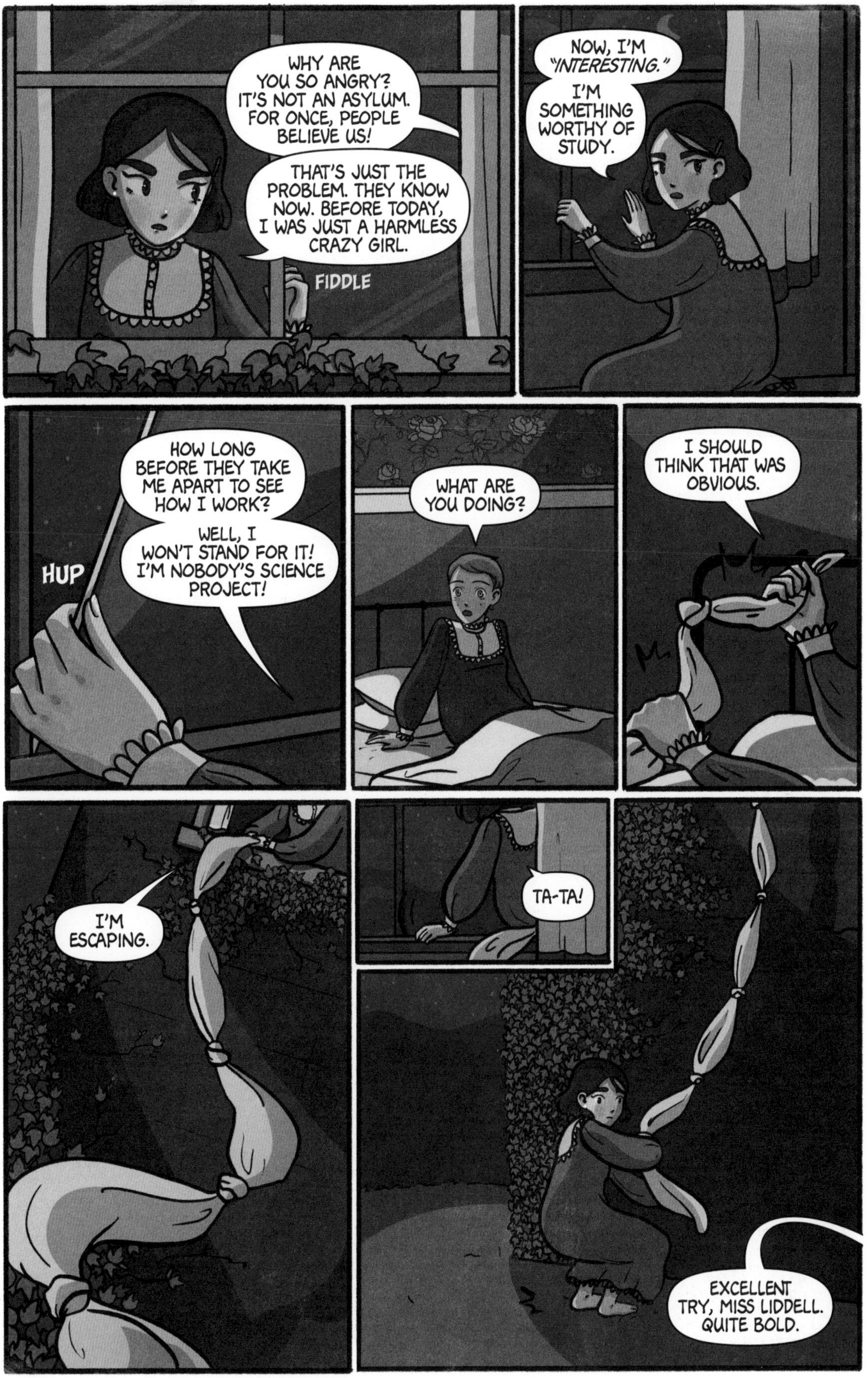
WHY ARE YOU SO ANGRY? IT'S NOT AN ASYLUM. FOR ONCE, PEOPLE BELIEVE US!
THAT'S JUST THE PROBLEM. THEY KNOW NOW. BEFORE TODAY, I WAS JUST A HARMLESS CRAZY GIRL.
FIDDLE
NOW, I'M *"INTERESTING."*
I'M SOMETHING WORTHY OF STUDY.
HOW LONG BEFORE THEY TAKE ME APART TO SEE HOW I WORK?
WELL, I WON'T STAND FOR IT! I'M NOBODY'S SCIENCE PROJECT!
HUP
WHAT ARE YOU DOING?
I SHOULD THINK THAT WAS OBVIOUS.
I'M ESCAPING.
TA-TA!
EXCELLENT TRY, MISS LIDDELL. QUITE BOLD.

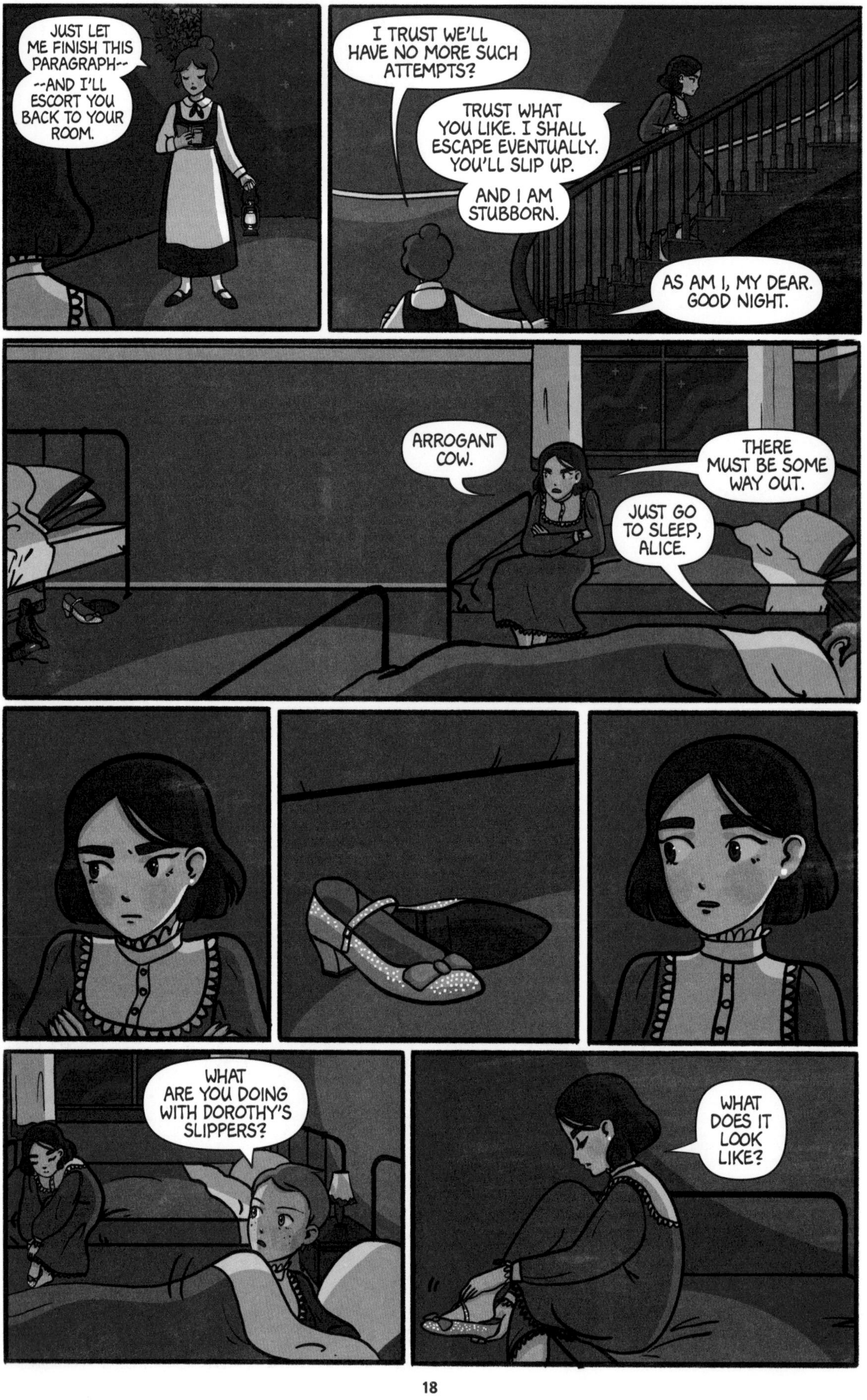
JUST LET ME FINISH THIS PARAGRAPH--
--AND I'LL ESCORT YOU BACK TO YOUR ROOM.
I TRUST WE'LL HAVE NO MORE SUCH ATTEMPTS?
TRUST WHAT YOU LIKE. I SHALL ESCAPE EVENTUALLY. YOU'LL SLIP UP.
AND I AM STUBBORN.
AS AM I, MY DEAR. GOOD NIGHT.
ARROGANT COW.
THERE MUST BE SOME WAY OUT.
JUST GO TO SLEEP, ALICE.
WHAT ARE YOU DOING WITH DOROTHY'S SLIPPERS?
WHAT DOES IT LOOK LIKE?

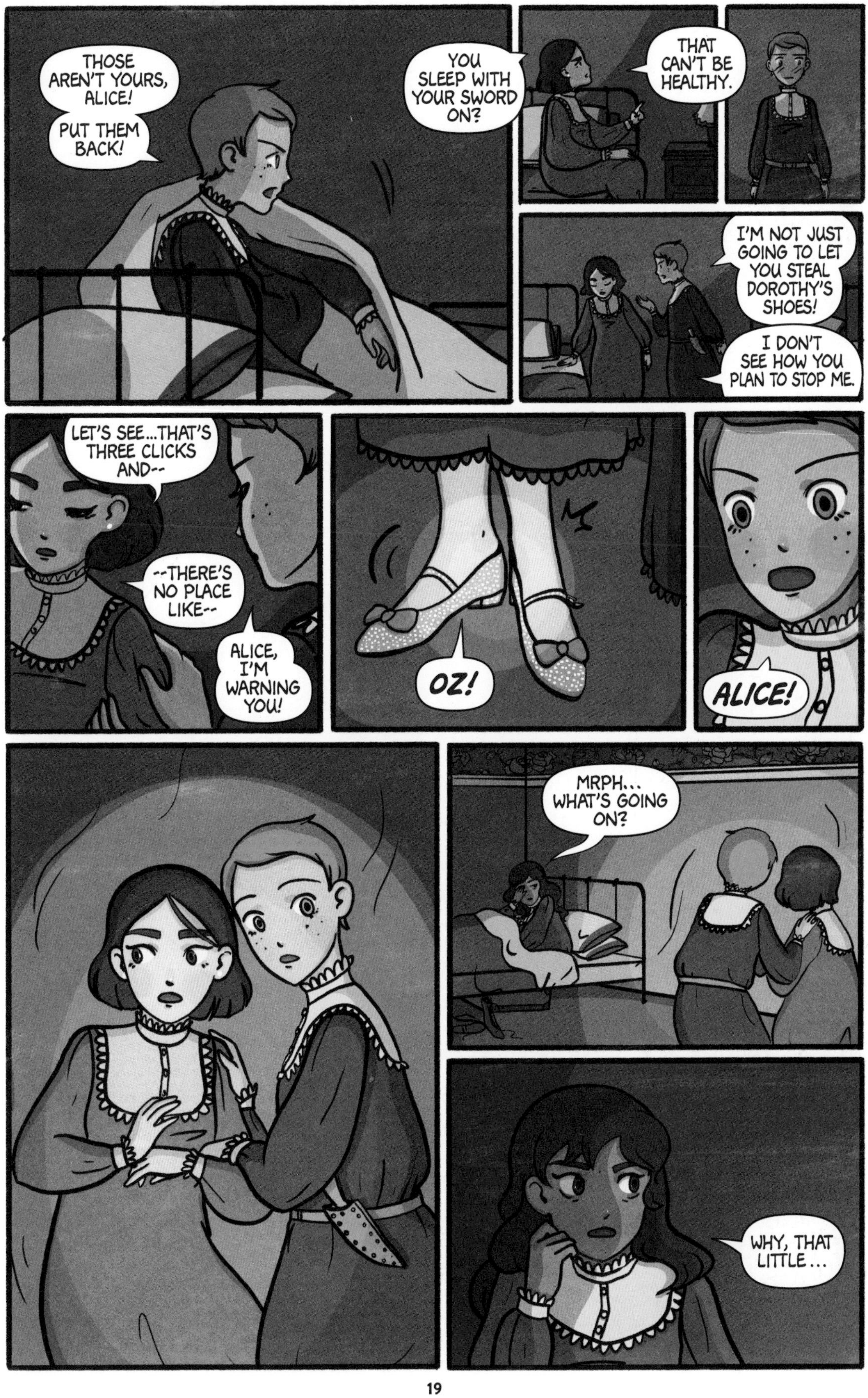
THOSE AREN'T YOURS, ALICE!
PUT THEM BACK!
YOU SLEEP WITH YOUR SWORD ON?
THAT CAN'T BE HEALTHY.
I'M NOT JUST GOING TO LET YOU STEAL DOROTHY'S SHOES!
I DON'T SEE HOW YOU PLAN TO STOP ME.
LET'S SEE...THAT'S THREE CLICKS AND--
--THERE'S NO PLACE LIKE--
ALICE, I'M WARNING YOU!
OZ!
ALICE!
MRPH... WHAT'S GOING ON?
WHY, THAT LITTLE...

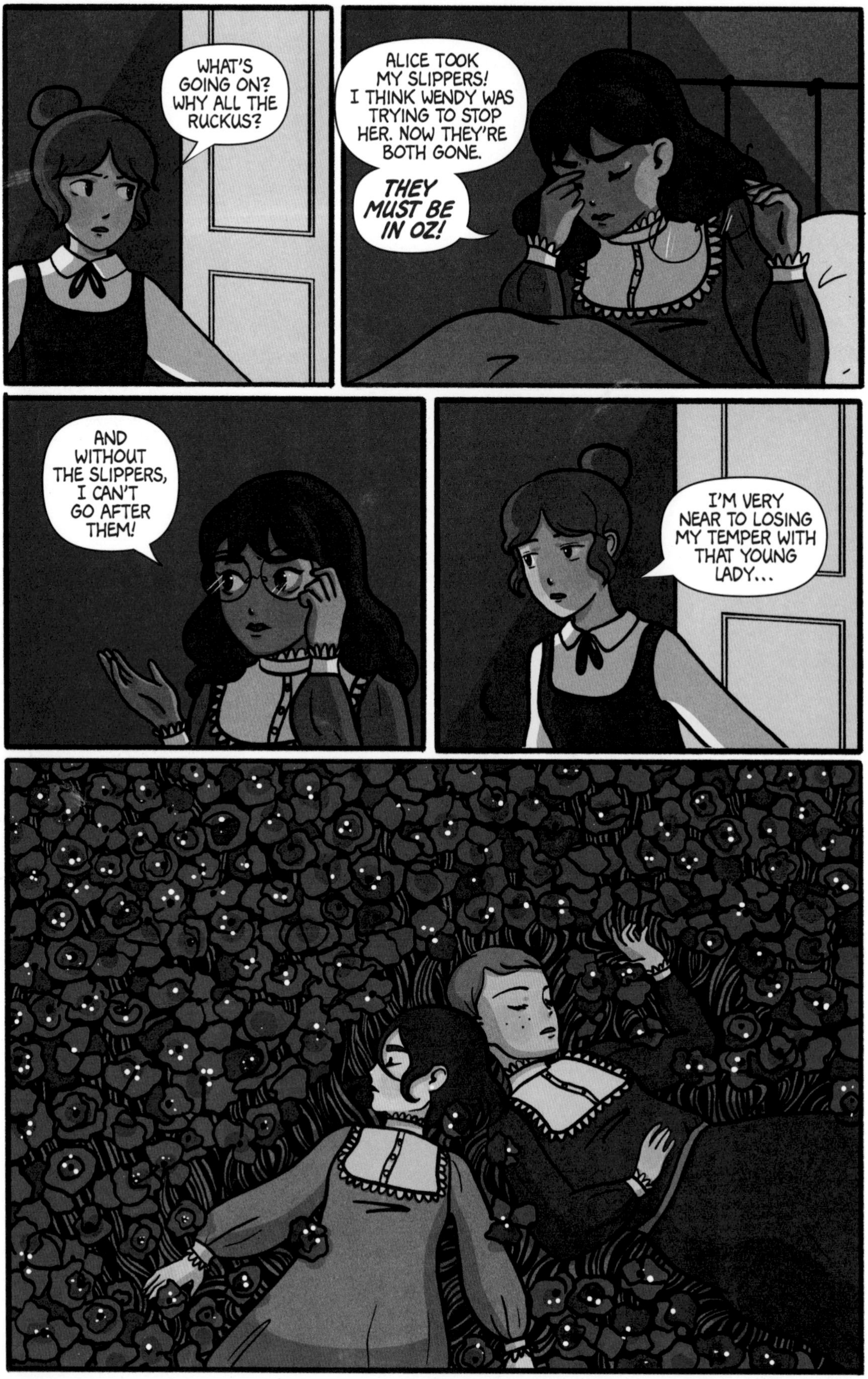
WHAT'S GOING ON? WHY ALL THE RUCKUS?
ALICE TOOK MY SLIPPERS! I THINK WENDY WAS TRYING TO STOP HER. NOW THEY'RE BOTH GONE.
THEY MUST BE IN OZ!
AND WITHOUT THE SLIPPERS, I CAN'T GO AFTER THEM!
I'M VERY NEAR TO LOSING MY TEMPER WITH THAT YOUNG LADY...

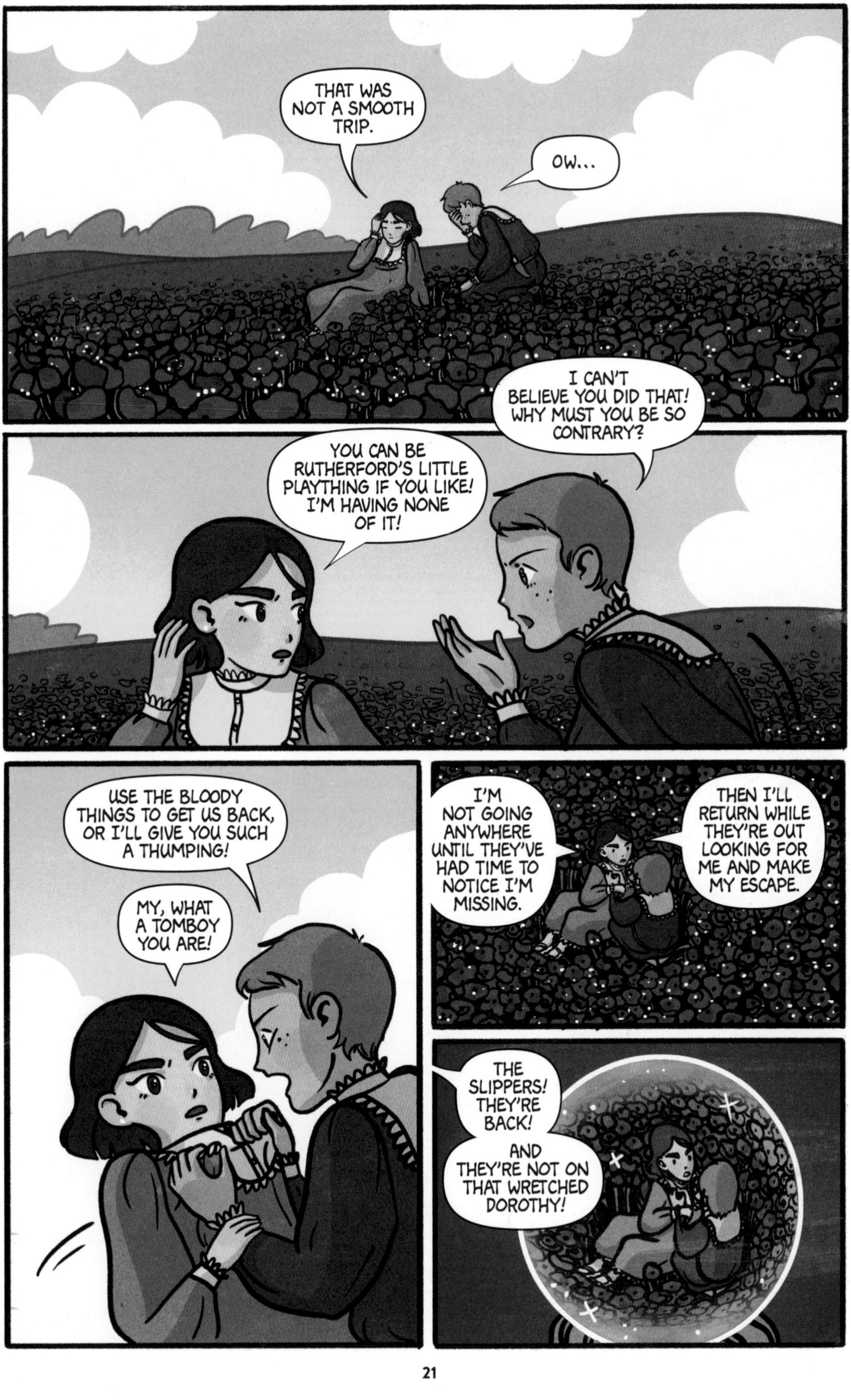
THAT WAS NOT A SMOOTH TRIP.
OW...
YOU CAN BE RUTHERFORD'S LITTLE PLAYTHING IF YOU LIKE! I'M HAVING NONE OF IT!
I CAN'T BELIEVE YOU DID THAT! WHY MUST YOU BE SO CONTRARY?
USE THE BLOODY THINGS TO GET US BACK, OR I'LL GIVE YOU SUCH A THUMPING!
MY, WHAT A TOMBOY YOU ARE!
I'M NOT GOING ANYWHERE UNTIL THEY'VE HAD TIME TO NOTICE I'M MISSING.
THEN I'LL RETURN WHILE THEY'RE OUT LOOKING FOR ME AND MAKE MY ESCAPE.
THE SLIPPERS! THEY'RE BACK!
AND THEY'RE NOT ON THAT WRETCHED DOROTHY!

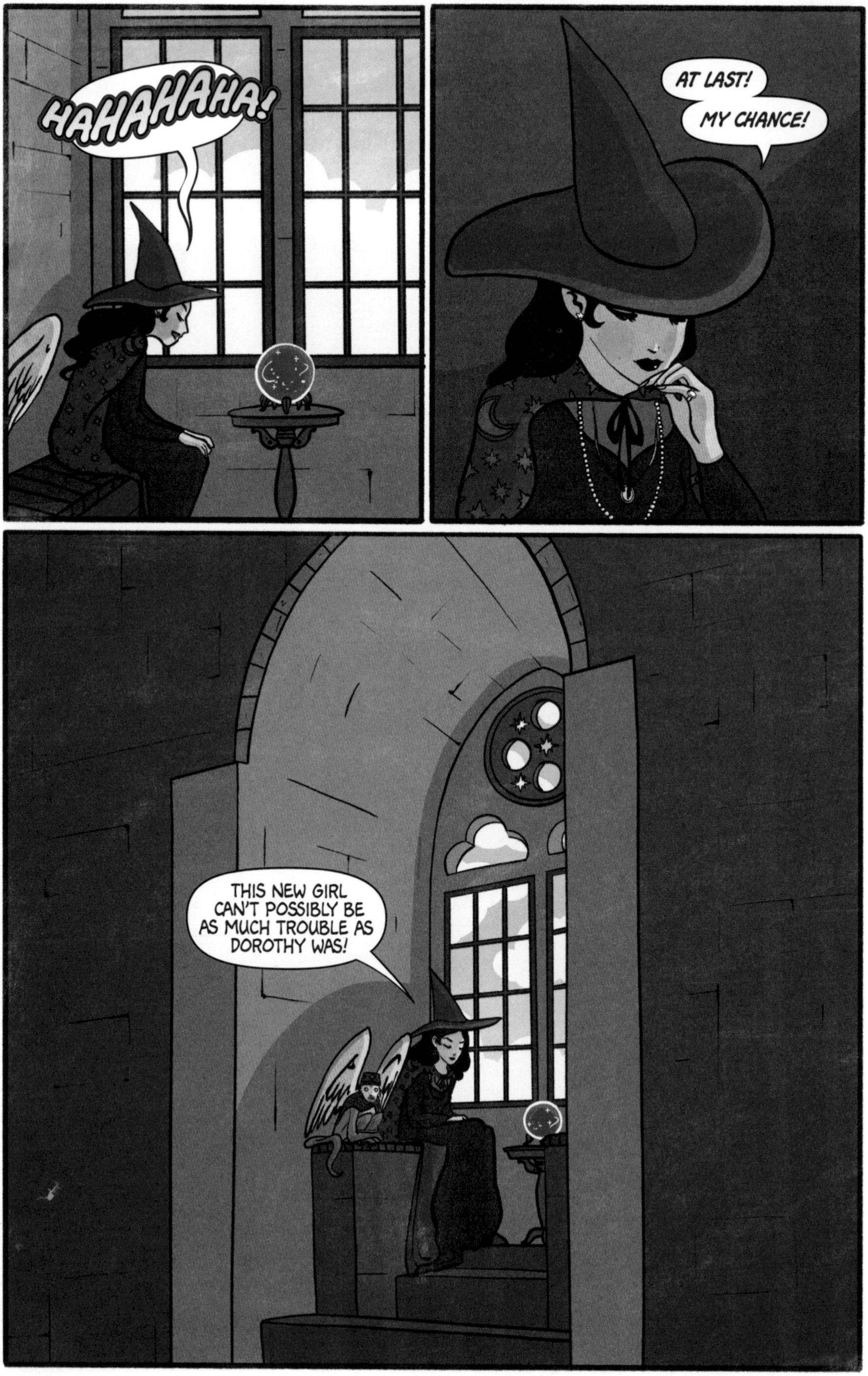
HAHAHAHA!
AT LAST!
MY CHANCE!
THIS NEW GIRL CAN'T POSSIBLY BE AS MUCH TROUBLE AS DOROTHY WAS!

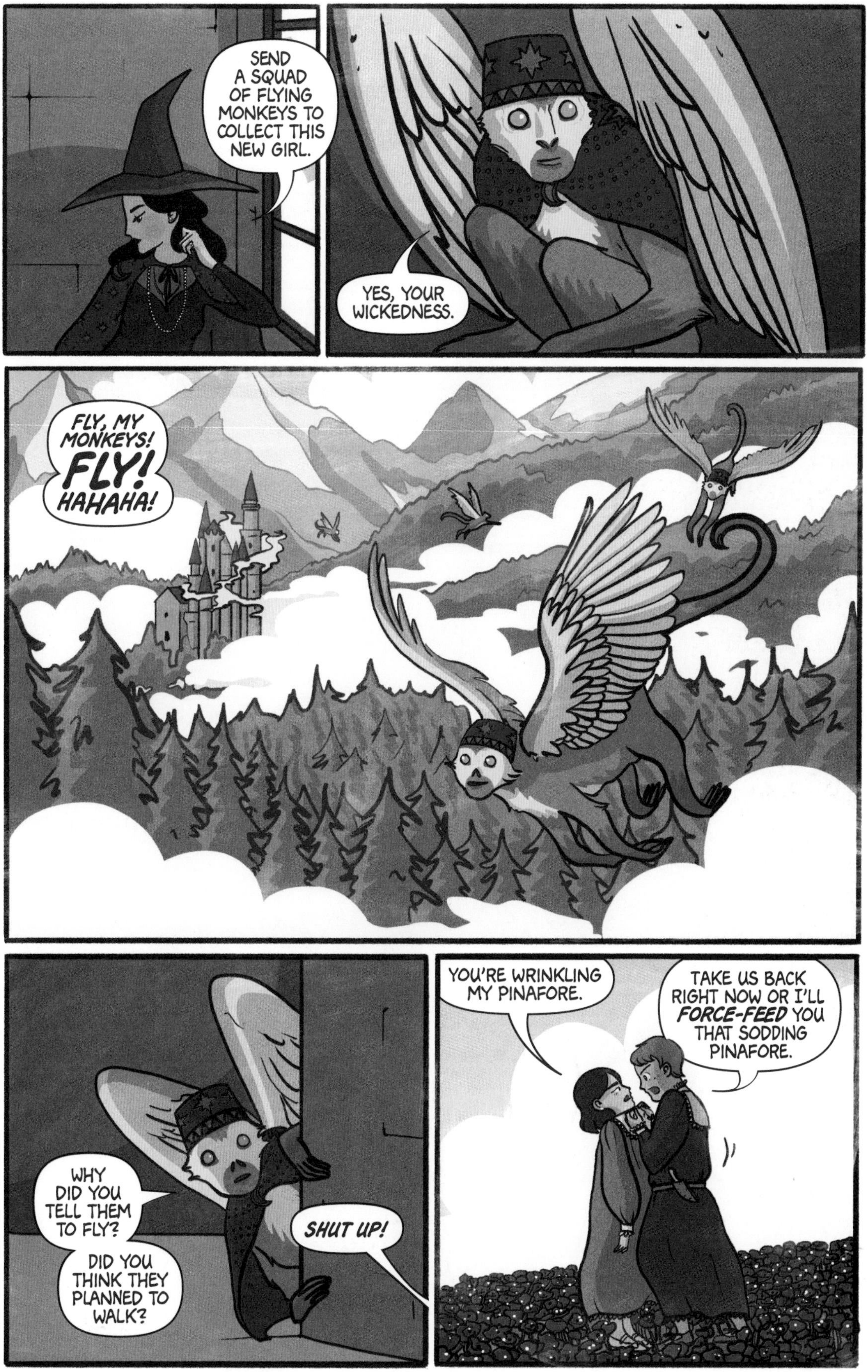
SEND A SQUAD OF FLYING MONKEYS TO COLLECT THIS NEW GIRL.
YES, YOUR WICKEDNESS.
FLY, MY MONKEYS! FLY! HAHAHA!
WHY DID YOU TELL THEM TO FLY?
DID YOU THINK THEY PLANNED TO WALK?
SHUT UP!
YOU'RE WRINKLING MY PINAFORE.
TAKE US BACK RIGHT NOW OR I'LL FORCE-FEED YOU THAT SODDING PINAFORE.

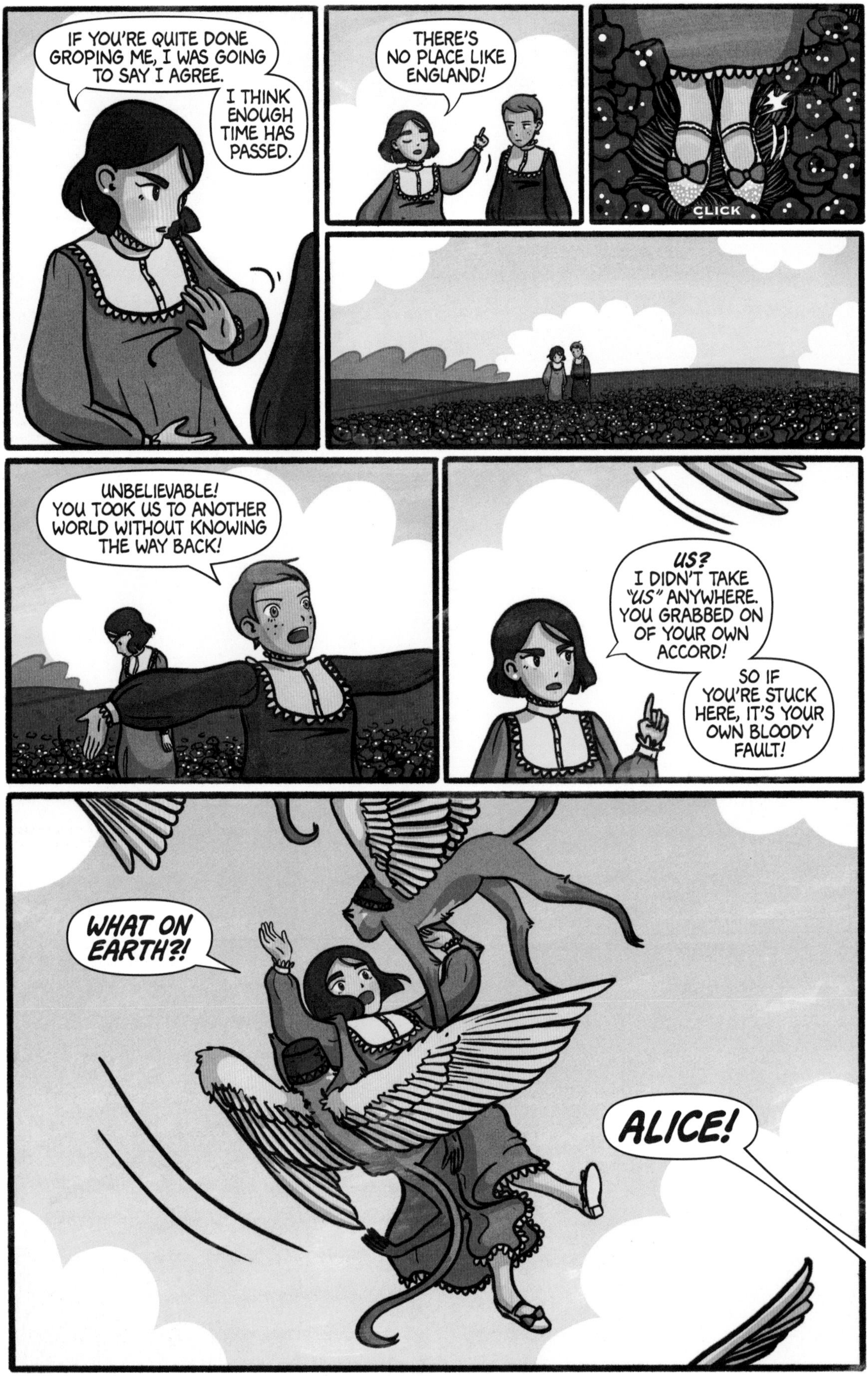
IF YOU'RE QUITE DONE GROPING ME, I WAS GOING TO SAY I AGREE.
I THINK ENOUGH TIME HAS PASSED.
THERE'S NO PLACE LIKE ENGLAND!
CLICK
UNBELIEVABLE! YOU TOOK US TO ANOTHER WORLD WITHOUT KNOWING THE WAY BACK!
US? I DIDN'T TAKE "US" ANYWHERE. YOU GRABBED ON OF YOUR OWN ACCORD!
SO IF YOU'RE STUCK HERE, IT'S YOUR OWN BLOODY FAULT!
WHAT ON EARTH?!
ALICE!

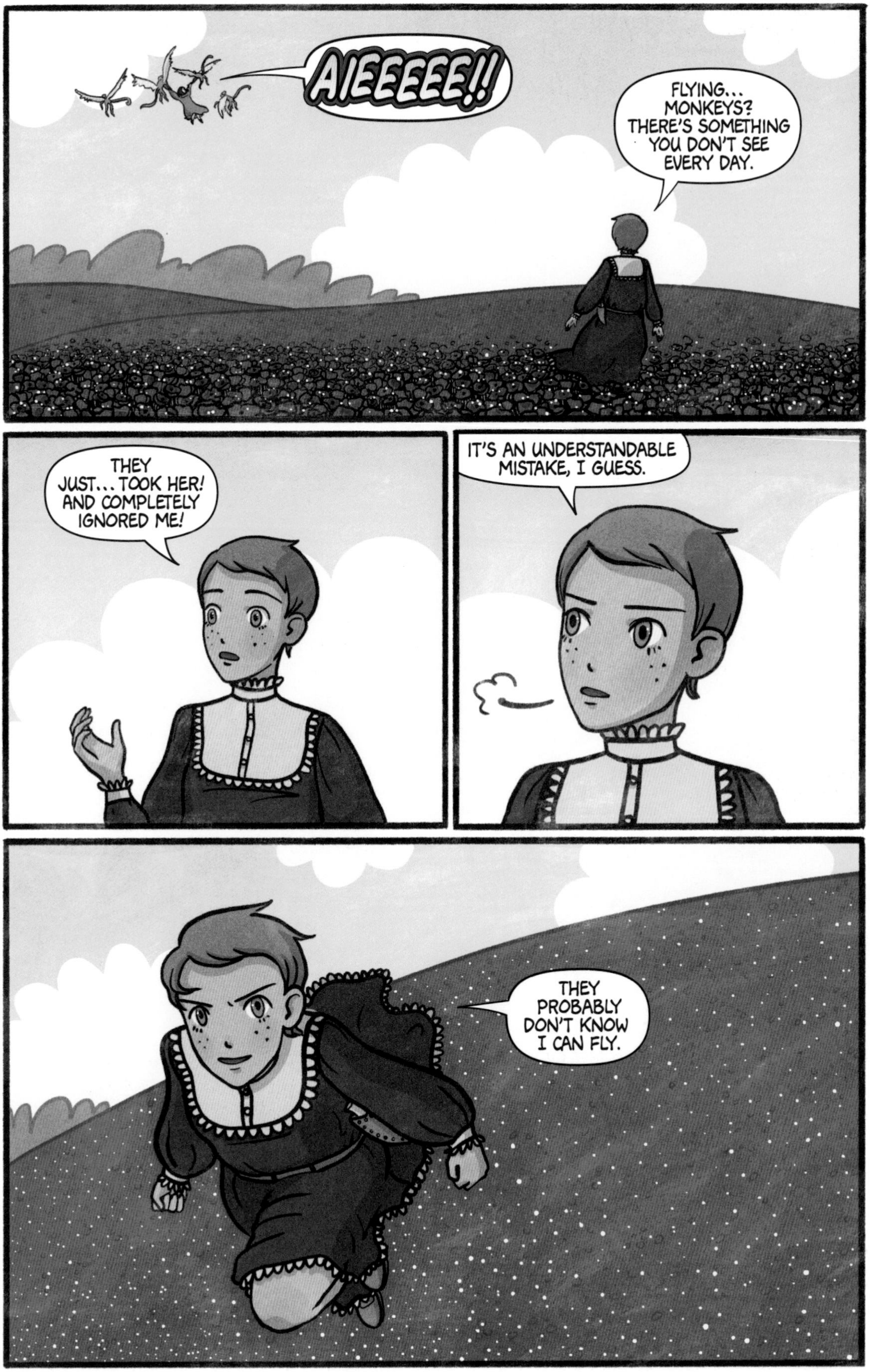
AIEEEEEE!!
FLYING... MONKEYS? THERE'S SOMETHING YOU DON'T SEE EVERY DAY.
THEY JUST... TOOK HER! AND COMPLETELY IGNORED ME!
IT'S AN UNDERSTANDABLE MISTAKE, I GUESS.
THEY PROBABLY DON'T KNOW I CAN FLY.

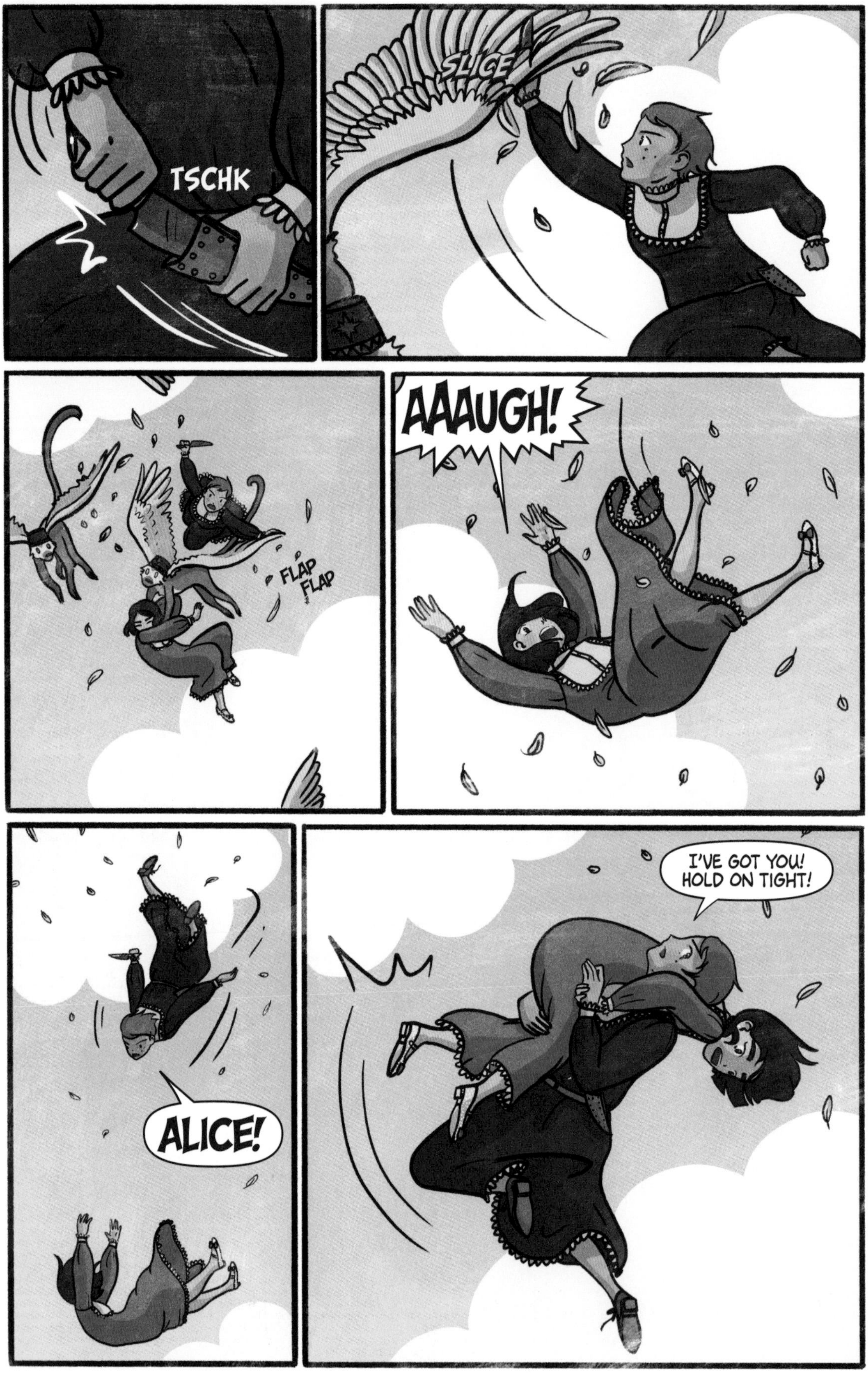
TSCHK
SLICE
FLAP FLAP
AAAUGH!
ALICE!
I'VE GOT YOU! HOLD ON TIGHT!

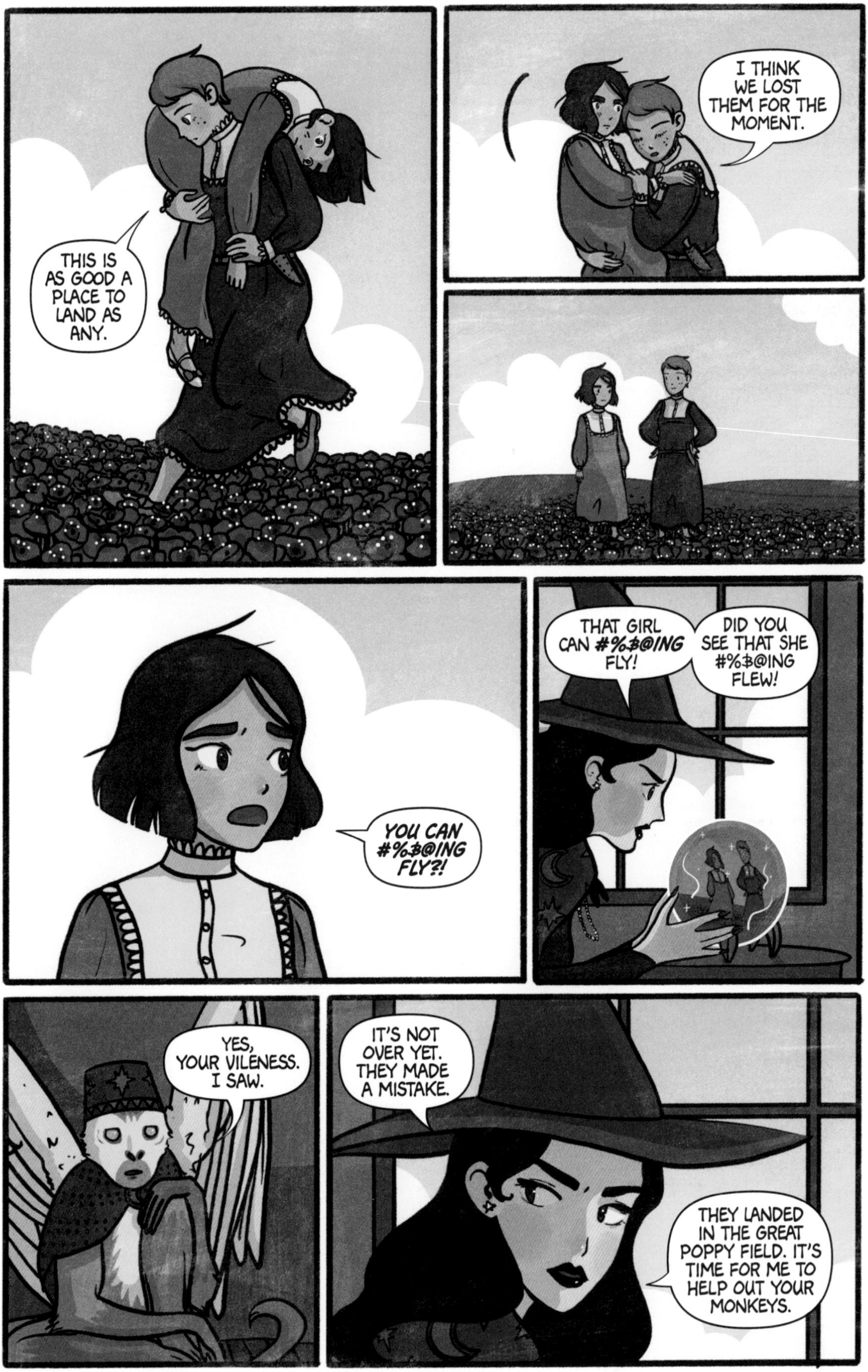
THIS IS AS GOOD A PLACE TO LAND AS ANY.
I THINK WE LOST THEM FOR THE MOMENT.
YOU CAN #%₿@ING FLY?!
THAT GIRL CAN #%₿@ING FLY!
DID YOU SEE THAT SHE #%₿@ING FLEW!
YES, YOUR VILENESS. I SAW.
IT'S NOT OVER YET. THEY MADE A MISTAKE.
THEY LANDED IN THE GREAT POPPY FIELD. IT'S TIME FOR ME TO HELP OUT YOUR MONKEYS.

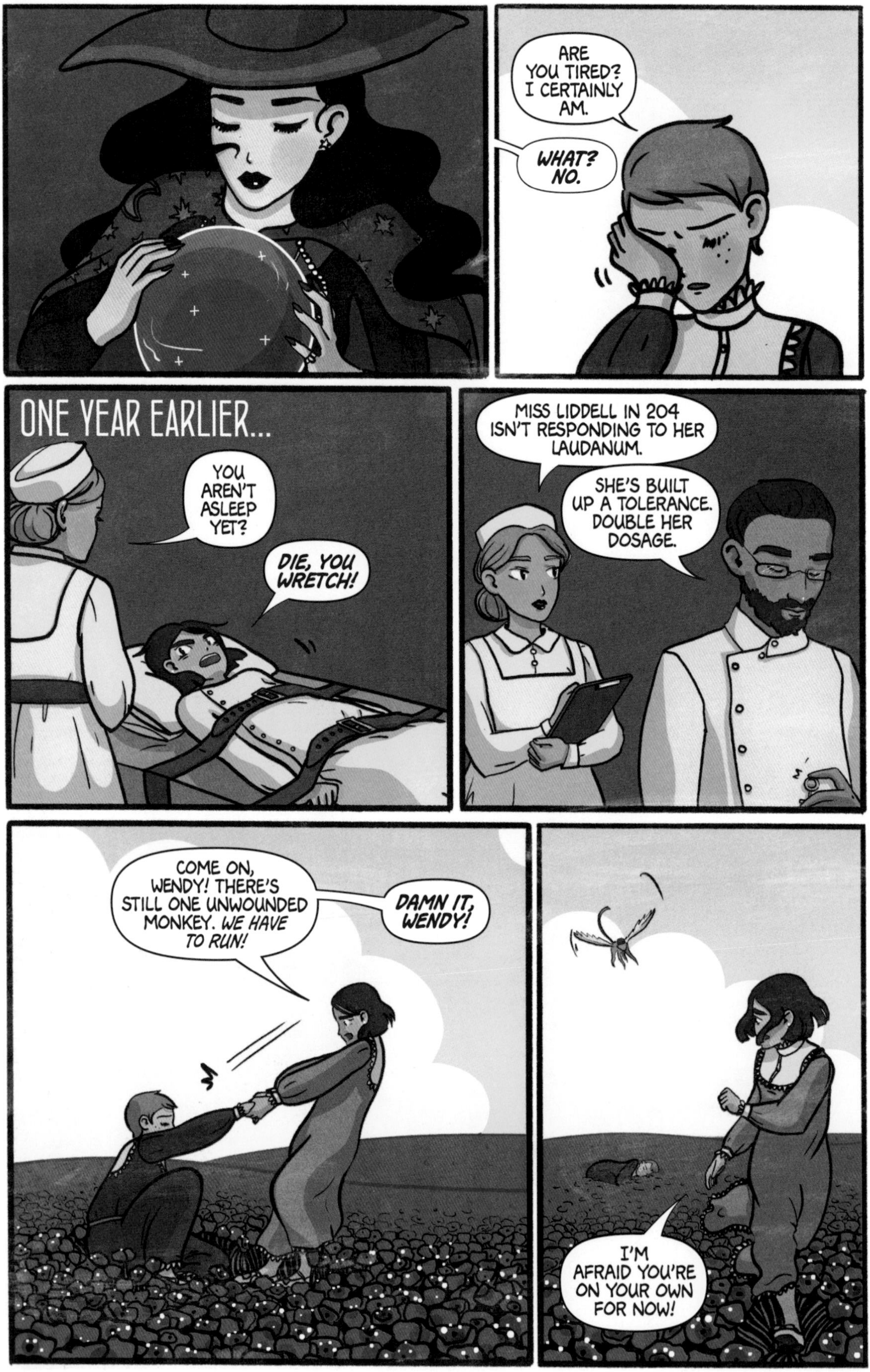
ARE YOU TIRED? I CERTAINLY AM.
WHAT? NO.
ONE YEAR EARLIER...
YOU AREN'T ASLEEP YET?
DIE, YOU WRETCH!
MISS LIDDELL IN 204 ISN'T RESPONDING TO HER LAUDANUM.
SHE'S BUILT UP A TOLERANCE. DOUBLE HER DOSAGE.
COME ON, WENDY! THERE'S STILL ONE UNWOUNDED MONKEY. *WE HAVE TO RUN!*
DAMN IT, WENDY!
I'M AFRAID YOU'RE ON YOUR OWN FOR NOW!

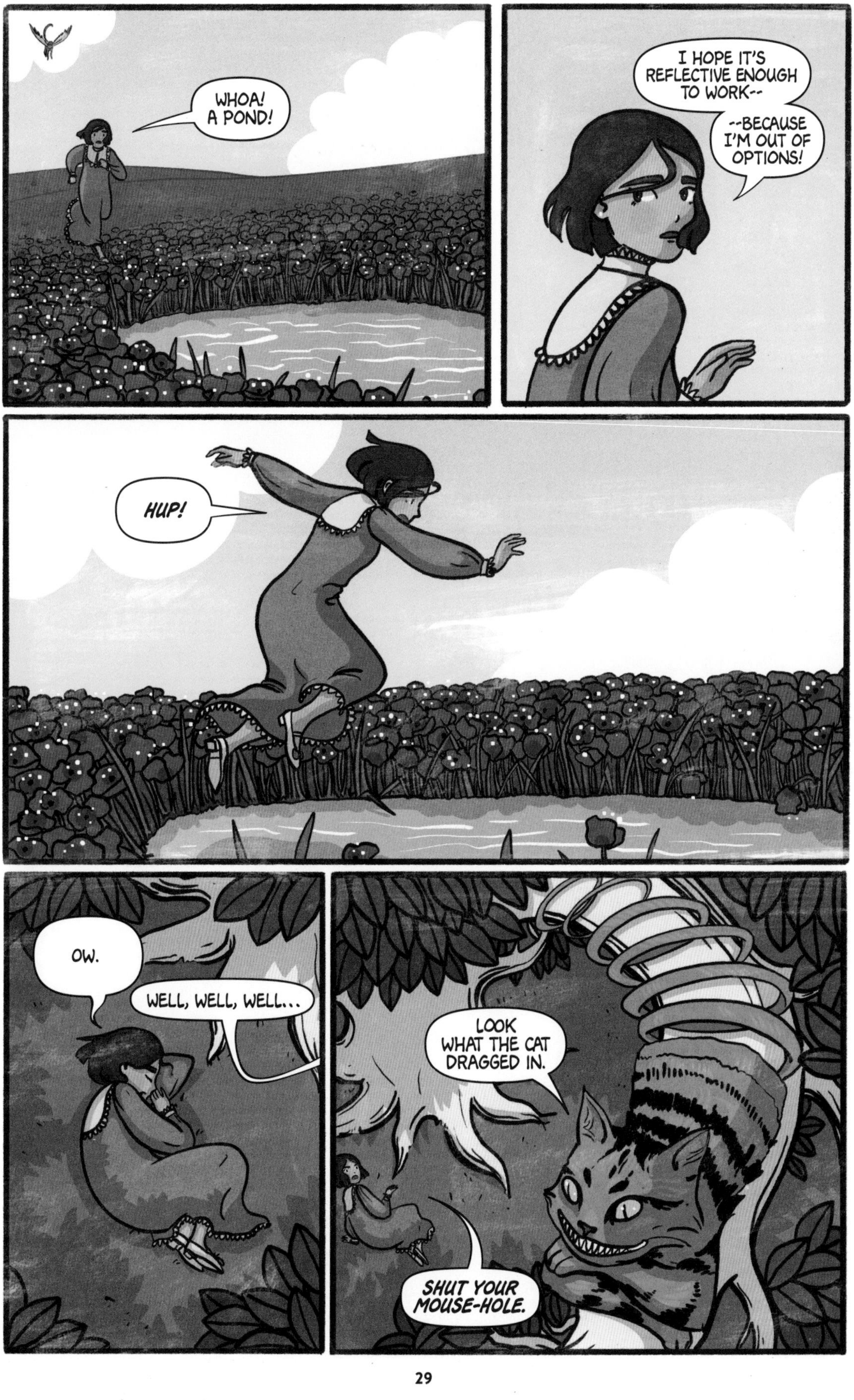
WHOA! A POND!
I HOPE IT'S REFLECTIVE ENOUGH TO WORK--
--BECAUSE I'M OUT OF OPTIONS!
HUP!
OW.
WELL, WELL, WELL...
LOOK WHAT THE CAT DRAGGED IN.
SHUT YOUR MOUSE-HOLE.

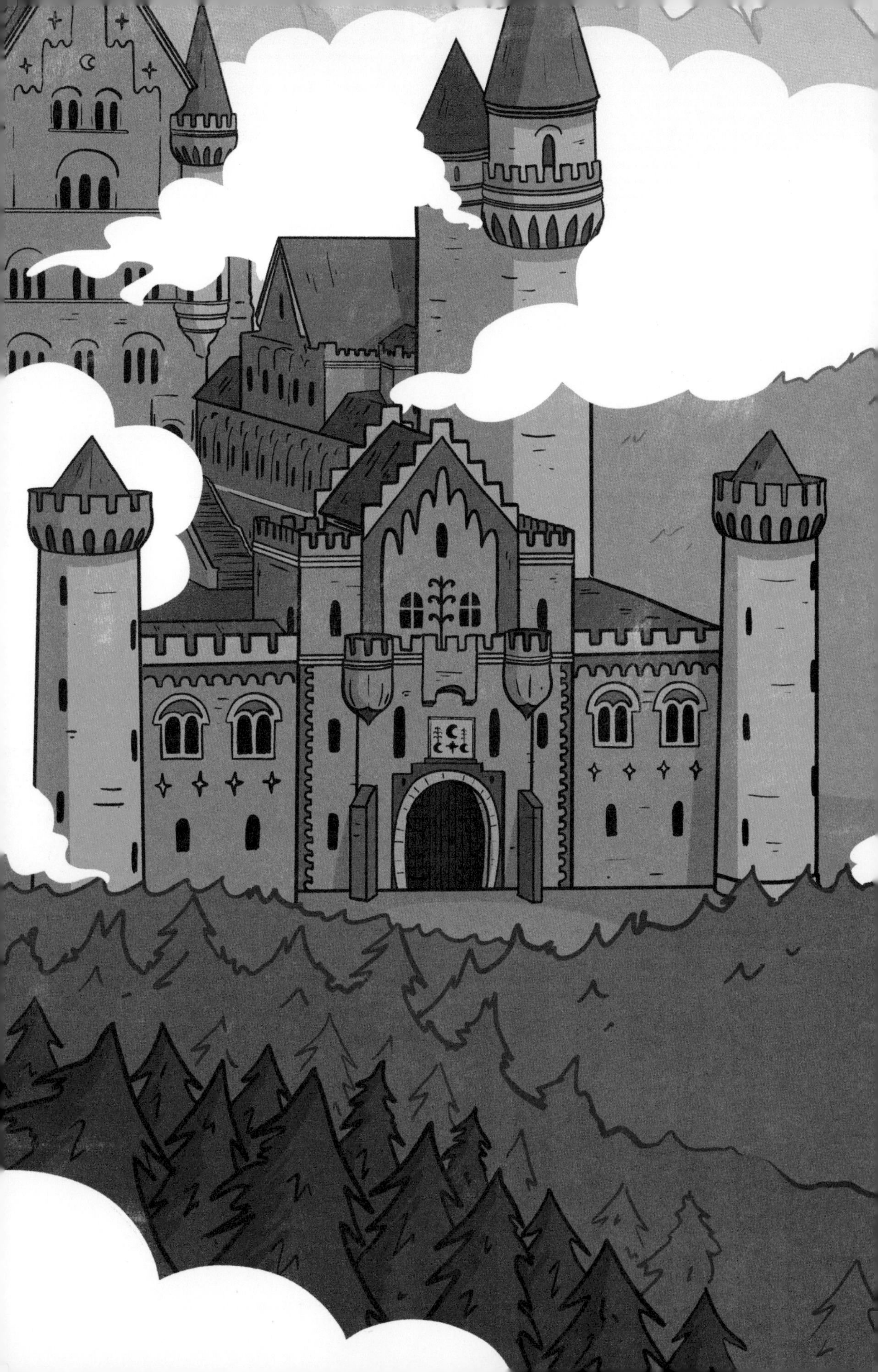

A VERY BAD WITCH

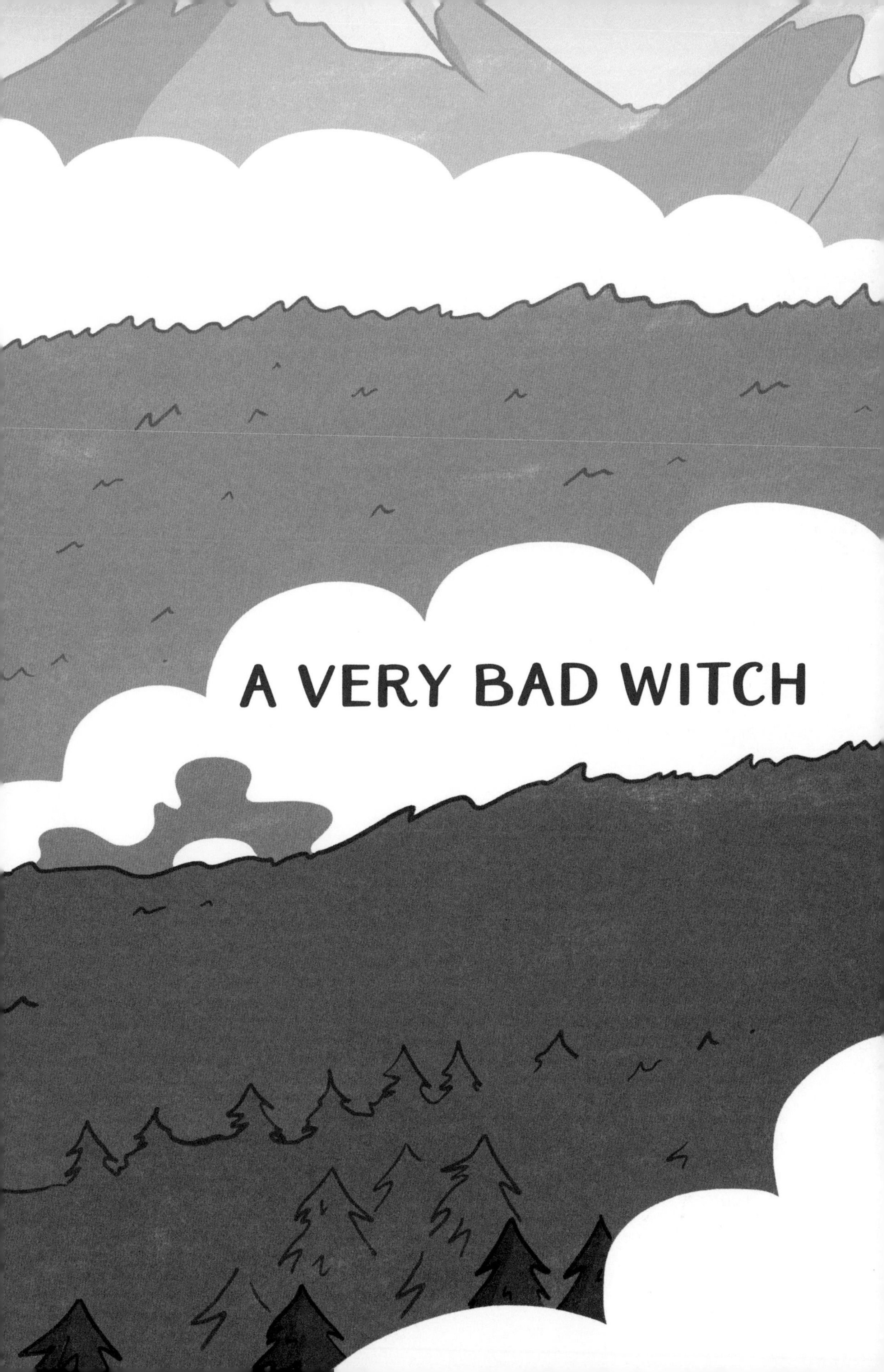

OZ

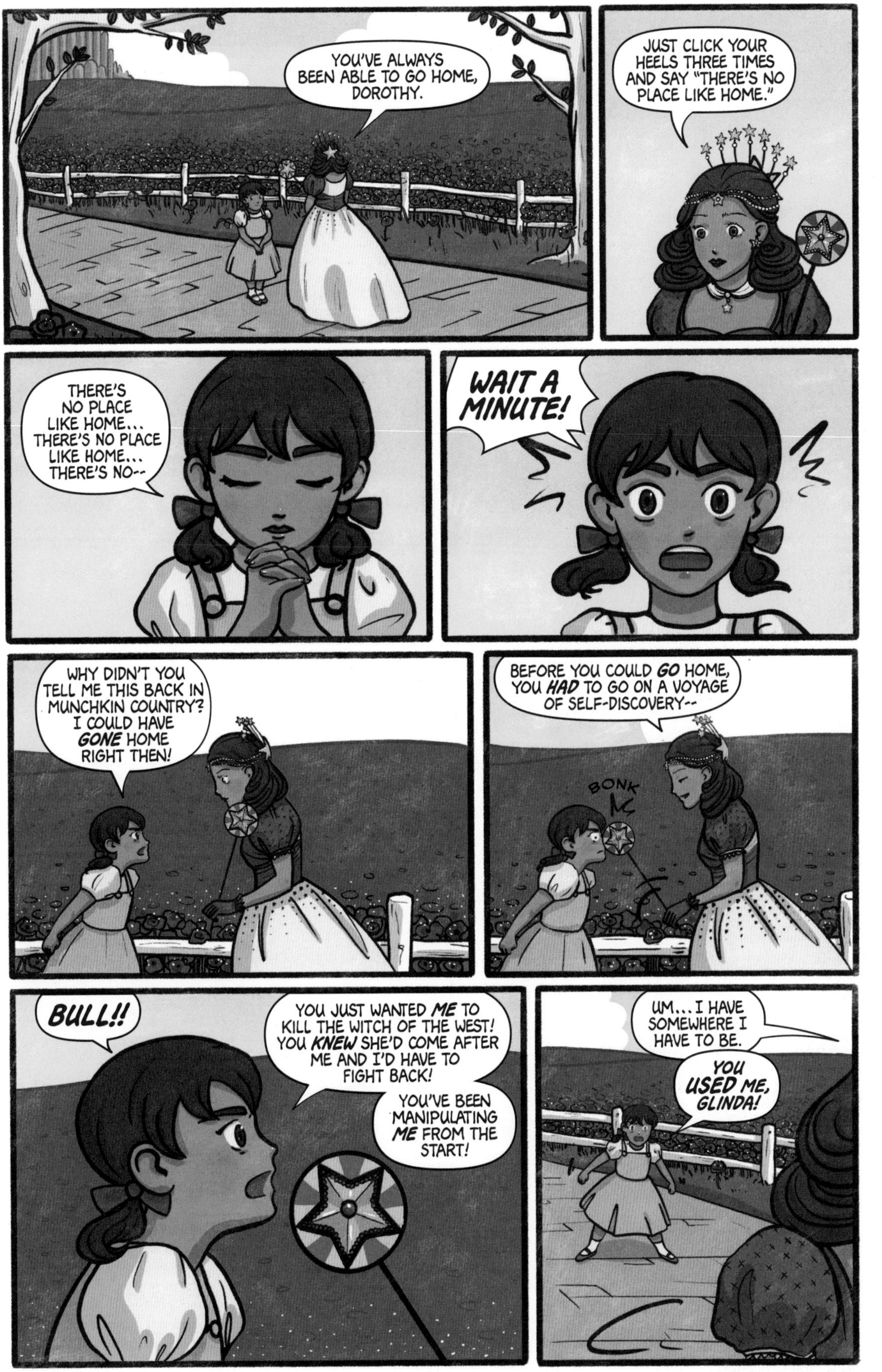
YOU'VE ALWAYS BEEN ABLE TO GO HOME, DOROTHY.
JUST CLICK YOUR HEELS THREE TIMES AND SAY "THERE'S NO PLACE LIKE HOME."
THERE'S NO PLACE LIKE HOME... THERE'S NO PLACE LIKE HOME... THERE'S NO--
WAIT A MINUTE!
WHY DIDN'T YOU TELL ME THIS BACK IN MUNCHKIN COUNTRY? I COULD HAVE GONE HOME RIGHT THEN!
BEFORE YOU COULD GO HOME, YOU HAD TO GO ON A VOYAGE OF SELF-DISCOVERY--
BONK
BULL!!
YOU JUST WANTED ME TO KILL THE WITCH OF THE WEST! YOU KNEW SHE'D COME AFTER ME AND I'D HAVE TO FIGHT BACK!
YOU'VE BEEN MANIPULATING ME FROM THE START!
UM... I HAVE SOMEWHERE I HAVE TO BE.
YOU USED ME, GLINDA!

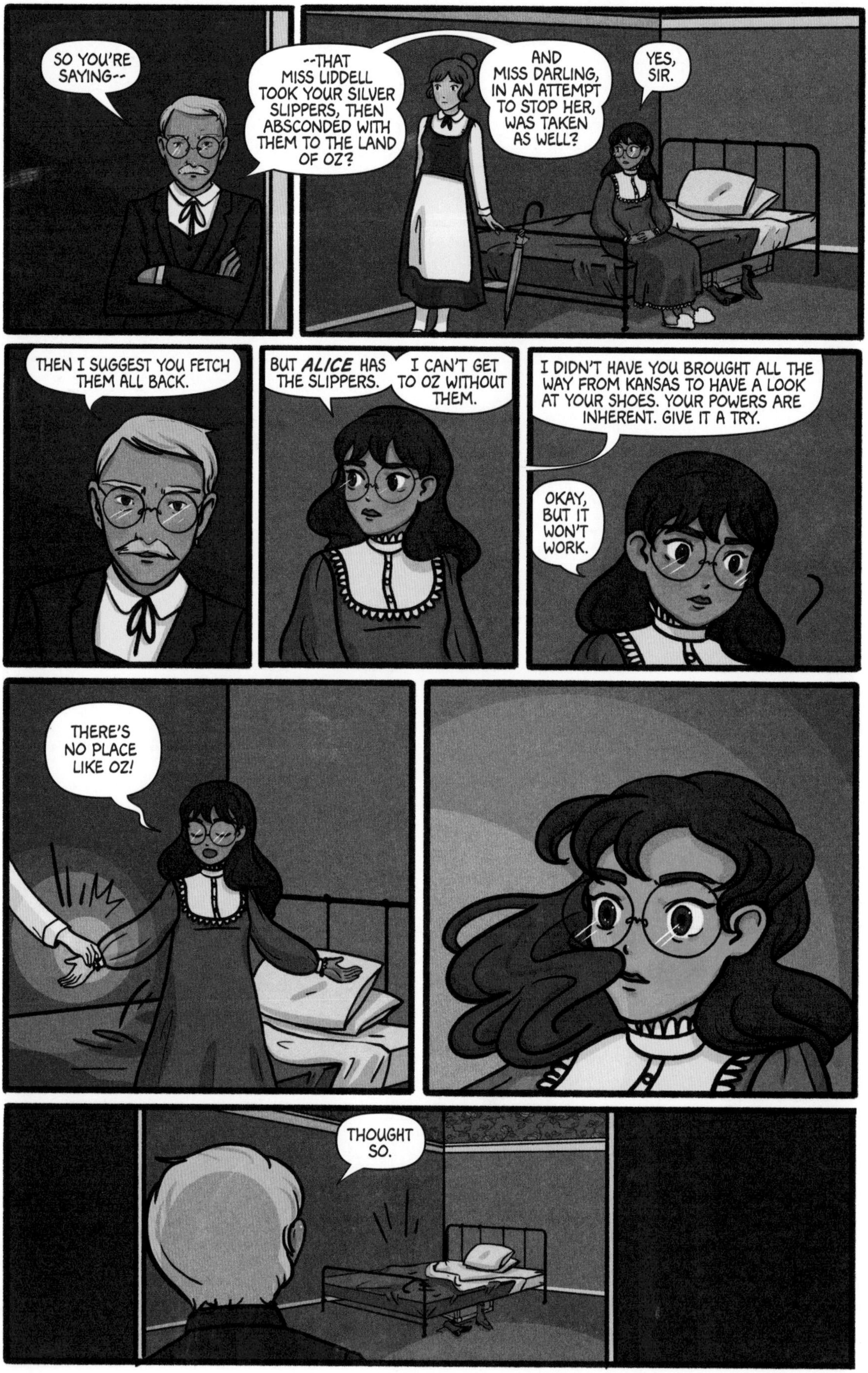
SO YOU'RE SAYING--
--THAT MISS LIDDELL TOOK YOUR SILVER SLIPPERS, THEN ABSCONDED WITH THEM TO THE LAND OF OZ?
AND MISS DARLING, IN AN ATTEMPT TO STOP HER, WAS TAKEN AS WELL?
YES, SIR.
THEN I SUGGEST YOU FETCH THEM ALL BACK.
BUT ALICE HAS THE SLIPPERS.
I CAN'T GET TO OZ WITHOUT THEM.
I DIDN'T HAVE YOU BROUGHT ALL THE WAY FROM KANSAS TO HAVE A LOOK AT YOUR SHOES. YOUR POWERS ARE INHERENT. GIVE IT A TRY.
OKAY, BUT IT WON'T WORK.
THERE'S NO PLACE LIKE OZ!
THOUGHT SO.

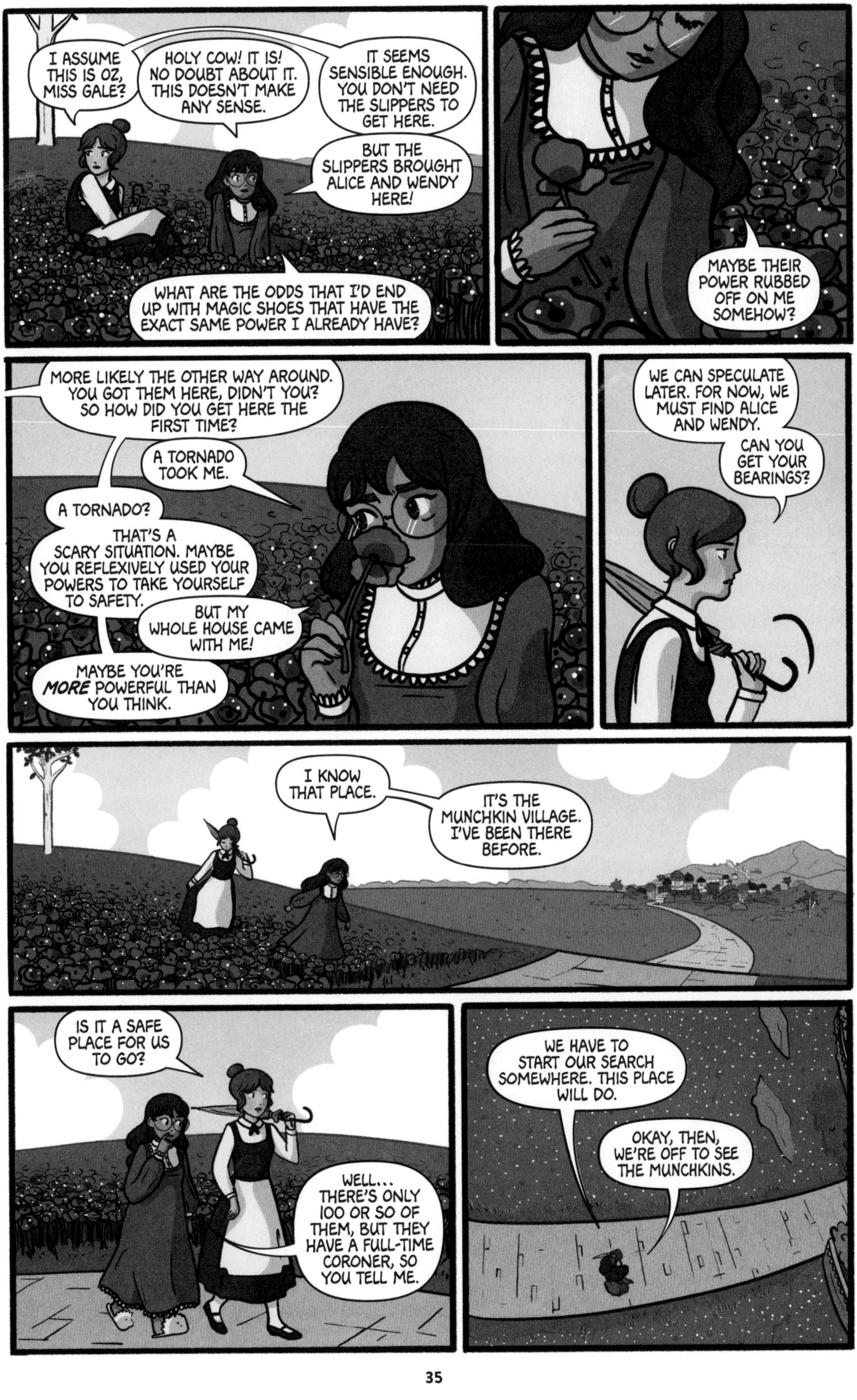
I ASSUME THIS IS OZ, MISS GALE?
HOLY COW! IT IS! NO DOUBT ABOUT IT. THIS DOESN'T MAKE ANY SENSE.
IT SEEMS SENSIBLE ENOUGH. YOU DON'T NEED THE SLIPPERS TO GET HERE.
BUT THE SLIPPERS BROUGHT ALICE AND WENDY HERE!
WHAT ARE THE ODDS THAT I'D END UP WITH MAGIC SHOES THAT HAVE THE EXACT SAME POWER I ALREADY HAVE?
MAYBE THEIR POWER RUBBED OFF ON ME SOMEHOW?
MORE LIKELY THE OTHER WAY AROUND. YOU GOT THEM HERE, DIDN'T YOU? SO HOW DID YOU GET HERE THE FIRST TIME?
A TORNADO TOOK ME.
A TORNADO?
THAT'S A SCARY SITUATION. MAYBE YOU REFLEXIVELY USED YOUR POWERS TO TAKE YOURSELF TO SAFETY.
BUT MY WHOLE HOUSE CAME WITH ME!
MAYBE YOU'RE ***MORE*** POWERFUL THAN YOU THINK.
WE CAN SPECULATE LATER. FOR NOW, WE MUST FIND ALICE AND WENDY.
CAN YOU GET YOUR BEARINGS?
I KNOW THAT PLACE.
IT'S THE MUNCHKIN VILLAGE. I'VE BEEN THERE BEFORE.
IS IT A SAFE PLACE FOR US TO GO?
WELL... THERE'S ONLY 100 OR SO OF THEM, BUT THEY HAVE A FULL-TIME CORONER, SO YOU TELL ME.
WE HAVE TO START OUR SEARCH SOMEWHERE. THIS PLACE WILL DO.
OKAY, THEN, WE'RE OFF TO SEE THE MUNCHKINS.

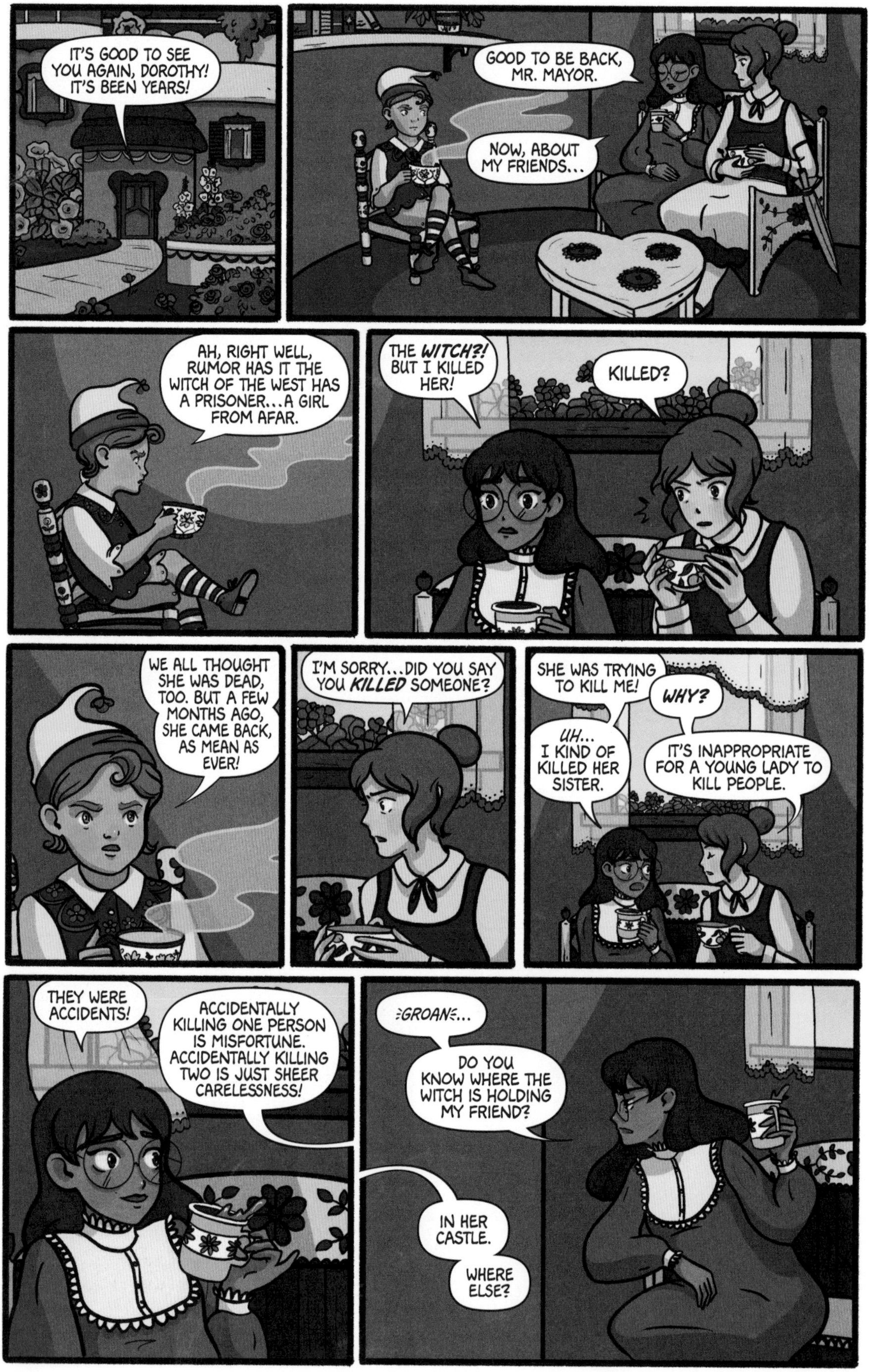

IT'S GOOD TO SEE YOU AGAIN, DOROTHY! IT'S BEEN YEARS!
GOOD TO BE BACK, MR. MAYOR.
NOW, ABOUT MY FRIENDS...
AH, RIGHT WELL, RUMOR HAS IT THE WITCH OF THE WEST HAS A PRISONER...A GIRL FROM AFAR.
THE *WITCH?!* BUT I KILLED HER!
KILLED?
WE ALL THOUGHT SHE WAS DEAD, TOO. BUT A FEW MONTHS AGO, SHE CAME BACK, AS MEAN AS EVER!
I'M SORRY...DID YOU SAY YOU *KILLED* SOMEONE?
SHE WAS TRYING TO KILL ME!
WHY?
UH... I KIND OF KILLED HER SISTER.
IT'S INAPPROPRIATE FOR A YOUNG LADY TO KILL PEOPLE.
THEY WERE ACCIDENTS!
ACCIDENTALLY KILLING ONE PERSON IS MISFORTUNE. ACCIDENTALLY KILLING TWO IS JUST SHEER CARELESSNESS!
GROAN...
DO YOU KNOW WHERE THE WITCH IS HOLDING MY FRIEND?
IN HER CASTLE.
WHERE ELSE?

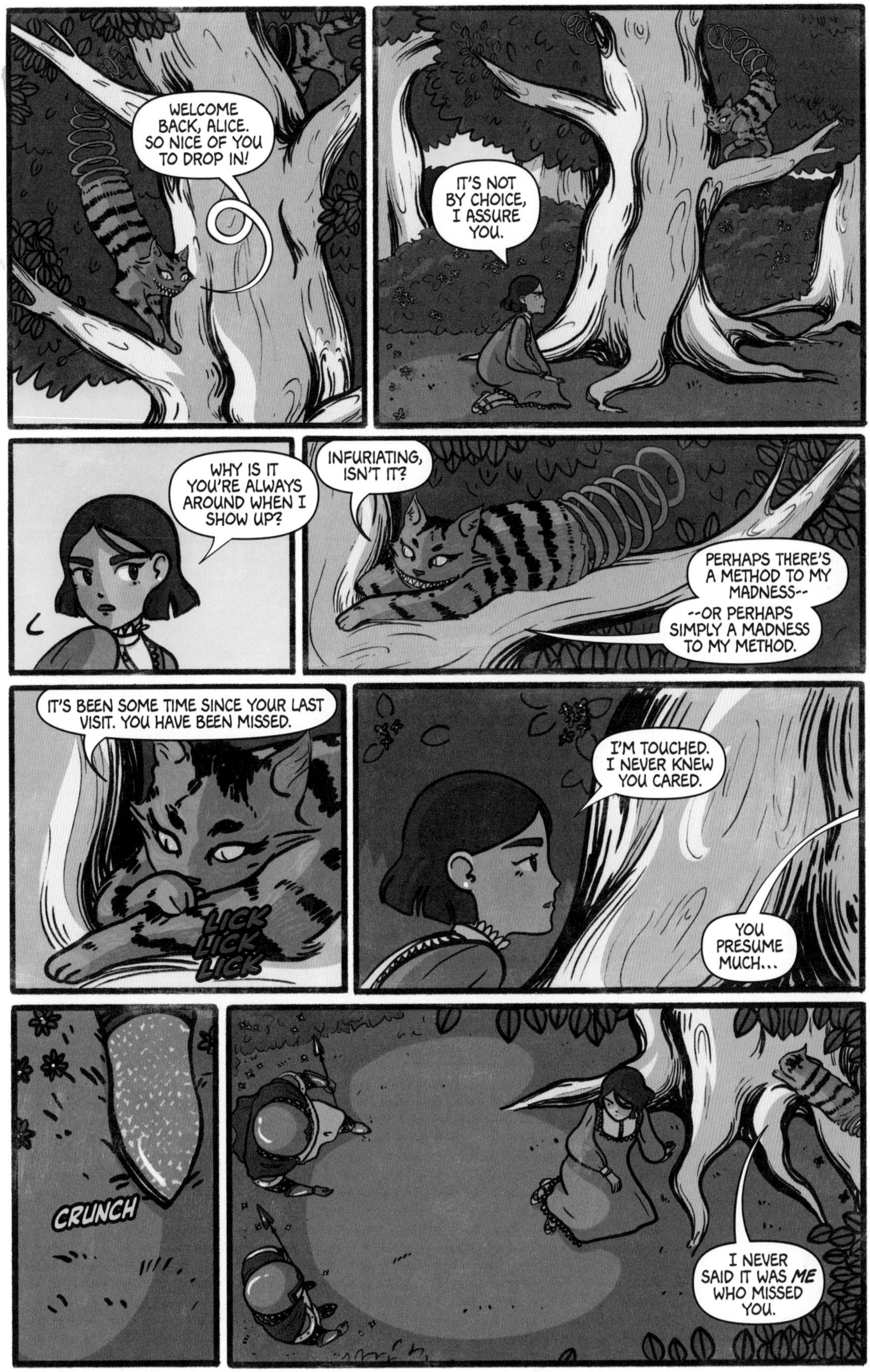
WELCOME BACK, ALICE. SO NICE OF YOU TO DROP IN!
IT'S NOT BY CHOICE, I ASSURE YOU.
WHY IS IT YOU'RE ALWAYS AROUND WHEN I SHOW UP?
INFURIATING, ISN'T IT?
PERHAPS THERE'S A METHOD TO MY MADNESS--
--OR PERHAPS SIMPLY A MADNESS TO MY METHOD.
IT'S BEEN SOME TIME SINCE YOUR LAST VISIT. YOU HAVE BEEN MISSED.
LICK LICK LICK
I'M TOUCHED. I NEVER KNEW YOU CARED.
YOU PRESUME MUCH...
CRUNCH
I NEVER SAID IT WAS *ME* WHO MISSED YOU.

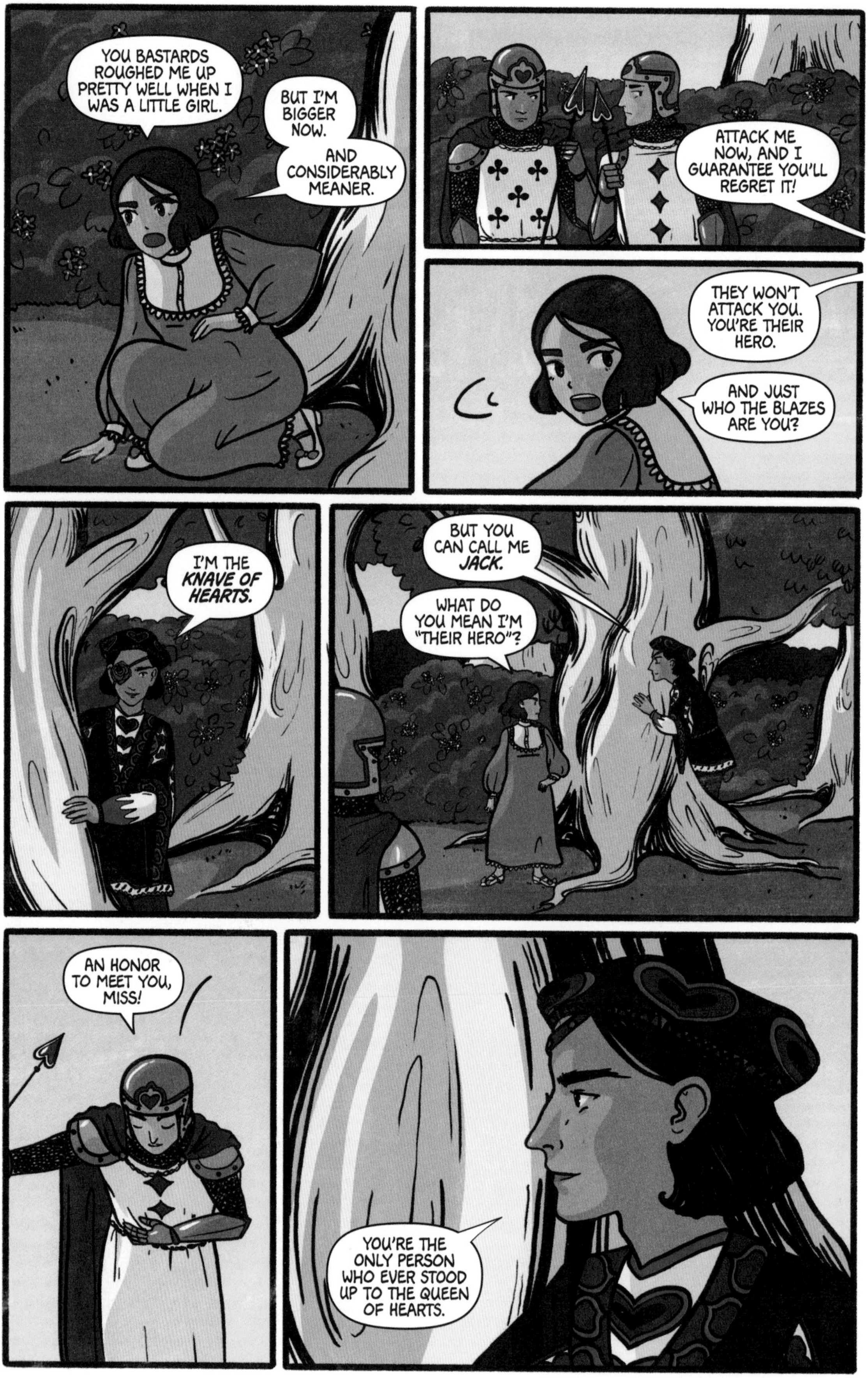
YOU BASTARDS ROUGHED ME UP PRETTY WELL WHEN I WAS A LITTLE GIRL.
BUT I'M BIGGER NOW.
AND CONSIDERABLY MEANER.
ATTACK ME NOW, AND I GUARANTEE YOU'LL REGRET IT!
THEY WON'T ATTACK YOU. YOU'RE THEIR HERO.
AND JUST WHO THE BLAZES ARE YOU?
I'M THE *KNAVE OF HEARTS.*
BUT YOU CAN CALL ME *JACK.*
WHAT DO YOU MEAN I'M "THEIR HERO"?
AN HONOR TO MEET YOU, MISS!
YOU'RE THE ONLY PERSON WHO EVER STOOD UP TO THE QUEEN OF HEARTS.

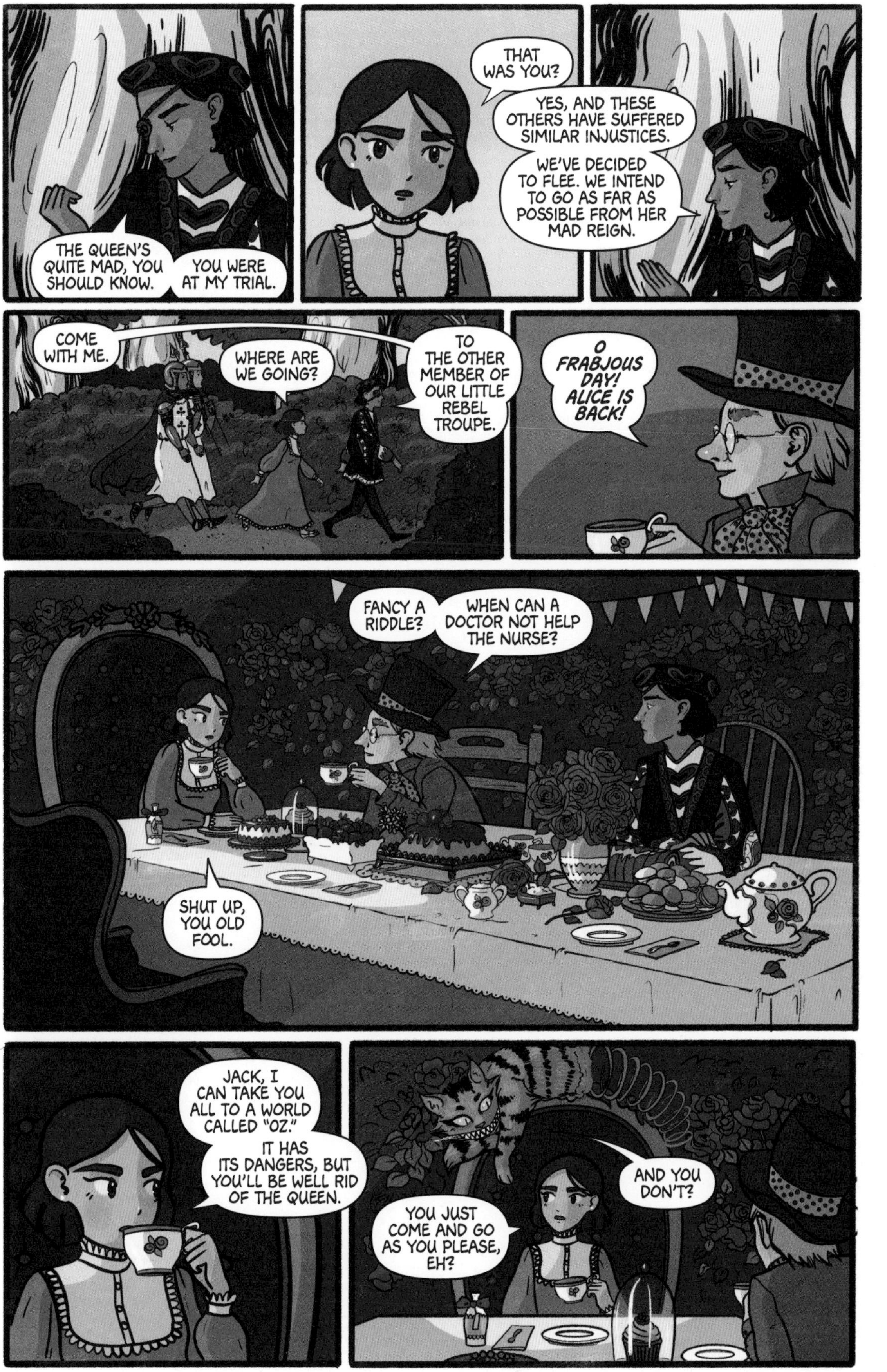
THE QUEEN'S QUITE MAD, YOU SHOULD KNOW.
YOU WERE AT MY TRIAL.
THAT WAS YOU?
YES, AND THESE OTHERS HAVE SUFFERED SIMILAR INJUSTICES.
WE'VE DECIDED TO FLEE. WE INTEND TO GO AS FAR AS POSSIBLE FROM HER MAD REIGN.
COME WITH ME.
WHERE ARE WE GOING?
TO THE OTHER MEMBER OF OUR LITTLE REBEL TROUPE.
O FRABJOUS DAY! ALICE IS BACK!
FANCY A RIDDLE?
WHEN CAN A DOCTOR NOT HELP THE NURSE?
SHUT UP, YOU OLD FOOL.
JACK, I CAN TAKE YOU ALL TO A WORLD CALLED "OZ."
IT HAS ITS DANGERS, BUT YOU'LL BE WELL RID OF THE QUEEN.
YOU JUST COME AND GO AS YOU PLEASE, EH?
AND YOU DON'T?

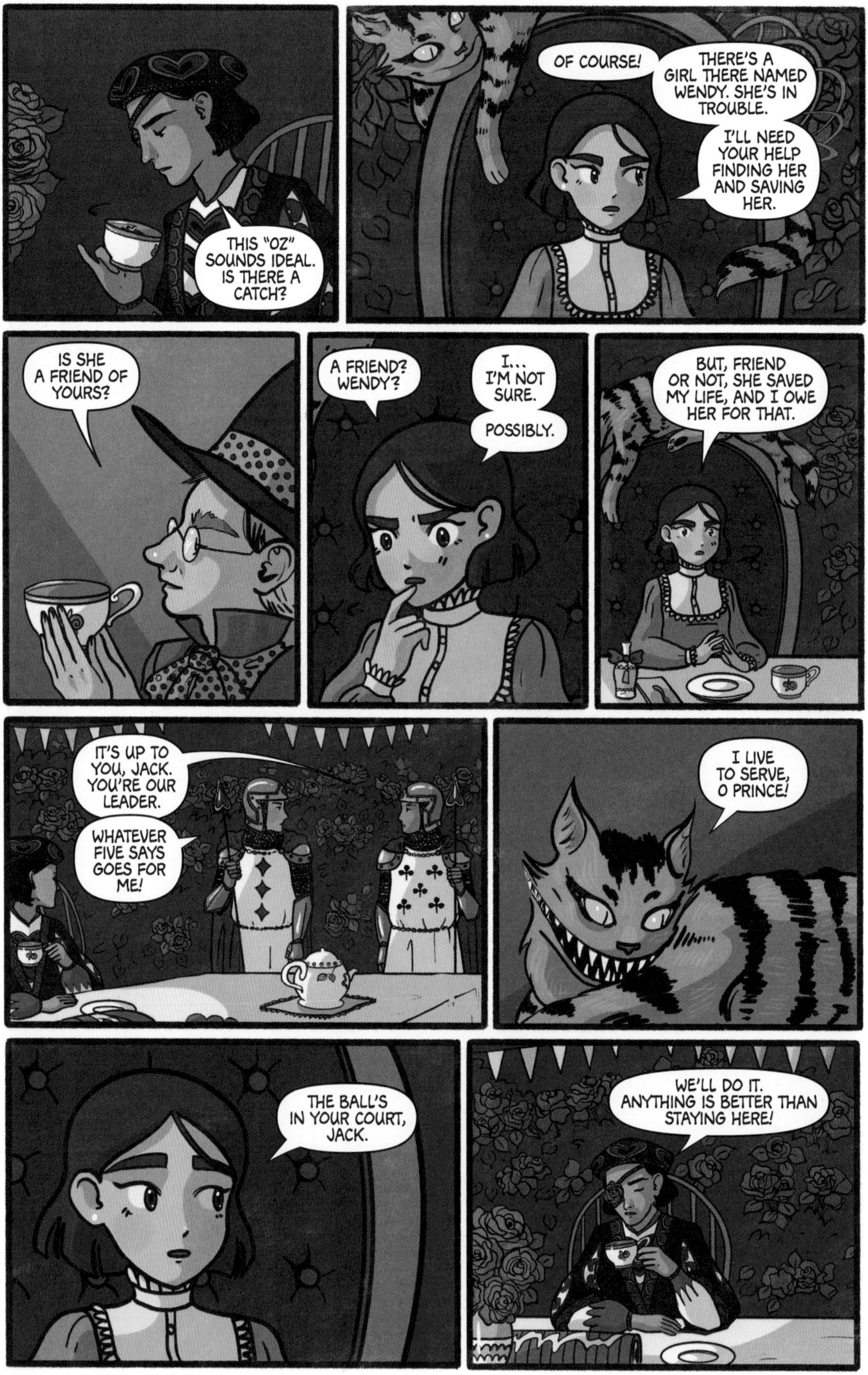
THIS "OZ" SOUNDS IDEAL. IS THERE A CATCH?
OF COURSE!
THERE'S A GIRL THERE NAMED WENDY. SHE'S IN TROUBLE.
I'LL NEED YOUR HELP FINDING HER AND SAVING HER.
IS SHE A FRIEND OF YOURS?
A FRIEND? WENDY?
I... I'M NOT SURE.
POSSIBLY.
BUT, FRIEND OR NOT, SHE SAVED MY LIFE, AND I OWE HER FOR THAT.
IT'S UP TO YOU, JACK. YOU'RE OUR LEADER.
WHATEVER FIVE SAYS GOES FOR ME!
I LIVE TO SERVE, O PRINCE!
THE BALL'S IN YOUR COURT, JACK.
WE'LL DO IT. ANYTHING IS BETTER THAN STAYING HERE!

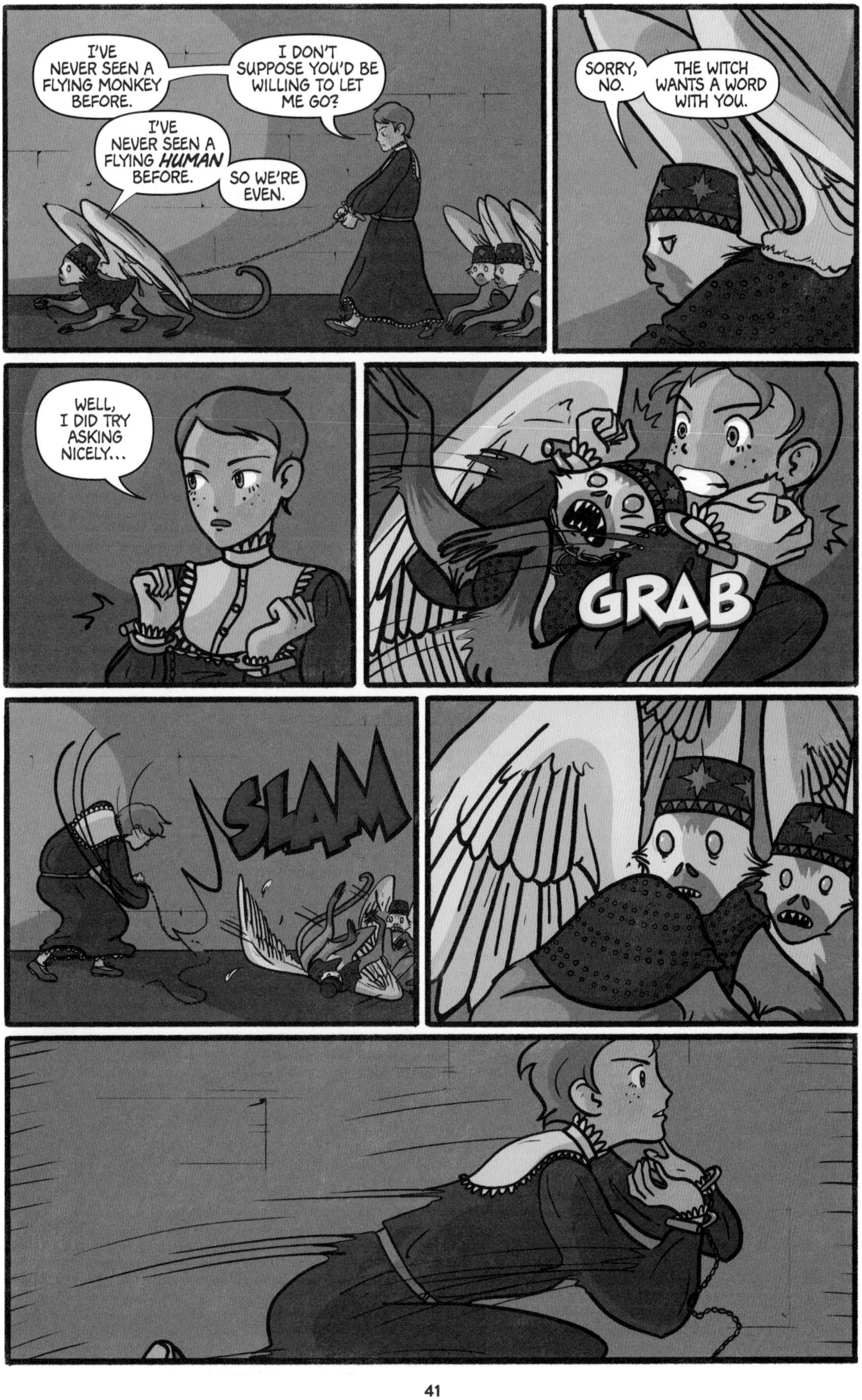
I'VE NEVER SEEN A FLYING MONKEY BEFORE.
I DON'T SUPPOSE YOU'D BE WILLING TO LET ME GO?
I'VE NEVER SEEN A FLYING HUMAN BEFORE.
SO WE'RE EVEN.
SORRY, NO.
THE WITCH WANTS A WORD WITH YOU.
WELL, I DID TRY ASKING NICELY...
GRAB
SLAM

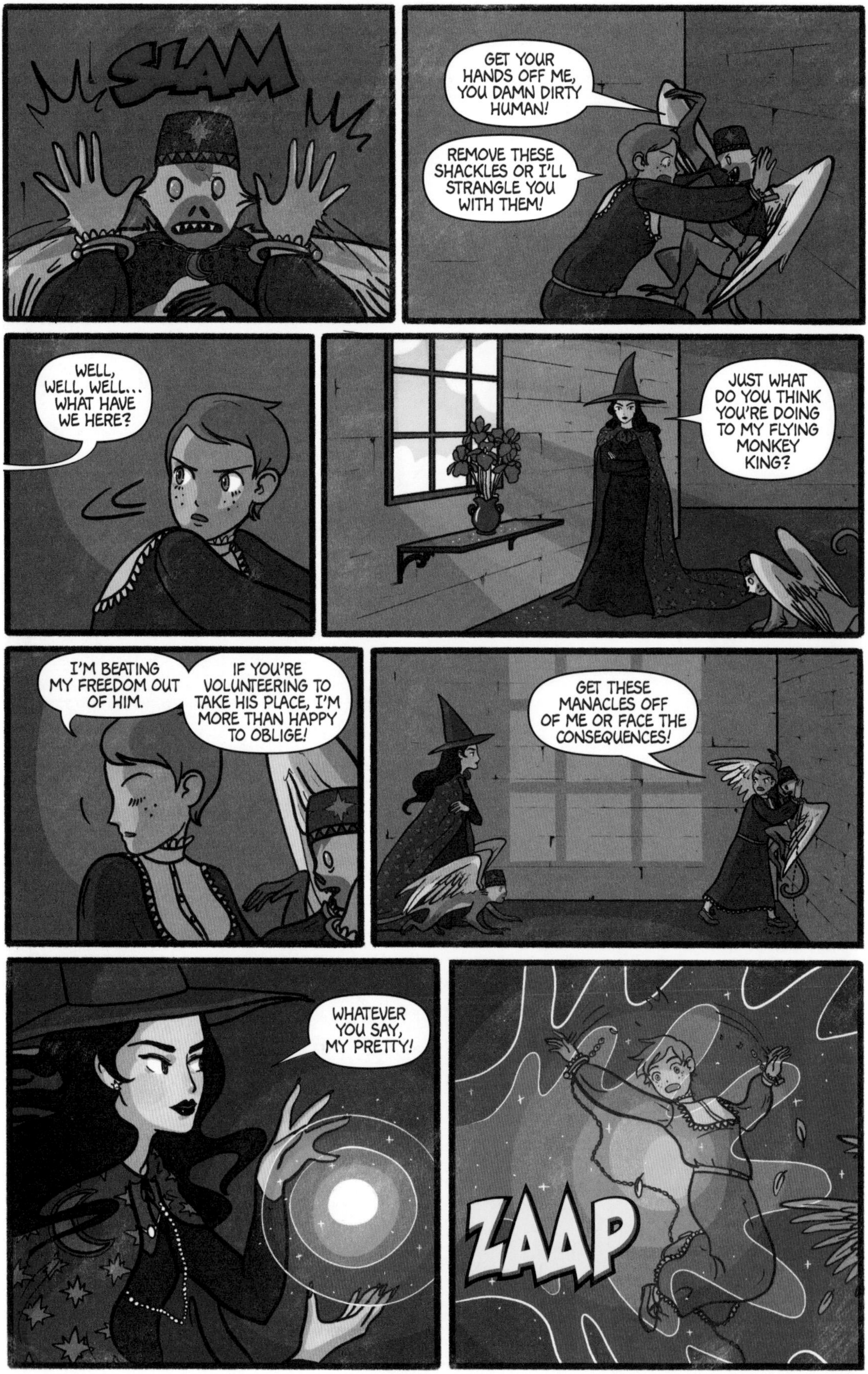
SLAM
GET YOUR HANDS OFF ME, YOU DAMN DIRTY HUMAN!
REMOVE THESE SHACKLES OR I'LL STRANGLE YOU WITH THEM!
WELL, WELL, WELL... WHAT HAVE WE HERE?
JUST WHAT DO YOU THINK YOU'RE DOING TO MY FLYING MONKEY KING?
I'M BEATING MY FREEDOM OUT OF HIM.
IF YOU'RE VOLUNTEERING TO TAKE HIS PLACE, I'M MORE THAN HAPPY TO OBLIGE!
GET THESE MANACLES OFF OF ME OR FACE THE CONSEQUENCES!
WHATEVER YOU SAY, MY PRETTY!
ZAAP

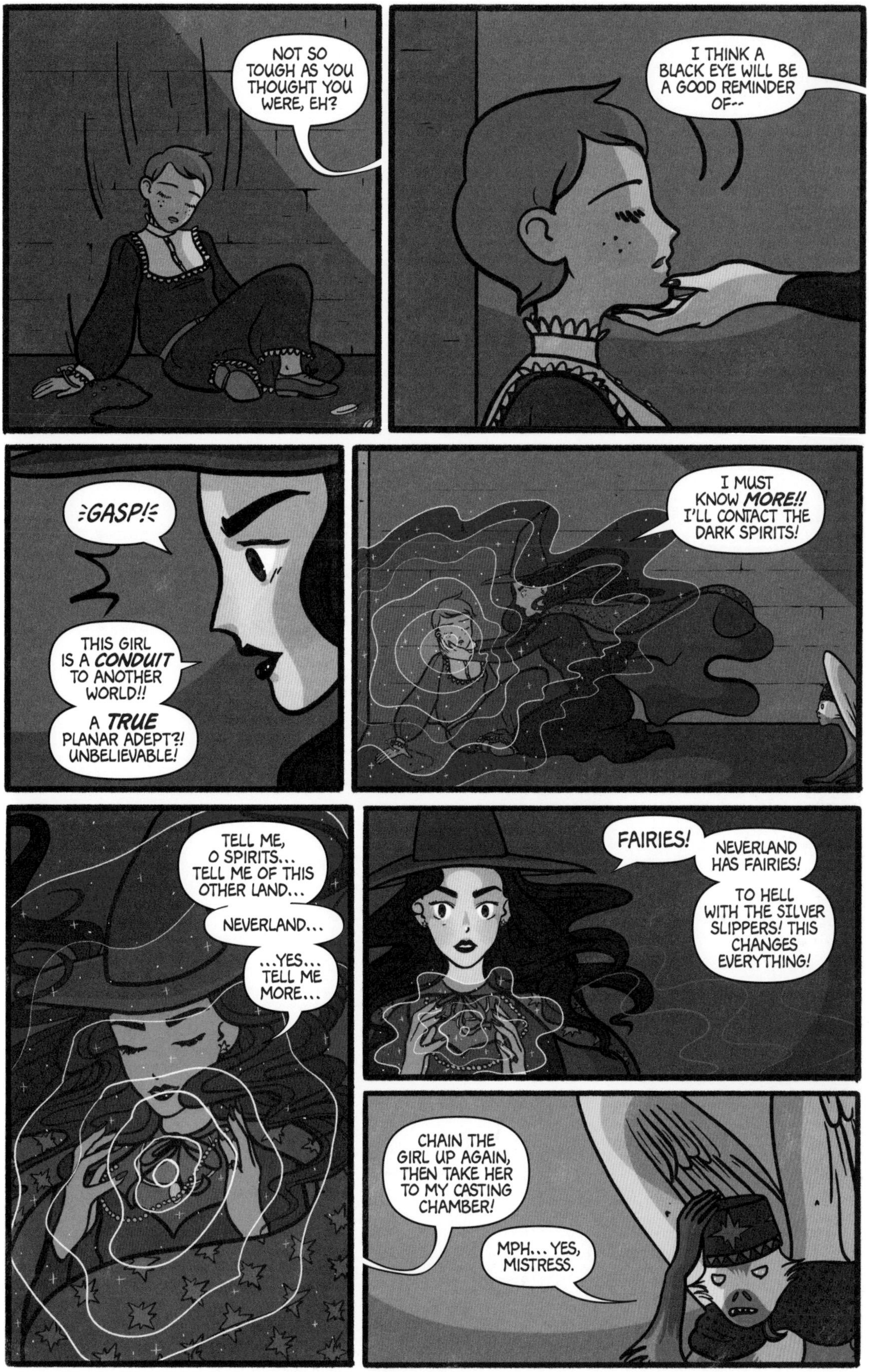
NOT SO TOUGH AS YOU THOUGHT YOU WERE, EH?
I THINK A BLACK EYE WILL BE A GOOD REMINDER OF--
GASP!
THIS GIRL IS A CONDUIT TO ANOTHER WORLD!!
A TRUE PLANAR ADEPT?! UNBELIEVABLE!
I MUST KNOW MORE!! I'LL CONTACT THE DARK SPIRITS!
TELL ME, O SPIRITS... TELL ME OF THIS OTHER LAND...
NEVERLAND...
...YES... TELL ME MORE...
FAIRIES!
NEVERLAND HAS FAIRIES!
TO HELL WITH THE SILVER SLIPPERS! THIS CHANGES EVERYTHING!
CHAIN THE GIRL UP AGAIN, THEN TAKE HER TO MY CASTING CHAMBER!
MPH... YES, MISTRESS.

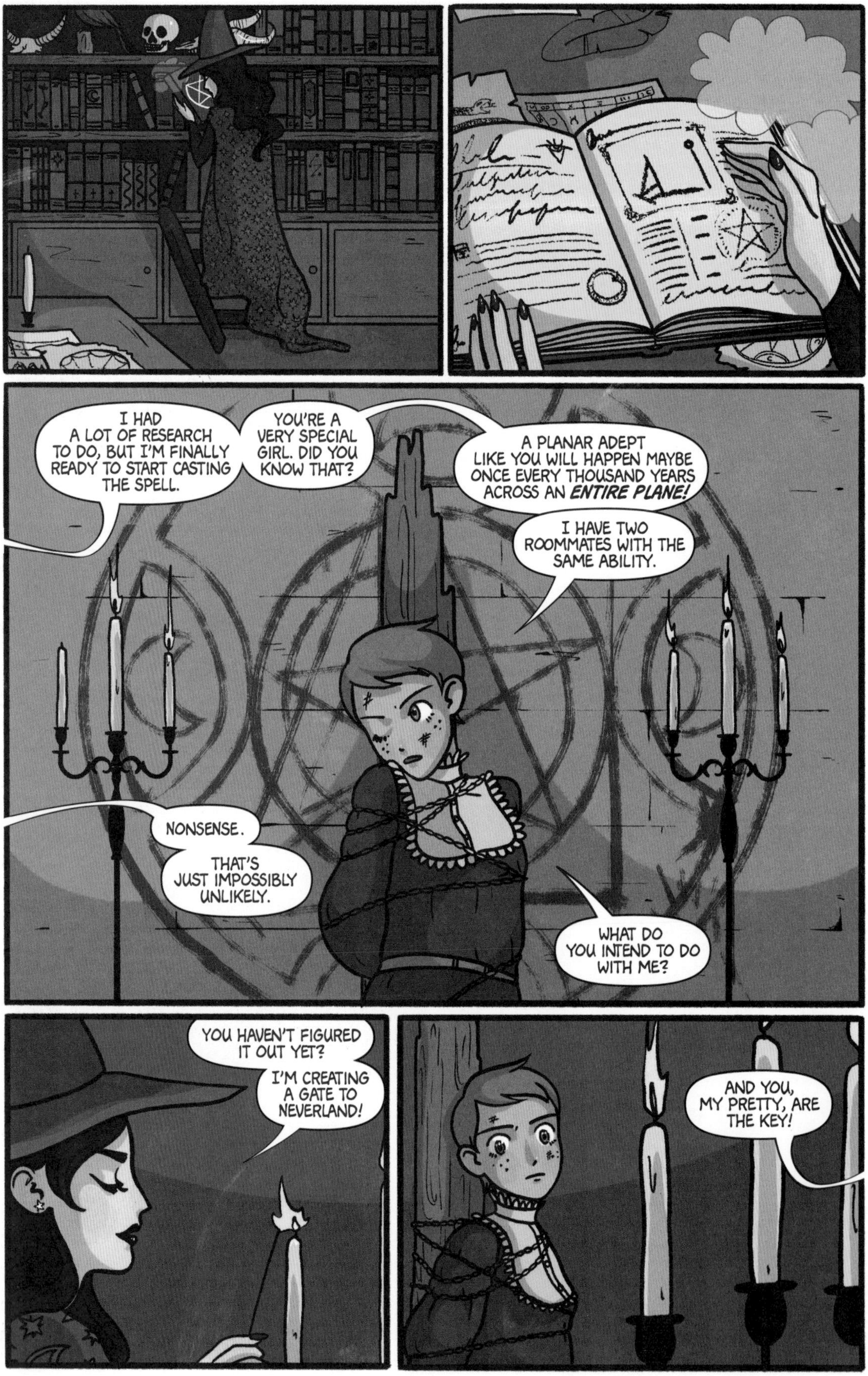
I HAD A LOT OF RESEARCH TO DO, BUT I'M FINALLY READY TO START CASTING THE SPELL.
YOU'RE A VERY SPECIAL GIRL. DID YOU KNOW THAT?
A PLANAR ADEPT LIKE YOU WILL HAPPEN MAYBE ONCE EVERY THOUSAND YEARS ACROSS AN ***ENTIRE PLANE!***
I HAVE TWO ROOMMATES WITH THE SAME ABILITY.
NONSENSE.
THAT'S JUST IMPOSSIBLY UNLIKELY.
WHAT DO YOU INTEND TO DO WITH ME?
YOU HAVEN'T FIGURED IT OUT YET?
I'M CREATING A GATE TO NEVERLAND!
AND YOU, MY PRETTY, ARE THE KEY!

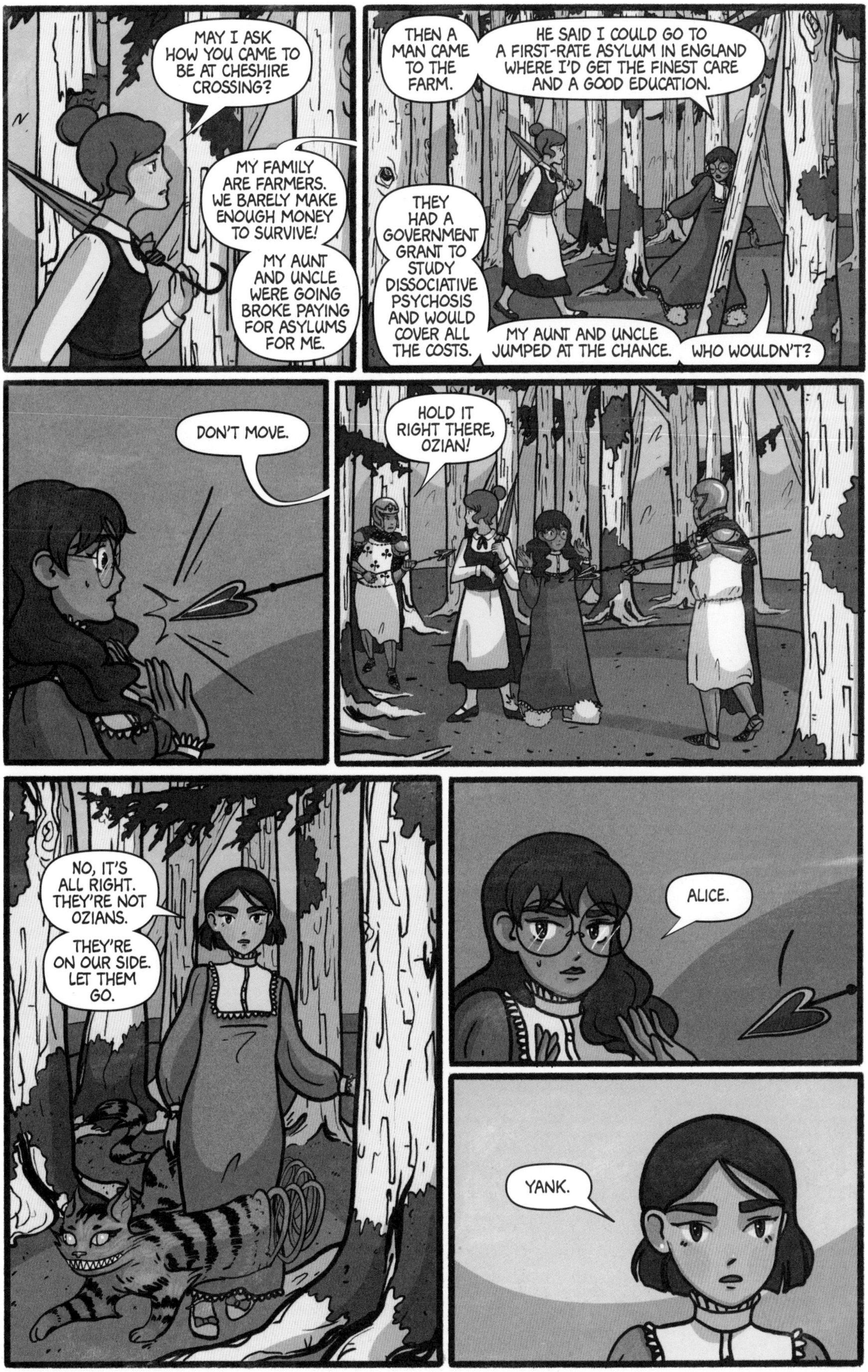
MAY I ASK HOW YOU CAME TO BE AT CHESHIRE CROSSING?
MY FAMILY ARE FARMERS. WE BARELY MAKE ENOUGH MONEY TO SURVIVE!
MY AUNT AND UNCLE WERE GOING BROKE PAYING FOR ASYLUMS FOR ME.
THEN A MAN CAME TO THE FARM.
HE SAID I COULD GO TO A FIRST-RATE ASYLUM IN ENGLAND WHERE I'D GET THE FINEST CARE AND A GOOD EDUCATION.
THEY HAD A GOVERNMENT GRANT TO STUDY DISSOCIATIVE PSYCHOSIS AND WOULD COVER ALL THE COSTS.
MY AUNT AND UNCLE JUMPED AT THE CHANCE.
WHO WOULDN'T?
DON'T MOVE.
HOLD IT RIGHT THERE, OZIAN!
NO, IT'S ALL RIGHT. THEY'RE NOT OZIANS.
THEY'RE ON OUR SIDE. LET THEM GO.
ALICE.
YANK.

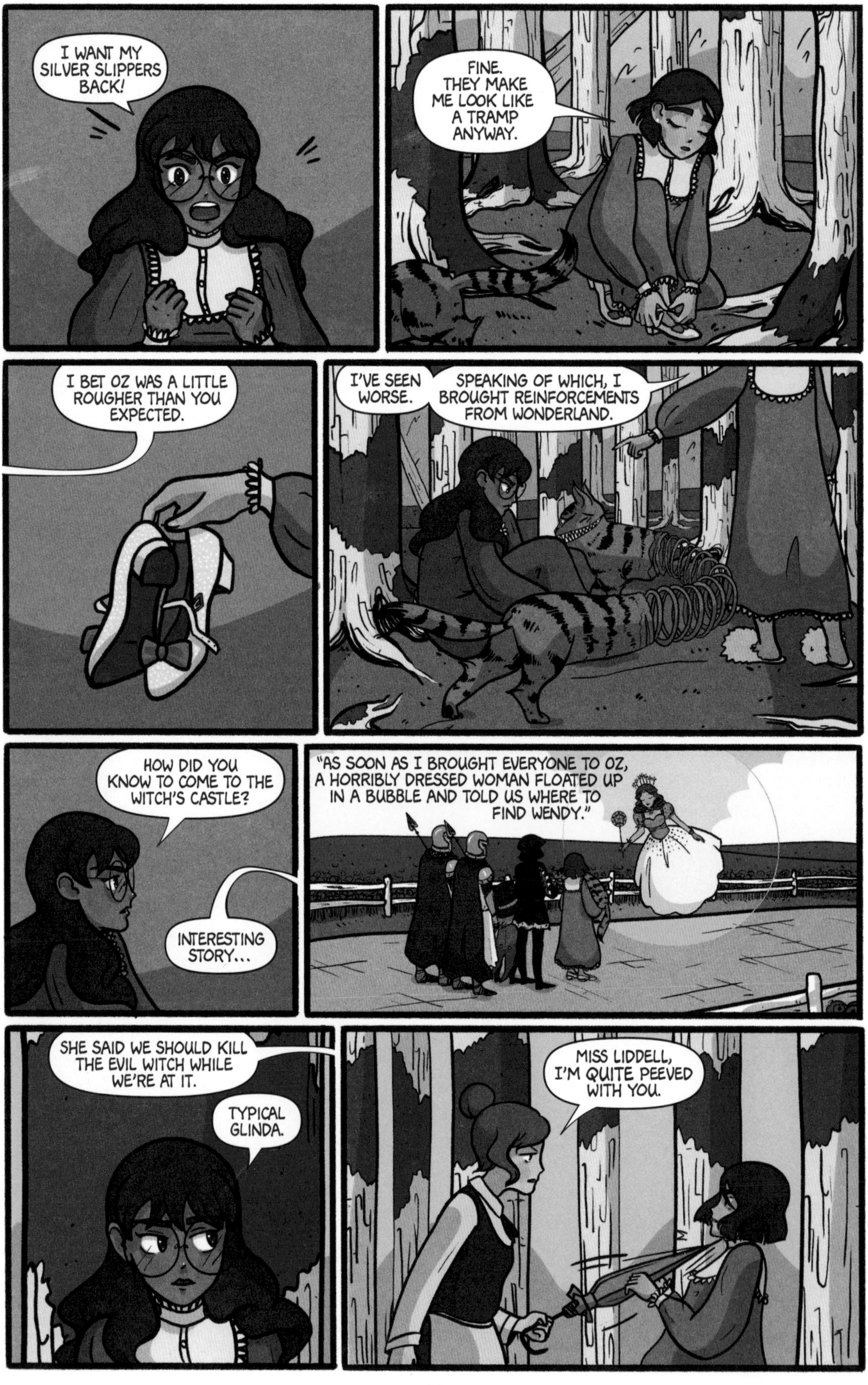
I WANT MY SILVER SLIPPERS BACK!
FINE. THEY MAKE ME LOOK LIKE A TRAMP ANYWAY.
I BET OZ WAS A LITTLE ROUGHER THAN YOU EXPECTED.
I'VE SEEN WORSE.
SPEAKING OF WHICH, I BROUGHT REINFORCEMENTS FROM WONDERLAND.
HOW DID YOU KNOW TO COME TO THE WITCH'S CASTLE?
INTERESTING STORY...
"AS SOON AS I BROUGHT EVERYONE TO OZ, A HORRIBLY DRESSED WOMAN FLOATED UP IN A BUBBLE AND TOLD US WHERE TO FIND WENDY."
SHE SAID WE SHOULD KILL THE EVIL WITCH WHILE WE'RE AT IT.
TYPICAL GLINDA.
MISS LIDDELL, I'M QUITE PEEVED WITH YOU.

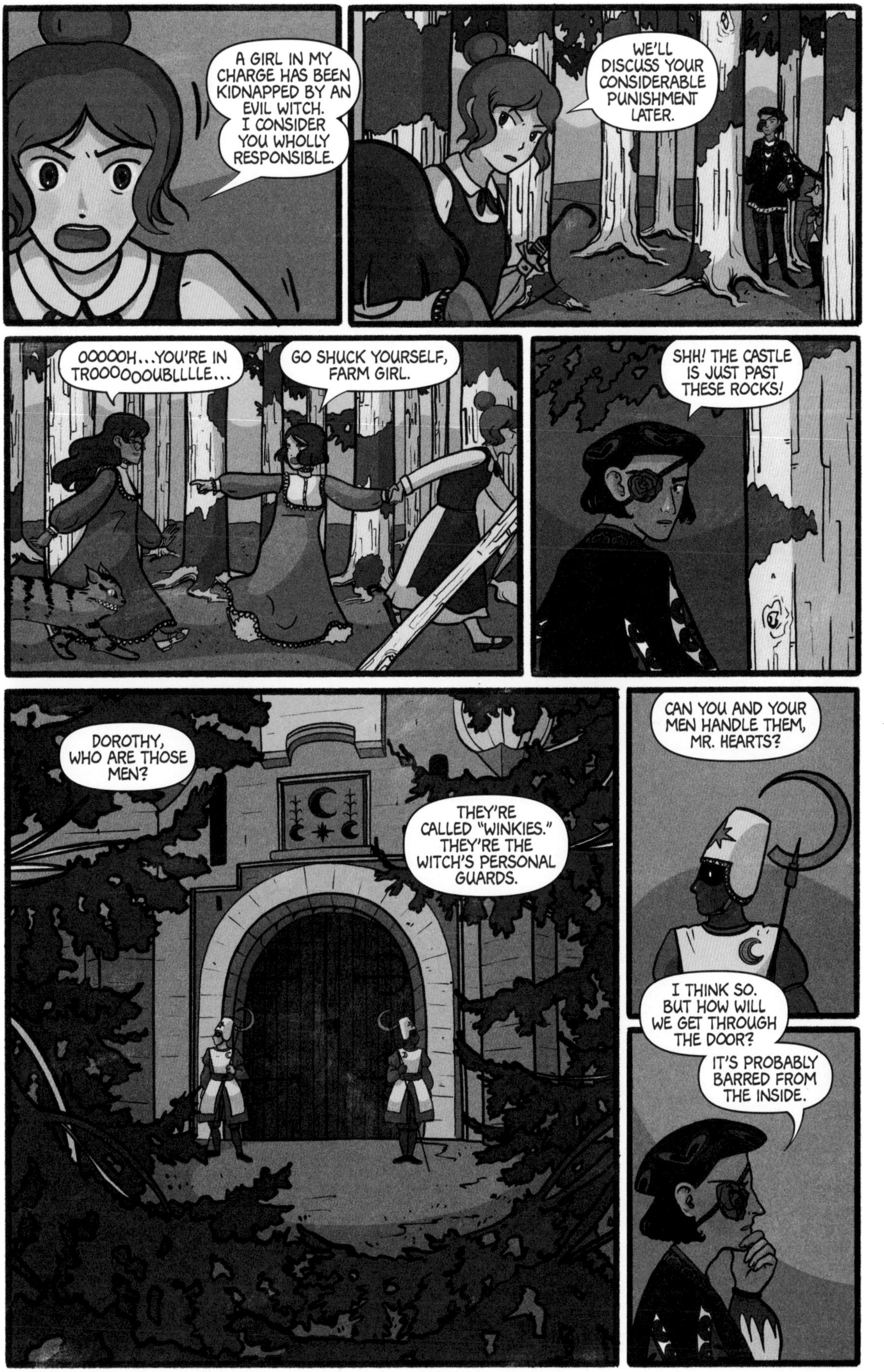
A GIRL IN MY CHARGE HAS BEEN KIDNAPPED BY AN EVIL WITCH. I CONSIDER YOU WHOLLY RESPONSIBLE.
WE'LL DISCUSS YOUR CONSIDERABLE PUNISHMENT LATER.
OOOOOH...YOU'RE IN TROOOOOOUBLLLLE...
GO SHUCK YOURSELF, FARM GIRL.
SHH! THE CASTLE IS JUST PAST THESE ROCKS!
DOROTHY, WHO ARE THOSE MEN?
THEY'RE CALLED "WINKIES." THEY'RE THE WITCH'S PERSONAL GUARDS.
CAN YOU AND YOUR MEN HANDLE THEM, MR. HEARTS?
I THINK SO. BUT HOW WILL WE GET THROUGH THE DOOR?
IT'S PROBABLY BARRED FROM THE INSIDE.

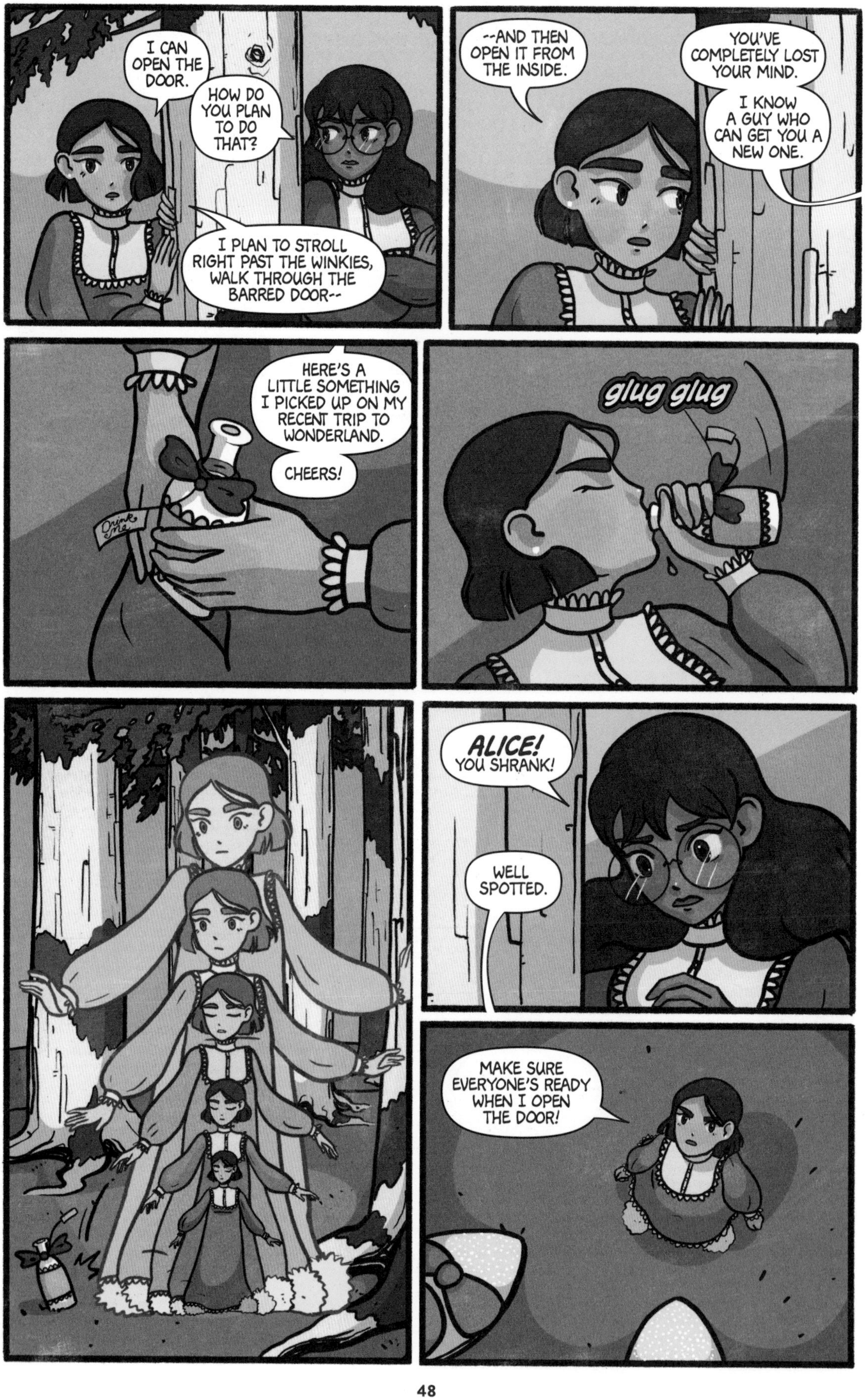
I CAN OPEN THE DOOR.
HOW DO YOU PLAN TO DO THAT?
I PLAN TO STROLL RIGHT PAST THE WINKIES, WALK THROUGH THE BARRED DOOR--
--AND THEN OPEN IT FROM THE INSIDE.
YOU'VE COMPLETELY LOST YOUR MIND.
I KNOW A GUY WHO CAN GET YOU A NEW ONE.
HERE'S A LITTLE SOMETHING I PICKED UP ON MY RECENT TRIP TO WONDERLAND.
CHEERS!
Drink Me
glug glug
ALICE! YOU SHRANK!
WELL SPOTTED.
MAKE SURE EVERYONE'S READY WHEN I OPEN THE DOOR!

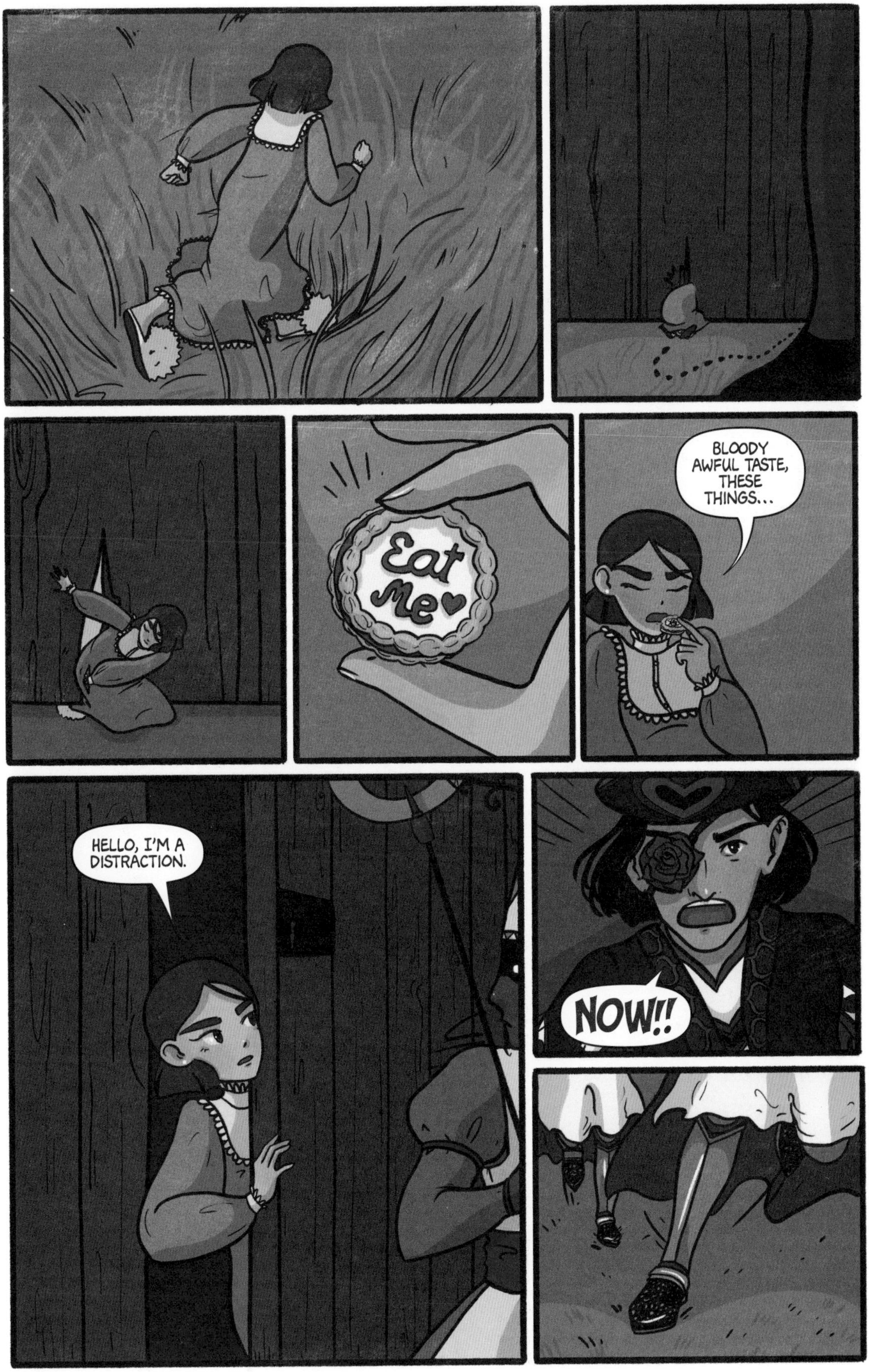
Eat Me
BLOODY AWFUL TASTE, THESE THINGS...
HELLO, I'M A DISTRACTION.
NOW!!

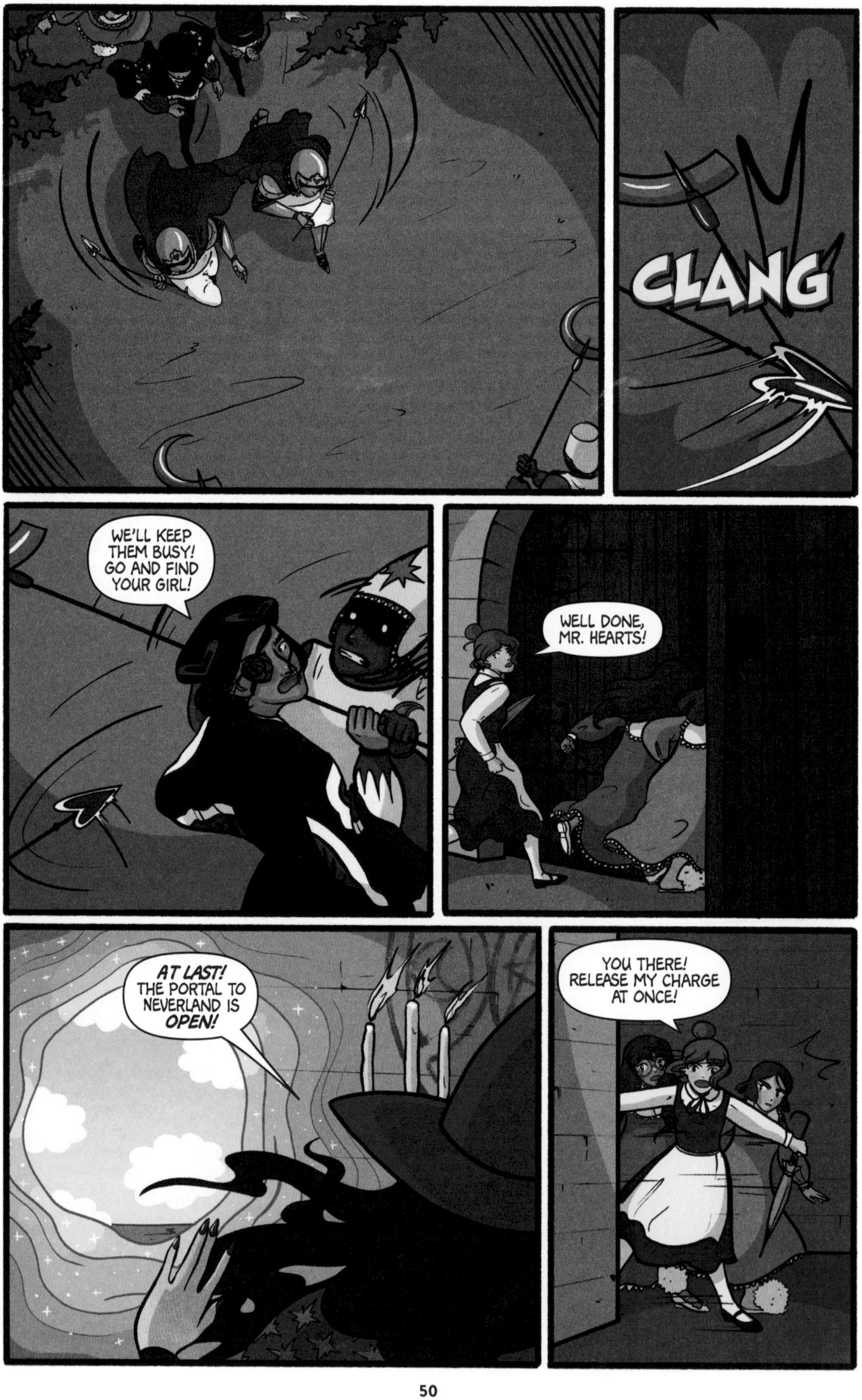
CLANG
WE'LL KEEP THEM BUSY! GO AND FIND YOUR GIRL!
WELL DONE, MR. HEARTS!
AT LAST! THE PORTAL TO NEVERLAND IS OPEN!
YOU THERE! RELEASE MY CHARGE AT ONCE!

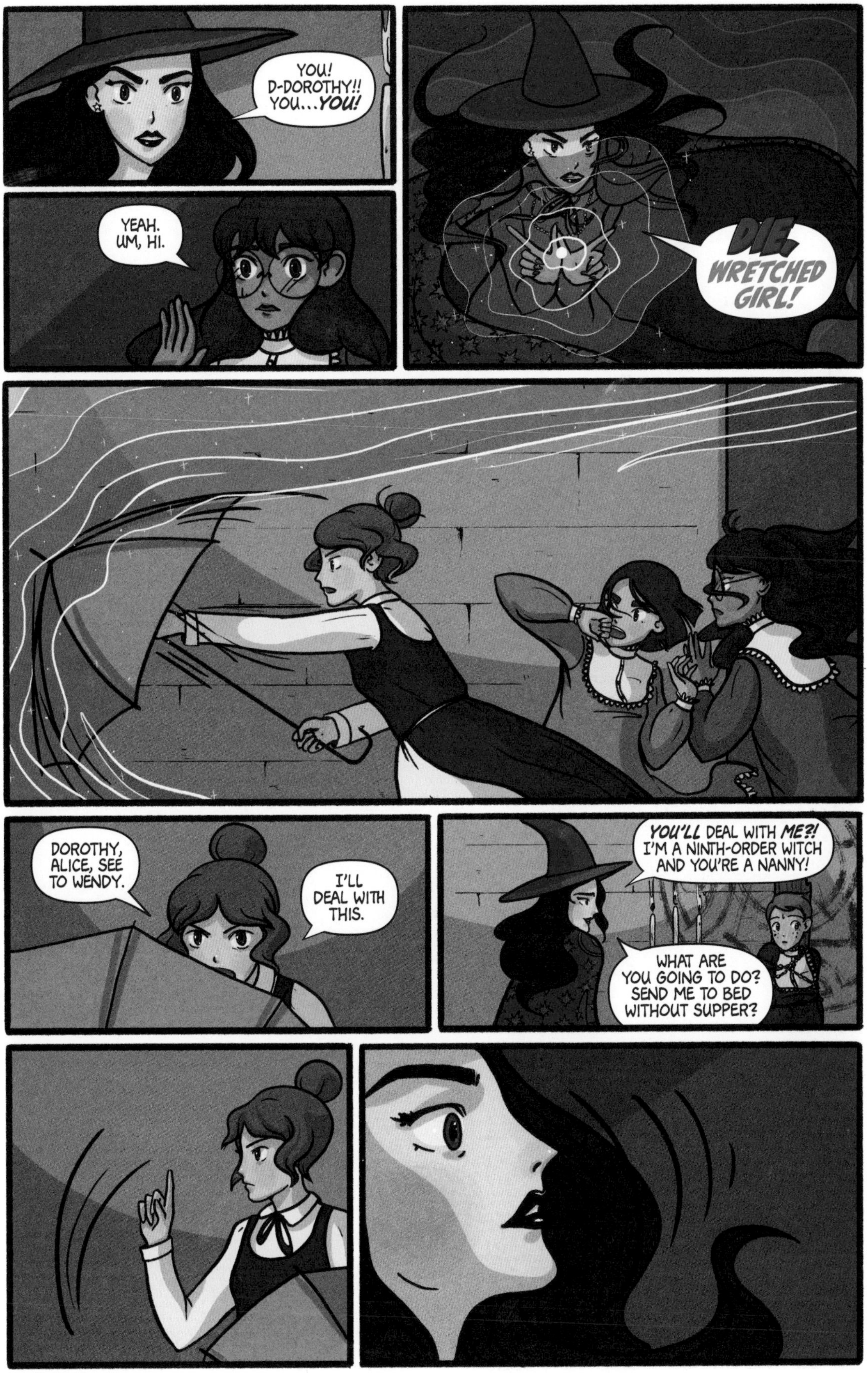
YOU! D-DOROTHY!! YOU...YOU!
YEAH. UM, HI.
DIE, WRETCHED GIRL!
DOROTHY, ALICE, SEE TO WENDY.
I'LL DEAL WITH THIS.
YOU'LL DEAL WITH ME?! I'M A NINTH-ORDER WITCH AND YOU'RE A NANNY!
WHAT ARE YOU GOING TO DO? SEND ME TO BED WITHOUT SUPPER?

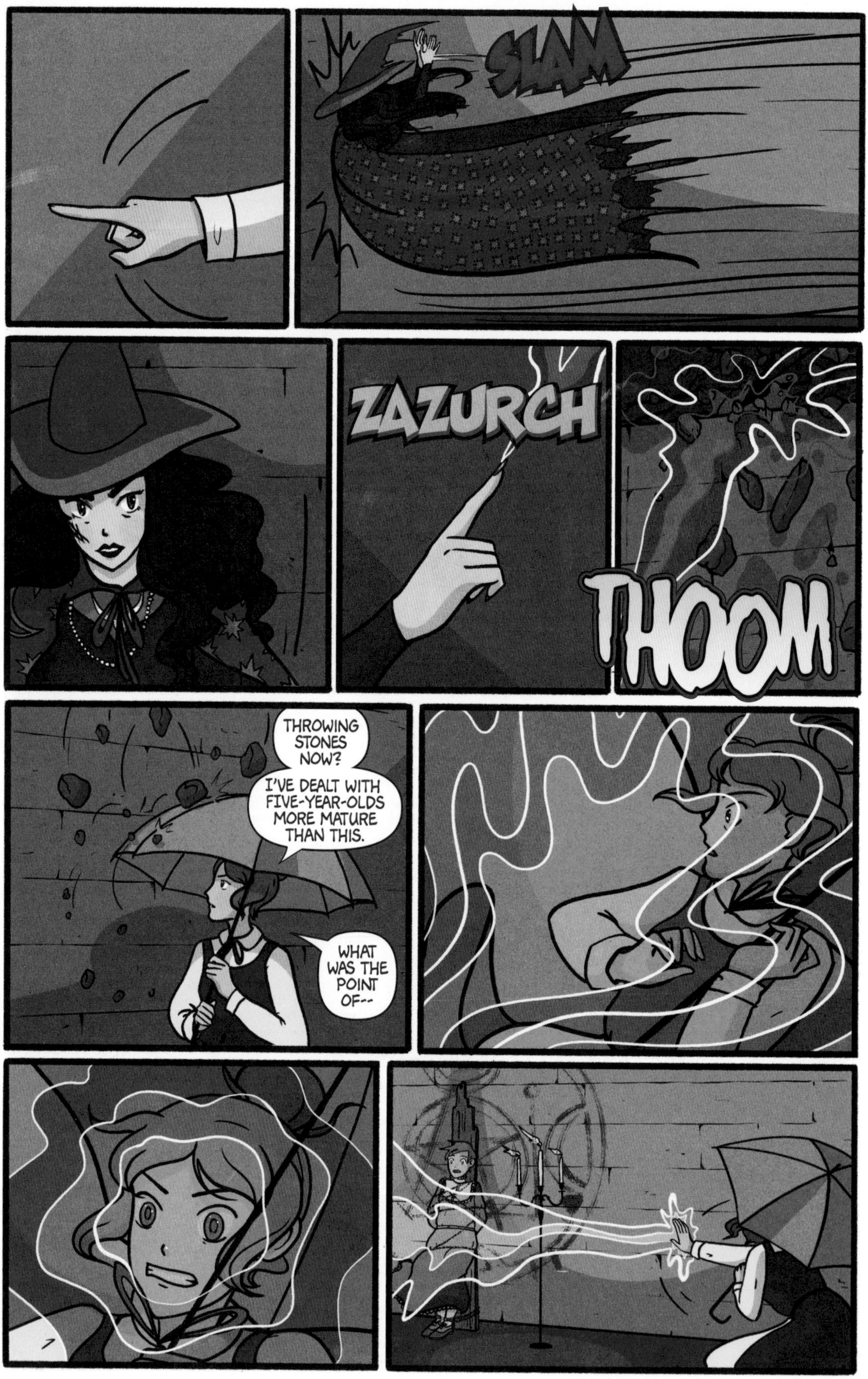
SLAM
ZAZURCH
THOOM
THROWING STONES NOW?
I'VE DEALT WITH FIVE-YEAR-OLDS MORE MATURE THAN THIS.
WHAT WAS THE POINT OF--

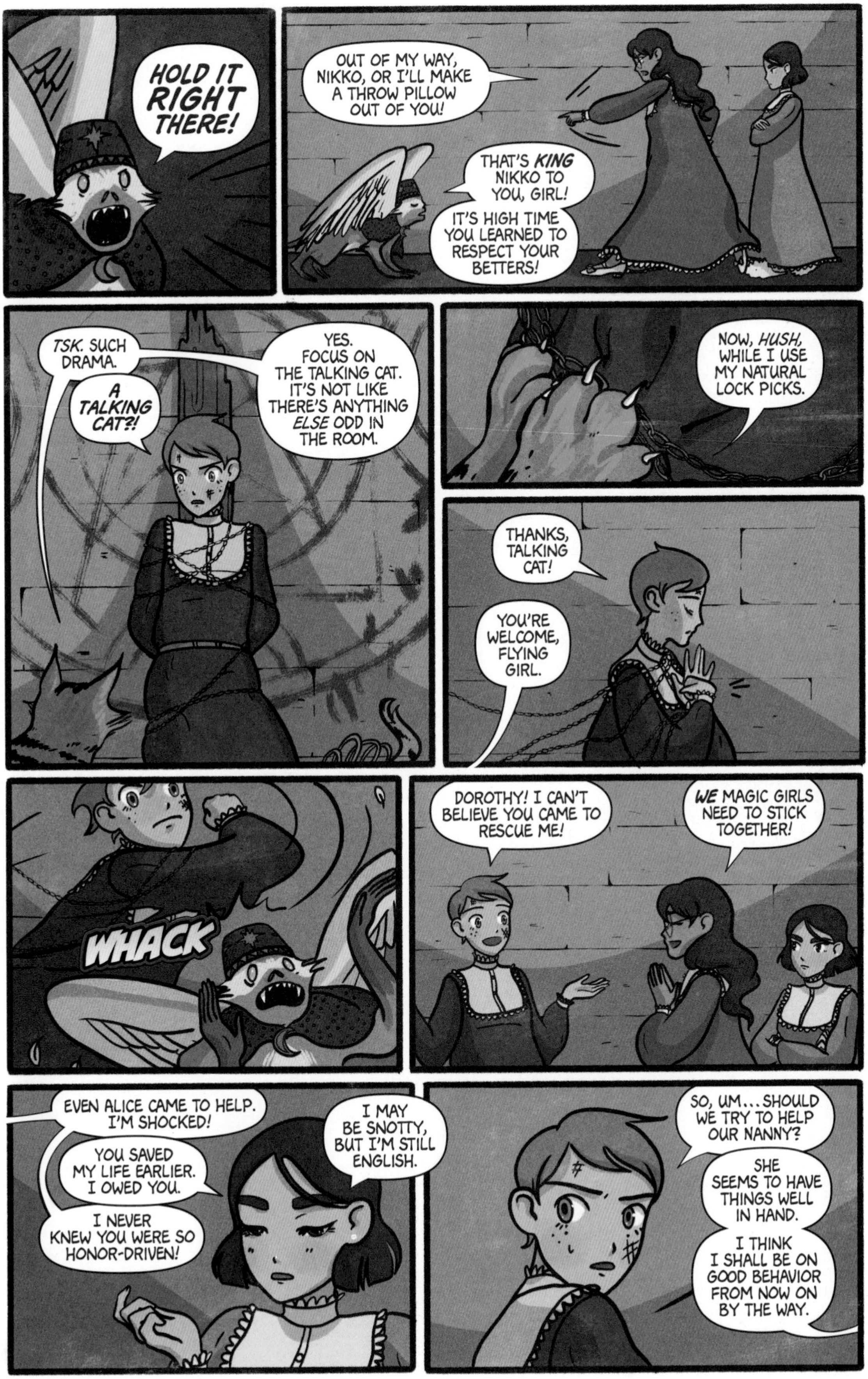
HOLD IT RIGHT THERE!
OUT OF MY WAY, NIKKO, OR I'LL MAKE A THROW PILLOW OUT OF YOU!
THAT'S *KING* NIKKO TO YOU, GIRL!
IT'S HIGH TIME YOU LEARNED TO RESPECT YOUR BETTERS!
TSK. SUCH DRAMA.
A TALKING CAT?!
YES. FOCUS ON THE TALKING CAT. IT'S NOT LIKE THERE'S ANYTHING *ELSE* ODD IN THE ROOM.
NOW, *HUSH,* WHILE I USE MY NATURAL LOCK PICKS.
THANKS, TALKING CAT!
YOU'RE WELCOME, FLYING GIRL.
WHACK
DOROTHY! I CAN'T BELIEVE YOU CAME TO RESCUE ME!
WE MAGIC GIRLS NEED TO STICK TOGETHER!
EVEN ALICE CAME TO HELP. I'M SHOCKED!
YOU SAVED MY LIFE EARLIER. I OWED YOU.
I NEVER KNEW YOU WERE SO HONOR-DRIVEN!
I MAY BE SNOTTY, BUT I'M STILL ENGLISH.
SO, UM...SHOULD WE TRY TO HELP OUR NANNY?
SHE SEEMS TO HAVE THINGS WELL IN HAND.
I THINK I SHALL BE ON GOOD BEHAVIOR FROM NOW ON BY THE WAY.

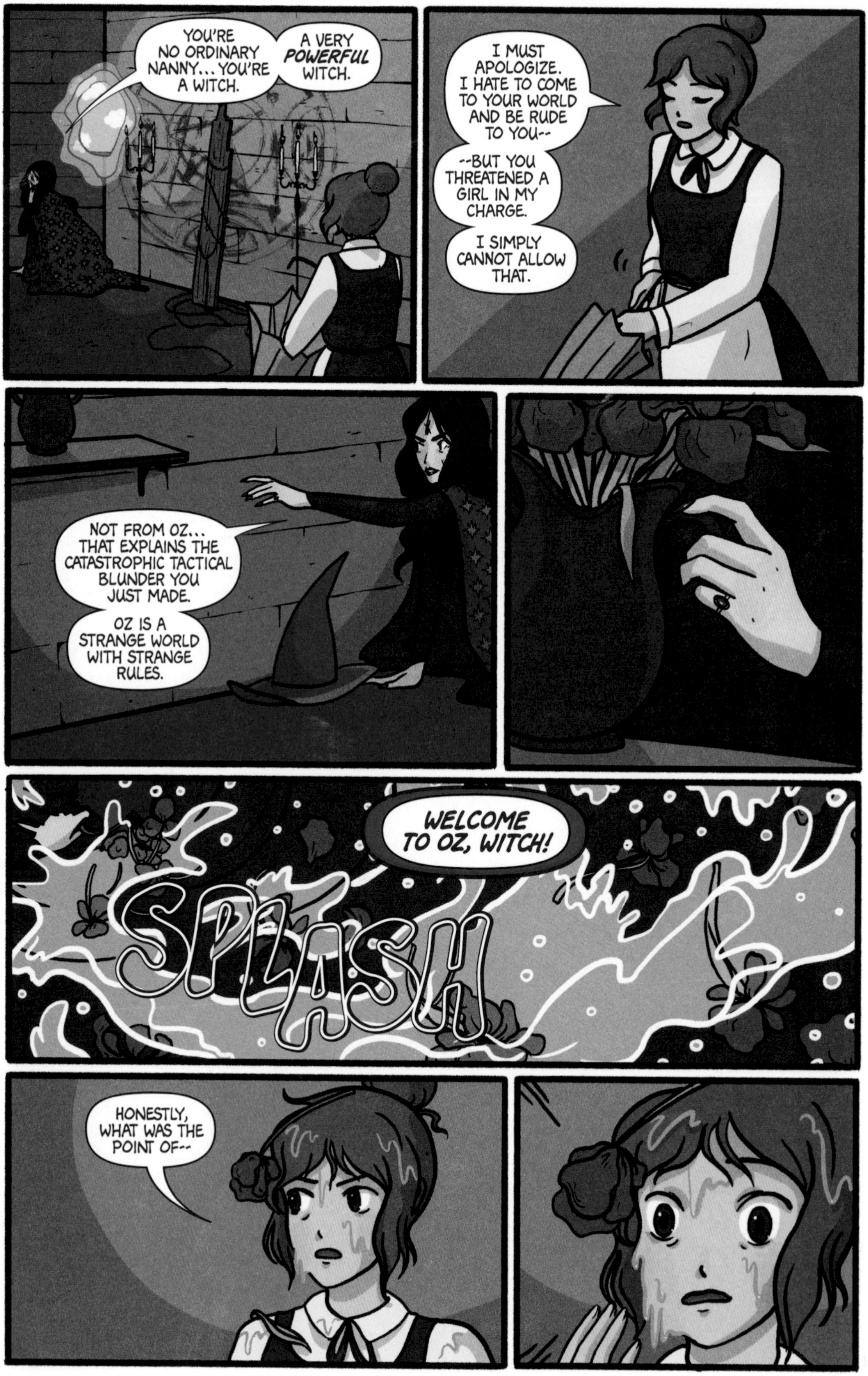
YOU'RE NO ORDINARY NANNY... YOU'RE A WITCH.
A VERY POWERFUL WITCH.
I MUST APOLOGIZE. I HATE TO COME TO YOUR WORLD AND BE RUDE TO YOU--
--BUT YOU THREATENED A GIRL IN MY CHARGE.
I SIMPLY CANNOT ALLOW THAT.
NOT FROM OZ... THAT EXPLAINS THE CATASTROPHIC TACTICAL BLUNDER YOU JUST MADE.
OZ IS A STRANGE WORLD WITH STRANGE RULES.
WELCOME TO OZ, WITCH!
SPLASH
HONESTLY, WHAT WAS THE POINT OF--

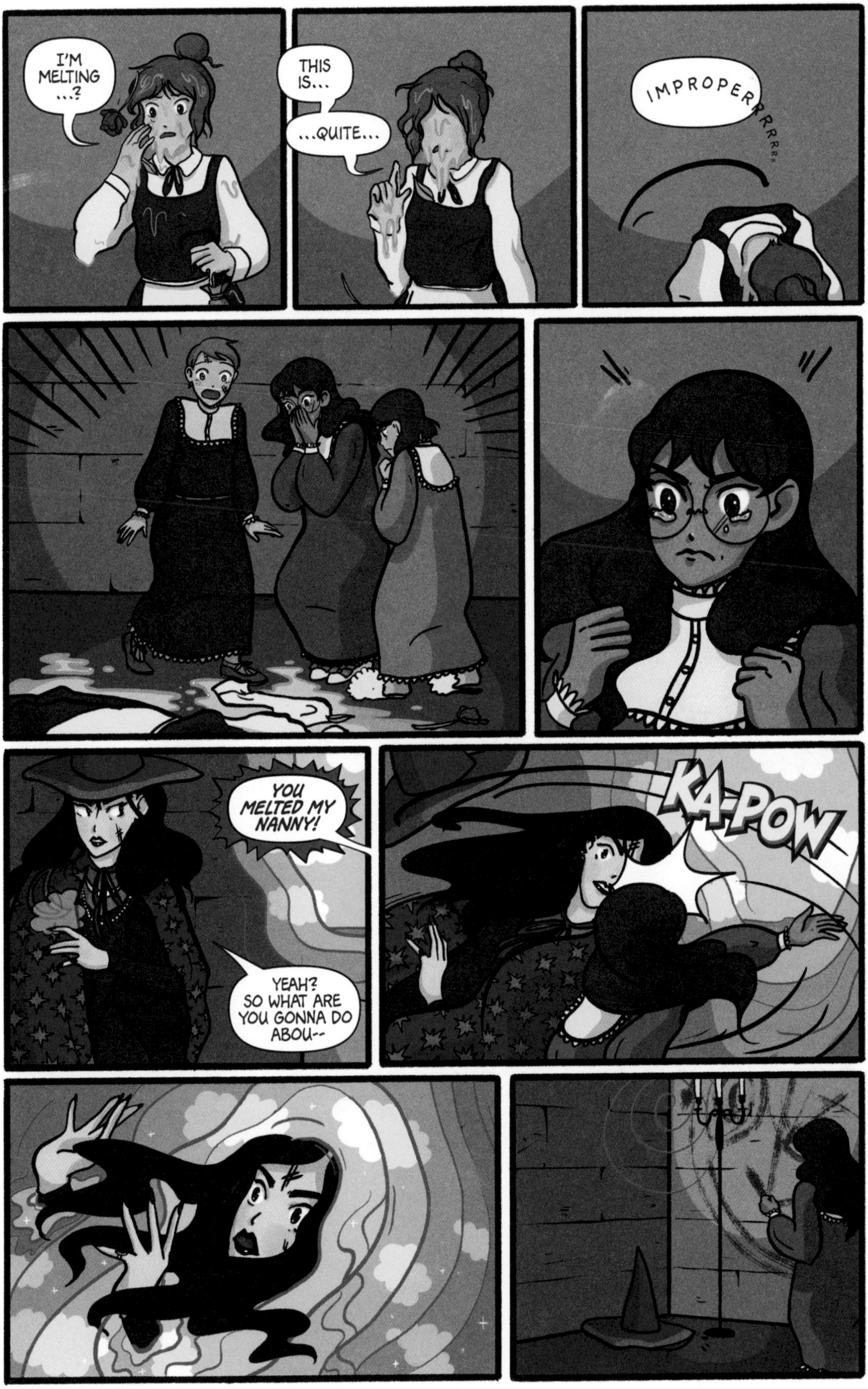
I'M MELTING ...?
THIS IS...
...QUITE...
IMPROPERRRRRR
YOU MELTED MY NANNY!
YEAH? SO WHAT ARE YOU GONNA DO ABOU--
KA-POW

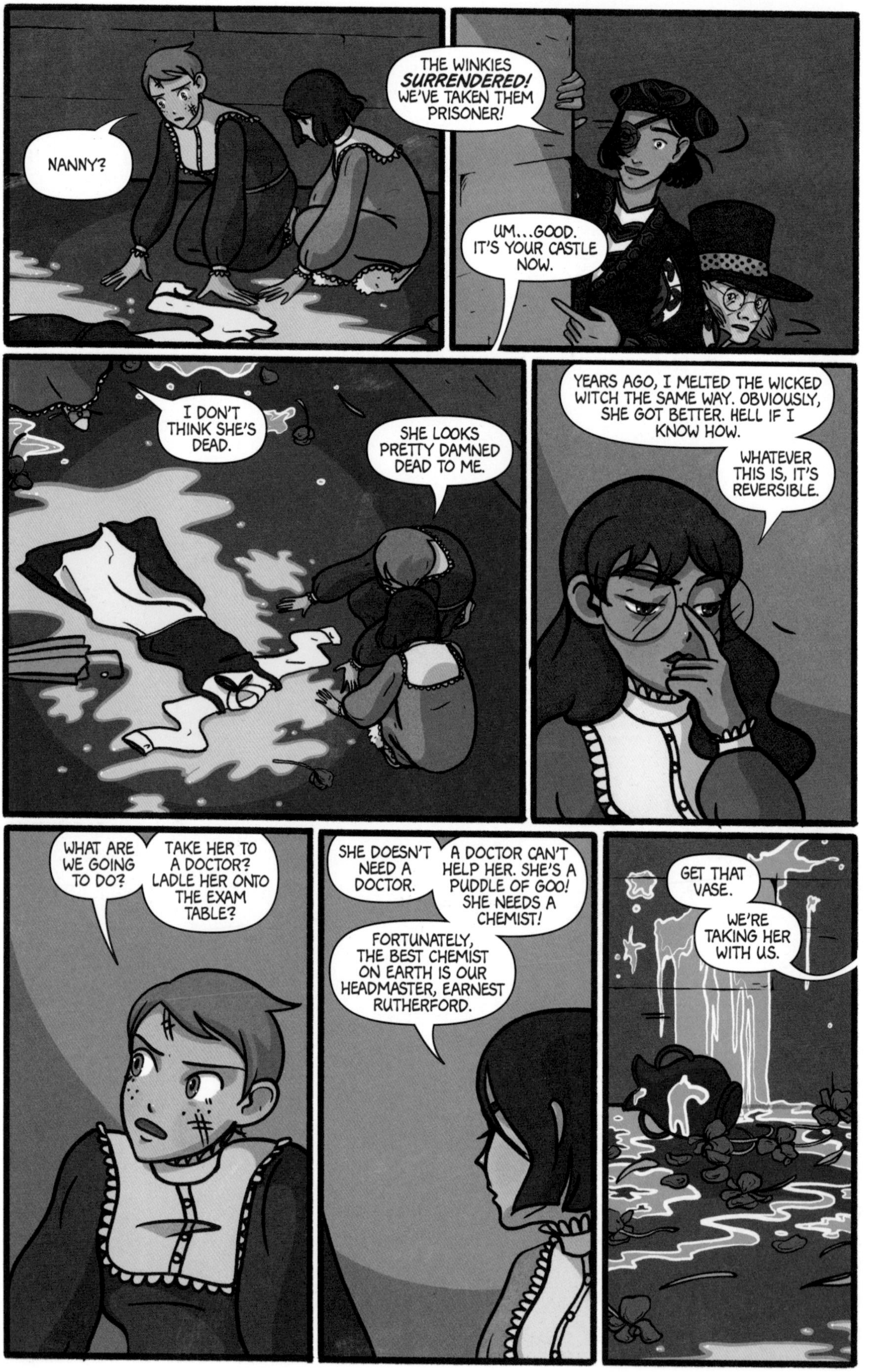
NANNY?
THE WINKIES SURRENDERED! WE'VE TAKEN THEM PRISONER!
UM...GOOD. IT'S YOUR CASTLE NOW.
I DON'T THINK SHE'S DEAD.
SHE LOOKS PRETTY DAMNED DEAD TO ME.
YEARS AGO, I MELTED THE WICKED WITCH THE SAME WAY. OBVIOUSLY, SHE GOT BETTER. HELL IF I KNOW HOW.
WHATEVER THIS IS, IT'S REVERSIBLE.
WHAT ARE WE GOING TO DO?
TAKE HER TO A DOCTOR? LADLE HER ONTO THE EXAM TABLE?
SHE DOESN'T NEED A DOCTOR.
A DOCTOR CAN'T HELP HER. SHE'S A PUDDLE OF GOO! SHE NEEDS A CHEMIST!
FORTUNATELY, THE BEST CHEMIST ON EARTH IS OUR HEADMASTER, EARNEST RUTHERFORD.
GET THAT VASE.
WE'RE TAKING HER WITH US.

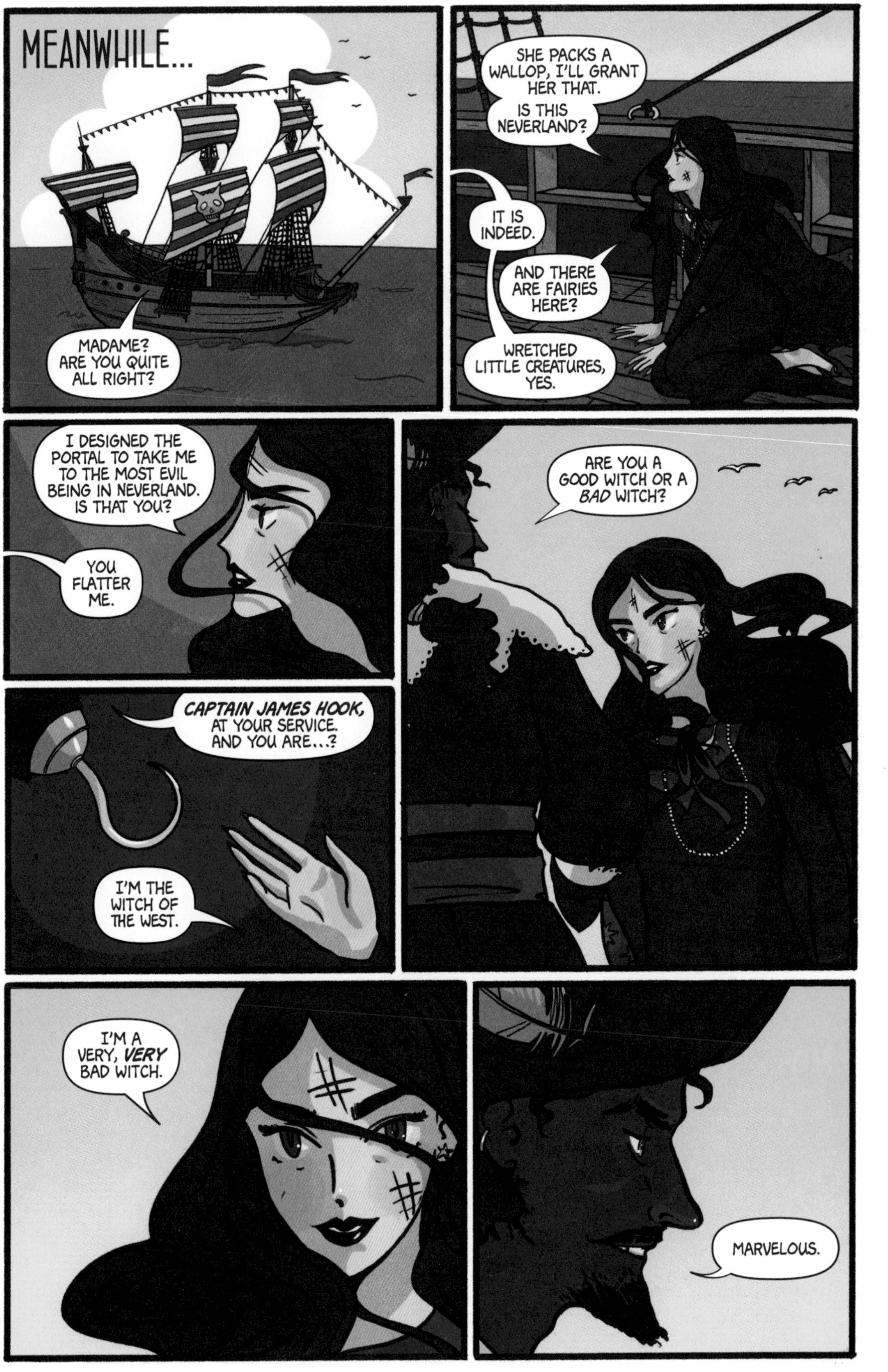
MEANWHILE...
MADAME? ARE YOU QUITE ALL RIGHT?
SHE PACKS A WALLOP, I'LL GRANT HER THAT.
IS THIS NEVERLAND?
IT IS INDEED.
AND THERE ARE FAIRIES HERE?
WRETCHED LITTLE CREATURES, YES.
I DESIGNED THE PORTAL TO TAKE ME TO THE MOST EVIL BEING IN NEVERLAND. IS THAT YOU?
YOU FLATTER ME.
CAPTAIN JAMES HOOK, AT YOUR SERVICE. AND YOU ARE...?
I'M THE WITCH OF THE WEST.
ARE YOU A GOOD WITCH OR A BAD WITCH?
I'M A VERY, VERY BAD WITCH.
MARVELOUS.

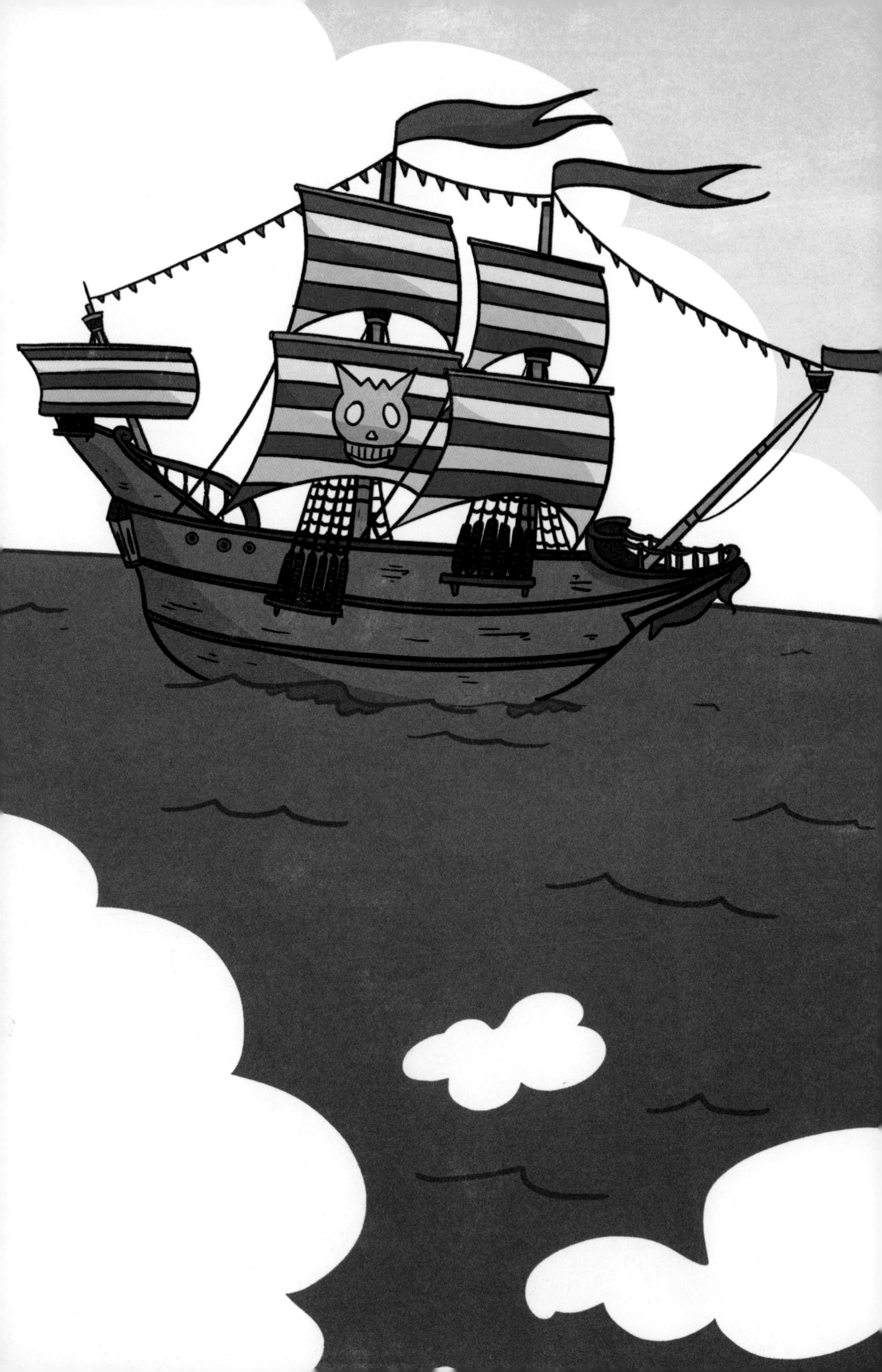

THROUGH THE LOOKING GLASS

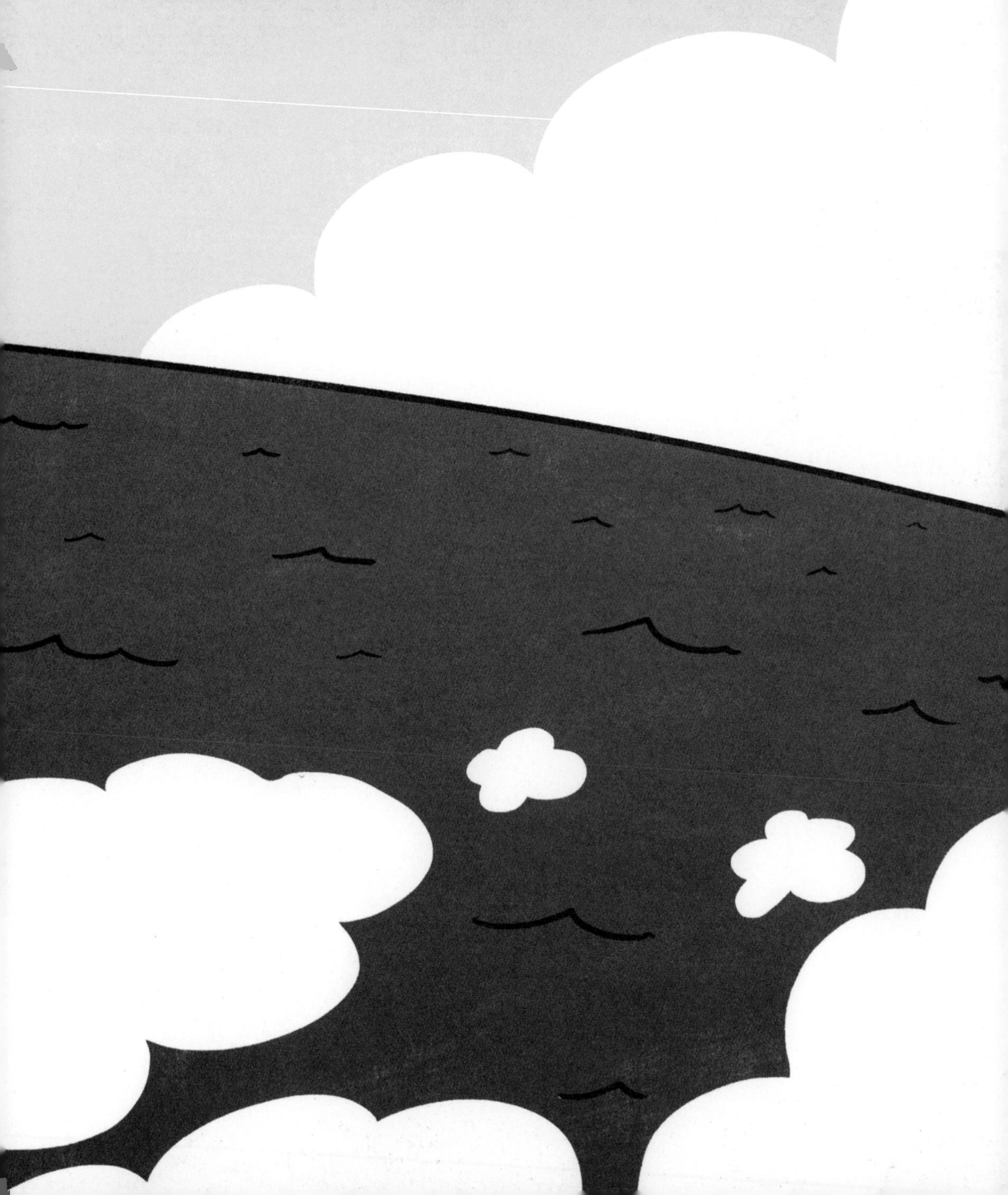

NEVERLAND

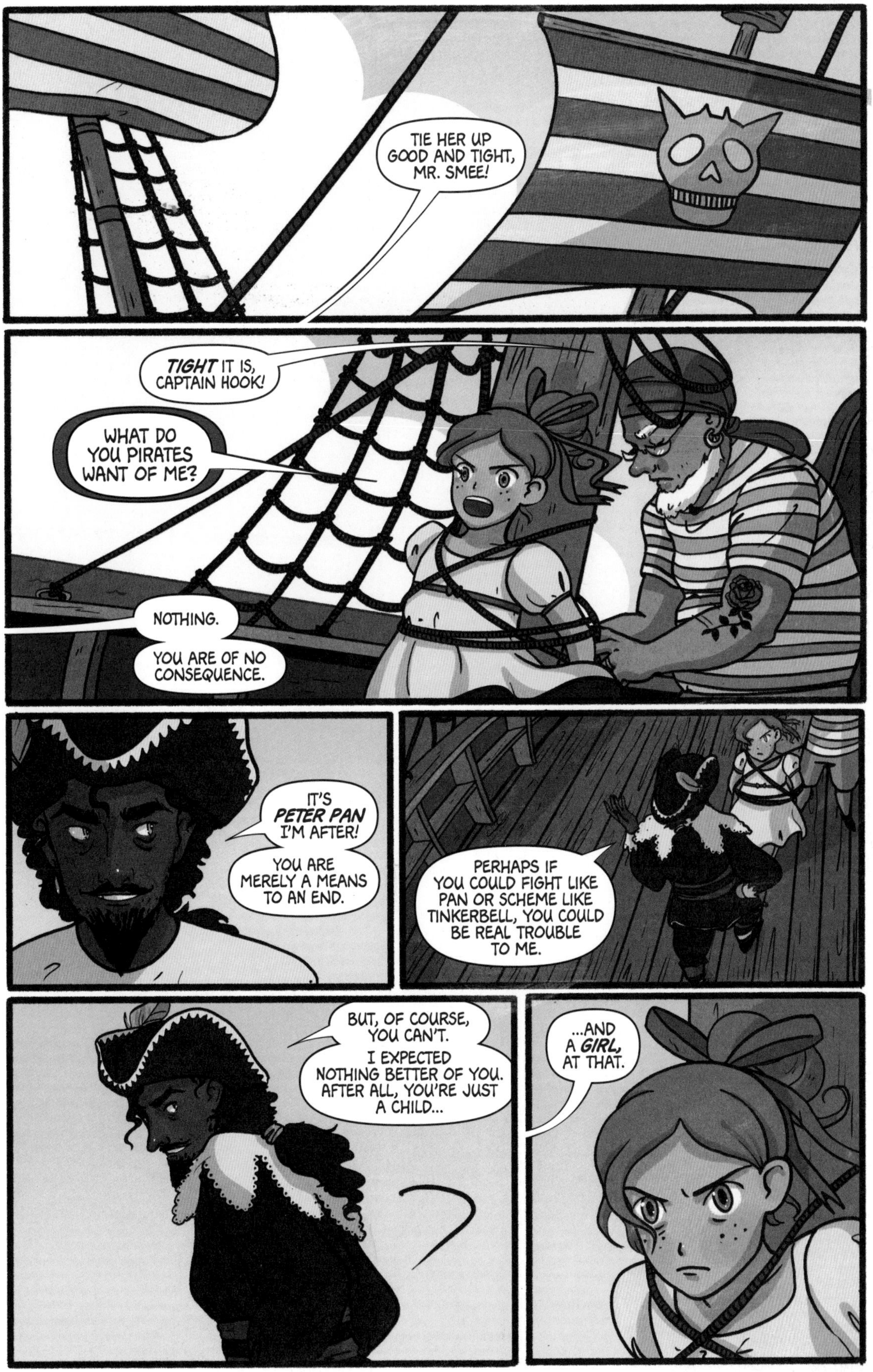
TIE HER UP GOOD AND TIGHT, MR. SMEE!
TIGHT IT IS, CAPTAIN HOOK!
WHAT DO YOU PIRATES WANT OF ME?
NOTHING.
YOU ARE OF NO CONSEQUENCE.
IT'S PETER PAN I'M AFTER!
YOU ARE MERELY A MEANS TO AN END.
PERHAPS IF YOU COULD FIGHT LIKE PAN OR SCHEME LIKE TINKERBELL, YOU COULD BE REAL TROUBLE TO ME.
BUT, OF COURSE, YOU CAN'T.
I EXPECTED NOTHING BETTER OF YOU. AFTER ALL, YOU'RE JUST A CHILD...
...AND A GIRL, AT THAT.

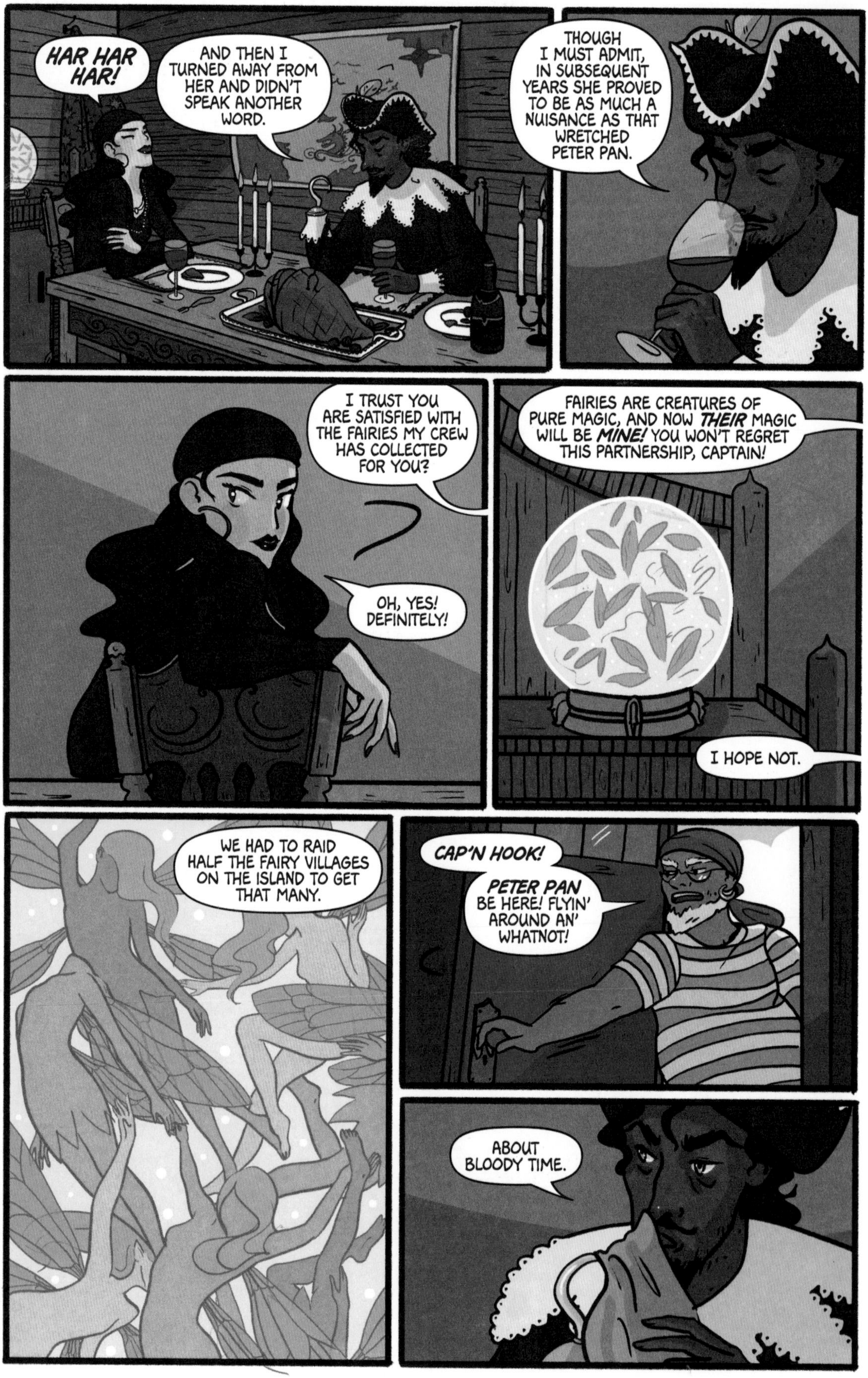
HAR HAR HAR!
AND THEN I TURNED AWAY FROM HER AND DIDN'T SPEAK ANOTHER WORD.
THOUGH I MUST ADMIT, IN SUBSEQUENT YEARS SHE PROVED TO BE AS MUCH A NUISANCE AS THAT WRETCHED PETER PAN.
I TRUST YOU ARE SATISFIED WITH THE FAIRIES MY CREW HAS COLLECTED FOR YOU?
OH, YES! DEFINITELY!
FAIRIES ARE CREATURES OF PURE MAGIC, AND NOW THEIR MAGIC WILL BE MINE! YOU WON'T REGRET THIS PARTNERSHIP, CAPTAIN!
I HOPE NOT.
WE HAD TO RAID HALF THE FAIRY VILLAGES ON THE ISLAND TO GET THAT MANY.
CAP'N HOOK!
PETER PAN BE HERE! FLYIN' AROUND AN' WHATNOT!
ABOUT BLOODY TIME.

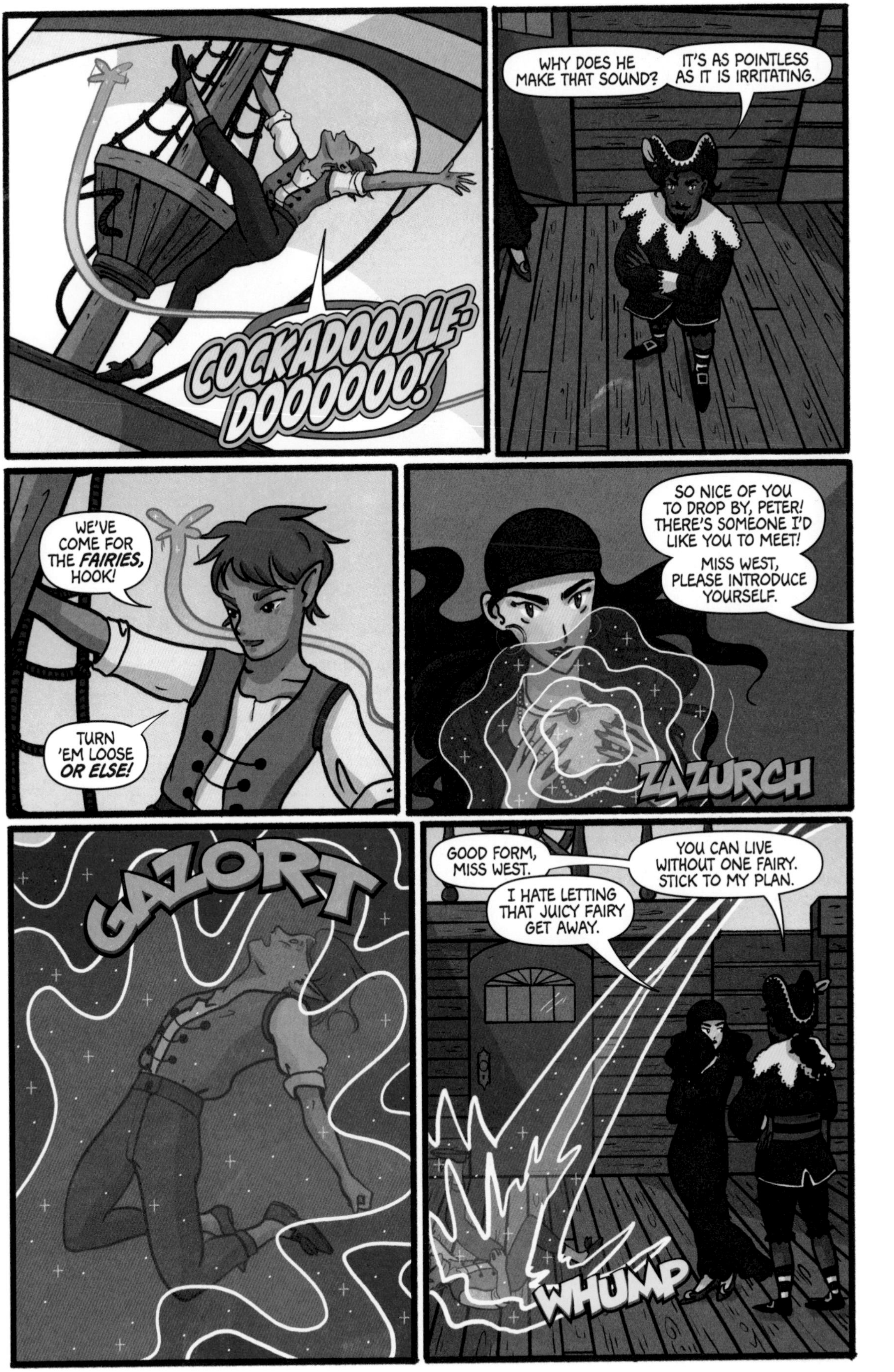

COCKADOODLE-DOOOOOO!
WHY DOES HE MAKE THAT SOUND?
IT'S AS POINTLESS AS IT IS IRRITATING.
WE'VE COME FOR THE *FAIRIES,* HOOK!
TURN 'EM LOOSE *OR ELSE!*
SO NICE OF YOU TO DROP BY, PETER! THERE'S SOMEONE I'D LIKE YOU TO MEET!
MISS WEST, PLEASE INTRODUCE YOURSELF.
ZAZURCH
GAZORT
GOOD FORM, MISS WEST.
I HATE LETTING THAT JUICY FAIRY GET AWAY.
YOU CAN LIVE WITHOUT ONE FAIRY. STICK TO MY PLAN.
WHUMP

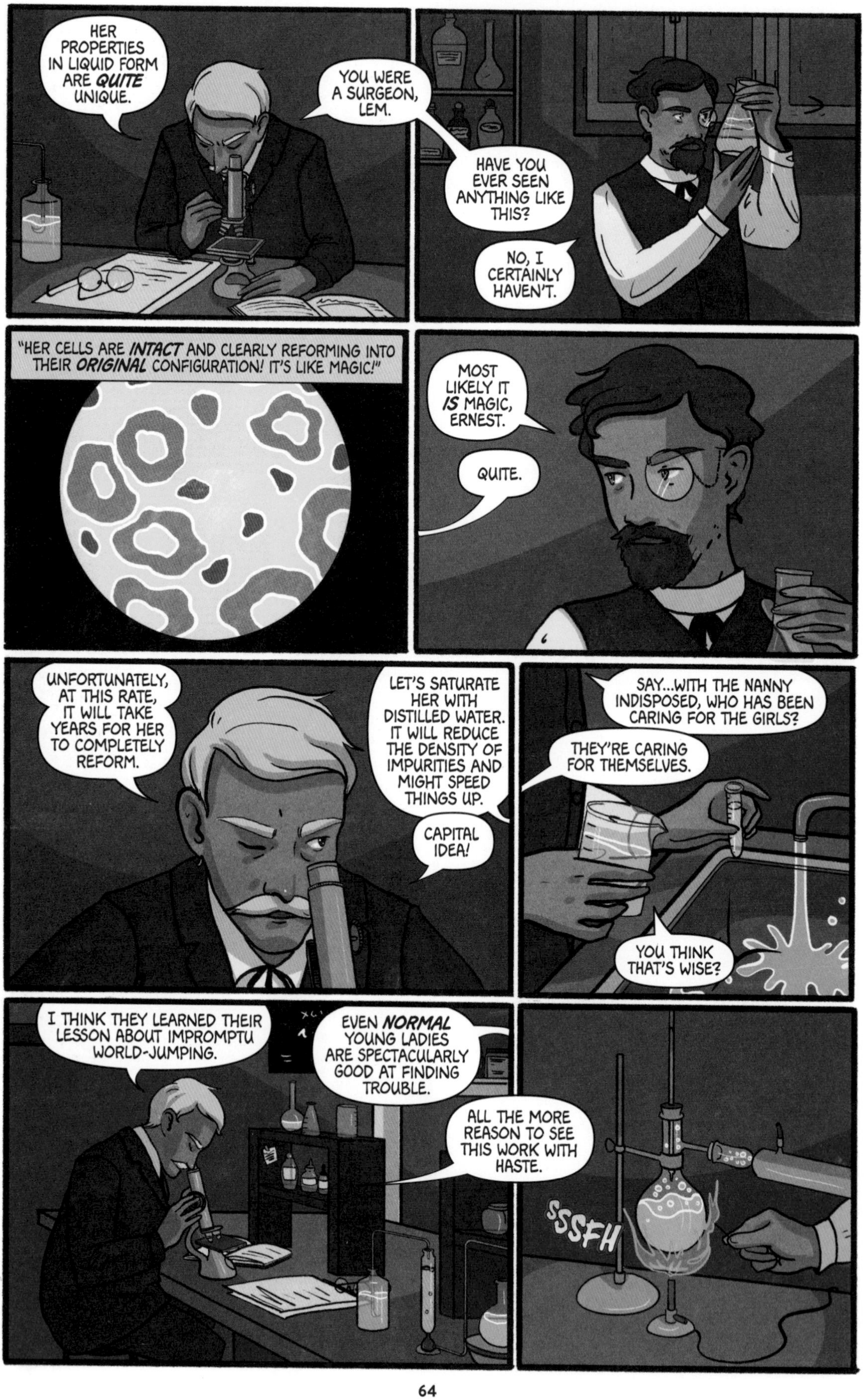
HER PROPERTIES IN LIQUID FORM ARE *QUITE* UNIQUE.
YOU WERE A SURGEON, LEM.
HAVE YOU EVER SEEN ANYTHING LIKE THIS?
NO, I CERTAINLY HAVEN'T.
"HER CELLS ARE *INTACT* AND CLEARLY REFORMING INTO THEIR *ORIGINAL* CONFIGURATION! IT'S LIKE MAGIC!"
MOST LIKELY IT *IS* MAGIC, ERNEST.
QUITE.
UNFORTUNATELY, AT THIS RATE, IT WILL TAKE YEARS FOR HER TO COMPLETELY REFORM.
LET'S SATURATE HER WITH DISTILLED WATER. IT WILL REDUCE THE DENSITY OF IMPURITIES AND MIGHT SPEED THINGS UP.
CAPITAL IDEA!
SAY...WITH THE NANNY INDISPOSED, WHO HAS BEEN CARING FOR THE GIRLS?
THEY'RE CARING FOR THEMSELVES.
YOU THINK THAT'S WISE?
I THINK THEY LEARNED THEIR LESSON ABOUT IMPROMPTU WORLD-JUMPING.
EVEN *NORMAL* YOUNG LADIES ARE SPECTACULARLY GOOD AT FINDING TROUBLE.
ALL THE MORE REASON TO SEE THIS WORK WITH HASTE.
SSSFH

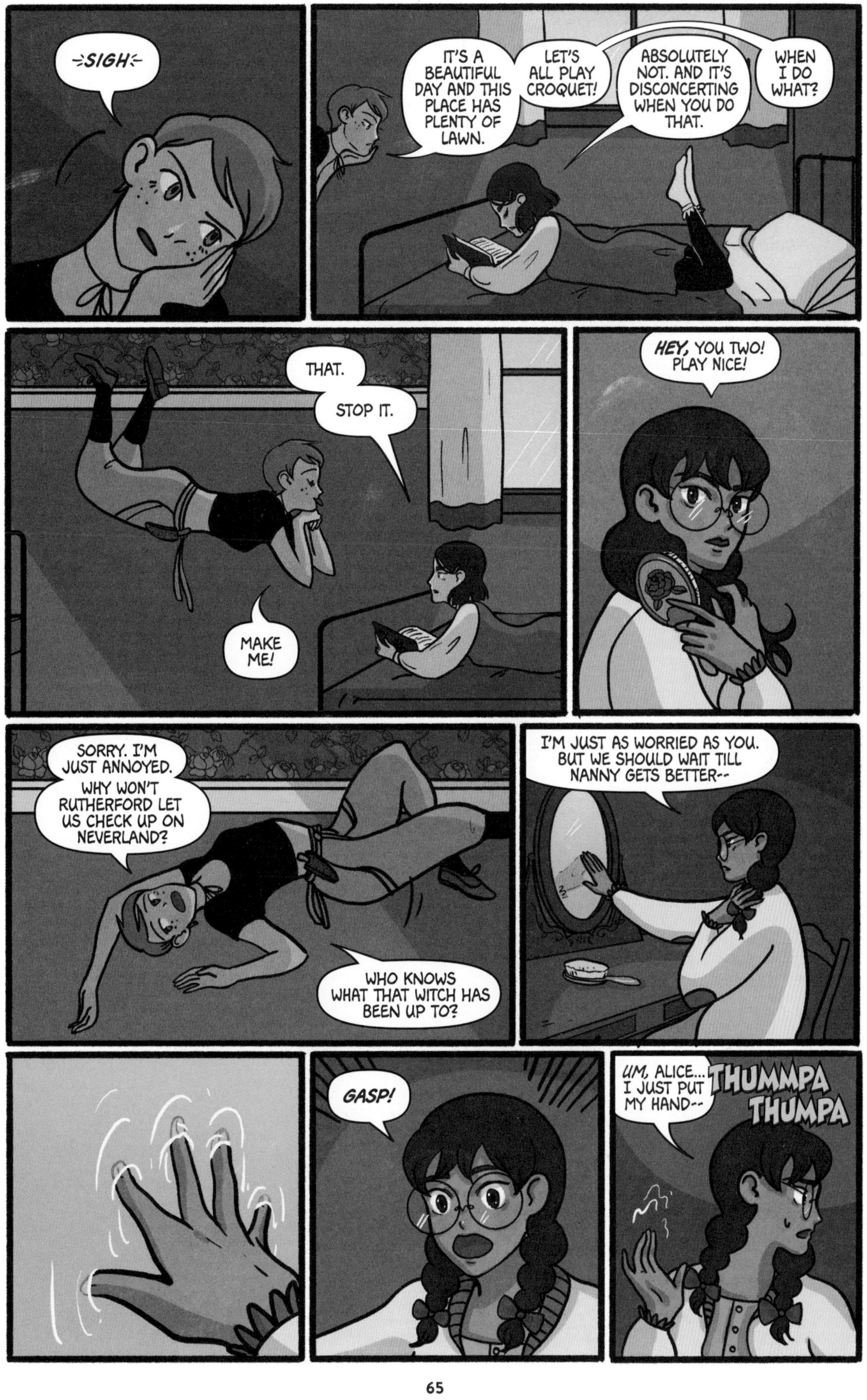

SIGH
IT'S A BEAUTIFUL DAY AND THIS PLACE HAS PLENTY OF LAWN.
LET'S ALL PLAY CROQUET!
ABSOLUTELY NOT. AND IT'S DISCONCERTING WHEN YOU DO THAT.
WHEN I DO WHAT?
THAT.
STOP IT.
MAKE ME!
HEY, YOU TWO! PLAY NICE!
SORRY. I'M JUST ANNOYED.
WHY WON'T RUTHERFORD LET US CHECK UP ON NEVERLAND?
WHO KNOWS WHAT THAT WITCH HAS BEEN UP TO?
I'M JUST AS WORRIED AS YOU. BUT WE SHOULD WAIT TILL NANNY GETS BETTER--
GASP!
UM, ALICE... I JUST PUT MY HAND--
THUMMPA THUMPA

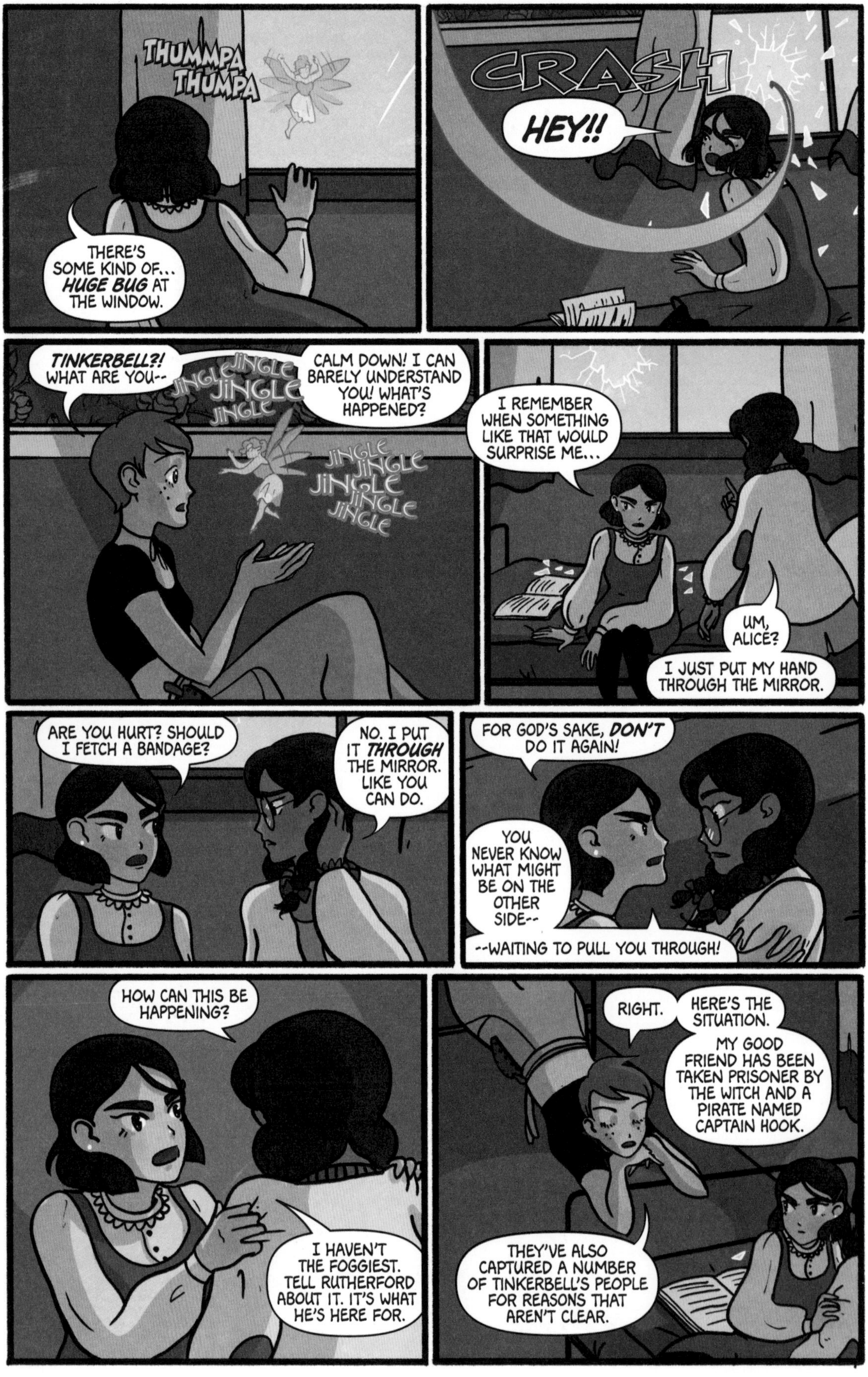
THUMMPA THUMPA
THERE'S SOME KIND OF... HUGE BUG AT THE WINDOW.
CRASH
HEY!!
TINKERBELL?! WHAT ARE YOU--
JINGLE JINGLE JINGLE JINGLE
CALM DOWN! I CAN BARELY UNDERSTAND YOU! WHAT'S HAPPENED?
JINGLE JINGLE JINGLE JINGLE JINGLE
I REMEMBER WHEN SOMETHING LIKE THAT WOULD SURPRISE ME...
UM, ALICE?
I JUST PUT MY HAND THROUGH THE MIRROR.
ARE YOU HURT? SHOULD I FETCH A BANDAGE?
NO. I PUT IT THROUGH THE MIRROR. LIKE YOU CAN DO.
FOR GOD'S SAKE, DON'T DO IT AGAIN!
YOU NEVER KNOW WHAT MIGHT BE ON THE OTHER SIDE--
--WAITING TO PULL YOU THROUGH!
HOW CAN THIS BE HAPPENING?
I HAVEN'T THE FOGGIEST. TELL RUTHERFORD ABOUT IT. IT'S WHAT HE'S HERE FOR.
RIGHT.
HERE'S THE SITUATION.
MY GOOD FRIEND HAS BEEN TAKEN PRISONER BY THE WITCH AND A PIRATE NAMED CAPTAIN HOOK.
THEY'VE ALSO CAPTURED A NUMBER OF TINKERBELL'S PEOPLE FOR REASONS THAT AREN'T CLEAR.

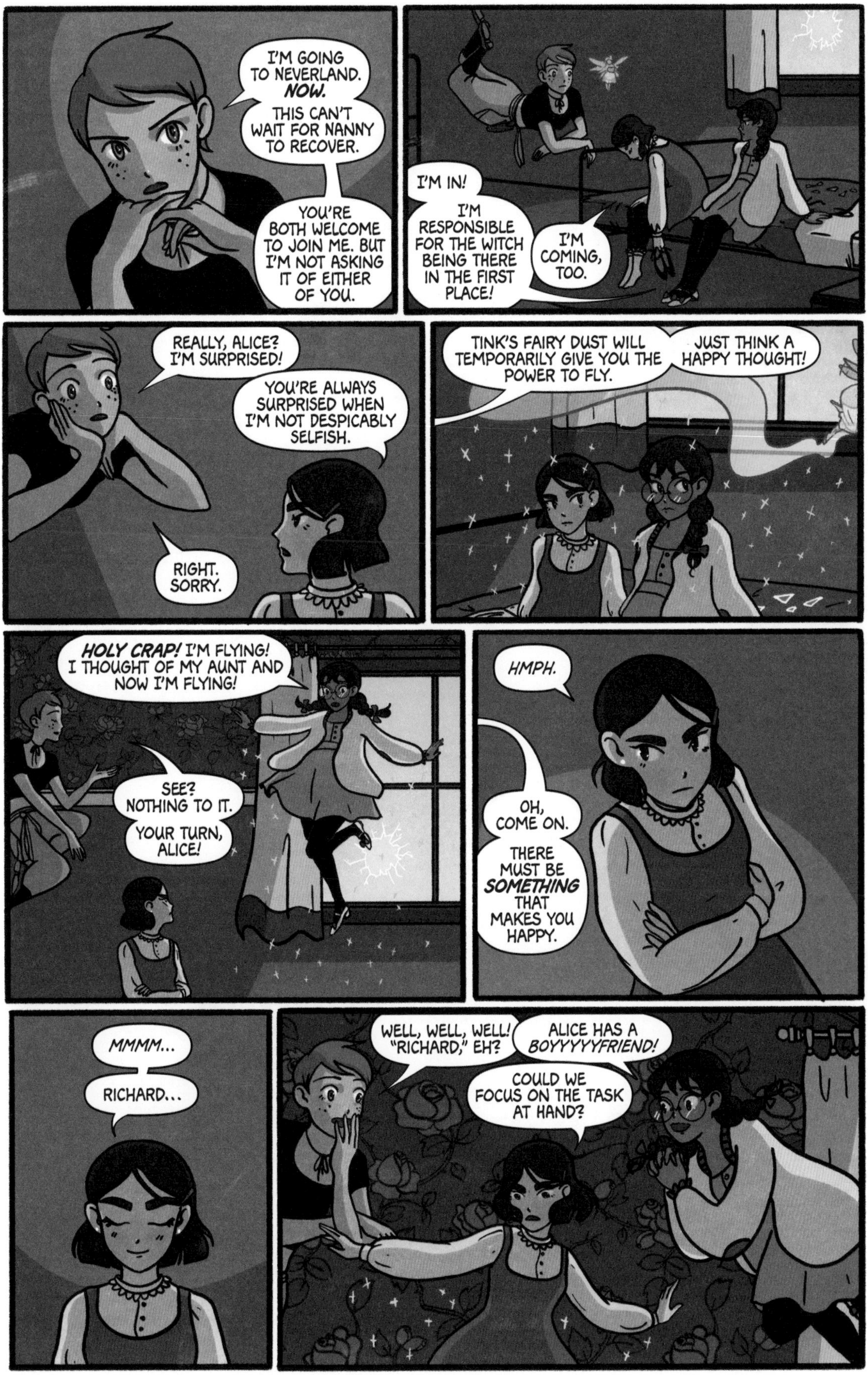
I'M GOING TO NEVERLAND. NOW.
THIS CAN'T WAIT FOR NANNY TO RECOVER.
YOU'RE BOTH WELCOME TO JOIN ME. BUT I'M NOT ASKING IT OF EITHER OF YOU.
I'M IN!
I'M RESPONSIBLE FOR THE WITCH BEING THERE IN THE FIRST PLACE!
I'M COMING, TOO.
REALLY, ALICE? I'M SURPRISED!
YOU'RE ALWAYS SURPRISED WHEN I'M NOT DESPICABLY SELFISH.
RIGHT. SORRY.
TINK'S FAIRY DUST WILL TEMPORARILY GIVE YOU THE POWER TO FLY.
JUST THINK A HAPPY THOUGHT!
HOLY CRAP! I'M FLYING! I THOUGHT OF MY AUNT AND NOW I'M FLYING!
SEE? NOTHING TO IT.
YOUR TURN, ALICE!
HMPH.
OH, COME ON.
THERE MUST BE SOMETHING THAT MAKES YOU HAPPY.
MMMM...
RICHARD...
WELL, WELL, WELL! "RICHARD," EH?
ALICE HAS A BOYYYYYFRIEND!
COULD WE FOCUS ON THE TASK AT HAND?

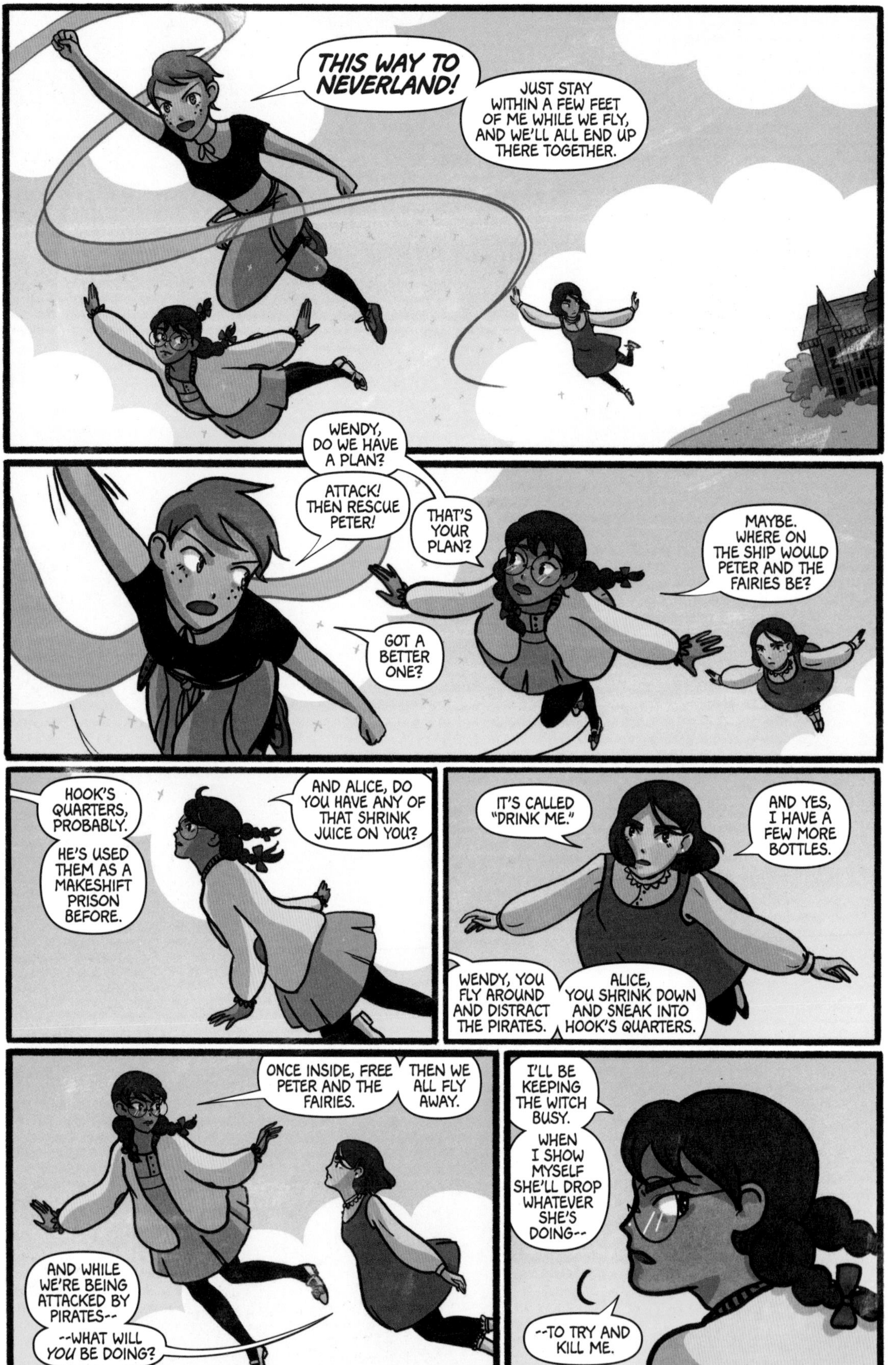
THIS WAY TO NEVERLAND!
JUST STAY WITHIN A FEW FEET OF ME WHILE WE FLY, AND WE'LL ALL END UP THERE TOGETHER.
WENDY, DO WE HAVE A PLAN?
ATTACK! THEN RESCUE PETER!
THAT'S YOUR PLAN?
GOT A BETTER ONE?
MAYBE. WHERE ON THE SHIP WOULD PETER AND THE FAIRIES BE?
HOOK'S QUARTERS, PROBABLY.
HE'S USED THEM AS A MAKESHIFT PRISON BEFORE.
AND ALICE, DO YOU HAVE ANY OF THAT SHRINK JUICE ON YOU?
IT'S CALLED "DRINK ME."
AND YES, I HAVE A FEW MORE BOTTLES.
WENDY, YOU FLY AROUND AND DISTRACT THE PIRATES.
ALICE, YOU SHRINK DOWN AND SNEAK INTO HOOK'S QUARTERS.
ONCE INSIDE, FREE PETER AND THE FAIRIES.
THEN WE ALL FLY AWAY.
AND WHILE WE'RE BEING ATTACKED BY PIRATES--
--WHAT WILL *YOU* BE DOING?
I'LL BE KEEPING THE WITCH BUSY.
WHEN I SHOW MYSELF SHE'LL DROP WHATEVER SHE'S DOING--
--TO TRY AND KILL ME.

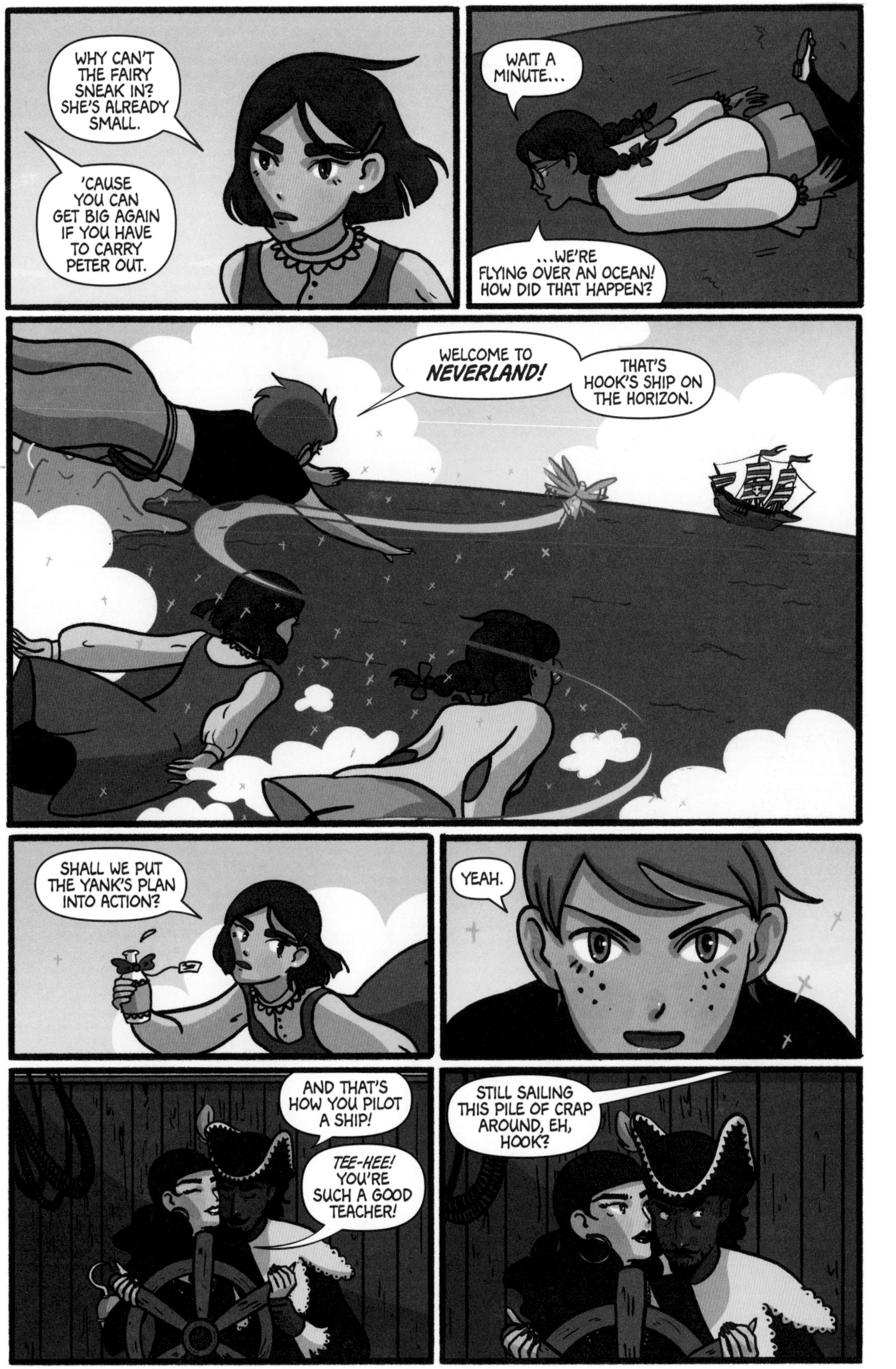
WHY CAN'T THE FAIRY SNEAK IN? SHE'S ALREADY SMALL.
'CAUSE YOU CAN GET BIG AGAIN IF YOU HAVE TO CARRY PETER OUT.
WAIT A MINUTE...
...WE'RE FLYING OVER AN OCEAN! HOW DID THAT HAPPEN?
WELCOME TO *NEVERLAND!*
THAT'S HOOK'S SHIP ON THE HORIZON.
SHALL WE PUT THE YANK'S PLAN INTO ACTION?
YEAH.
AND THAT'S HOW YOU PILOT A SHIP!
TEE-HEE! YOU'RE SUCH A GOOD TEACHER!
STILL SAILING THIS PILE OF CRAP AROUND, EH, HOOK?

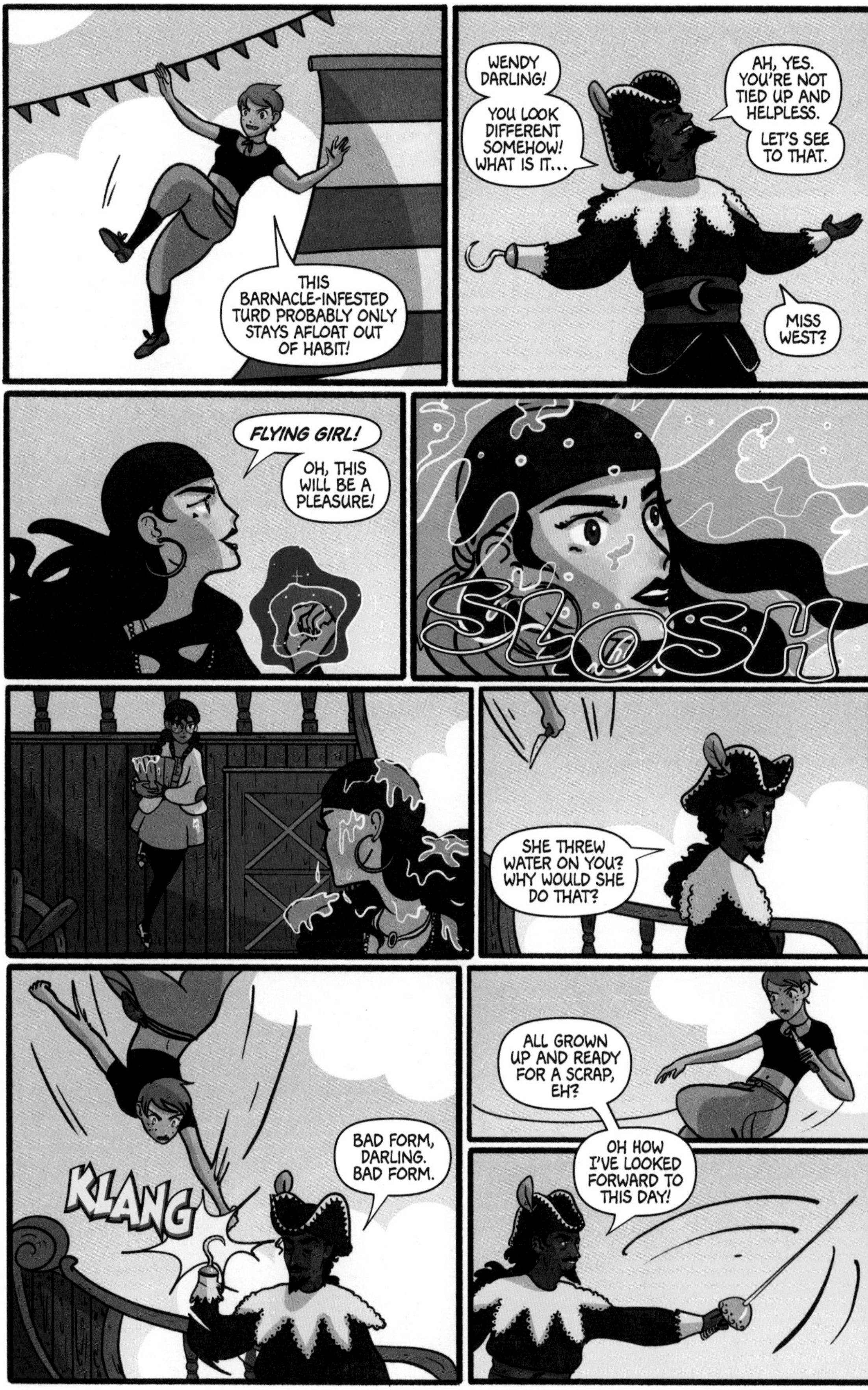
THIS BARNACLE-INFESTED TURD PROBABLY ONLY STAYS AFLOAT OUT OF HABIT!
WENDY DARLING!
YOU LOOK DIFFERENT SOMEHOW! WHAT IS IT...
AH, YES. YOU'RE NOT TIED UP AND HELPLESS.
LET'S SEE TO THAT.
MISS WEST?
FLYING GIRL!
OH, THIS WILL BE A PLEASURE!
SLOSH
SHE THREW WATER ON YOU? WHY WOULD SHE DO THAT?
KLANG
BAD FORM, DARLING. BAD FORM.
ALL GROWN UP AND READY FOR A SCRAP, EH?
OH HOW I'VE LOOKED FORWARD TO THIS DAY!

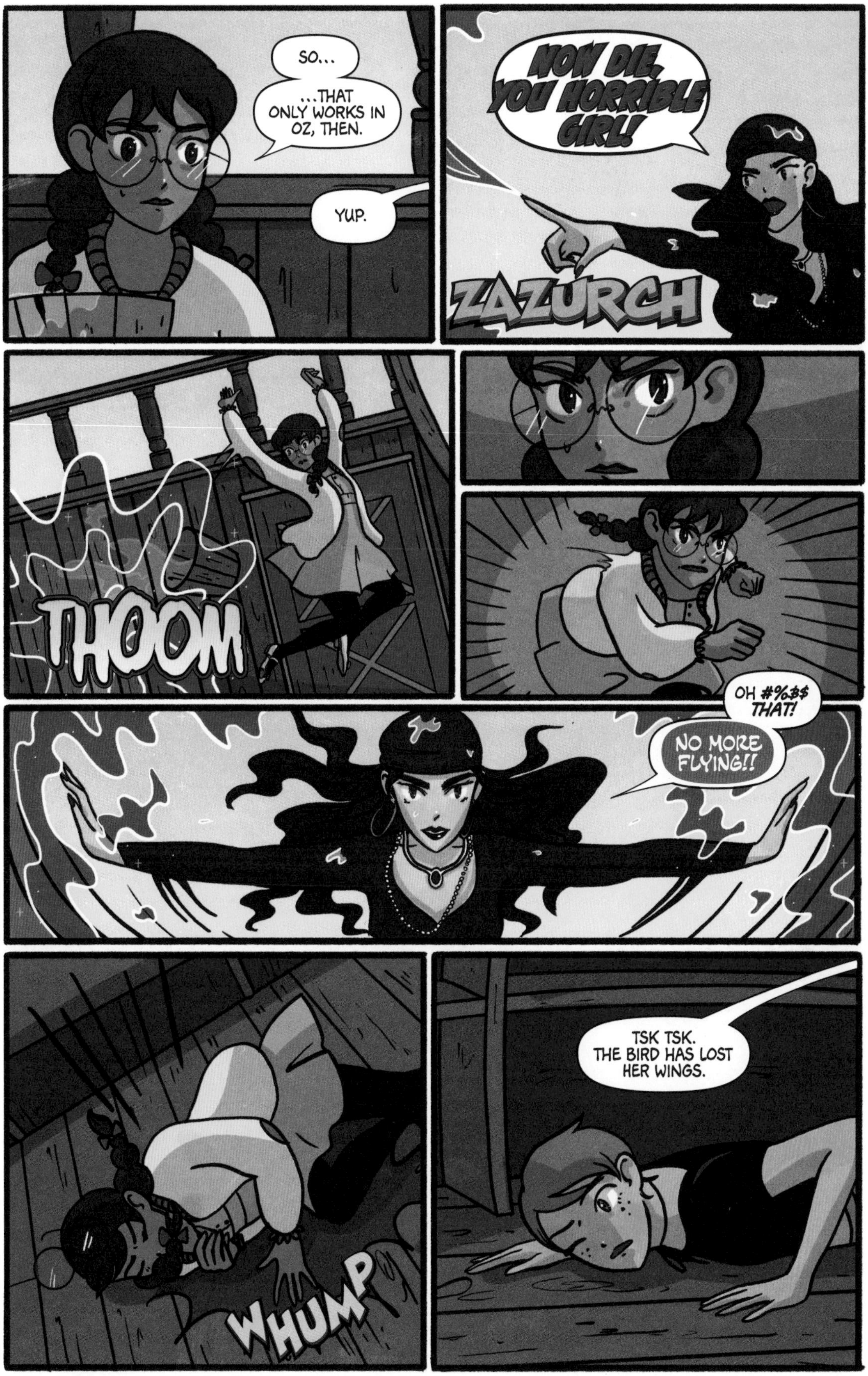

SO...
...THAT ONLY WORKS IN OZ, THEN.
YUP.
NOW DIE, YOU HORRIBLE GIRL!
ZAZURCH
THOOM
OH #%$$ THAT!
NO MORE FLYING!!
WHUMP
TSK TSK. THE BIRD HAS LOST HER WINGS.

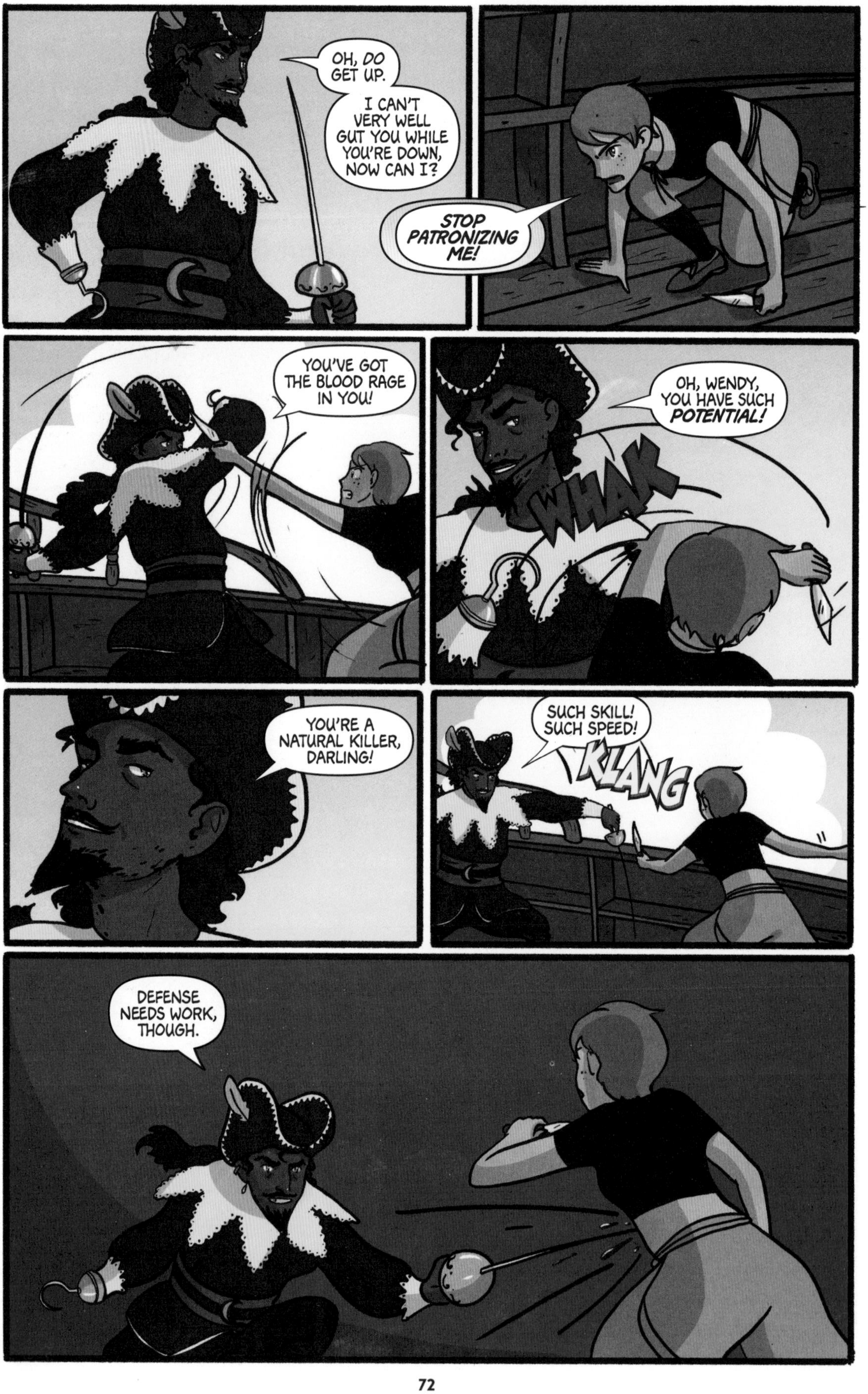
OH, *DO* GET UP.
I CAN'T VERY WELL GUT YOU WHILE YOU'RE DOWN, NOW CAN I?
STOP PATRONIZING ME!
YOU'VE GOT THE BLOOD RAGE IN YOU!
OH, WENDY, YOU HAVE SUCH ***POTENTIAL!***
WHAK
YOU'RE A NATURAL KILLER, DARLING!
SUCH SKILL! SUCH SPEED!
KLANG
DEFENSE NEEDS WORK, THOUGH.

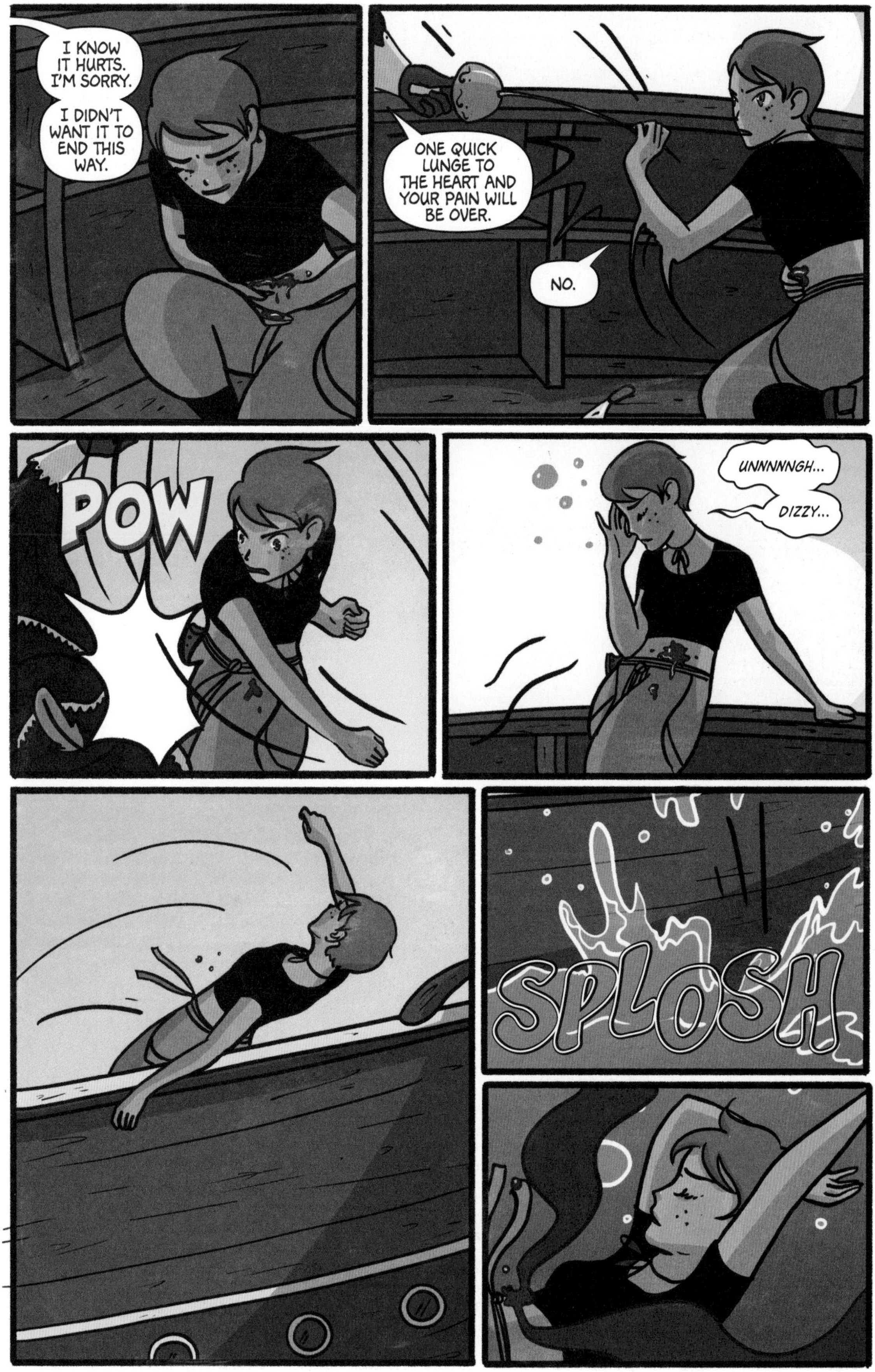
I KNOW IT HURTS. I'M SORRY.
I DIDN'T WANT IT TO END THIS WAY.
ONE QUICK LUNGE TO THE HEART AND YOUR PAIN WILL BE OVER.
NO.
POW
UNNNNNGH...
DIZZY...
SPLOSH

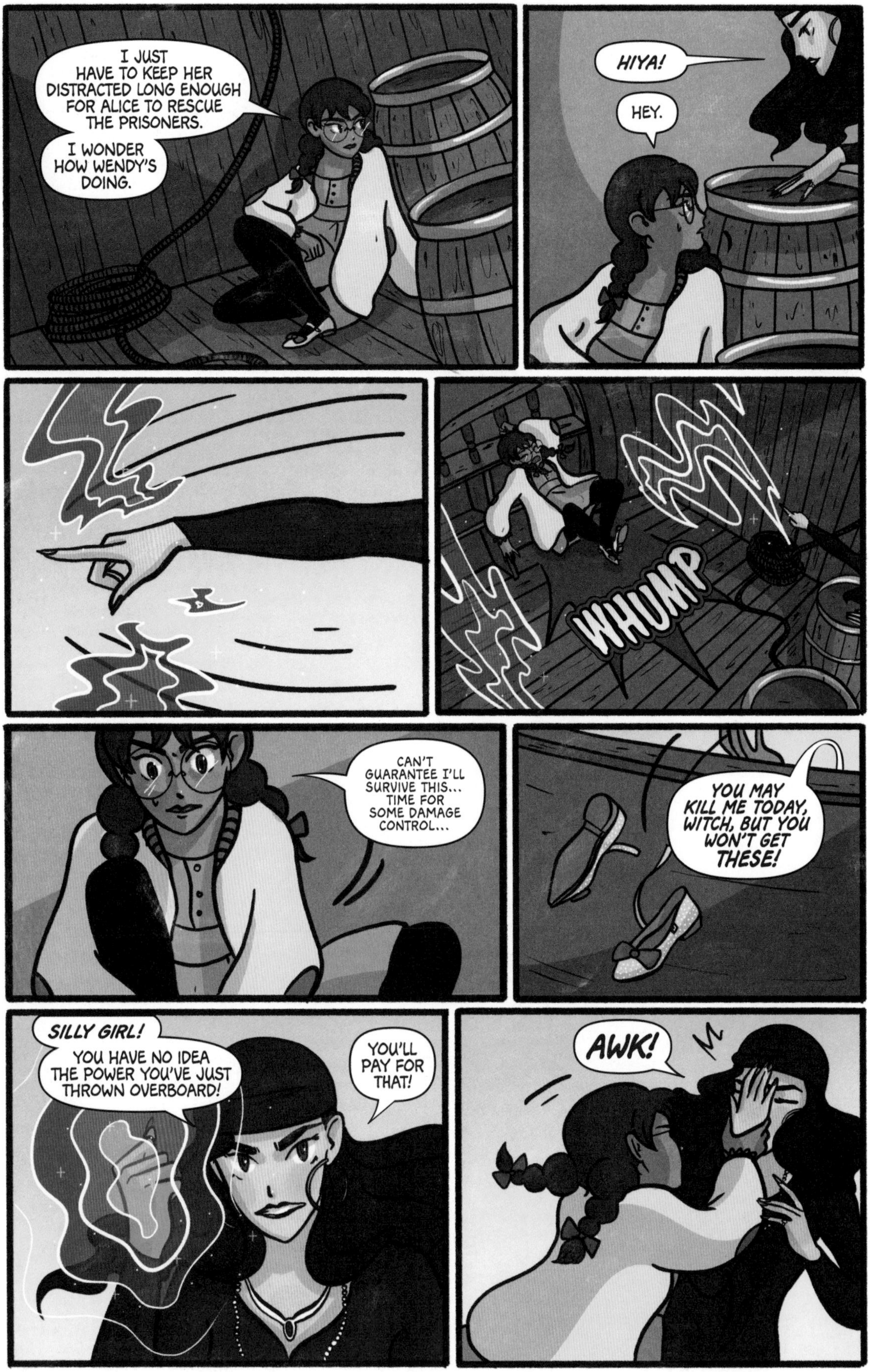
I JUST HAVE TO KEEP HER DISTRACTED LONG ENOUGH FOR ALICE TO RESCUE THE PRISONERS.
I WONDER HOW WENDY'S DOING.
HIYA!
HEY.
WHUMP
CAN'T GUARANTEE I'LL SURVIVE THIS... TIME FOR SOME DAMAGE CONTROL...
YOU MAY KILL ME TODAY, WITCH, BUT YOU WON'T GET THESE!
SILLY GIRL!
YOU HAVE NO IDEA THE POWER YOU'VE JUST THROWN OVERBOARD!
YOU'LL PAY FOR THAT!
AWK!

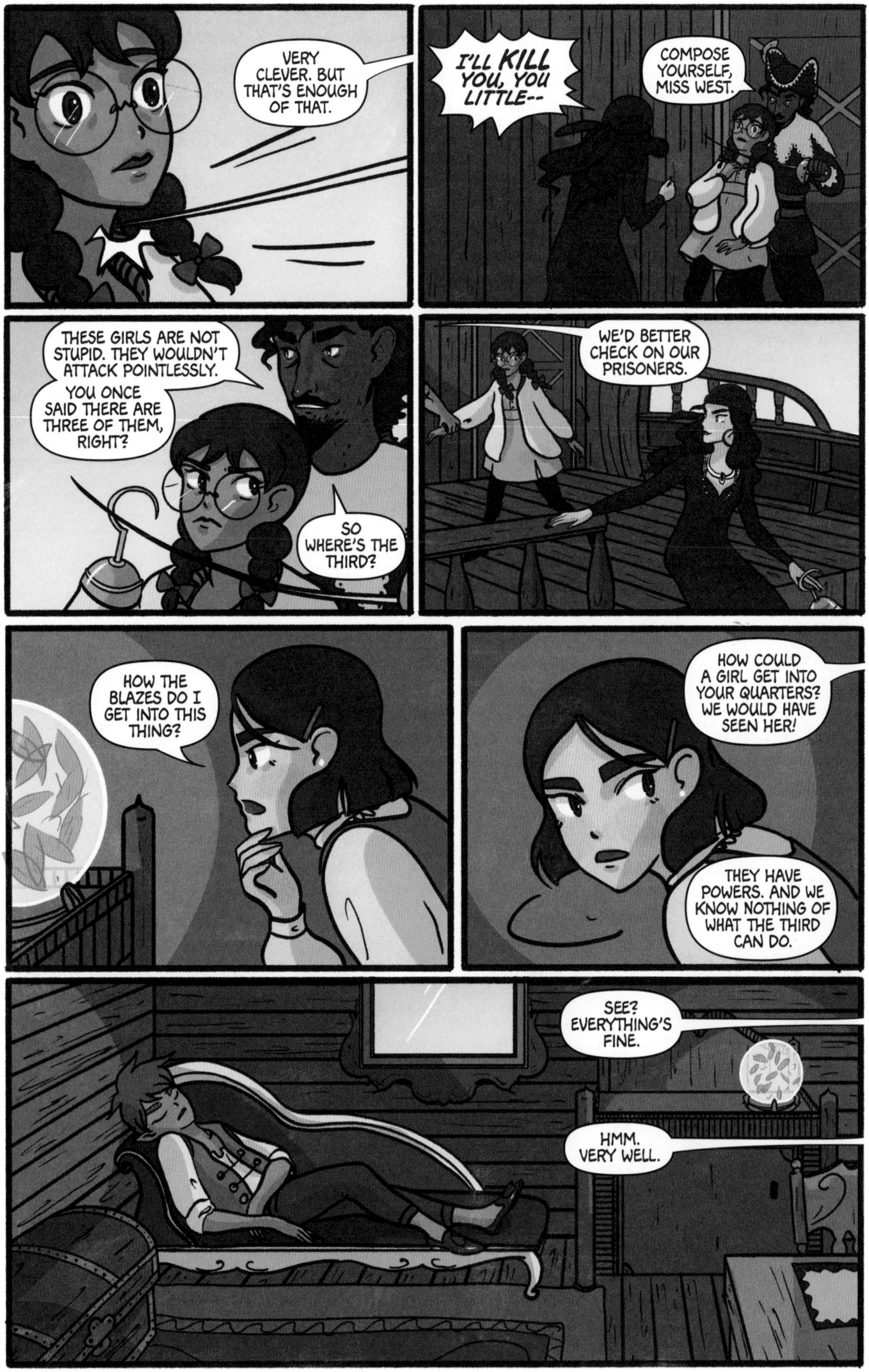
VERY CLEVER. BUT THAT'S ENOUGH OF THAT.
I'LL **KILL** YOU, YOU LITTLE--
COMPOSE YOURSELF, MISS WEST.
THESE GIRLS ARE NOT STUPID. THEY WOULDN'T ATTACK POINTLESSLY.
YOU ONCE SAID THERE ARE THREE OF THEM, RIGHT?
SO WHERE'S THE THIRD?
WE'D BETTER CHECK ON OUR PRISONERS.
HOW THE BLAZES DO I GET INTO THIS THING?
HOW COULD A GIRL GET INTO YOUR QUARTERS? WE WOULD HAVE SEEN HER!
THEY HAVE POWERS. AND WE KNOW NOTHING OF WHAT THE THIRD CAN DO.
SEE? EVERYTHING'S FINE.
HMM. VERY WELL.

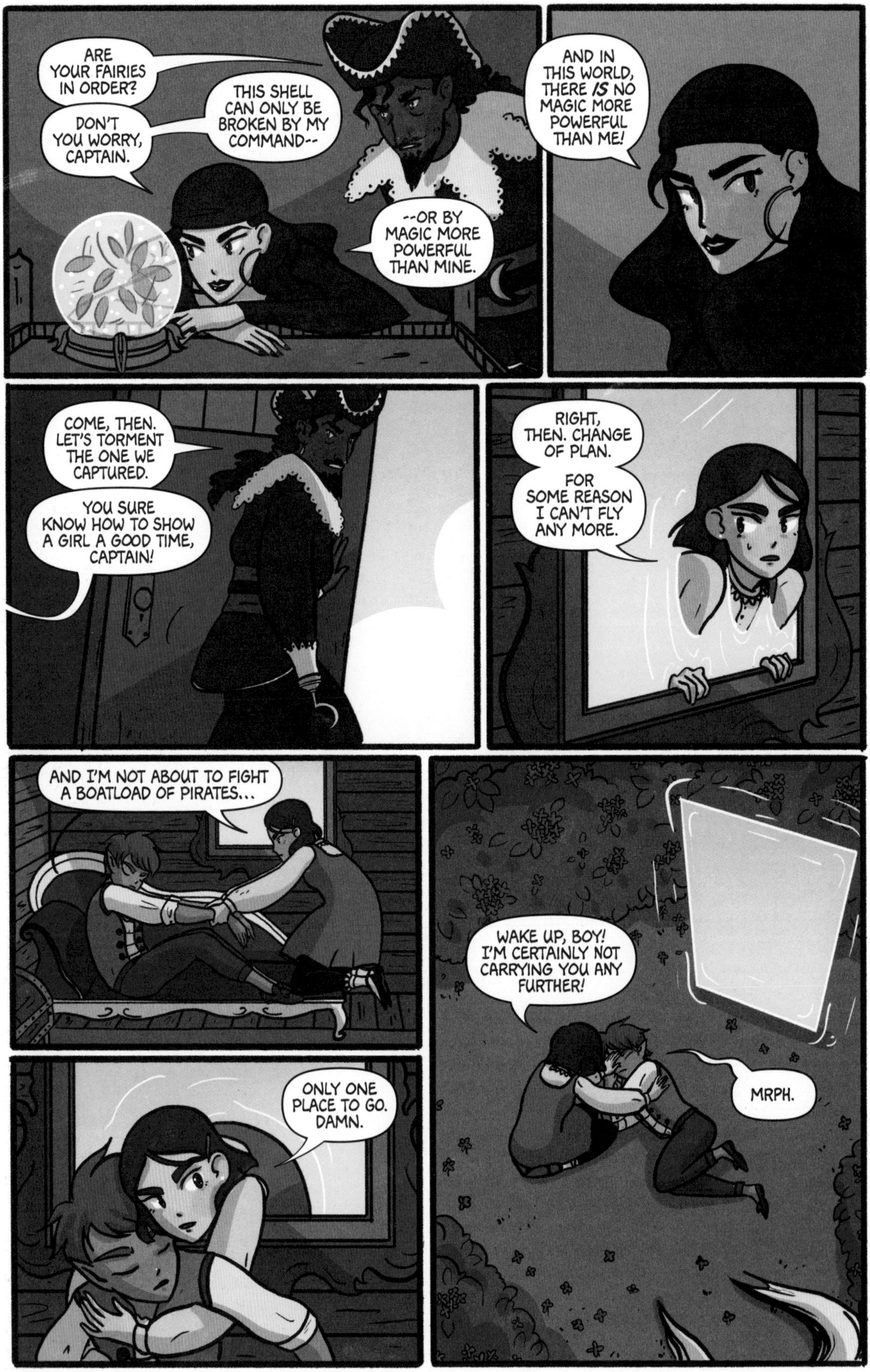
ARE YOUR FAIRIES IN ORDER?
DON'T YOU WORRY, CAPTAIN.
THIS SHELL CAN ONLY BE BROKEN BY MY COMMAND--
--OR BY MAGIC MORE POWERFUL THAN MINE.
AND IN THIS WORLD, THERE *IS* NO MAGIC MORE POWERFUL THAN ME!
COME, THEN. LET'S TORMENT THE ONE WE CAPTURED.
YOU SURE KNOW HOW TO SHOW A GIRL A GOOD TIME, CAPTAIN!
RIGHT, THEN. CHANGE OF PLAN.
FOR SOME REASON I CAN'T FLY ANY MORE.
AND I'M NOT ABOUT TO FIGHT A BOATLOAD OF PIRATES...
ONLY ONE PLACE TO GO. DAMN.
WAKE UP, BOY! I'M CERTAINLY NOT CARRYING YOU ANY FURTHER!
MRPH.

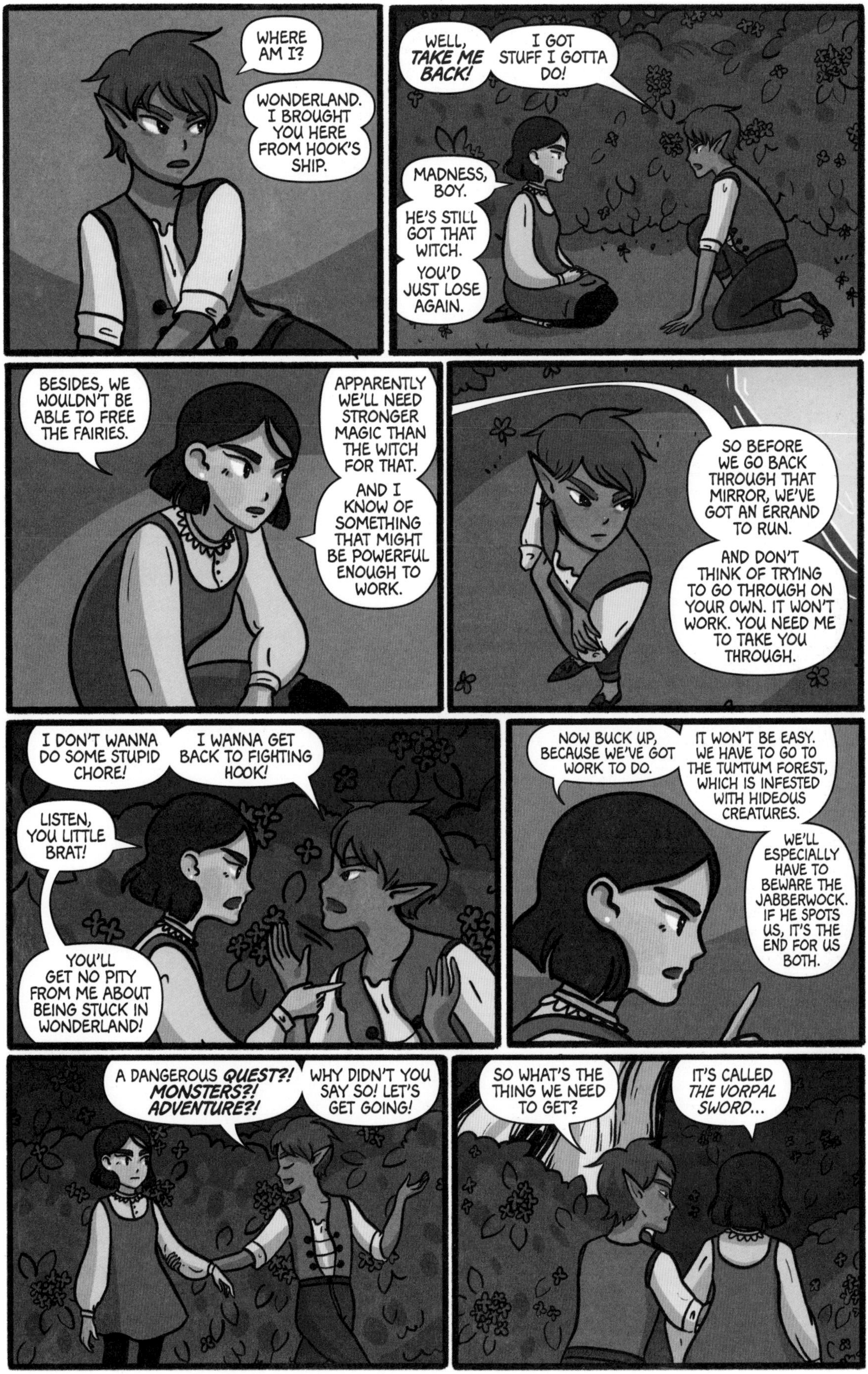
WHERE AM I?
WONDERLAND. I BROUGHT YOU HERE FROM HOOK'S SHIP.
WELL, ***TAKE ME BACK!***
I GOT STUFF I GOTTA DO!
MADNESS, BOY.
HE'S STILL GOT THAT WITCH.
YOU'D JUST LOSE AGAIN.
BESIDES, WE WOULDN'T BE ABLE TO FREE THE FAIRIES.
APPARENTLY WE'LL NEED STRONGER MAGIC THAN THE WITCH FOR THAT.
AND I KNOW OF SOMETHING THAT MIGHT BE POWERFUL ENOUGH TO WORK.
SO BEFORE WE GO BACK THROUGH THAT MIRROR, WE'VE GOT AN ERRAND TO RUN.
AND DON'T THINK OF TRYING TO GO THROUGH ON YOUR OWN. IT WON'T WORK. YOU NEED ME TO TAKE YOU THROUGH.
I DON'T WANNA DO SOME STUPID CHORE!
I WANNA GET BACK TO FIGHTING HOOK!
LISTEN, YOU LITTLE BRAT!
YOU'LL GET NO PITY FROM ME ABOUT BEING STUCK IN WONDERLAND!
NOW BUCK UP, BECAUSE WE'VE GOT WORK TO DO.
IT WON'T BE EASY. WE HAVE TO GO TO THE TUMTUM FOREST, WHICH IS INFESTED WITH HIDEOUS CREATURES.
WE'LL ESPECIALLY HAVE TO BEWARE THE JABBERWOCK. IF HE SPOTS US, IT'S THE END FOR US BOTH.
A DANGEROUS ***QUEST?!*** ***MONSTERS?!*** ***ADVENTURE?!***
WHY DIDN'T YOU SAY SO! LET'S GET GOING!
SO WHAT'S THE THING WE NEED TO GET?
IT'S CALLED *THE VORPAL SWORD*...

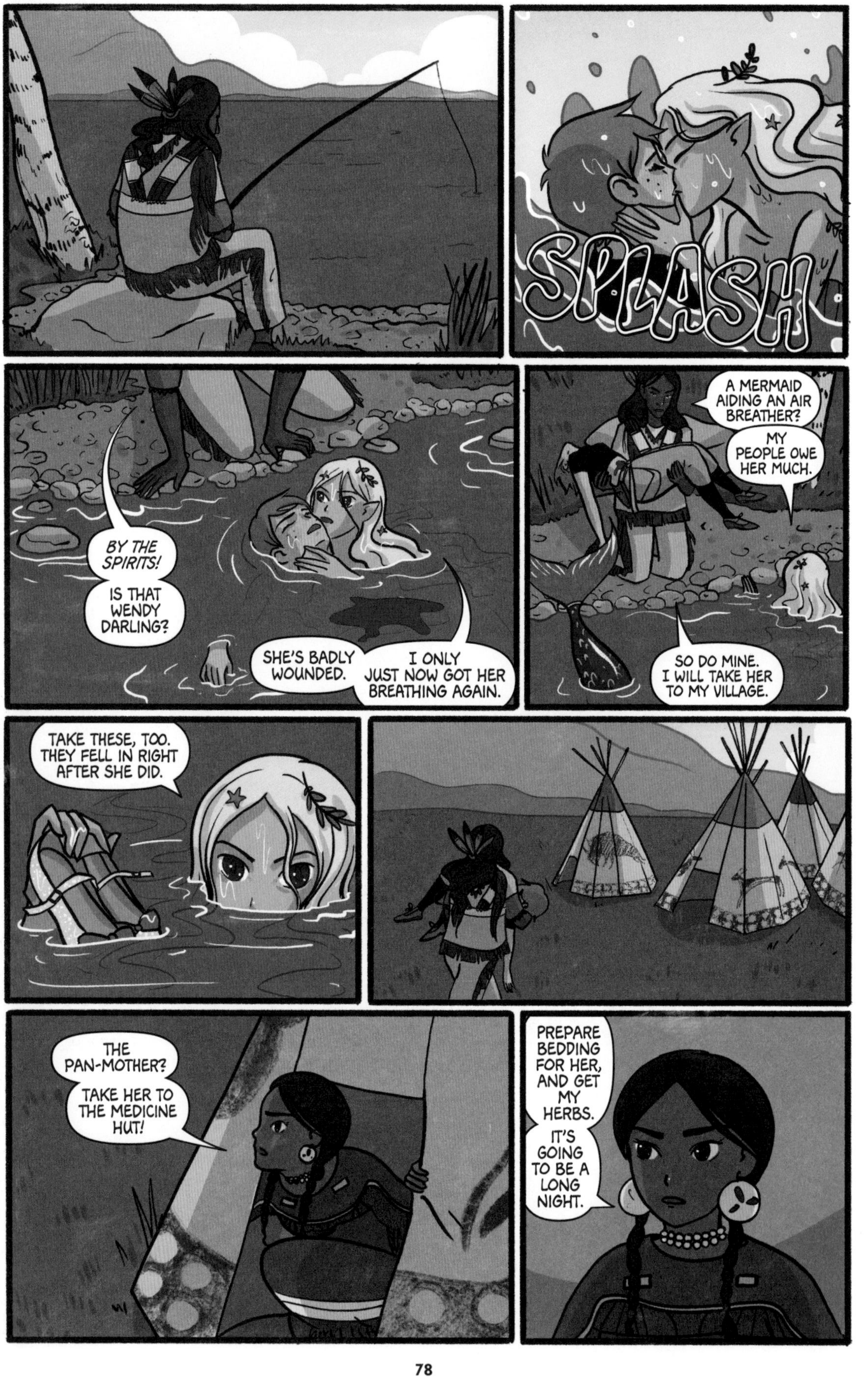
SPLASH
BY THE SPIRITS!
IS THAT WENDY DARLING?
SHE'S BADLY WOUNDED.
I ONLY JUST NOW GOT HER BREATHING AGAIN.
A MERMAID AIDING AN AIR BREATHER?
MY PEOPLE OWE HER MUCH.
SO DO MINE. I WILL TAKE HER TO MY VILLAGE.
TAKE THESE, TOO. THEY FELL IN RIGHT AFTER SHE DID.
THE PAN-MOTHER?
TAKE HER TO THE MEDICINE HUT!
PREPARE BEDDING FOR HER, AND GET MY HERBS.
IT'S GOING TO BE A LONG NIGHT.

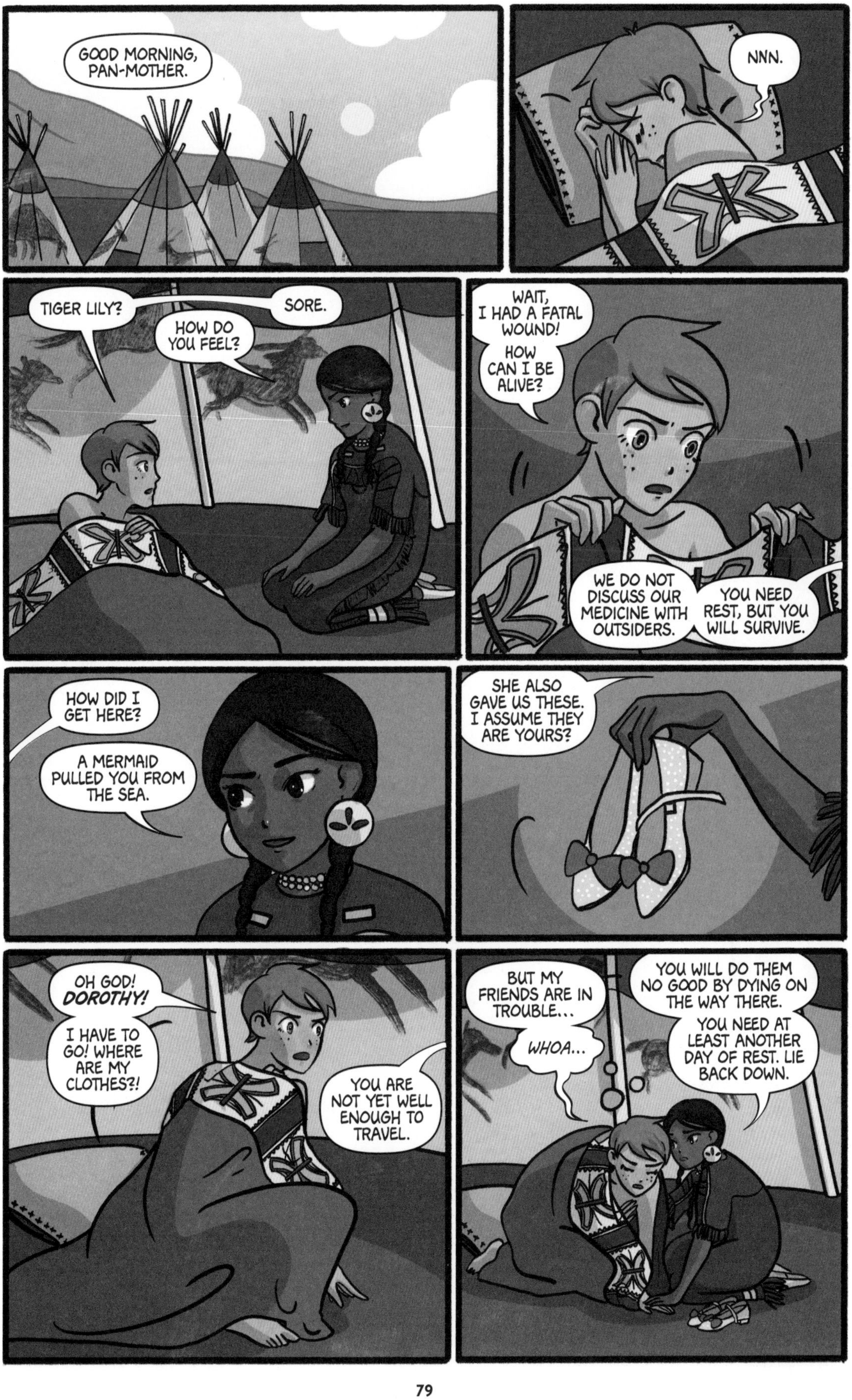
GOOD MORNING, PAN-MOTHER.
NNN.
TIGER LILY?
HOW DO YOU FEEL?
SORE.
WAIT, I HAD A FATAL WOUND!
HOW CAN I BE ALIVE?
WE DO NOT DISCUSS OUR MEDICINE WITH OUTSIDERS.
YOU NEED REST, BUT YOU WILL SURVIVE.
HOW DID I GET HERE?
A MERMAID PULLED YOU FROM THE SEA.
SHE ALSO GAVE US THESE. I ASSUME THEY ARE YOURS?
OH GOD! ***DOROTHY!***
I HAVE TO GO! WHERE ARE MY CLOTHES?!
YOU ARE NOT YET WELL ENOUGH TO TRAVEL.
BUT MY FRIENDS ARE IN TROUBLE...
WHOA...
YOU WILL DO THEM NO GOOD BY DYING ON THE WAY THERE.
YOU NEED AT LEAST ANOTHER DAY OF REST. LIE BACK DOWN.

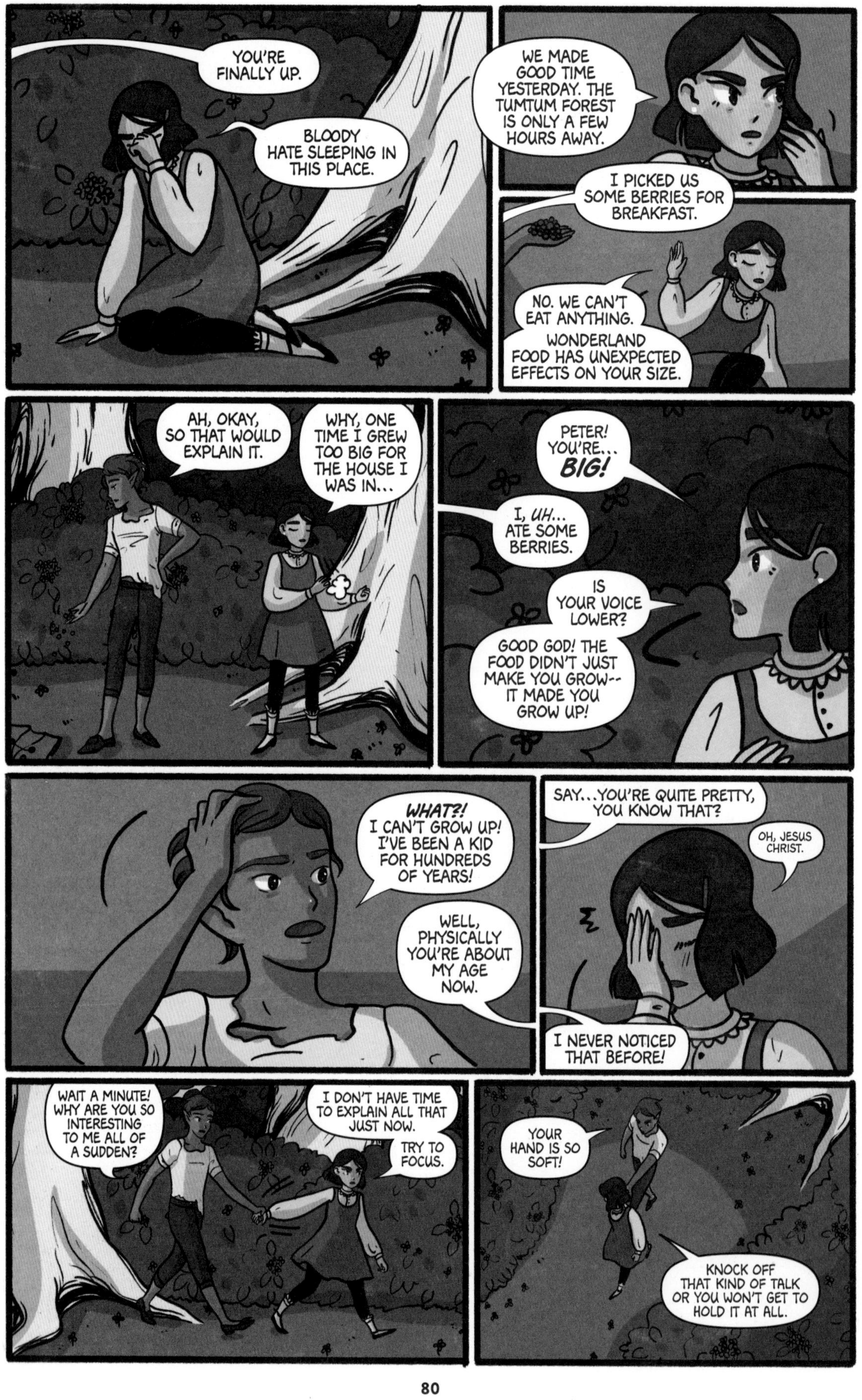
YOU'RE FINALLY UP.
BLOODY HATE SLEEPING IN THIS PLACE.
WE MADE GOOD TIME YESTERDAY. THE TUMTUM FOREST IS ONLY A FEW HOURS AWAY.
I PICKED US SOME BERRIES FOR BREAKFAST.
NO. WE CAN'T EAT ANYTHING.
WONDERLAND FOOD HAS UNEXPECTED EFFECTS ON YOUR SIZE.
AH, OKAY, SO THAT WOULD EXPLAIN IT.
WHY, ONE TIME I GREW TOO BIG FOR THE HOUSE I WAS IN...
PETER! YOU'RE... BIG!
I, UH... ATE SOME BERRIES.
IS YOUR VOICE LOWER?
GOOD GOD! THE FOOD DIDN'T JUST MAKE YOU GROW-- IT MADE YOU GROW UP!
WHAT?! I CAN'T GROW UP! I'VE BEEN A KID FOR HUNDREDS OF YEARS!
WELL, PHYSICALLY YOU'RE ABOUT MY AGE NOW.
SAY...YOU'RE QUITE PRETTY, YOU KNOW THAT?
OH, JESUS CHRIST.
I NEVER NOTICED THAT BEFORE!
WAIT A MINUTE! WHY ARE YOU SO INTERESTING TO ME ALL OF A SUDDEN?
I DON'T HAVE TIME TO EXPLAIN ALL THAT JUST NOW.
TRY TO FOCUS.
YOUR HAND IS SO SOFT!
KNOCK OFF THAT KIND OF TALK OR YOU WON'T GET TO HOLD IT AT ALL.

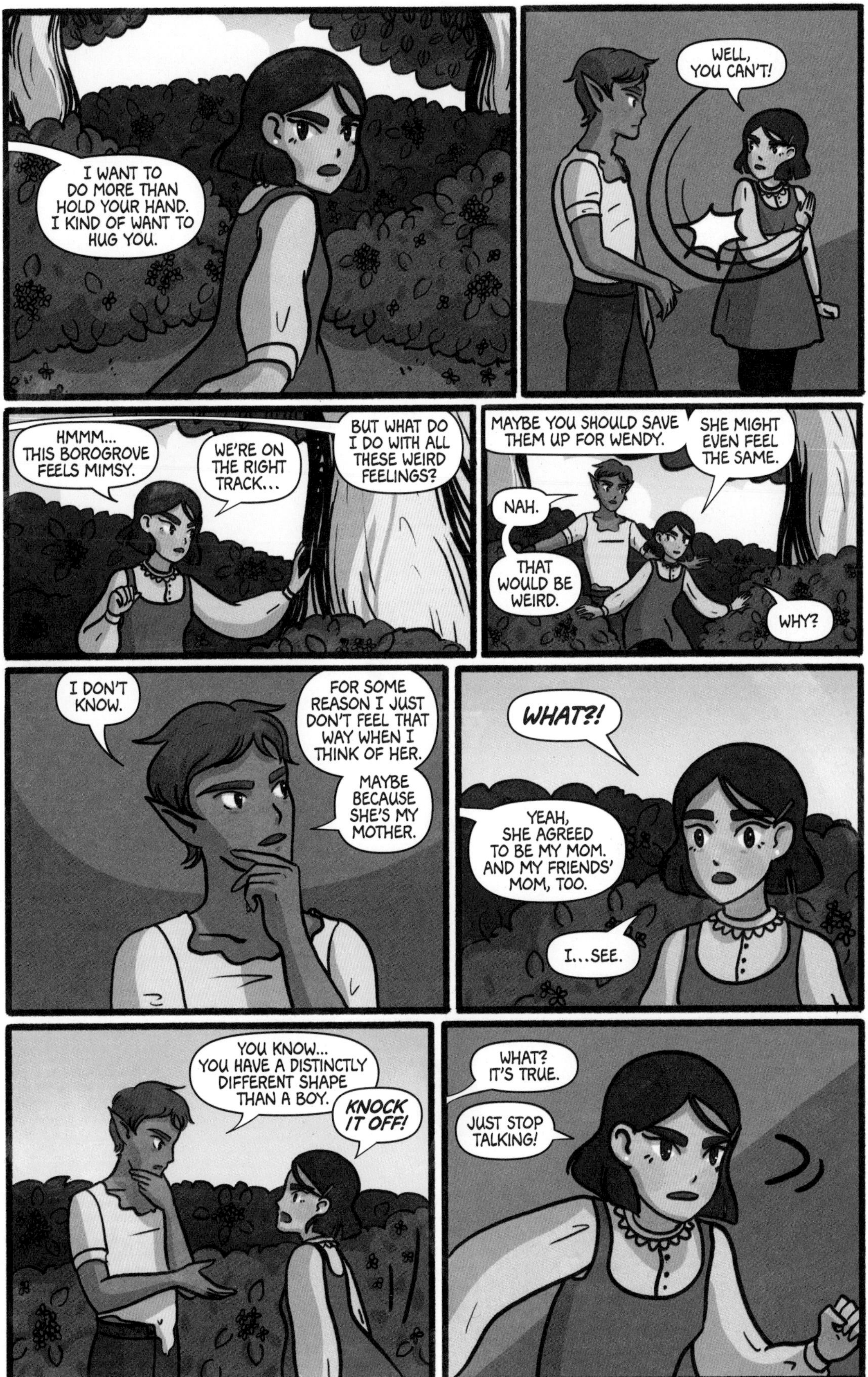
I WANT TO DO MORE THAN HOLD YOUR HAND. I KIND OF WANT TO HUG YOU.
WELL, YOU CAN'T!
HMMM... THIS BOROGROVE FEELS MIMSY.
WE'RE ON THE RIGHT TRACK...
BUT WHAT DO I DO WITH ALL THESE WEIRD FEELINGS?
MAYBE YOU SHOULD SAVE THEM UP FOR WENDY.
SHE MIGHT EVEN FEEL THE SAME.
NAH.
THAT WOULD BE WEIRD.
WHY?
I DON'T KNOW.
FOR SOME REASON I JUST DON'T FEEL THAT WAY WHEN I THINK OF HER.
MAYBE BECAUSE SHE'S MY MOTHER.
WHAT?!
YEAH, SHE AGREED TO BE MY MOM. AND MY FRIENDS' MOM, TOO.
I...SEE.
YOU KNOW... YOU HAVE A DISTINCTLY DIFFERENT SHAPE THAN A BOY.
KNOCK IT OFF!
WHAT? IT'S TRUE.
JUST STOP TALKING!

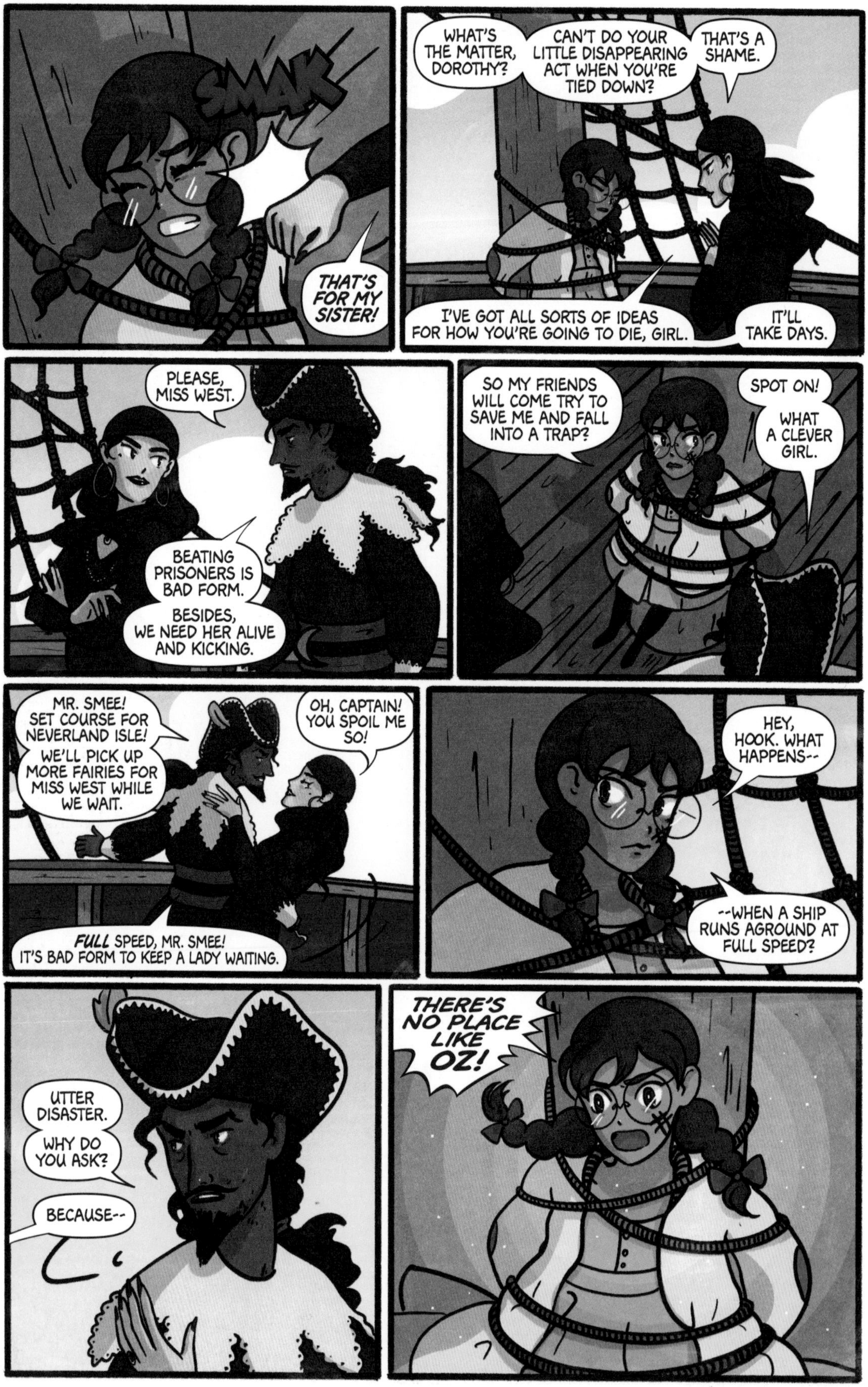
SMAK
THAT'S FOR MY SISTER!
WHAT'S THE MATTER, DOROTHY?
CAN'T DO YOUR LITTLE DISAPPEARING ACT WHEN YOU'RE TIED DOWN?
THAT'S A SHAME.
I'VE GOT ALL SORTS OF IDEAS FOR HOW YOU'RE GOING TO DIE, GIRL.
IT'LL TAKE DAYS.
PLEASE, MISS WEST.
BEATING PRISONERS IS BAD FORM.
BESIDES, WE NEED HER ALIVE AND KICKING.
SO MY FRIENDS WILL COME TRY TO SAVE ME AND FALL INTO A TRAP?
SPOT ON!
WHAT A CLEVER GIRL.
MR. SMEE! SET COURSE FOR NEVERLAND ISLE!
WE'LL PICK UP MORE FAIRIES FOR MISS WEST WHILE WE WAIT.
OH, CAPTAIN! YOU SPOIL ME SO!
FULL SPEED, MR. SMEE! IT'S BAD FORM TO KEEP A LADY WAITING.
HEY, HOOK. WHAT HAPPENS--
--WHEN A SHIP RUNS AGROUND AT FULL SPEED?
UTTER DISASTER.
WHY DO YOU ASK?
BECAUSE--
THERE'S NO PLACE LIKE OZ!

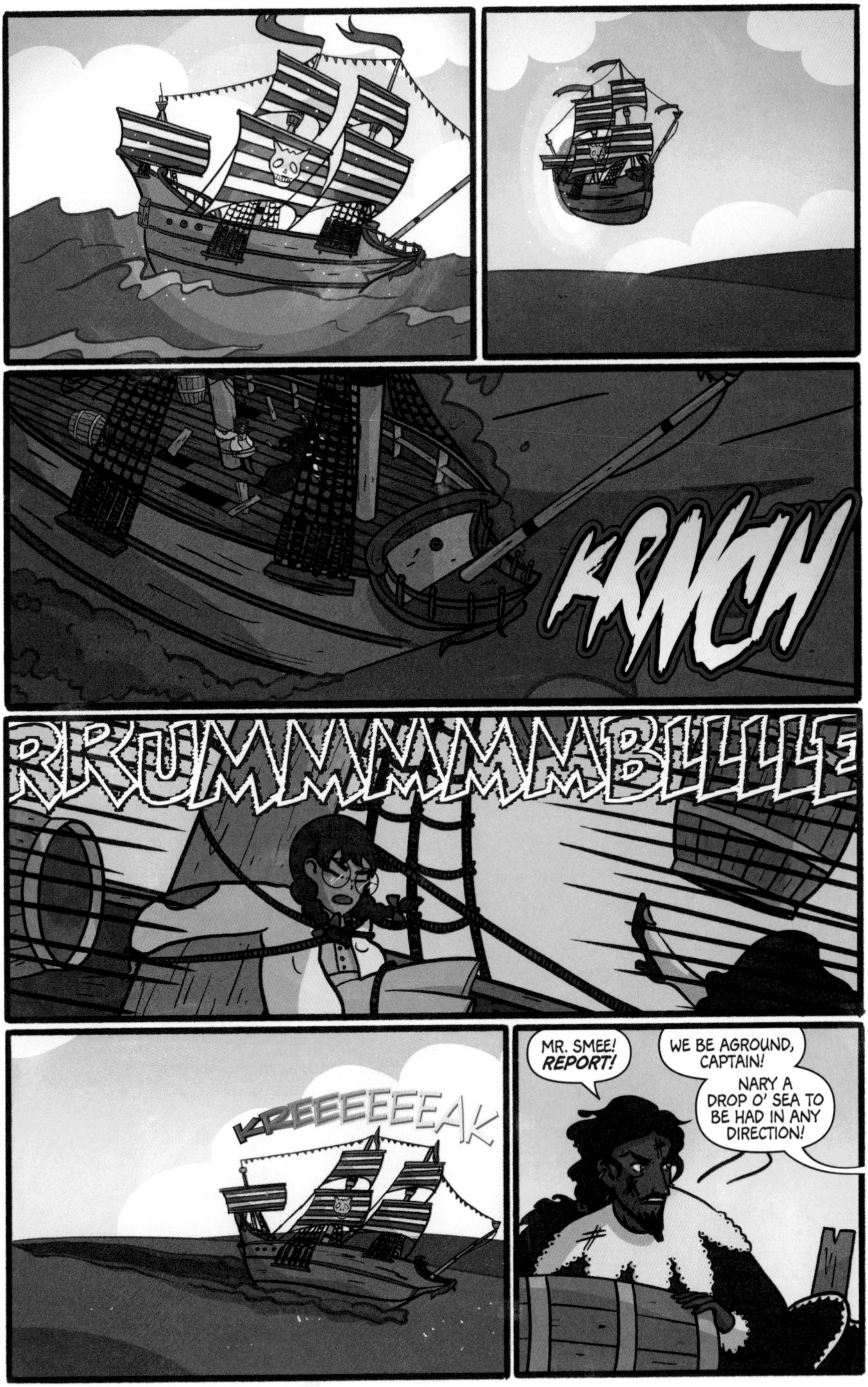
KRNCH
RRUMMMMMMBLLLLE
KREEEEEEEAK
MR. SMEE! **REPORT!**
WE BE AGROUND, CAPTAIN!
NARY A DROP O' SEA TO BE HAD IN ANY DIRECTION!

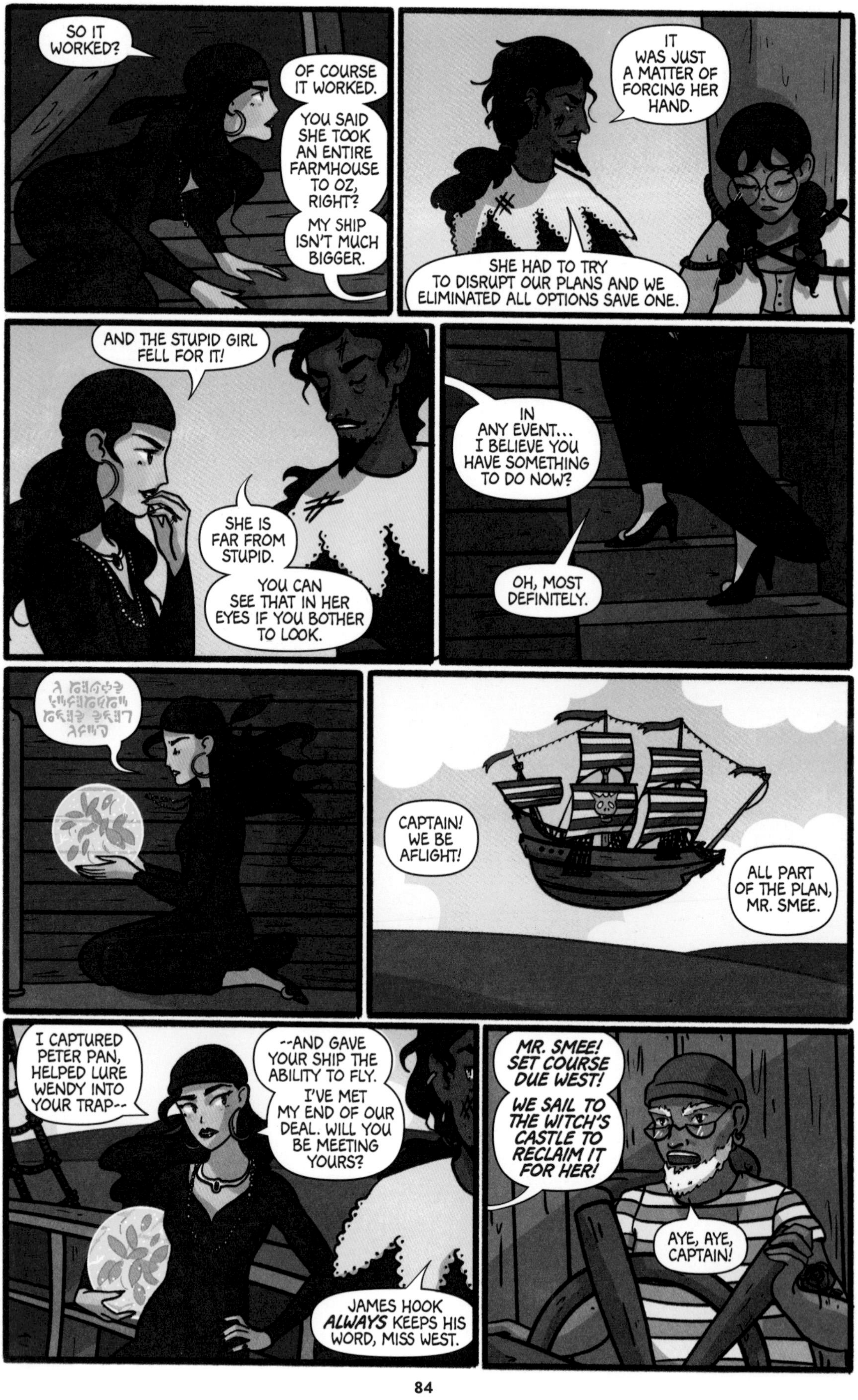
SO IT WORKED?
OF COURSE IT WORKED.
YOU SAID SHE TOOK AN ENTIRE FARMHOUSE TO OZ, RIGHT?
MY SHIP ISN'T MUCH BIGGER.
IT WAS JUST A MATTER OF FORCING HER HAND.
SHE HAD TO TRY TO DISRUPT OUR PLANS AND WE ELIMINATED ALL OPTIONS SAVE ONE.
AND THE STUPID GIRL FELL FOR IT!
SHE IS FAR FROM STUPID.
YOU CAN SEE THAT IN HER EYES IF YOU BOTHER TO LOOK.
IN ANY EVENT... I BELIEVE YOU HAVE SOMETHING TO DO NOW?
OH, MOST DEFINITELY.
CAPTAIN! WE BE AFLIGHT!
ALL PART OF THE PLAN, MR. SMEE.
I CAPTURED PETER PAN, HELPED LURE WENDY INTO YOUR TRAP--
--AND GAVE YOUR SHIP THE ABILITY TO FLY.
I'VE MET MY END OF OUR DEAL. WILL YOU BE MEETING YOURS?
JAMES HOOK **ALWAYS** KEEPS HIS WORD, MISS WEST.
MR. SMEE! SET COURSE DUE WEST!
WE SAIL TO THE WITCH'S CASTLE TO RECLAIM IT FOR HER!
AYE, AYE, CAPTAIN!

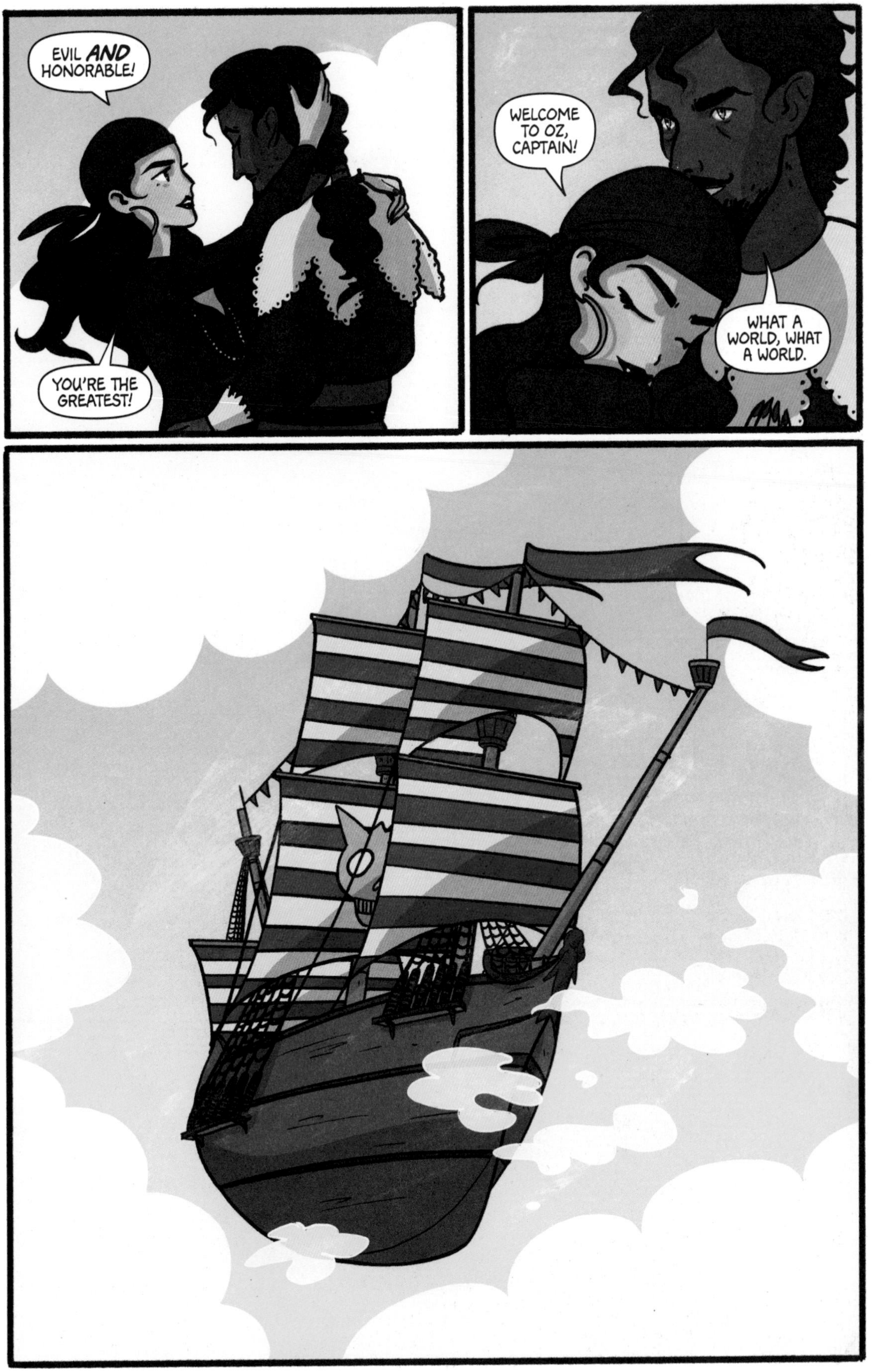
EVIL AND HONORABLE!
YOU'RE THE GREATEST!
WELCOME TO OZ, CAPTAIN!
WHAT A WORLD, WHAT A WORLD.

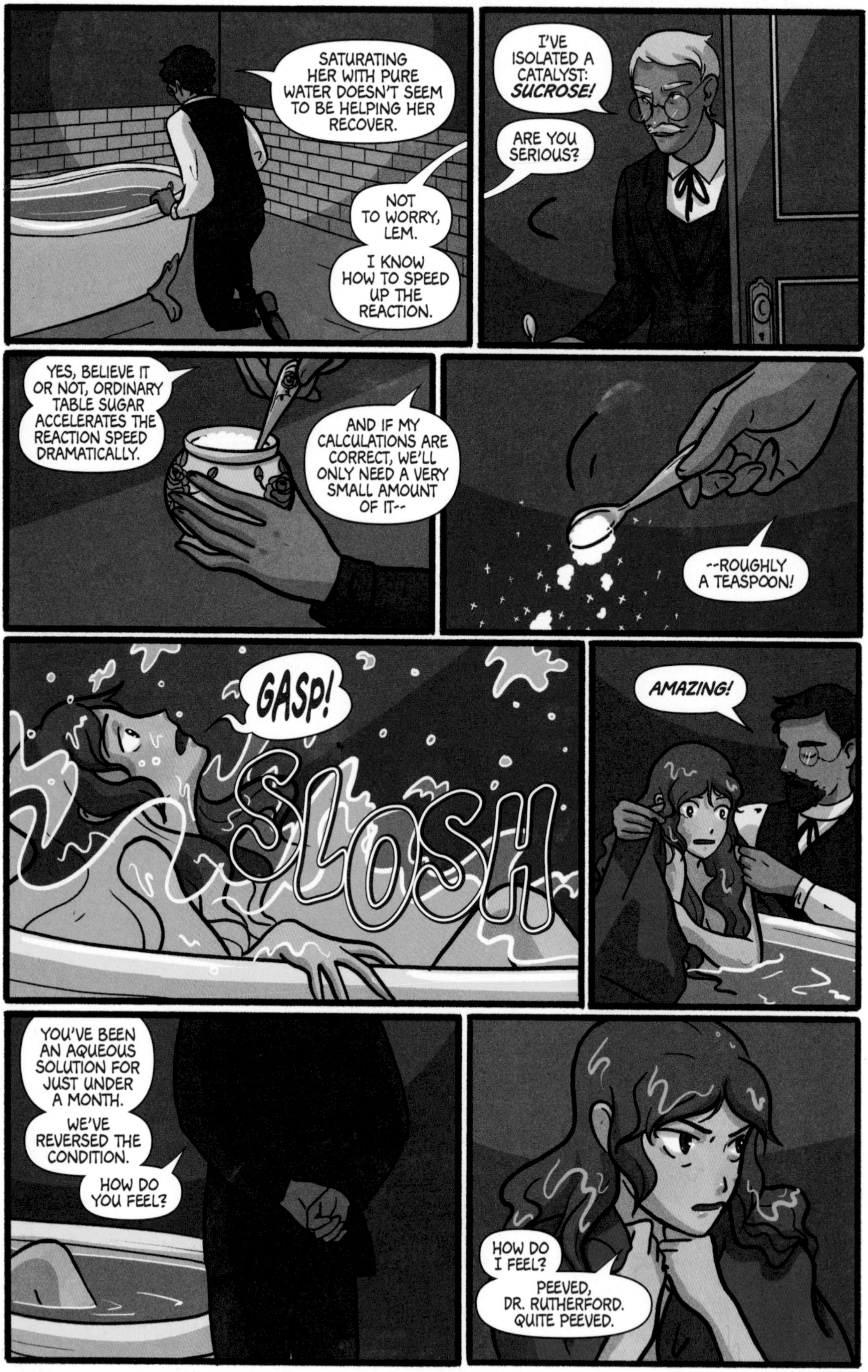
SATURATING HER WITH PURE WATER DOESN'T SEEM TO BE HELPING HER RECOVER.
NOT TO WORRY, LEM.
I KNOW HOW TO SPEED UP THE REACTION.
I'VE ISOLATED A CATALYST: SUCROSE!
ARE YOU SERIOUS?
YES, BELIEVE IT OR NOT, ORDINARY TABLE SUGAR ACCELERATES THE REACTION SPEED DRAMATICALLY.
AND IF MY CALCULATIONS ARE CORRECT, WE'LL ONLY NEED A VERY SMALL AMOUNT OF IT--
--ROUGHLY A TEASPOON!
GASP!
SLOSH
AMAZING!
YOU'VE BEEN AN AQUEOUS SOLUTION FOR JUST UNDER A MONTH.
WE'VE REVERSED THE CONDITION.
HOW DO YOU FEEL?
HOW DO I FEEL?
PEEVED, DR. RUTHERFORD. QUITE PEEVED.

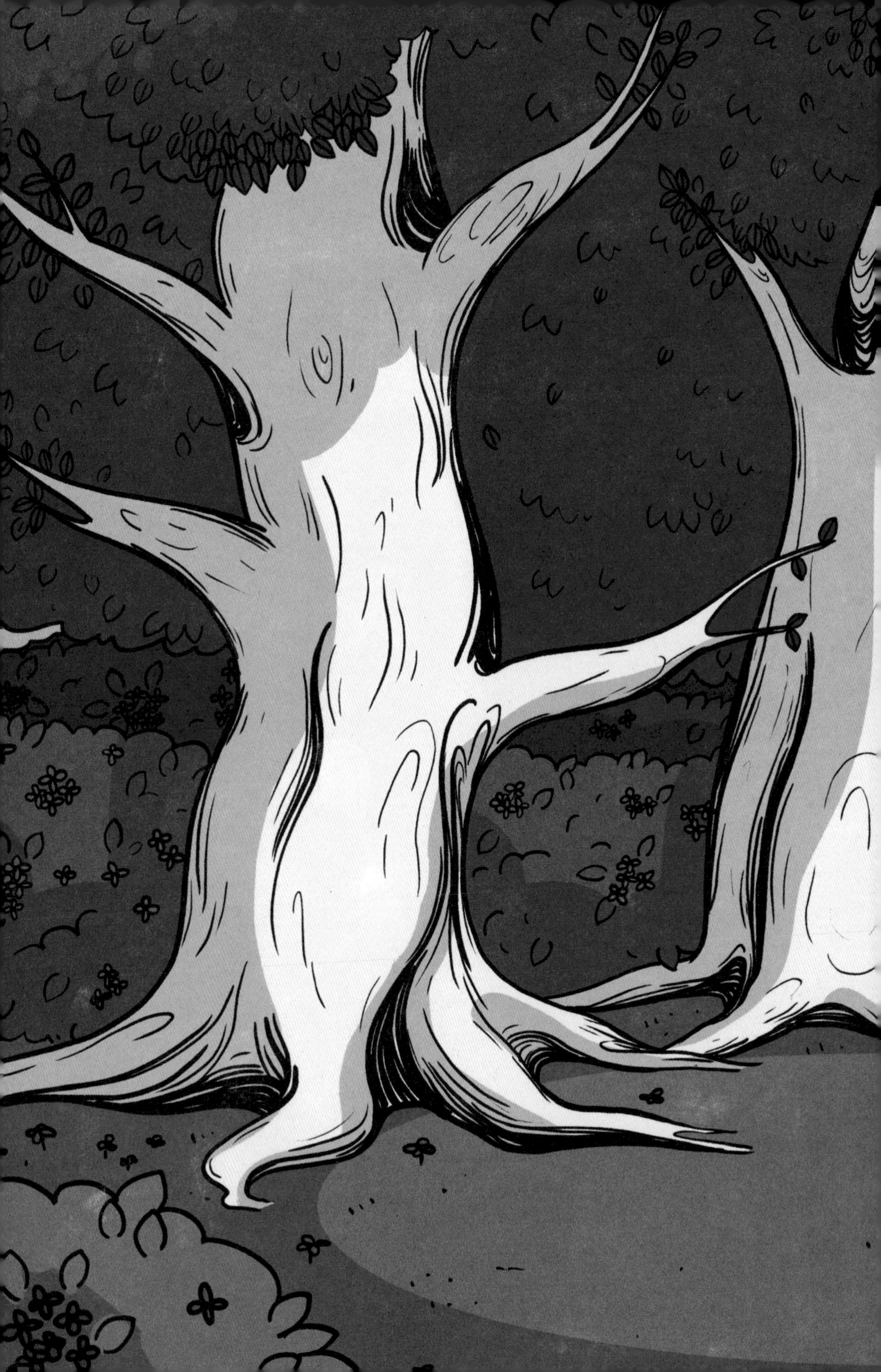

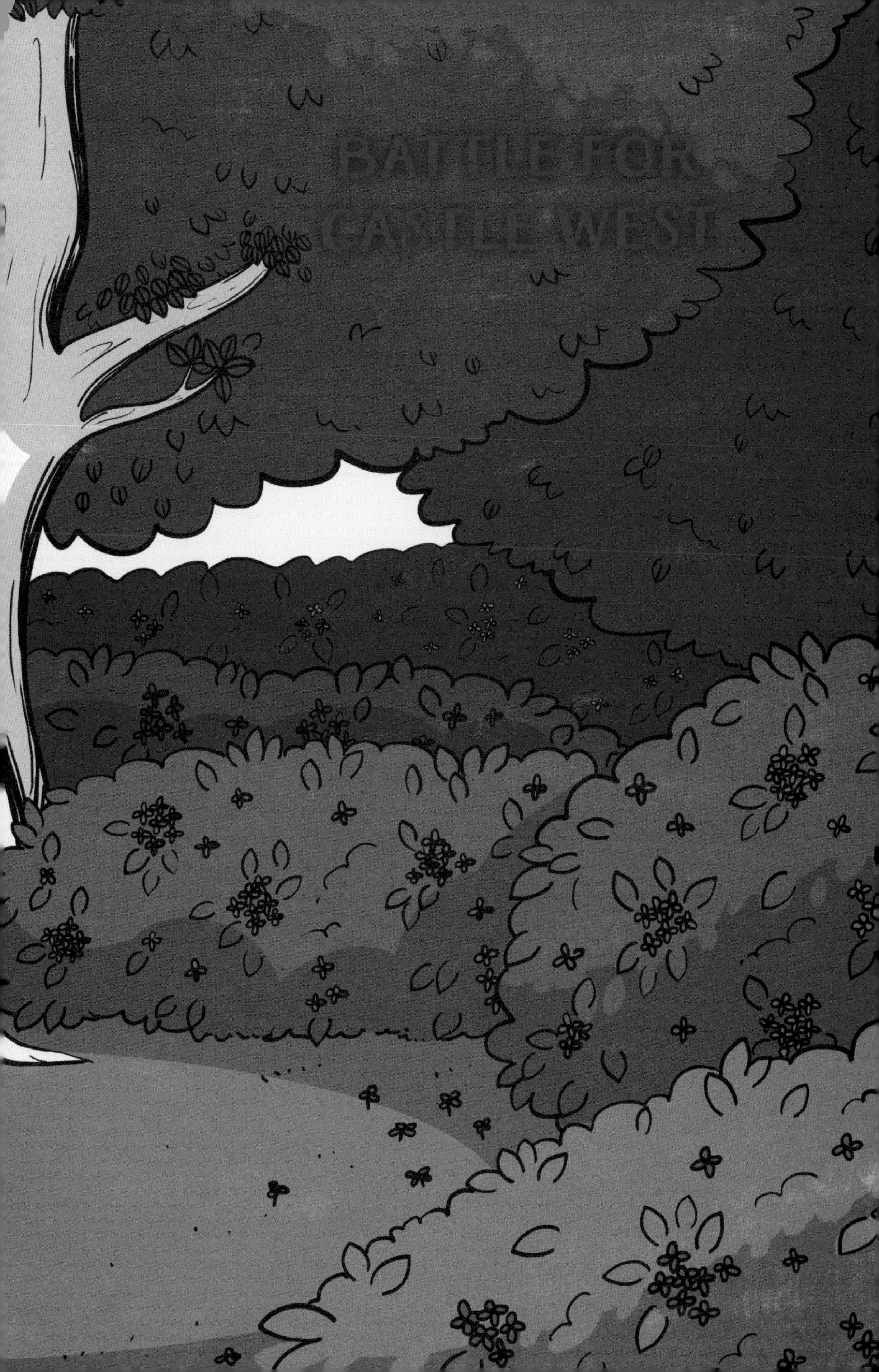
BATTLE FOR
CASTLE WEST

OZ

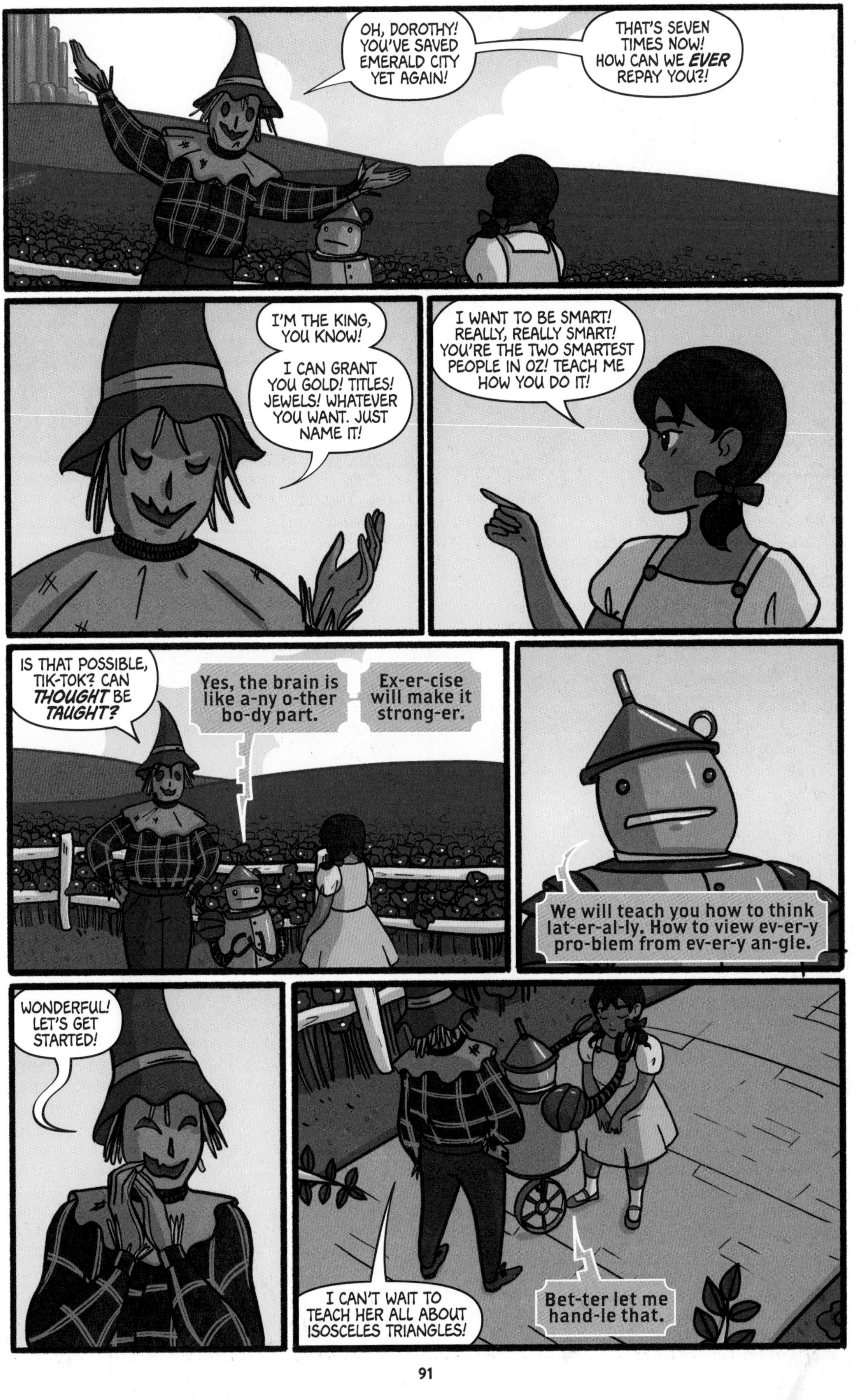
OH, DOROTHY! YOU'VE SAVED EMERALD CITY YET AGAIN!
THAT'S SEVEN TIMES NOW! HOW CAN WE *EVER* REPAY YOU?!
I'M THE KING, YOU KNOW!
I CAN GRANT YOU GOLD! TITLES! JEWELS! WHATEVER YOU WANT. JUST NAME IT!
I WANT TO BE SMART! REALLY, REALLY SMART! YOU'RE THE TWO SMARTEST PEOPLE IN OZ! TEACH ME HOW YOU DO IT!
IS THAT POSSIBLE, TIK-TOK? CAN *THOUGHT* BE *TAUGHT?*
Yes, the brain is like a-ny o-ther bo-dy part.
Ex-er-cise will make it strong-er.
We will teach you how to think lat-er-al-ly. How to view ev-er-y pro-blem from ev-er-y an-gle.
WONDERFUL! LET'S GET STARTED!
I CAN'T WAIT TO TEACH HER ALL ABOUT ISOSCELES TRIANGLES!
Bet-ter let me hand-le that.

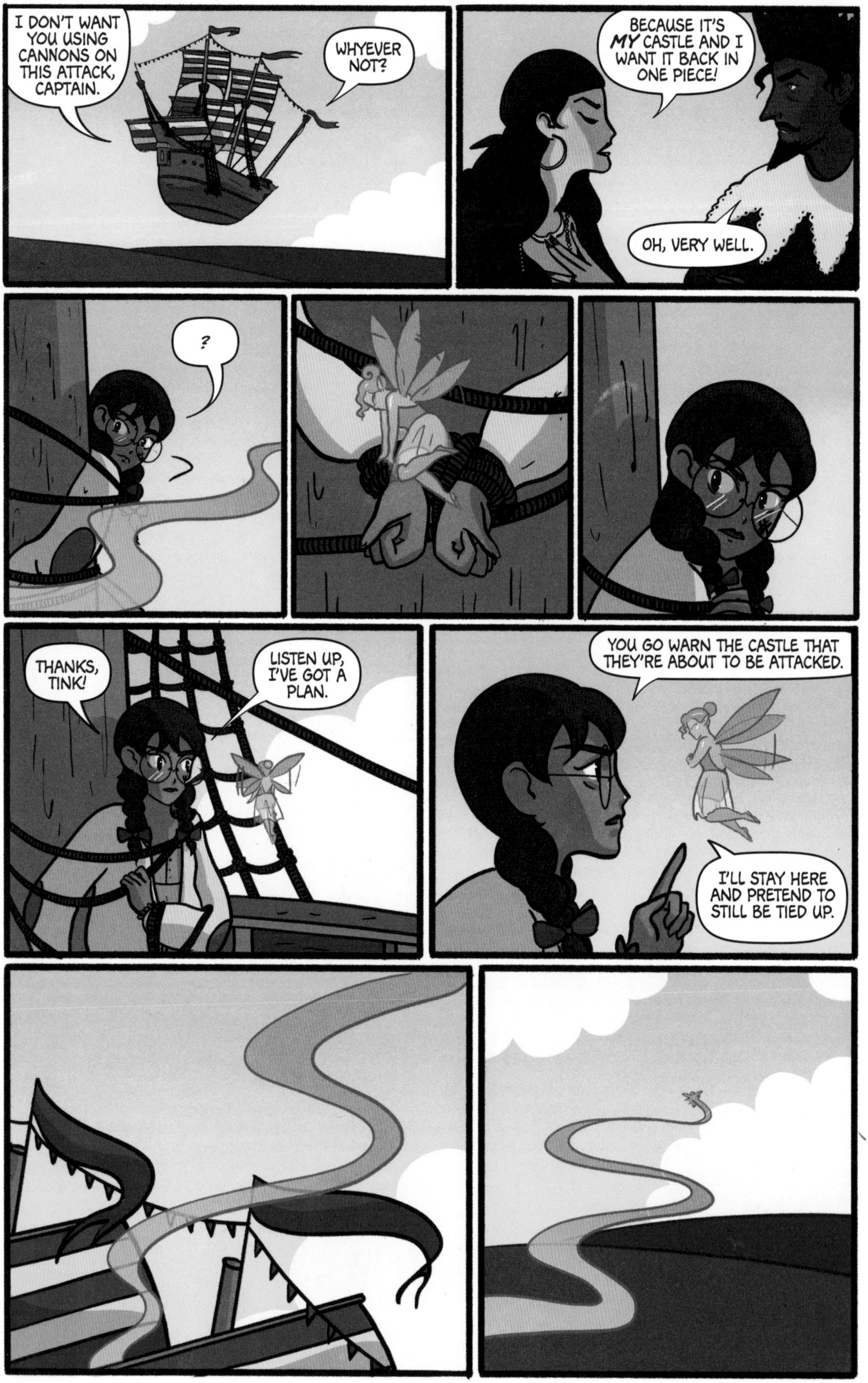
I DON'T WANT YOU USING CANNONS ON THIS ATTACK, CAPTAIN.
WHYEVER NOT?
BECAUSE IT'S MY CASTLE AND I WANT IT BACK IN ONE PIECE!
OH, VERY WELL.
?
THANKS, TINK!
LISTEN UP, I'VE GOT A PLAN.
YOU GO WARN THE CASTLE THAT THEY'RE ABOUT TO BE ATTACKED.
I'LL STAY HERE AND PRETEND TO STILL BE TIED UP.

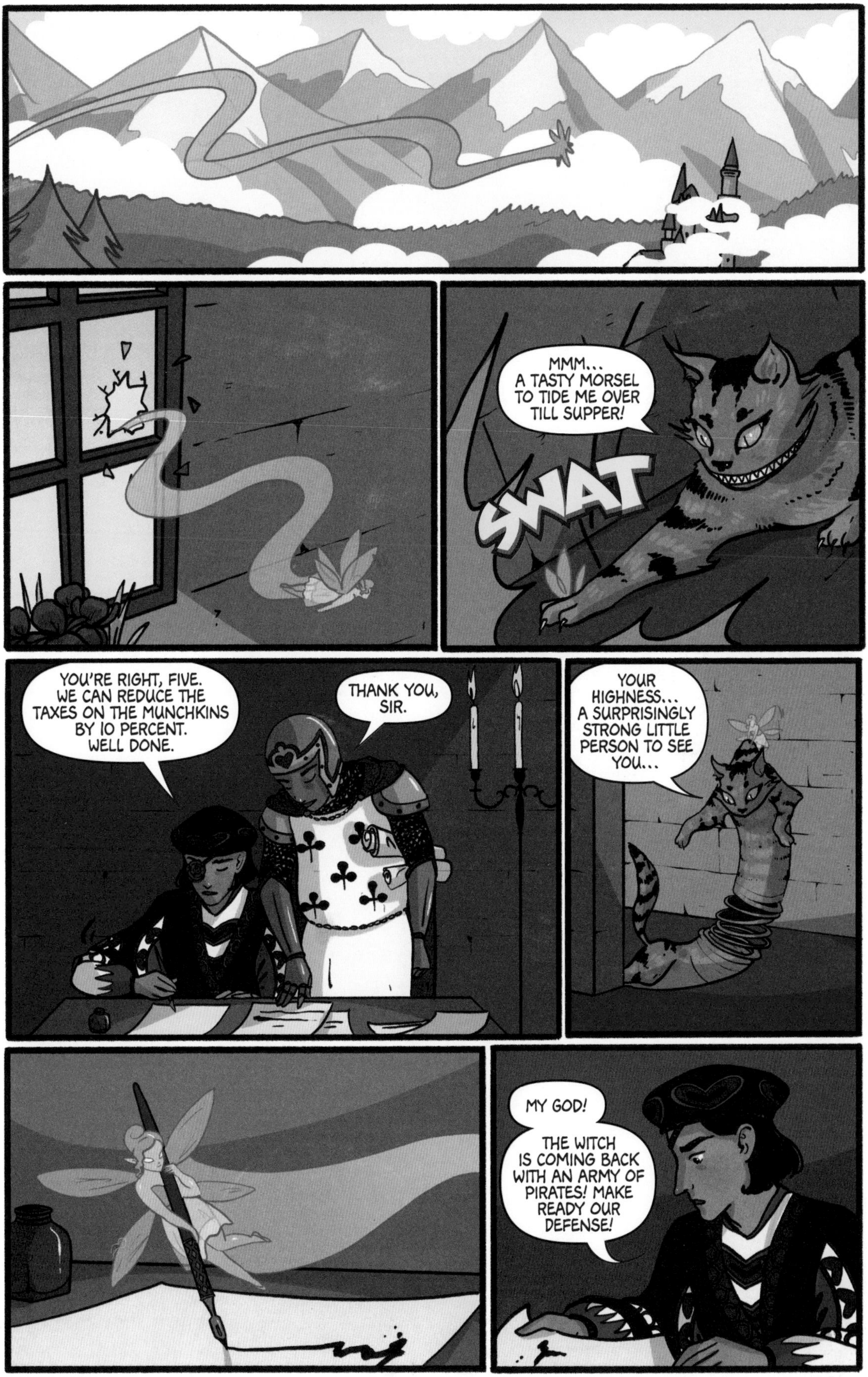
MMM... A TASTY MORSEL TO TIDE ME OVER TILL SUPPER!
SWAT
YOU'RE RIGHT, FIVE. WE CAN REDUCE THE TAXES ON THE MUNCHKINS BY 10 PERCENT. WELL DONE.
THANK YOU, SIR.
YOUR HIGHNESS... A SURPRISINGLY STRONG LITTLE PERSON TO SEE YOU...
MY GOD!
THE WITCH IS COMING BACK WITH AN ARMY OF PIRATES! MAKE READY OUR DEFENSE!

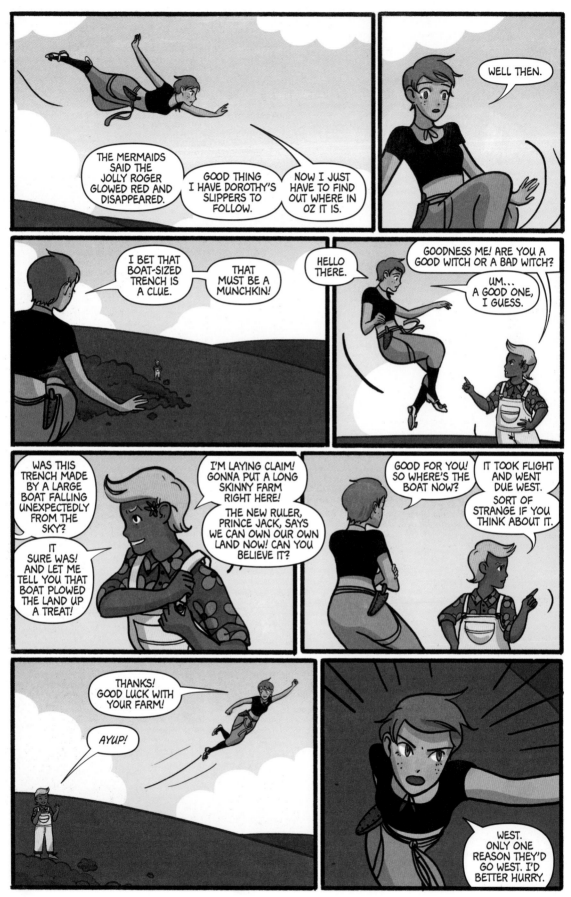

THE MERMAIDS SAID THE JOLLY ROGER GLOWED RED AND DISAPPEARED.

GOOD THING I HAVE DOROTHY'S SLIPPERS TO FOLLOW.

NOW I JUST HAVE TO FIND OUT WHERE IN OZ IT IS.

WELL THEN.

I BET THAT BOAT-SIZED TRENCH IS A CLUE.

THAT MUST BE A MUNCHKIN!

HELLO THERE.

GOODNESS ME! ARE YOU A GOOD WITCH OR A BAD WITCH?

UM... A GOOD ONE, I GUESS.

WAS THIS TRENCH MADE BY A LARGE BOAT FALLING UNEXPECTEDLY FROM THE SKY?

IT SURE WAS! AND LET ME TELL YOU THAT BOAT PLOWED THE LAND UP A TREAT!

I'M LAYING CLAIM! GONNA PUT A LONG SKINNY FARM RIGHT HERE!

THE NEW RULER, PRINCE JACK, SAYS WE CAN OWN OUR OWN LAND NOW! CAN YOU BELIEVE IT?

GOOD FOR YOU! SO WHERE'S THE BOAT NOW?

IT TOOK FLIGHT AND WENT DUE WEST. SORT OF STRANGE IF YOU THINK ABOUT IT.

THANKS! GOOD LUCK WITH YOUR FARM!

AYUP!

WEST. ONLY ONE REASON THEY'D GO WEST. I'D BETTER HURRY.

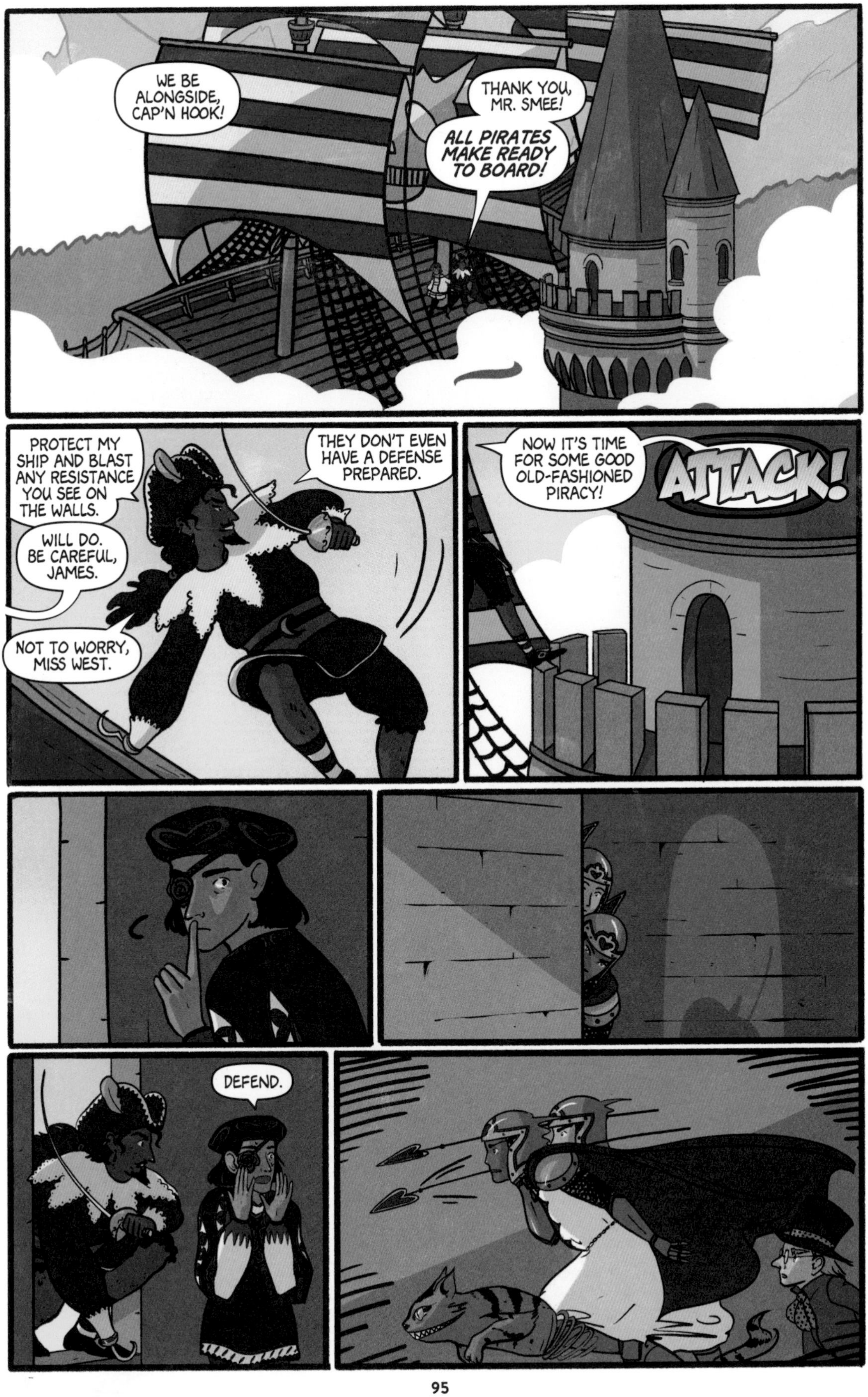
WE BE ALONGSIDE, CAP'N HOOK!
THANK YOU, MR. SMEE!
ALL PIRATES MAKE READY TO BOARD!
PROTECT MY SHIP AND BLAST ANY RESISTANCE YOU SEE ON THE WALLS.
THEY DON'T EVEN HAVE A DEFENSE PREPARED.
WILL DO. BE CAREFUL, JAMES.
NOT TO WORRY, MISS WEST.
NOW IT'S TIME FOR SOME GOOD OLD-FASHIONED PIRACY!
ATTACK!
DEFEND.

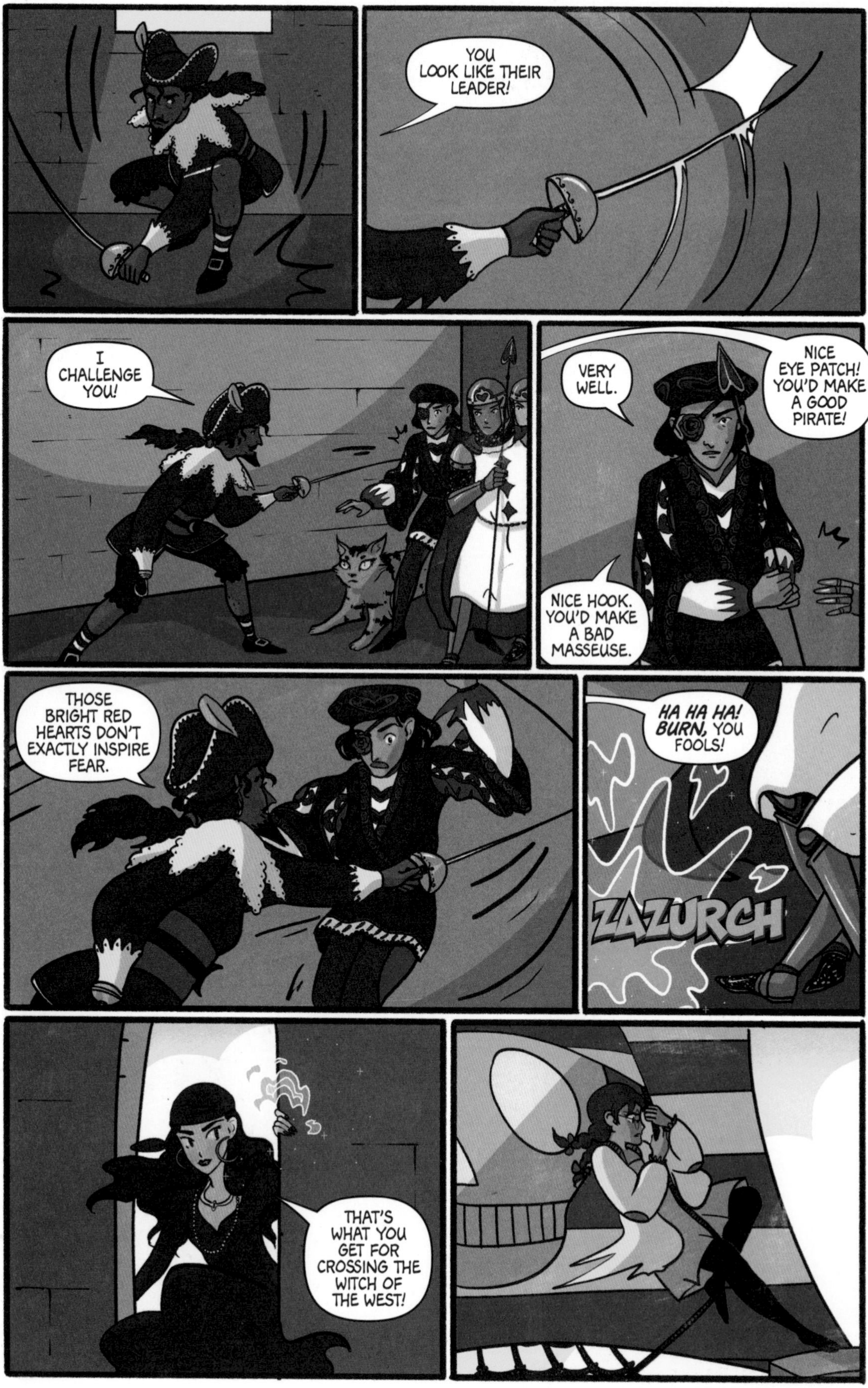
YOU LOOK LIKE THEIR LEADER!
I CHALLENGE YOU!
VERY WELL.
NICE EYE PATCH! YOU'D MAKE A GOOD PIRATE!
NICE HOOK. YOU'D MAKE A BAD MASSEUSE.
THOSE BRIGHT RED HEARTS DON'T EXACTLY INSPIRE FEAR.
HA HA HA! BURN, YOU FOOLS!
ZAZURCH
THAT'S WHAT YOU GET FOR CROSSING THE WITCH OF THE WEST!

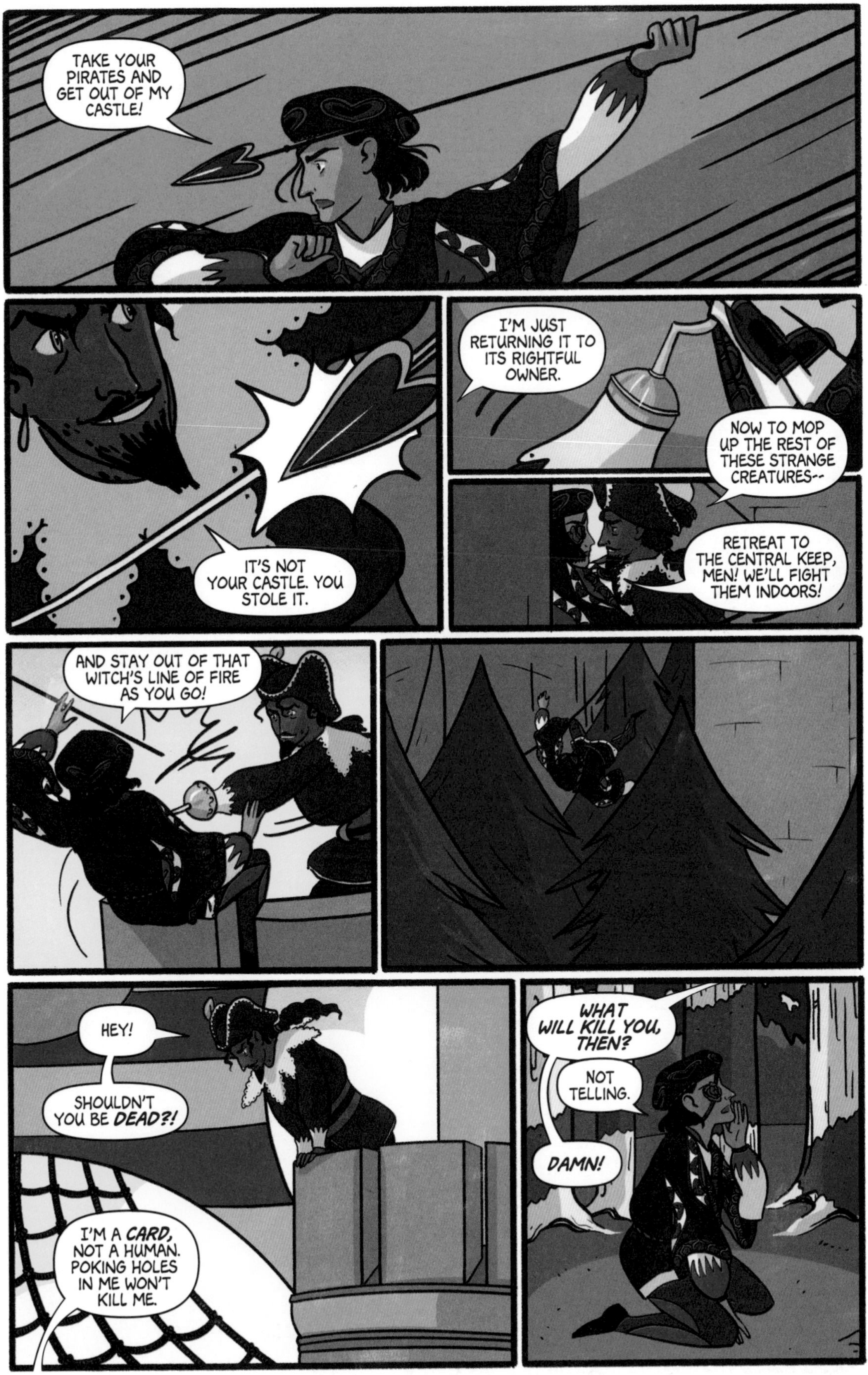
TAKE YOUR PIRATES AND GET OUT OF MY CASTLE!
IT'S NOT YOUR CASTLE. YOU STOLE IT.
I'M JUST RETURNING IT TO ITS RIGHTFUL OWNER.
NOW TO MOP UP THE REST OF THESE STRANGE CREATURES--
RETREAT TO THE CENTRAL KEEP, MEN! WE'LL FIGHT THEM INDOORS!
AND STAY OUT OF THAT WITCH'S LINE OF FIRE AS YOU GO!
HEY!
SHOULDN'T YOU BE DEAD?!
I'M A CARD, NOT A HUMAN. POKING HOLES IN ME WON'T KILL ME.
WHAT WILL KILL YOU, THEN?
NOT TELLING.
DAMN!

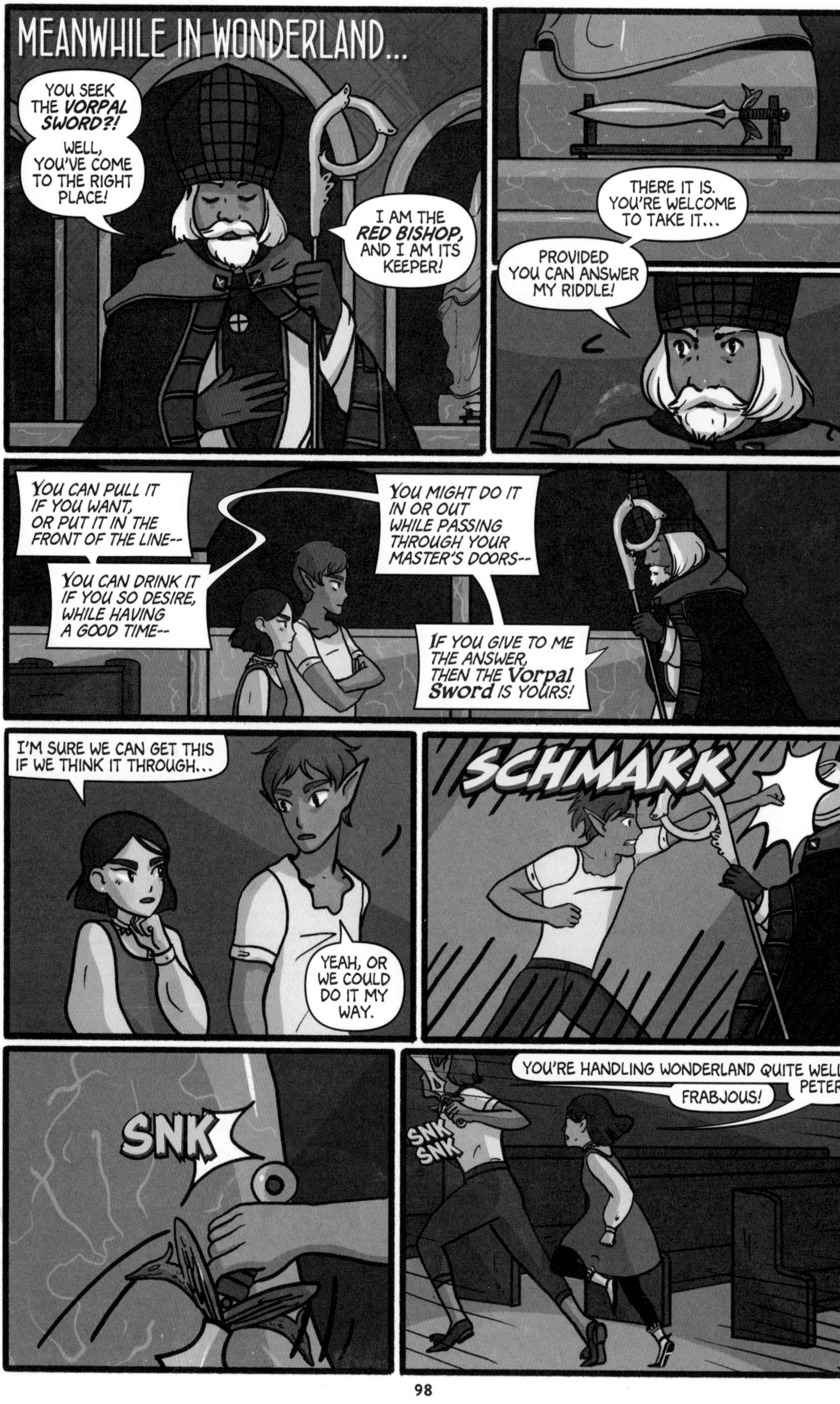
MEANWHILE IN WONDERLAND...
YOU SEEK THE VORPAL SWORD?!
WELL, YOU'VE COME TO THE RIGHT PLACE!
I AM THE RED BISHOP, AND I AM ITS KEEPER!
THERE IT IS. YOU'RE WELCOME TO TAKE IT...
PROVIDED YOU CAN ANSWER MY RIDDLE!
YOU CAN PULL IT IF YOU WANT, OR PUT IT IN THE FRONT OF THE LINE--
YOU CAN DRINK IT IF YOU SO DESIRE, WHILE HAVING A GOOD TIME--
YOU MIGHT DO IT IN OR OUT WHILE PASSING THROUGH YOUR MASTER'S DOORS--
IF YOU GIVE TO ME THE ANSWER, THEN THE Vorpal Sword IS YOURS!
I'M SURE WE CAN GET THIS IF WE THINK IT THROUGH...
YEAH, OR WE COULD DO IT MY WAY.
SCHMAKK
SNK
SNK SNK
YOU'RE HANDLING WONDERLAND QUITE WELL, PETER.
FRABJOUS!

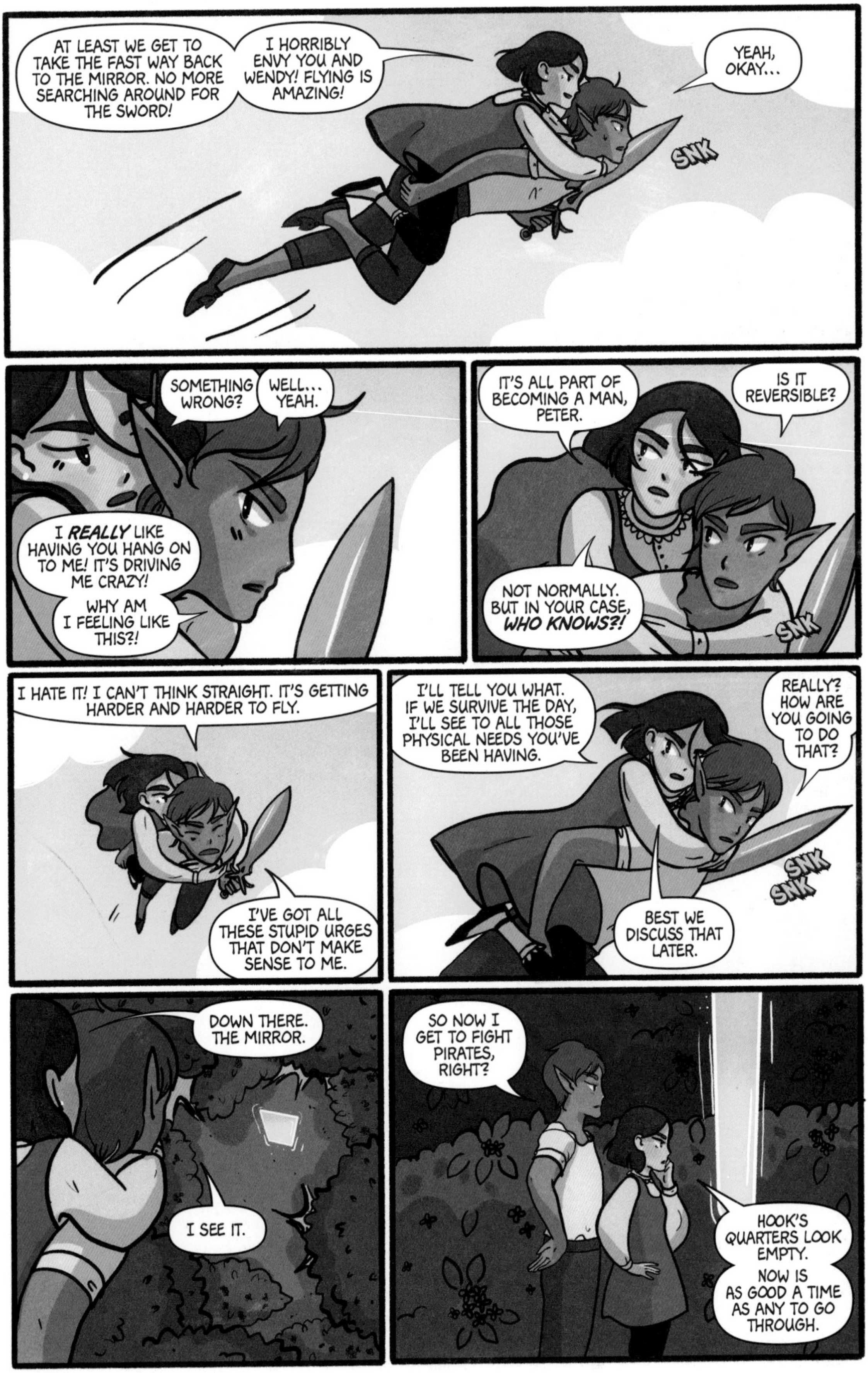
AT LEAST WE GET TO TAKE THE FAST WAY BACK TO THE MIRROR. NO MORE SEARCHING AROUND FOR THE SWORD!
I HORRIBLY ENVY YOU AND WENDY! FLYING IS AMAZING!
YEAH, OKAY...
SNK
SOMETHING WRONG?
WELL... YEAH.
I REALLY LIKE HAVING YOU HANG ON TO ME! IT'S DRIVING ME CRAZY!
WHY AM I FEELING LIKE THIS?!
IT'S ALL PART OF BECOMING A MAN, PETER.
IS IT REVERSIBLE?
NOT NORMALLY. BUT IN YOUR CASE, WHO KNOWS?!
SNK
I HATE IT! I CAN'T THINK STRAIGHT. IT'S GETTING HARDER AND HARDER TO FLY.
I'VE GOT ALL THESE STUPID URGES THAT DON'T MAKE SENSE TO ME.
I'LL TELL YOU WHAT. IF WE SURVIVE THE DAY, I'LL SEE TO ALL THOSE PHYSICAL NEEDS YOU'VE BEEN HAVING.
REALLY? HOW ARE YOU GOING TO DO THAT?
SNK
SNK
BEST WE DISCUSS THAT LATER.
DOWN THERE. THE MIRROR.
I SEE IT.
SO NOW I GET TO FIGHT PIRATES, RIGHT?
HOOK'S QUARTERS LOOK EMPTY.
NOW IS AS GOOD A TIME AS ANY TO GO THROUGH.

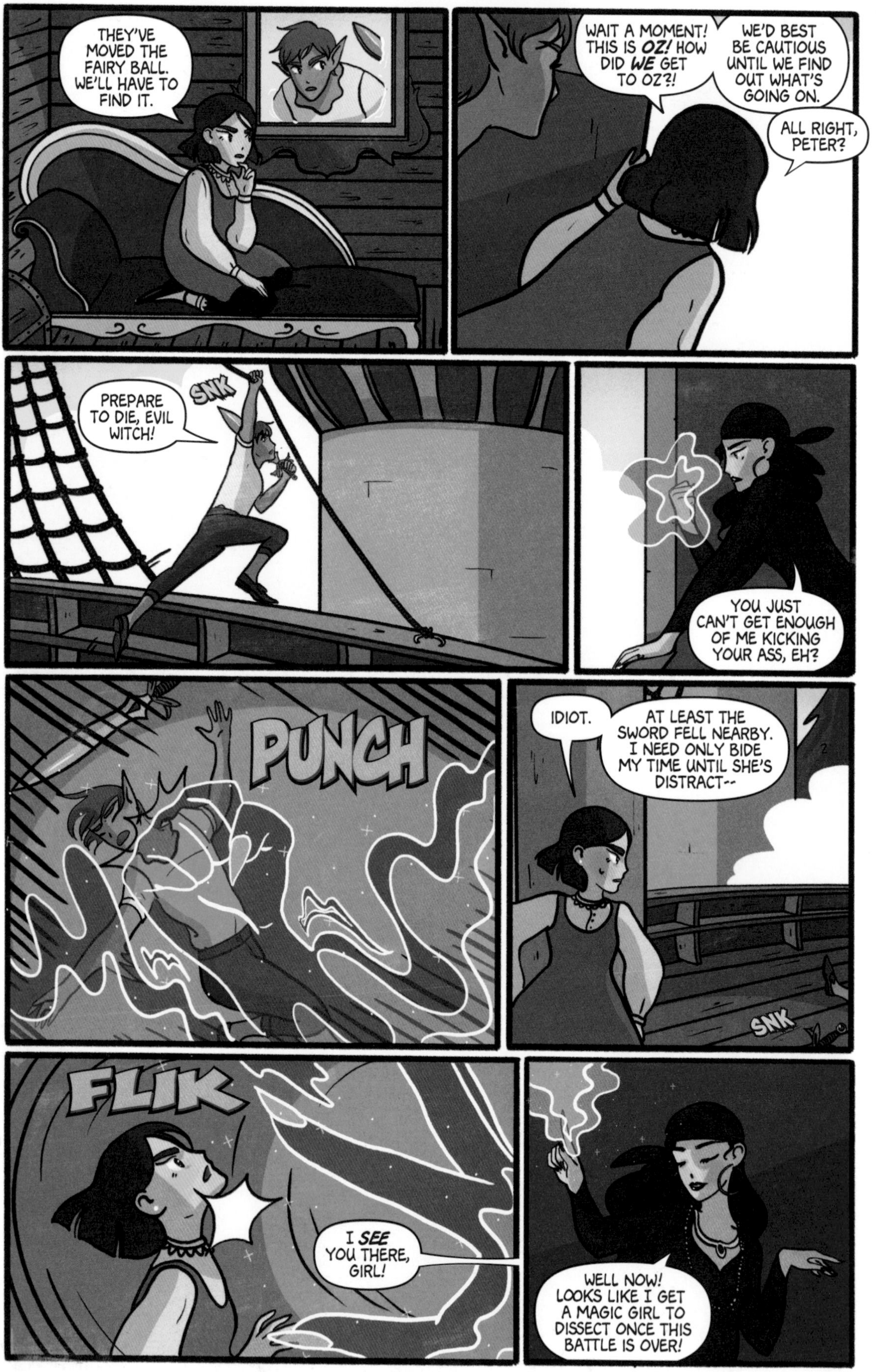
THEY'VE MOVED THE FAIRY BALL. WE'LL HAVE TO FIND IT.
WAIT A MOMENT! THIS IS *OZ!* HOW DID *WE* GET TO OZ?!
WE'D BEST BE CAUTIOUS UNTIL WE FIND OUT WHAT'S GOING ON.
ALL RIGHT, PETER?
PREPARE TO DIE, EVIL WITCH!
SNK
YOU JUST CAN'T GET ENOUGH OF ME KICKING YOUR ASS, EH?
PUNCH
IDIOT.
AT LEAST THE SWORD FELL NEARBY. I NEED ONLY BIDE MY TIME UNTIL SHE'S DISTRACT--
SNK
FLIK
I *SEE* YOU THERE, GIRL!
WELL NOW! LOOKS LIKE I GET A MAGIC GIRL TO DISSECT ONCE THIS BATTLE IS OVER!

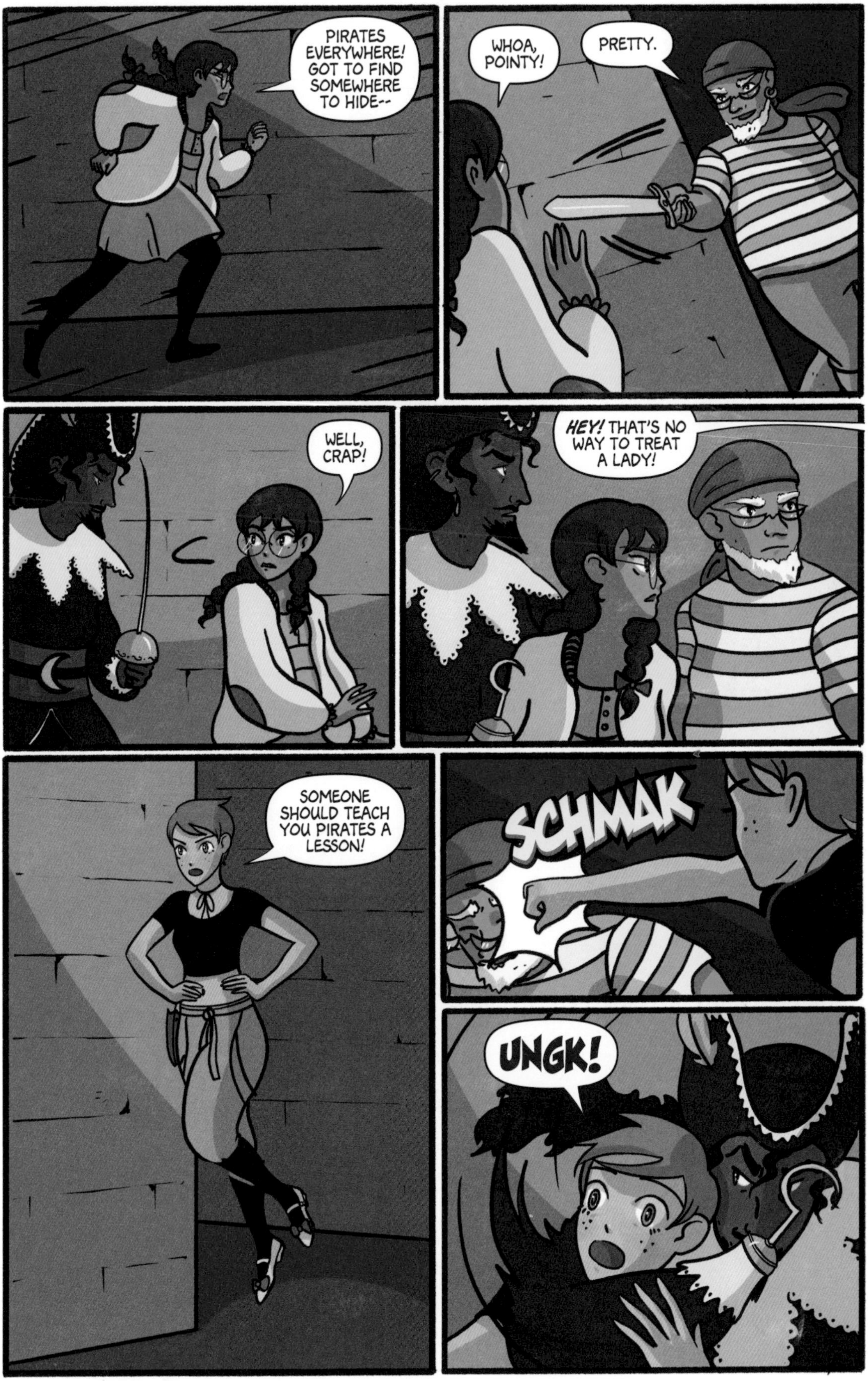
PIRATES EVERYWHERE! GOT TO FIND SOMEWHERE TO HIDE--
WHOA, POINTY!
PRETTY.
WELL, CRAP!
HEY! THAT'S NO WAY TO TREAT A LADY!
SOMEONE SHOULD TEACH YOU PIRATES A LESSON!
SCHMAK
UNGK!

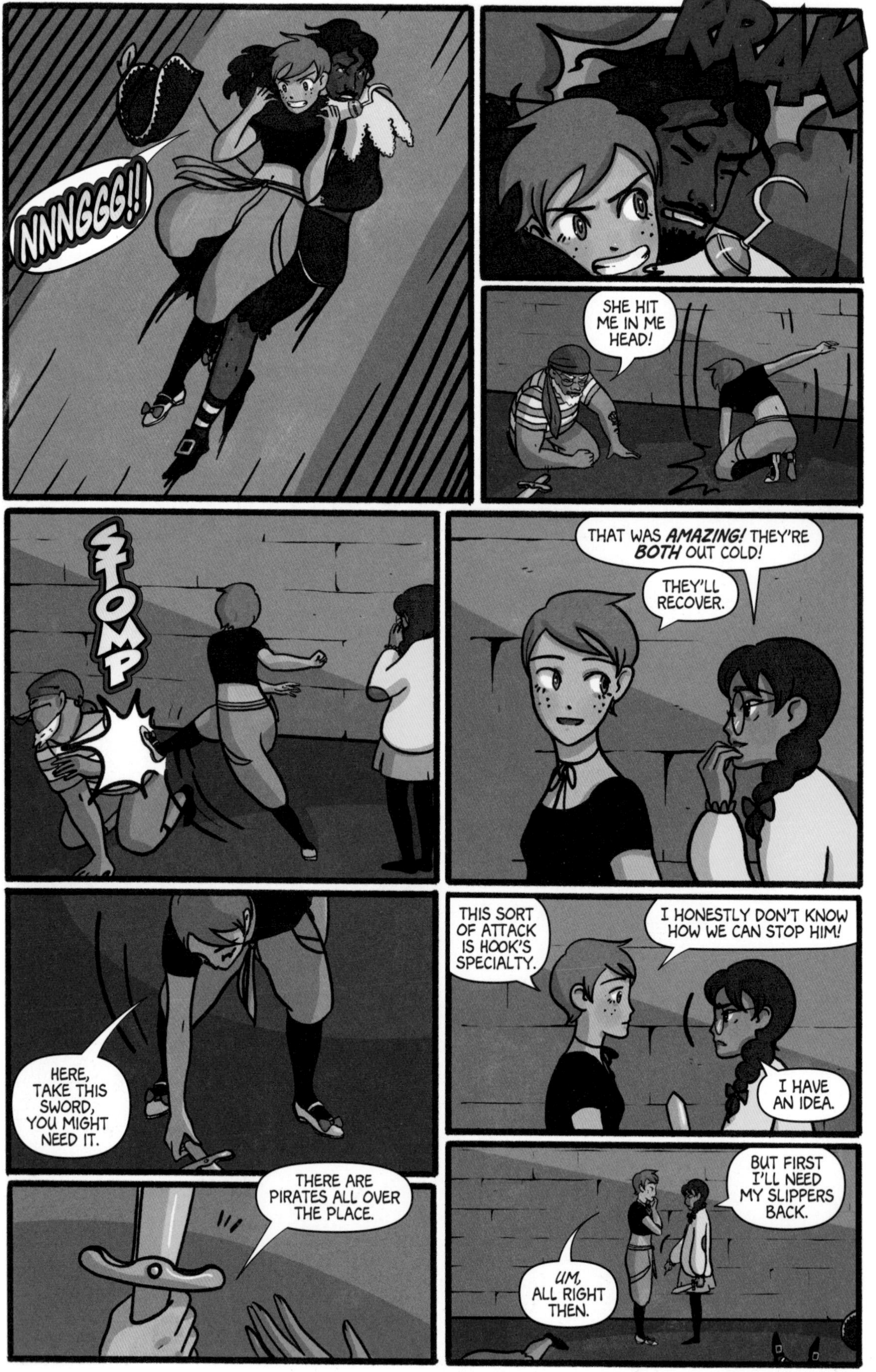
NNNGGG!!
KRAK
SHE HIT ME IN ME HEAD!
STOMP
THAT WAS *AMAZING!* THEY'RE *BOTH* OUT COLD!
THEY'LL RECOVER.
HERE, TAKE THIS SWORD, YOU MIGHT NEED IT.
THERE ARE PIRATES ALL OVER THE PLACE.
THIS SORT OF ATTACK IS HOOK'S SPECIALTY.
I HONESTLY DON'T KNOW HOW WE CAN STOP HIM!
I HAVE AN IDEA.
BUT FIRST I'LL NEED MY SLIPPERS BACK.
UM, ALL RIGHT THEN.

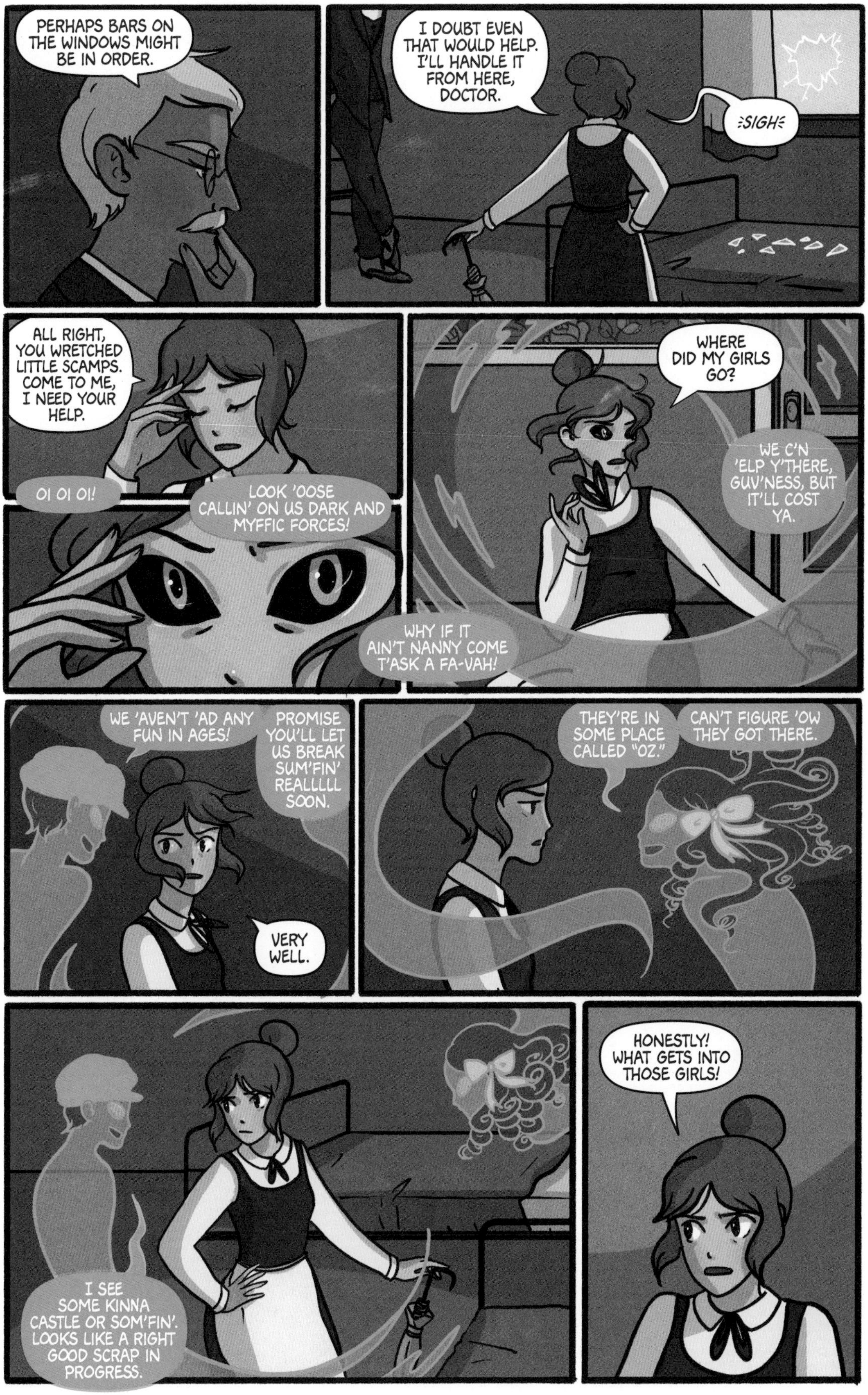
PERHAPS BARS ON THE WINDOWS MIGHT BE IN ORDER.
I DOUBT EVEN THAT WOULD HELP. I'LL HANDLE IT FROM HERE, DOCTOR.
SIGH
ALL RIGHT, YOU WRETCHED LITTLE SCAMPS. COME TO ME, I NEED YOUR HELP.
OI OI OI!
LOOK 'OOSE CALLIN' ON US DARK AND MYFFIC FORCES!
WHERE DID MY GIRLS GO?
WE C'N 'ELP Y'THERE, GUV'NESS, BUT IT'LL COST YA.
WHY IF IT AIN'T NANNY COME T'ASK A FA-VAH!
WE 'AVEN'T 'AD ANY FUN IN AGES!
PROMISE YOU'LL LET US BREAK SUM'FIN' REALLLLL SOON.
VERY WELL.
THEY'RE IN SOME PLACE CALLED "OZ."
CAN'T FIGURE 'OW THEY GOT THERE.
I SEE SOME KINNA CASTLE OR SOM'FIN'. LOOKS LIKE A RIGHT GOOD SCRAP IN PROGRESS.
HONESTLY! WHAT GETS INTO THOSE GIRLS!

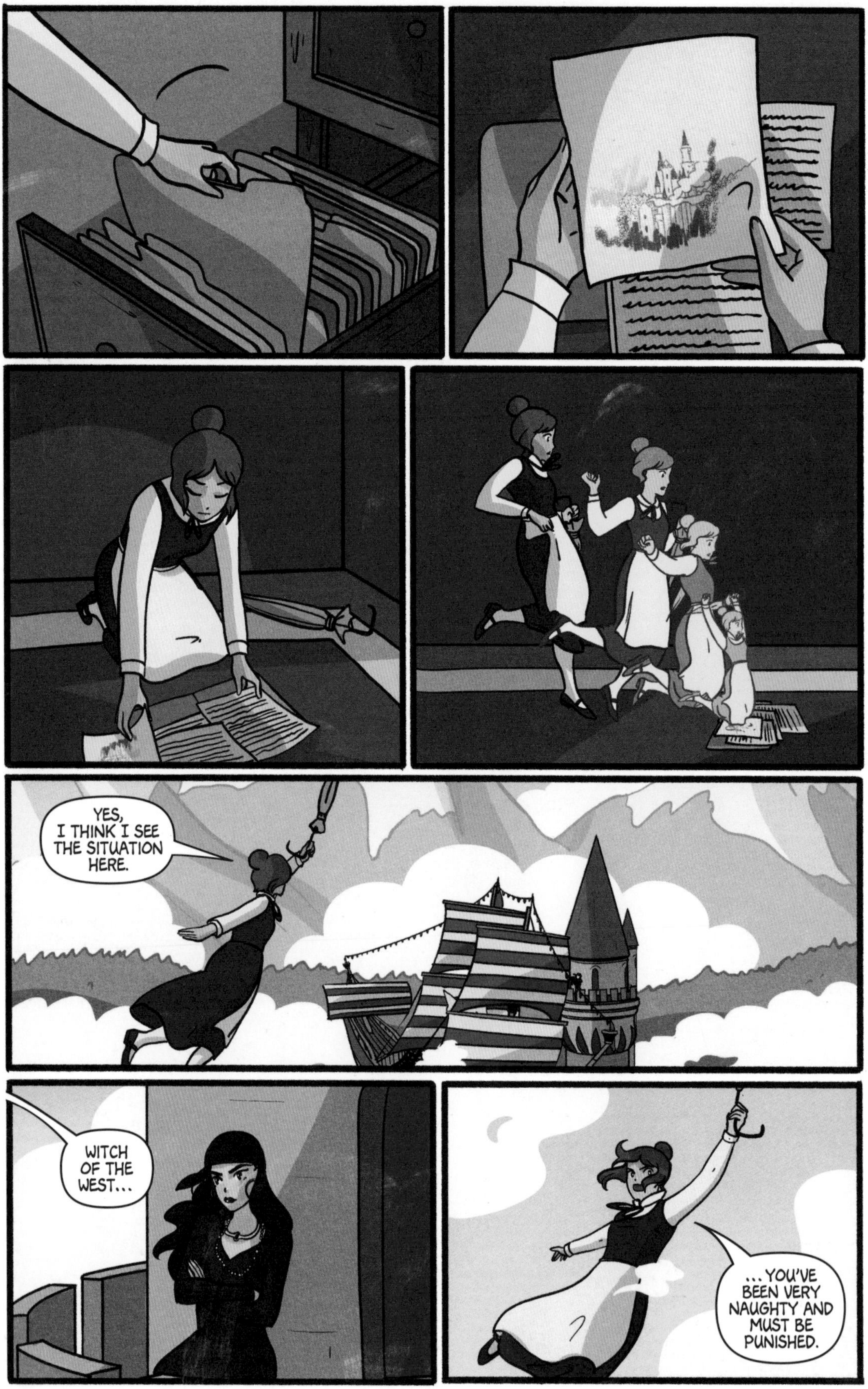
YES, I THINK I SEE THE SITUATION HERE.
WITCH OF THE WEST...
...YOU'VE BEEN VERY NAUGHTY AND MUST BE PUNISHED.

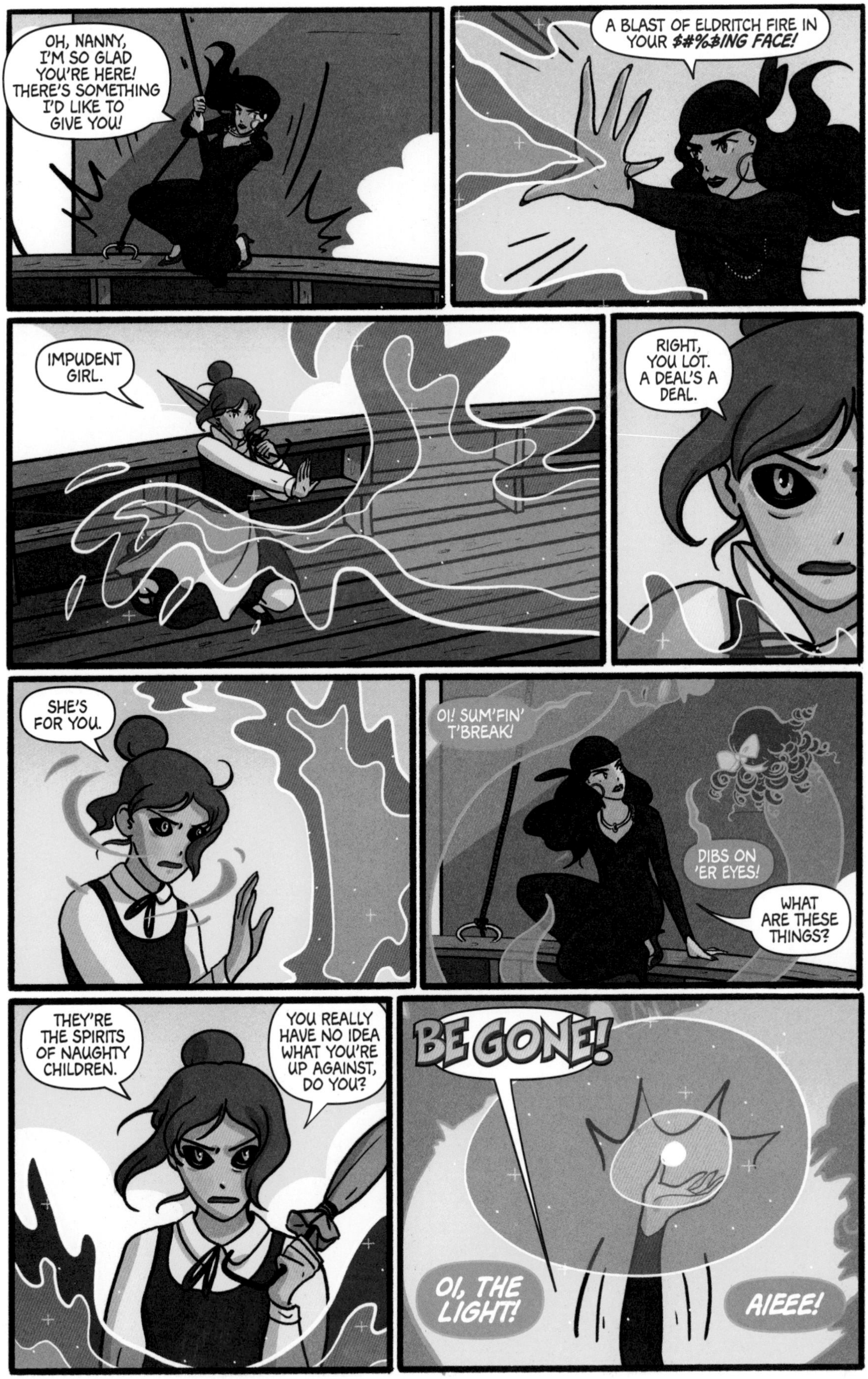
OH, NANNY, I'M SO GLAD YOU'RE HERE! THERE'S SOMETHING I'D LIKE TO GIVE YOU!
A BLAST OF ELDRITCH FIRE IN YOUR $#%$ING FACE!
IMPUDENT GIRL.
RIGHT, YOU LOT. A DEAL'S A DEAL.
SHE'S FOR YOU.
OI! SUM'FIN' T'BREAK!
DIBS ON 'ER EYES!
WHAT ARE THESE THINGS?
THEY'RE THE SPIRITS OF NAUGHTY CHILDREN.
YOU REALLY HAVE NO IDEA WHAT YOU'RE UP AGAINST, DO YOU?
BE GONE!
OI, THE LIGHT!
AIEEE!

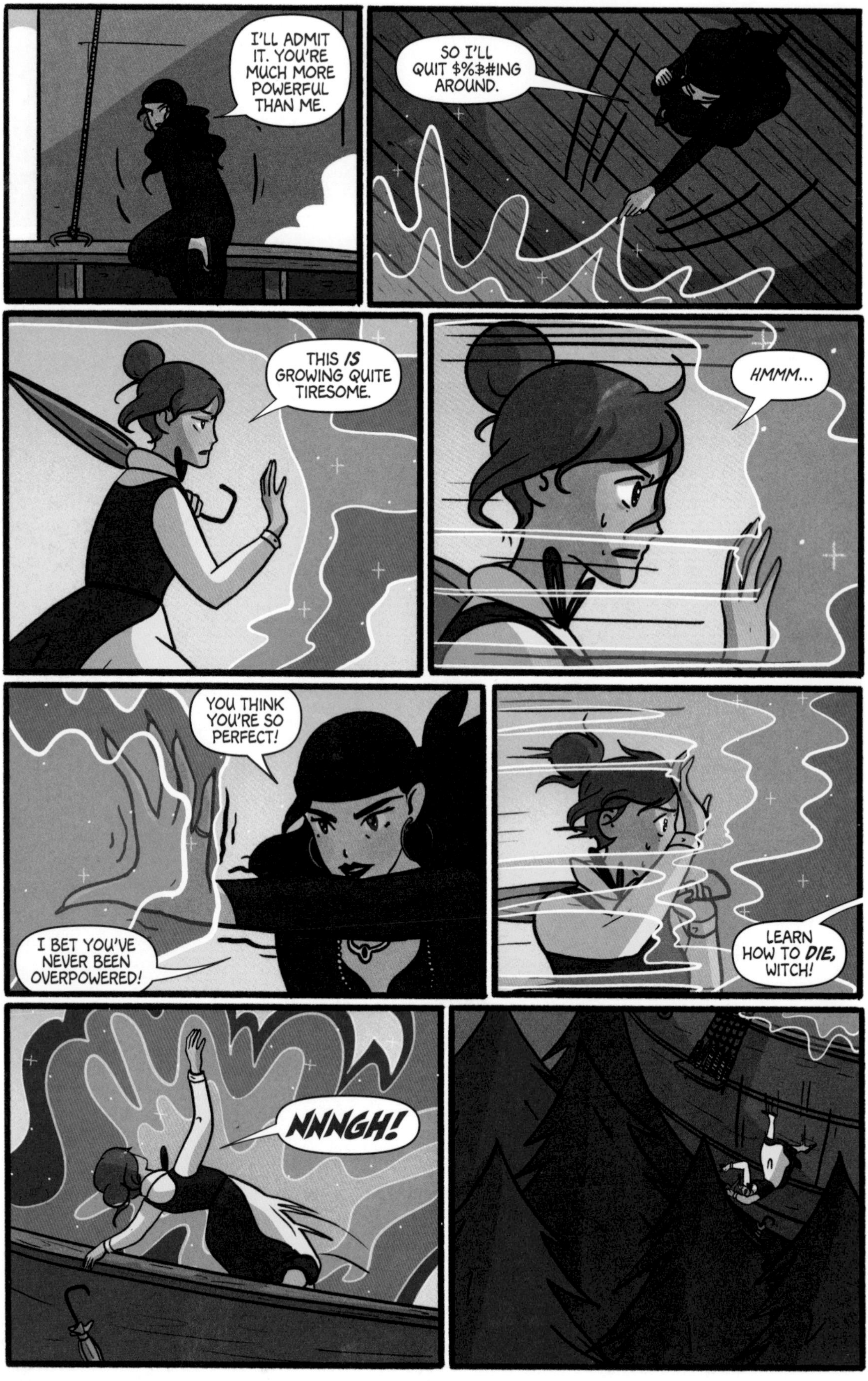
I'LL ADMIT IT. YOU'RE MUCH MORE POWERFUL THAN ME.
SO I'LL QUIT $%$#ING AROUND.
THIS *IS* GROWING QUITE TIRESOME.
HMMM...
YOU THINK YOU'RE SO PERFECT!
I BET YOU'VE NEVER BEEN OVERPOWERED!
LEARN HOW TO *DIE*, WITCH!
NNNGH!

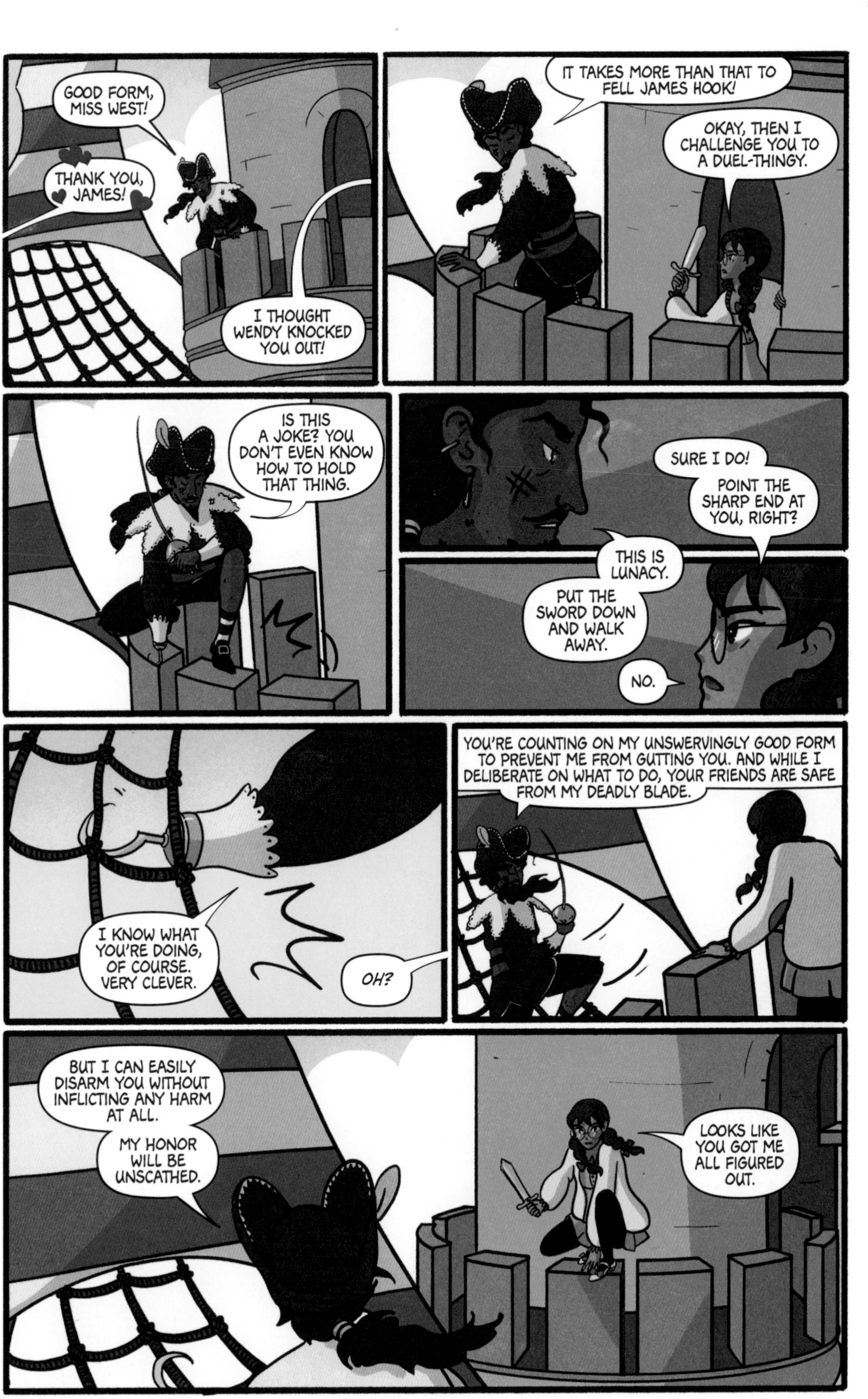
GOOD FORM, MISS WEST!
THANK YOU, JAMES!
I THOUGHT WENDY KNOCKED YOU OUT!
IT TAKES MORE THAN THAT TO FELL JAMES HOOK!
OKAY, THEN I CHALLENGE YOU TO A DUEL-THINGY.
IS THIS A JOKE? YOU DON'T EVEN KNOW HOW TO HOLD THAT THING.
SURE I DO!
POINT THE SHARP END AT YOU, RIGHT?
THIS IS LUNACY.
PUT THE SWORD DOWN AND WALK AWAY.
NO.
I KNOW WHAT YOU'RE DOING, OF COURSE. VERY CLEVER.
OH?
YOU'RE COUNTING ON MY UNSWERVINGLY GOOD FORM TO PREVENT ME FROM GUTTING YOU. AND WHILE I DELIBERATE ON WHAT TO DO, YOUR FRIENDS ARE SAFE FROM MY DEADLY BLADE.
BUT I CAN EASILY DISARM YOU WITHOUT INFLICTING ANY HARM AT ALL.
MY HONOR WILL BE UNSCATHED.
LOOKS LIKE YOU GOT ME ALL FIGURED OUT.

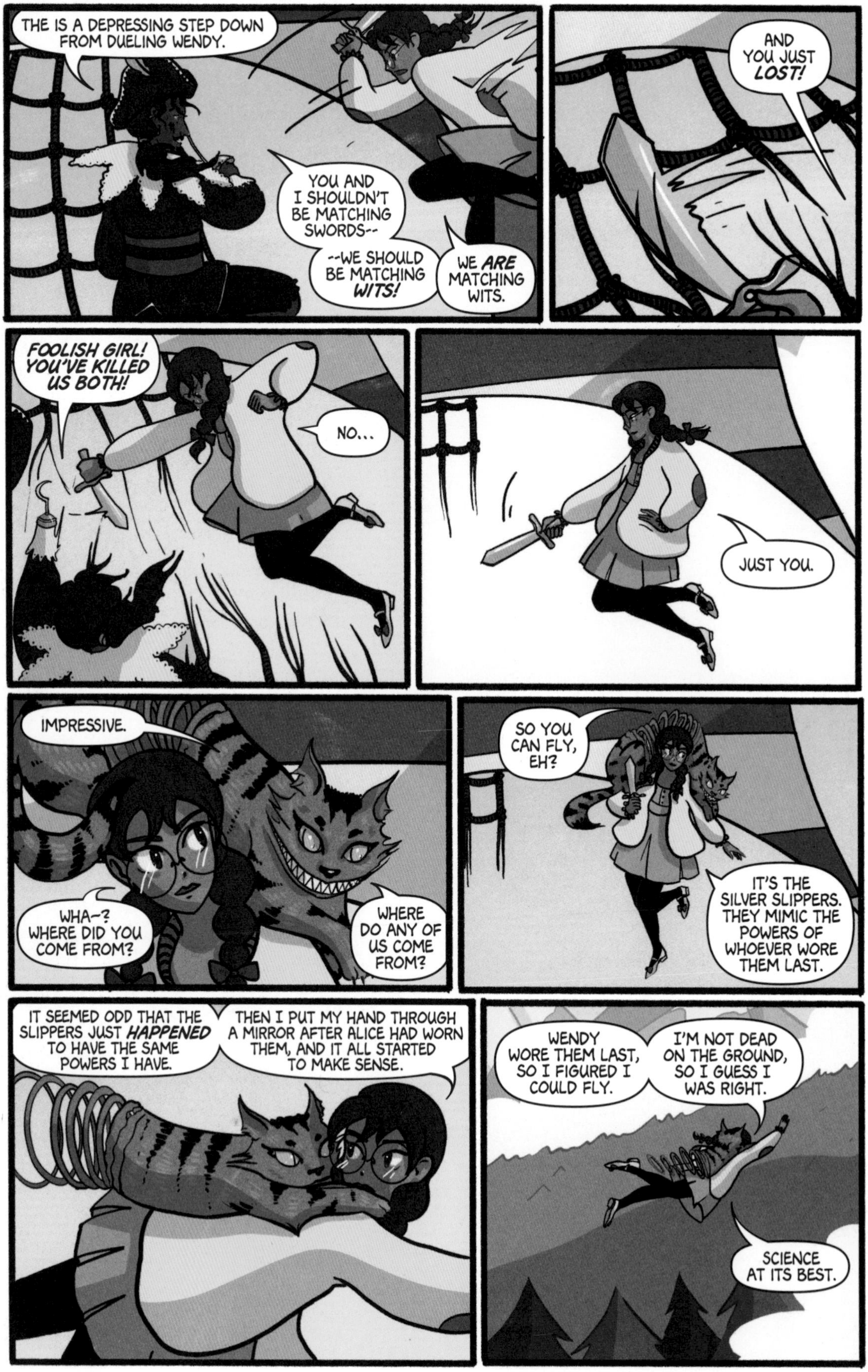
THE IS A DEPRESSING STEP DOWN FROM DUELING WENDY.
YOU AND I SHOULDN'T BE MATCHING SWORDS--
--WE SHOULD BE MATCHING WITS!
WE ARE MATCHING WITS.
AND YOU JUST LOST!
FOOLISH GIRL! YOU'VE KILLED US BOTH!
NO...
JUST YOU.
IMPRESSIVE.
WHA-? WHERE DID YOU COME FROM?
WHERE DO ANY OF US COME FROM?
SO YOU CAN FLY, EH?
IT'S THE SILVER SLIPPERS. THEY MIMIC THE POWERS OF WHOEVER WORE THEM LAST.
IT SEEMED ODD THAT THE SLIPPERS JUST HAPPENED TO HAVE THE SAME POWERS I HAVE.
THEN I PUT MY HAND THROUGH A MIRROR AFTER ALICE HAD WORN THEM, AND IT ALL STARTED TO MAKE SENSE.
WENDY WORE THEM LAST, SO I FIGURED I COULD FLY.
I'M NOT DEAD ON THE GROUND, SO I GUESS I WAS RIGHT.
SCIENCE AT ITS BEST.

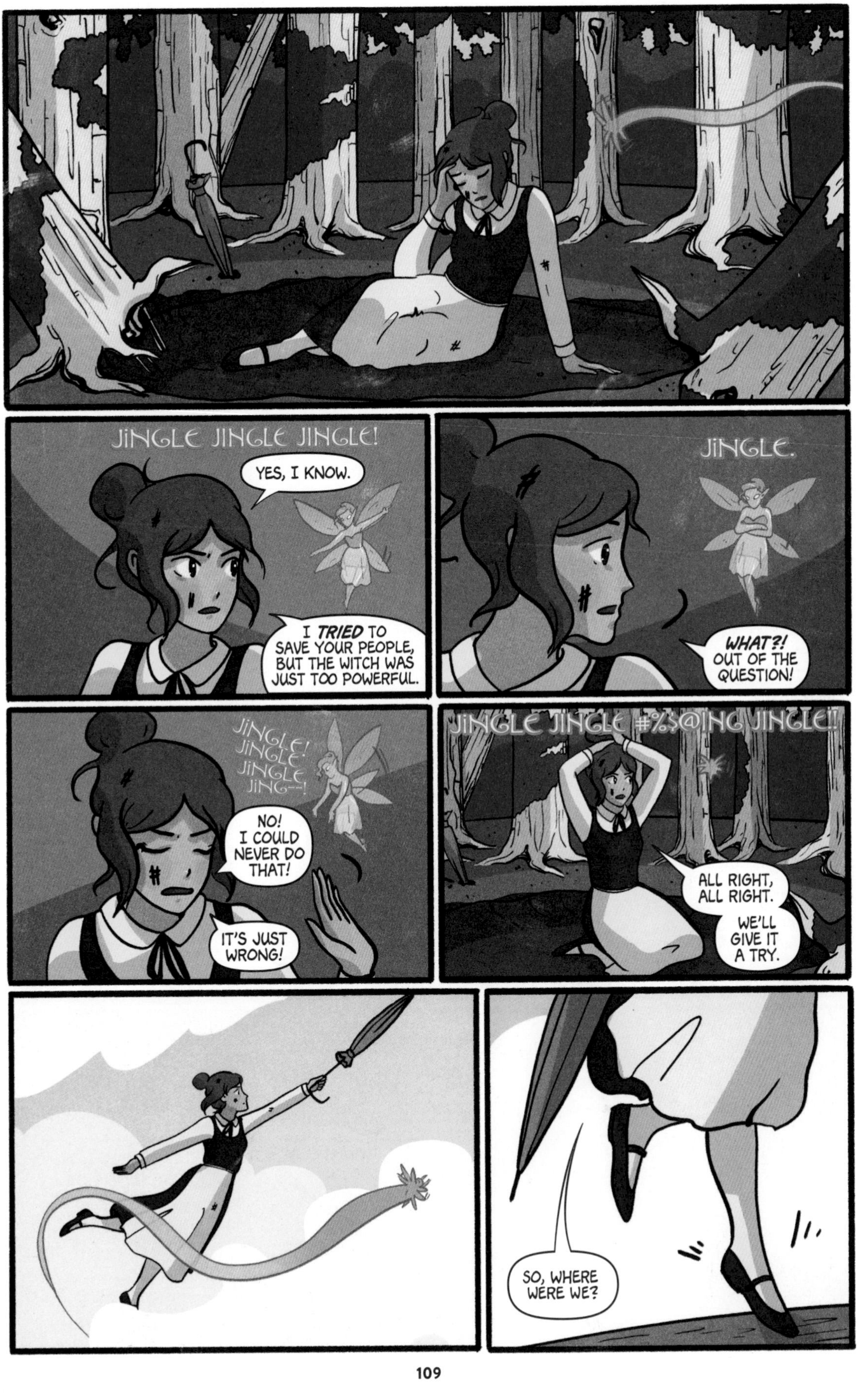
JiNGLE JiNGLE JiNGLE!
YES, I KNOW.
I **TRIED** TO SAVE YOUR PEOPLE, BUT THE WITCH WAS JUST TOO POWERFUL.
JiNGLE.
WHAT?! OUT OF THE QUESTION!
JiNGLE! JiNGLE! JiNGLE JiNG--!
NO! I COULD NEVER DO THAT!
IT'S JUST WRONG!
JiNGLE JiNGLE #%$@iNG JiNGLE!!
ALL RIGHT, ALL RIGHT.
WE'LL GIVE IT A TRY.
SO, WHERE WERE WE?

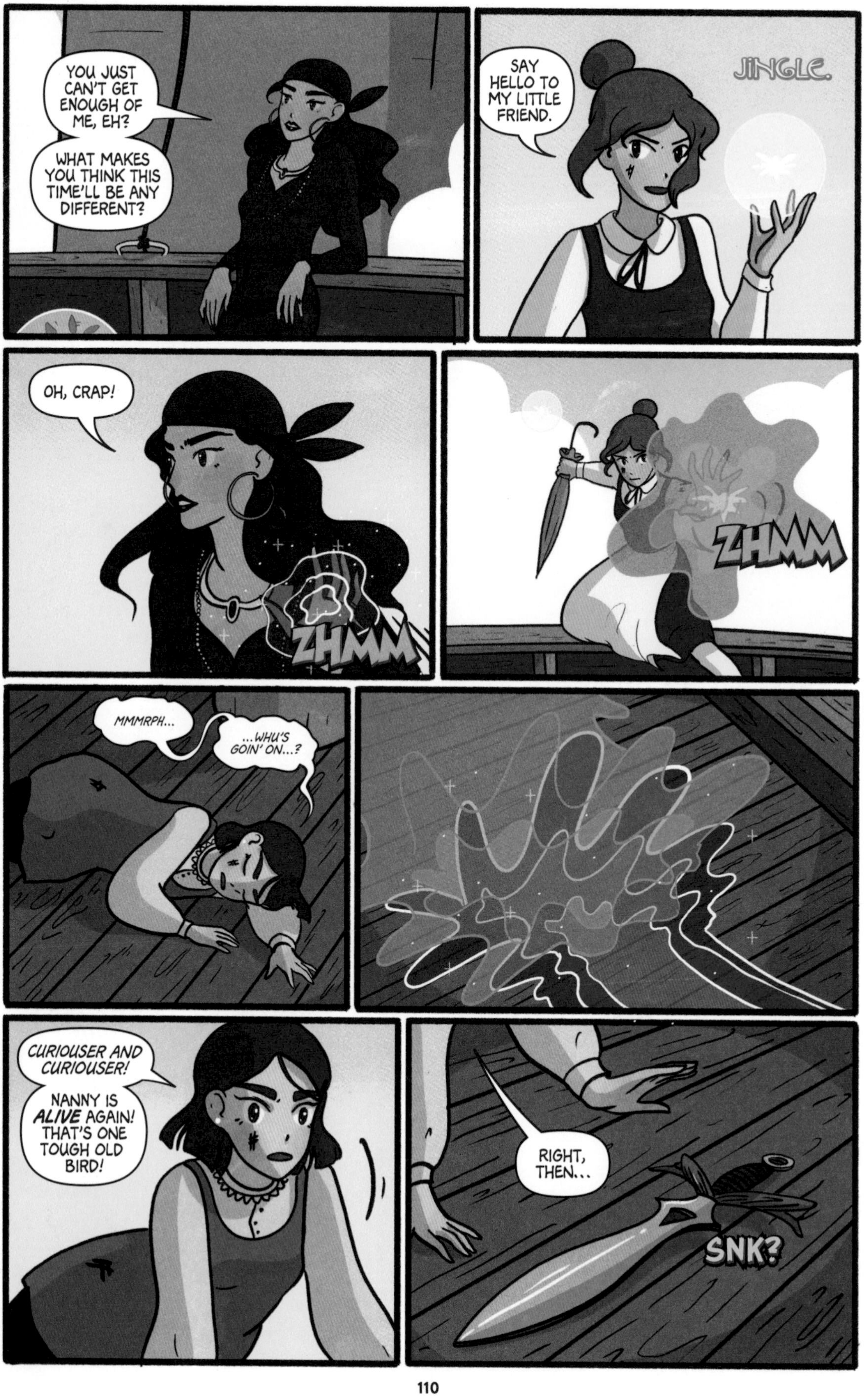
YOU JUST CAN'T GET ENOUGH OF ME, EH?
WHAT MAKES YOU THINK THIS TIME'LL BE ANY DIFFERENT?
SAY HELLO TO MY LITTLE FRIEND.
JINGLE.
OH, CRAP!
ZHMM
ZHMM
MMMRPH...
...WHU'S GOIN' ON...?
CURIOUSER AND CURIOUSER!
NANNY IS *ALIVE* AGAIN! THAT'S ONE TOUGH OLD BIRD!
RIGHT, THEN...
SNK?

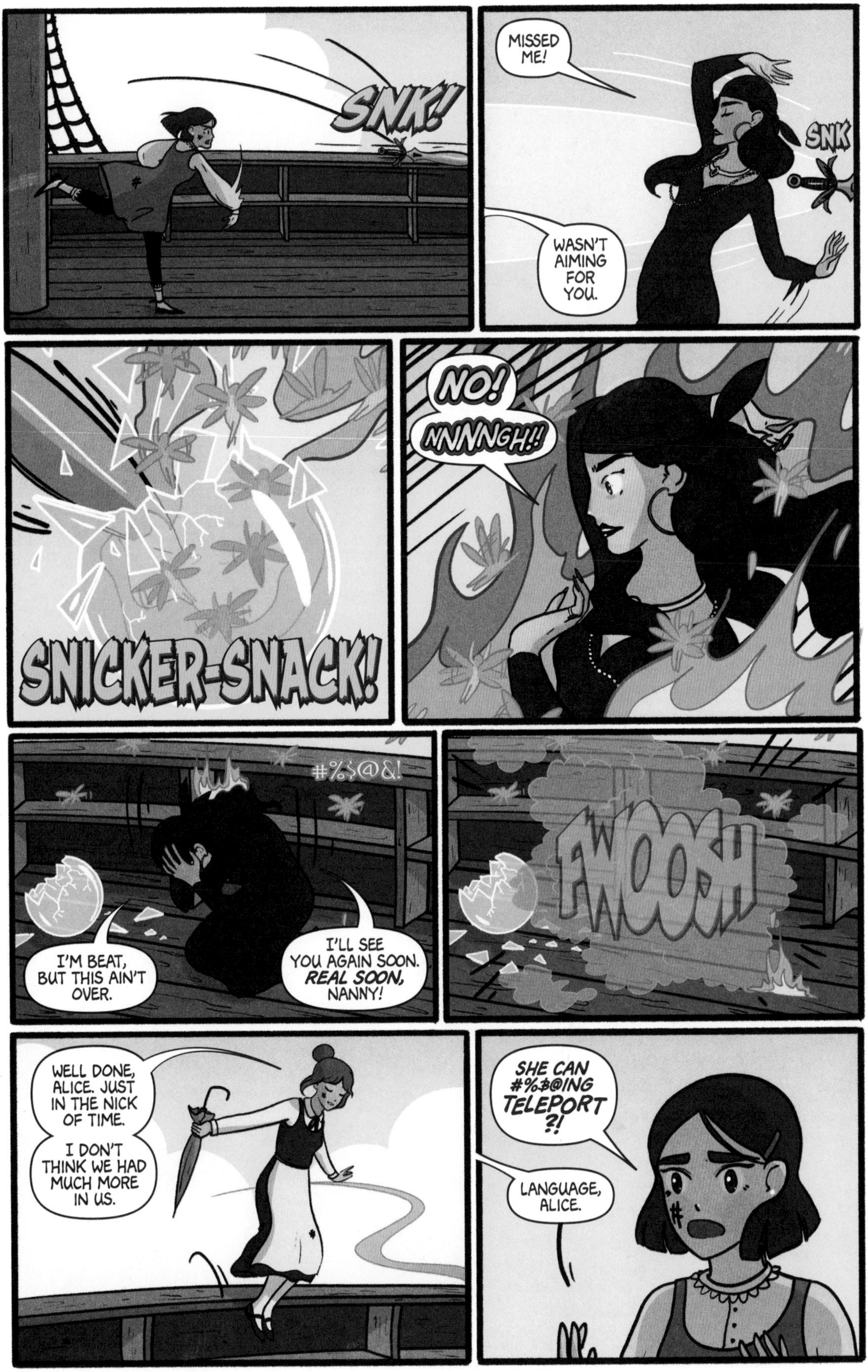
SNK!
MISSED ME!
WASN'T AIMING FOR YOU.
SNK
SNICKER-SNACK!
NO!
NNNNGH!!
#%$@&!
I'M BEAT, BUT THIS AIN'T OVER.
I'LL SEE YOU AGAIN SOON. REAL SOON, NANNY!
FWOOSH
WELL DONE, ALICE. JUST IN THE NICK OF TIME.
I DON'T THINK WE HAD MUCH MORE IN US.
SHE CAN #%$@ING TELEPORT ?!
LANGUAGE, ALICE.

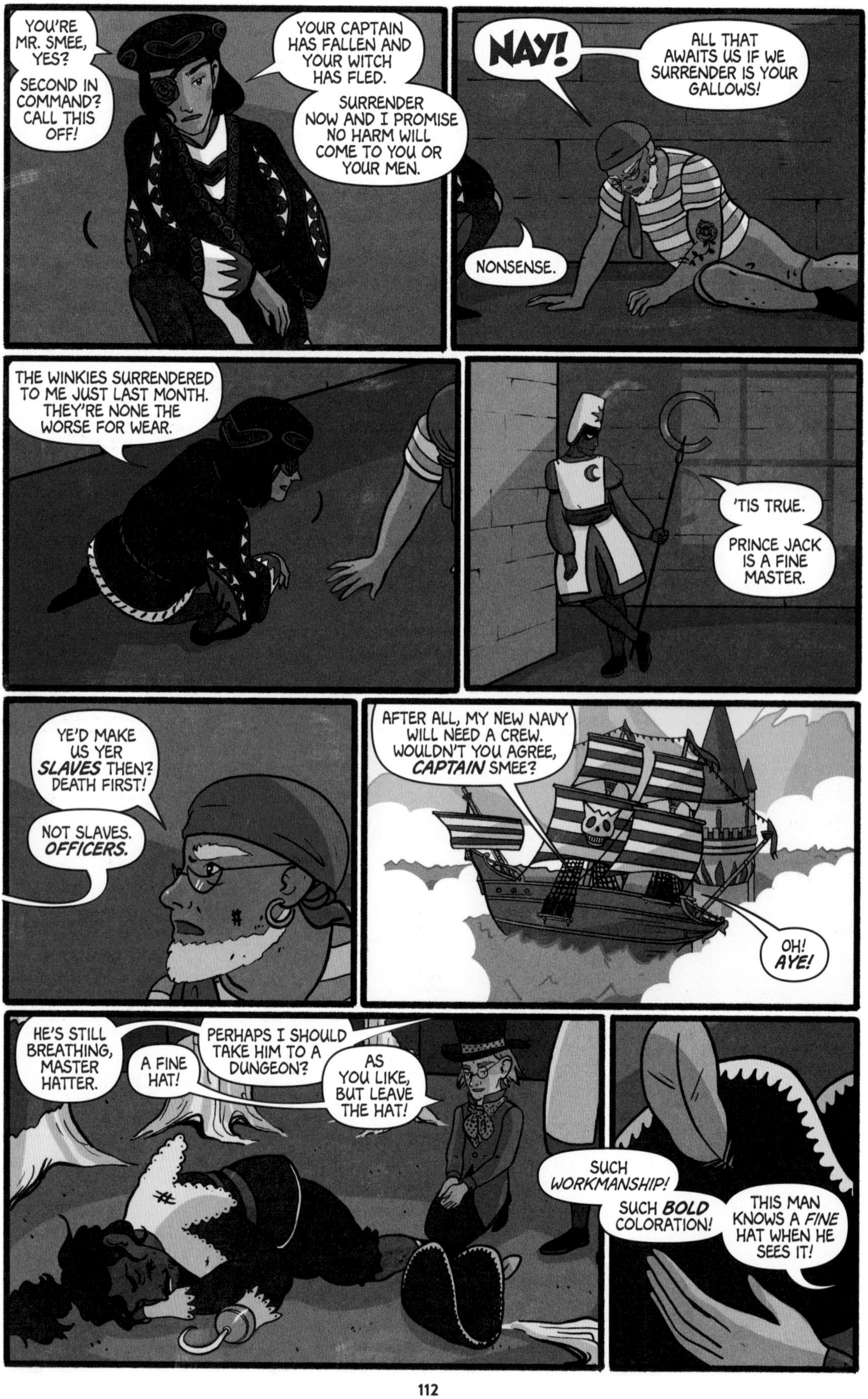
YOU'RE MR. SMEE, YES?
SECOND IN COMMAND? CALL THIS OFF!
YOUR CAPTAIN HAS FALLEN AND YOUR WITCH HAS FLED.
SURRENDER NOW AND I PROMISE NO HARM WILL COME TO YOU OR YOUR MEN.
NAY!
ALL THAT AWAITS US IF WE SURRENDER IS YOUR GALLOWS!
NONSENSE.
THE WINKIES SURRENDERED TO ME JUST LAST MONTH. THEY'RE NONE THE WORSE FOR WEAR.
'TIS TRUE.
PRINCE JACK IS A FINE MASTER.
YE'D MAKE US YER SLAVES THEN? DEATH FIRST!
NOT SLAVES. OFFICERS.
AFTER ALL, MY NEW NAVY WILL NEED A CREW. WOULDN'T YOU AGREE, CAPTAIN SMEE?
OH! AYE!
HE'S STILL BREATHING, MASTER HATTER.
PERHAPS I SHOULD TAKE HIM TO A DUNGEON?
A FINE HAT!
AS YOU LIKE, BUT LEAVE THE HAT!
SUCH WORKMANSHIP!
SUCH BOLD COLORATION!
THIS MAN KNOWS A FINE HAT WHEN HE SEES IT!

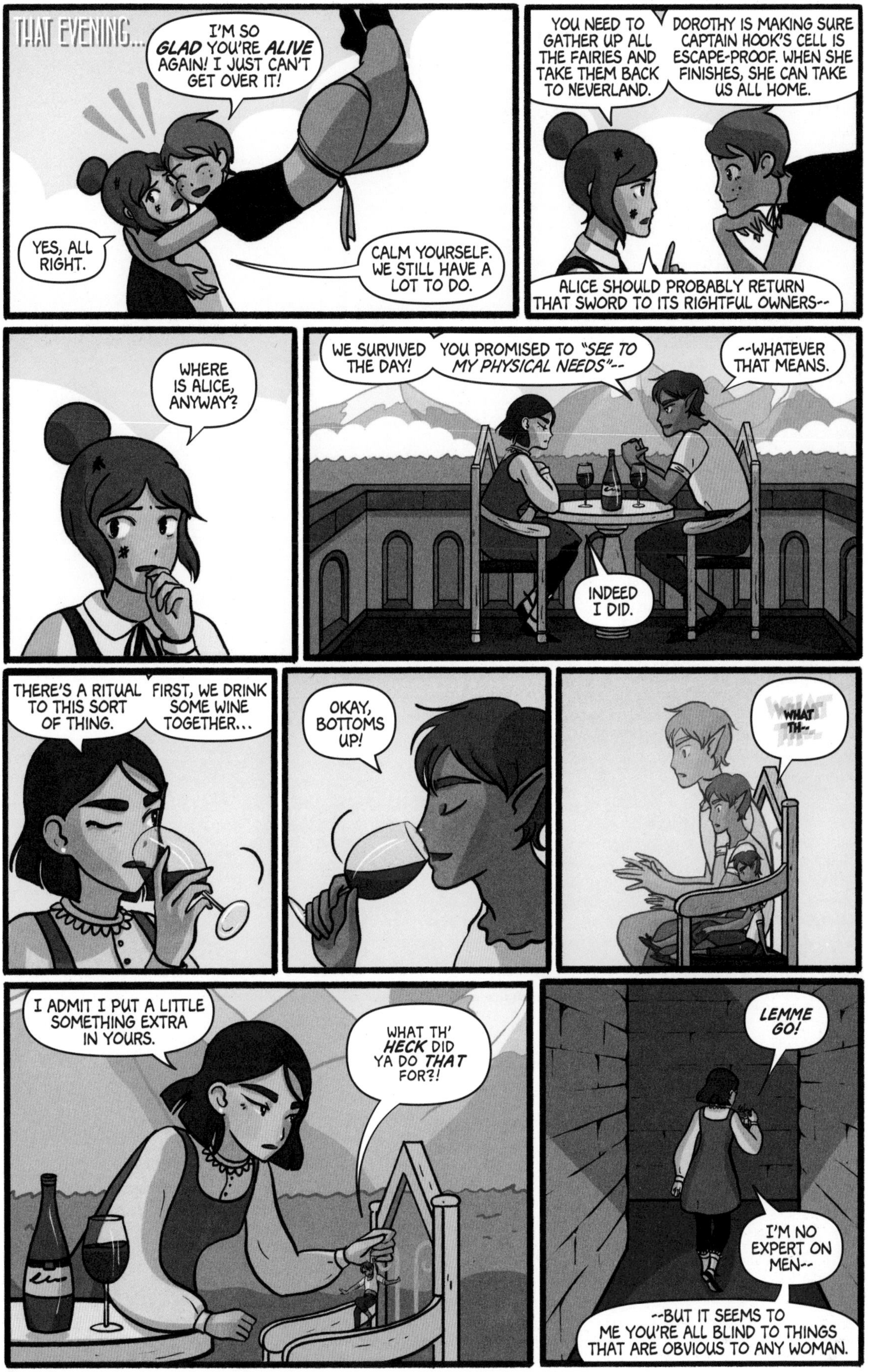
THAT EVENING...
I'M SO GLAD YOU'RE ALIVE AGAIN! I JUST CAN'T GET OVER IT!
YES, ALL RIGHT.
CALM YOURSELF. WE STILL HAVE A LOT TO DO.
YOU NEED TO GATHER UP ALL THE FAIRIES AND TAKE THEM BACK TO NEVERLAND.
DOROTHY IS MAKING SURE CAPTAIN HOOK'S CELL IS ESCAPE-PROOF. WHEN SHE FINISHES, SHE CAN TAKE US ALL HOME.
ALICE SHOULD PROBABLY RETURN THAT SWORD TO ITS RIGHTFUL OWNERS--
WHERE IS ALICE, ANYWAY?
WE SURVIVED THE DAY!
YOU PROMISED TO "SEE TO MY PHYSICAL NEEDS"--
--WHATEVER THAT MEANS.
INDEED I DID.
THERE'S A RITUAL TO THIS SORT OF THING.
FIRST, WE DRINK SOME WINE TOGETHER...
OKAY, BOTTOMS UP!
WHAT TH--
I ADMIT I PUT A LITTLE SOMETHING EXTRA IN YOURS.
WHAT TH' HECK DID YA DO THAT FOR?!
LEMME GO!
I'M NO EXPERT ON MEN--
--BUT IT SEEMS TO ME YOU'RE ALL BLIND TO THINGS THAT ARE OBVIOUS TO ANY WOMAN.

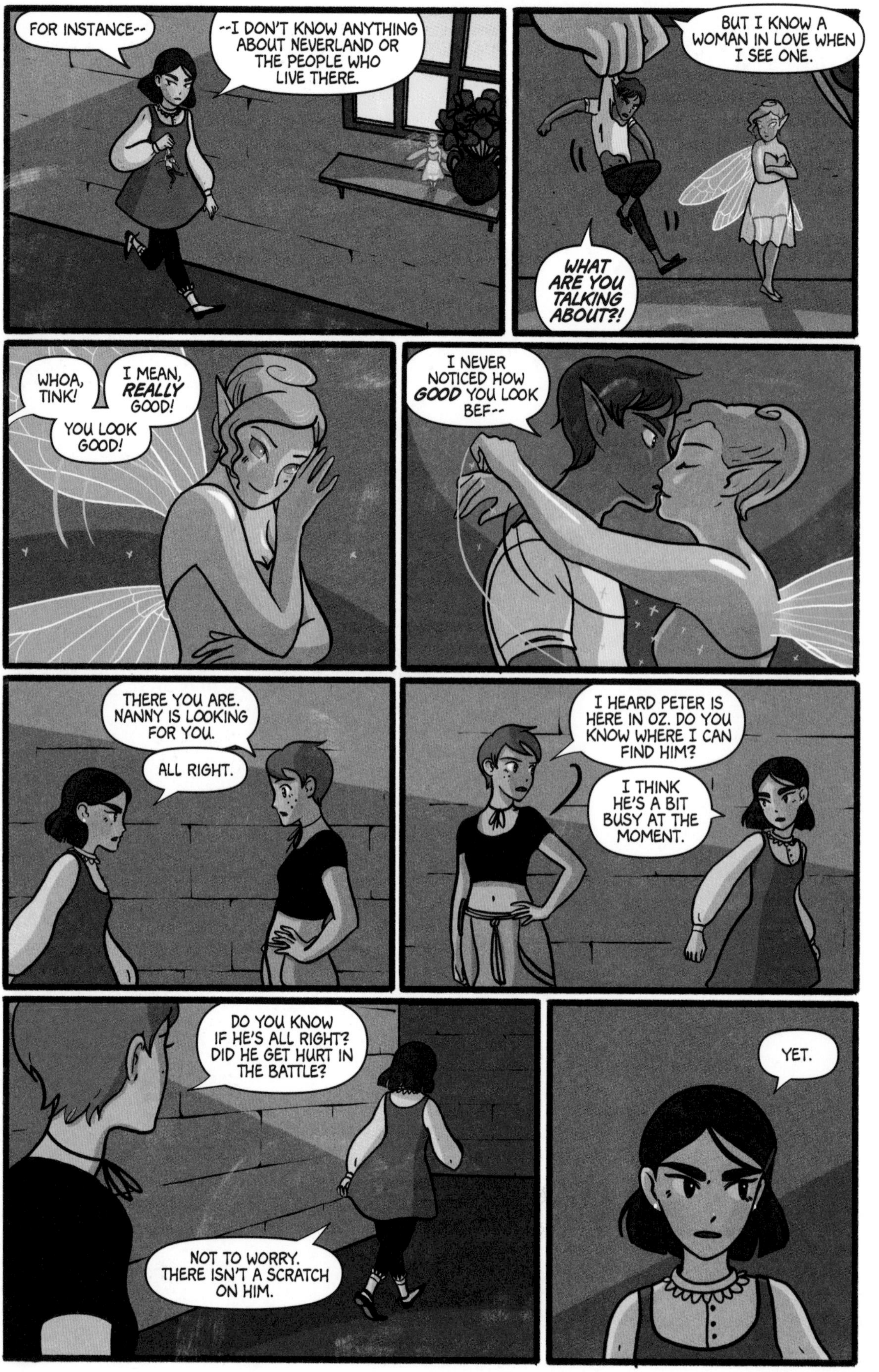
FOR INSTANCE--
--I DON'T KNOW ANYTHING ABOUT NEVERLAND OR THE PEOPLE WHO LIVE THERE.
BUT I KNOW A WOMAN IN LOVE WHEN I SEE ONE.
WHAT ARE YOU TALKING ABOUT?!
WHOA, TINK!
YOU LOOK GOOD!
I MEAN, REALLY GOOD!
I NEVER NOTICED HOW GOOD YOU LOOK BEF--
THERE YOU ARE. NANNY IS LOOKING FOR YOU.
ALL RIGHT.
I HEARD PETER IS HERE IN OZ. DO YOU KNOW WHERE I CAN FIND HIM?
I THINK HE'S A BIT BUSY AT THE MOMENT.
DO YOU KNOW IF HE'S ALL RIGHT? DID HE GET HURT IN THE BATTLE?
NOT TO WORRY. THERE ISN'T A SCRATCH ON HIM.
YET.

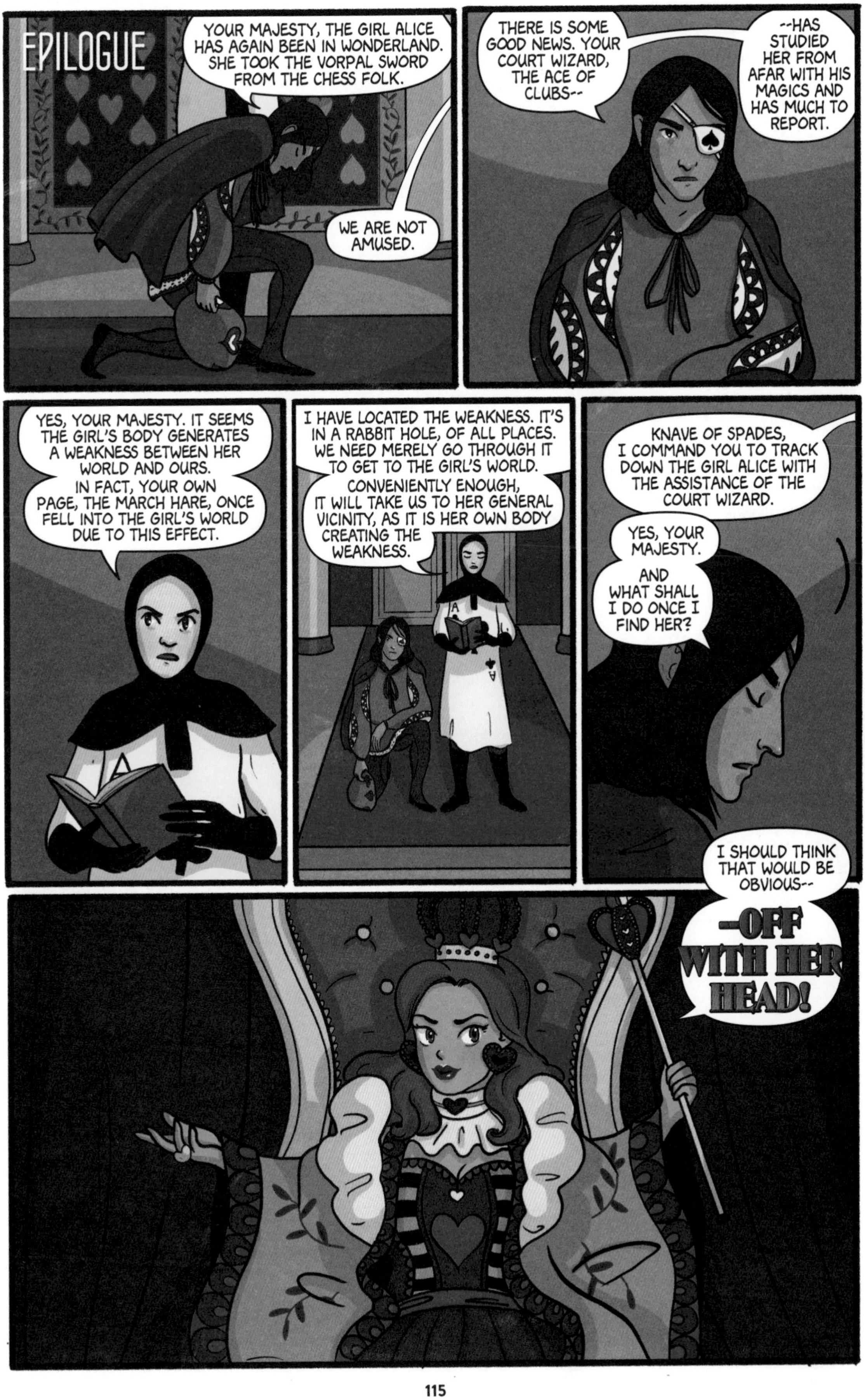
EPILOGUE
YOUR MAJESTY, THE GIRL ALICE HAS AGAIN BEEN IN WONDERLAND. SHE TOOK THE VORPAL SWORD FROM THE CHESS FOLK.
WE ARE NOT AMUSED.
THERE IS SOME GOOD NEWS. YOUR COURT WIZARD, THE ACE OF CLUBS--
--HAS STUDIED HER FROM AFAR WITH HIS MAGICS AND HAS MUCH TO REPORT.
YES, YOUR MAJESTY. IT SEEMS THE GIRL'S BODY GENERATES A WEAKNESS BETWEEN HER WORLD AND OURS. IN FACT, YOUR OWN PAGE, THE MARCH HARE, ONCE FELL INTO THE GIRL'S WORLD DUE TO THIS EFFECT.
I HAVE LOCATED THE WEAKNESS. IT'S IN A RABBIT HOLE, OF ALL PLACES. WE NEED MERELY GO THROUGH IT TO GET TO THE GIRL'S WORLD.
CONVENIENTLY ENOUGH, IT WILL TAKE US TO HER GENERAL VICINITY, AS IT IS HER OWN BODY CREATING THE WEAKNESS.
KNAVE OF SPADES, I COMMAND YOU TO TRACK DOWN THE GIRL ALICE WITH THE ASSISTANCE OF THE COURT WIZARD.
YES, YOUR MAJESTY.
AND WHAT SHALL I DO ONCE I FIND HER?
I SHOULD THINK THAT WOULD BE OBVIOUS--
--OFF WITH HER HEAD!

ACKNOWLEDGMENTS

ANDY: My gratitude goes out to illustrator Sarah Andersen for her beautiful illustrations as well as Alison George, Kayla Bickers, and Dave Lanphear for their color work and lettering. Many thanks to the people who worked behind the scenes to bring this book to life, including Julian Pavia, Patrick Barb, Ashley Pierce, Mikayla Butchart, Chloe Rawlins, Jane Chinn, Natalie Mulford, Daniel Wikey, Windy Dorresteyn, Hannah Rahill, and Aaron Wehner.

SARAH: Thank you to Adrienne McWhorter Bamford and Michael Son of Tapas Media for years of *Sarah's Scribbles* support as well as the opportunity to try something new and exciting. Thank you to my agent Seth Fishman for having my back and encouraging my work. Thank you to the brilliant colorists Alison George and Kayla Bickers who made *Cheshire Crossing* look the very best it possibly could. Lastly, an eternal thank-you to my friends and family who always push me to be my best.

ABOUT THE AUTHOR AND ILLUSTRATOR

ANDY WEIR built a career as a software engineer until the success of his first published novel, *The Martian*, allowed him to live out his dream of writing full-time. He is a lifelong space nerd and a devoted hobbyist of subjects such as relativistic physics, orbital mechanics, and the history of manned spaceflight. He also mixes a mean cocktail. He lives in California.

SARAH ANDERSEN is a 26-year-old cartoonist and illustrator. She graduated from the Maryland Institute College of Art in 2014 and currently lives in Norwalk, Connecticut. She is known for the webcomic *Sarah's Scribbles* and is a three-time Goodreads Choice Award winner. She is also a proud black cat owner.

Published in the United States by Ten Speed Press, an imprint of
Random House, a division of Penguin Random House LLC, New York.
www.crownpublishing.com
www.tenspeed.com

Ten Speed Press and the Ten Speed Press colophon are registered
trademarks of Penguin Random House LLC.

Originally published in four separate volumes in 2006, 2007, and
2008 in a different form by the author on www.cheshirecrossing.net.

Library of Congress Control Number: 2019930344

Trade Paperback ISBN: 978-0-399-58207-3
eBook ISBN: 978-0-399-58208-0

Printed in China

Editors: Julian Pavia, Patrick Barb, and Michael Son (Tapas Media)
Design: Chloe Rawlins
Colors: Alison George
Color Assists: Kayla Bickers and Dojo Gubser
Lettering: Dave Lanphear
In association with Tapas Media

10 9 8 7 6 5 4 3 2 1

First Edition